Over The Horizon belongs on every bookshelf! As commanding officer of Midway during the book's time period, it is impossible to describe in words how accurately this story captures the essence of Midway Magic.....A spellbinding tale of a fascinating part of American history.
RADM E. Inman Carmichael, USN; Commanding Officer
USS Midway, 1979-81

A must read!!! So realistic, you will forget the book is historical fiction. I know...I was there! Experience the Navy's foreign legion and its incredible adventures at sea, in the air, and in the exotic ports of call that welcomed Midway with open arms.
CAPT Robert 'Magnum' Wittenberg USN; Commanding Officer,
VA-115; 1981-82

Resurrects in vivid detail a time and place largely forgotten in recent history, as America's 'foreign legion' confronts its Cold War foes while deployed to the Western Pacific....puts a human face on both those who served and the indigenous people who supported the U.S. Navy ashore.
Peter Hunt, former Intruder pilot; Author of Angles of
Attack and The Lost Intruder

OVER THE HORIZON

ISBN-10: 1718971354

Over The Horizon

Luke Ridenhour

Edited By Hal Fletcher
Cover Design by Vinny DiGirolamo

ABOUT THE AUTHOR

A North Carolina native, Luke Ridenhour is a 1978 graduate of the U.S. Naval Academy. In addition to being a Naval Aviator, he was designated a U.S. Army parachutist and a Naval Parachutist. He was the recipient of the 1989 David S. Ingalls Award, presented annually to the number one flight instructor in the Naval Air Training Command. He is a designated U.S. Navy Proven Subspecialist in Education and Training.

During his career, he logged over 6,000 accident-free flight hours, the majority in the A-6 Intruder and A-4 Skyhawk. He logged 455 aircraft carrier landings, including 160 at night, in the Western Pacific, Atlantic, Indian Ocean, Mediterranean, and Caribbean theaters of operation. He is a centurion (100+ landings) on the aircraft carrier USS Forrestal (CV-59) and a double centurion on the aircraft carrier USS Midway (CV-41). He was formally recognized by the U.S. Navy and a prestigious aviation safety magazine for piloting a T-2 Buckeye jet with no fore-aft flight controls over 120 miles to a safe landing.

ACKNOWLEDGEMENTS

God, who provided divine intervention in the air, and the Navy's enlisted personnel who kept my jet safe and airworthy from my first takeoff to my very last landing;

The U.S. Naval Academy Class of 1978, most especially Sixth Company, with whom my journey to the far side of the world began in the sweltering summer of 1974; and the officers and men of Attack Squadron 115 during the period 1980-1982, most notably the residents of Bunkroom Eight, the Midway Oasis;

Stephen Coonts, who introduced our jet to the world with Flight of the Intruder;

Lea Tsokris, an enchanting Greek beauty whose deep-rooted heritage, untouchable wit, and captivating personality took this book and my heart to rarified places;

Vinny DiGirolamo, USNA classmate, Navy pilot, and exceptional artist;

Leland Shanle, Peter Hunt, and John Schork, former naval aviators and published authors, whose literary advice and friendship was and always will be invaluable;

Doug Hegdahl, former Vietnam POW who agreed I could share his story. We first met in 1980 at the Navy's SERE school on opposite sides of the interrogation rooms;

Rear Admiral E. Inman 'Hoagy' Carmichael, USN; CO, USS Midway (1979-1981);

Rear Admiral Ken Carlsen, USN; Midway's XO (1980-1981), who, as VAQ-136 CO in the summer of '77, enabled me, then a midshipman, to log ten carrier landings on USS Independence in his squadron's jets, confirming my desire to be a Navy flyboy;

The late Capt. Roger Flower, USN (ret), Commander, Carrier Air Wing Five, 1980-81;

Ramona Noles, who unselfishly shared her incredible tale as a child in a concentration camp following an escape attempt from communist Romania;

LCDR Dennis 'Seadog' Seipel, USN, and LCDR Brian McMahon, USNR, two of my very best friends, who died in A-6 Intruder crashes in the same Pacific waters where Midway once roamed. Their spirit is resurrected in many of the book's characters;

Inspirational friends and contributors: Nelson Cayabyab, Don Owen, Andy Howard, Lenny Shores, Sale Lilly, David Gruber, 'Whip' Johnson, Bob Backus, Wes Olsen, Dr. John McHugh, Dr. Duane Caneva, Ron Henderson, 'Mac' Williams, Marti Williams, Paul Summerville, Jim Hoffman, Patti Eller Sprouse, Don Beverlin, Sharon Napora, Bill Dennis, Kristi and Pat Brennan, Michael O'Brien, John Carmichael, John Indorf, Paul Liberatore, Evan 'Buzz' Nau, Jeffery Lay, Jim Beaver, VT-4 Class 8402, the late Ann E. King, flight school classmate and pioneer among women naval aviators; and

Capt. Bob Wittenberg, USN (ret), friend and respected leader, who, as the VA-115 prospective commanding officer, selected me to fill a vacancy in the squadron, spawning a trajectory that ended in this tale. Arigatou Gozaimashita, Skipper.

AUTHOR'S NOTES

Over The Horizon is historical fiction based on actual events in the western Pacific during 1980-1982, an active but little regarded time period in which impactful incidents and exercises, along with colorful events at sea and ashore, unfolded long before the rise and impact of the Internet and a 24-hour news cycle. To facilitate the telling of this tale, some liberties have been taken in describing actual places, procedures, events, dates, and timelines.

Operating out of sight and out of mind to virtually all Americans, the Cold War in Asia was simmering and often hot, and 'cat and mouse' episodes with potential enemies were not uncommon during the book's timeline. The two Koreas had yet to sign a peace treaty on a peninsula that was far more volatile than peaceful. The Soviet Union was playing 'catch up' with its own tactical and strategic fleets, as well as increasing its persecution and incarceration of Christian families inside and outside its borders. In America, the government was transitioning from a 'peacenik' president to a president who brought a 'big stick swagger' and a 'trust but verify' mentality to the tensions boiling in the Far East.

This novel is centered on Attack Squadron 115, a Navy medium attack squadron to which the author was assigned as a junior officer and aviator. Nicknamed the Eagles, VA-115 was a component of Carrier Air Wing Five onboard the aircraft carrier USS Midway, then permanently homeported in Yokosuka, Japan, and now based in San Diego as one of the top five museums in the country.

The Eagles flew the Grumman A-6 Intruder, a twin engine, carrier-based, all-weather attack jet. The Intruder was so lethal, especially at night and/or in bad weather, that it was the only Navy attack jet never exported to any foreign country, no matter the obscene amount of money or blank checks offered.

PREFACE

In October, 1973, with little fanfare, the United States Navy established what was, effectively, a foreign legion on the far side of the planet. Baptized in the deep, cold waters of the Pacific Ocean, it was christened with a harmless, government-issued name: Overseas Family Residency Program. The innocent title allowed sailors' families across fifty states to sleep peacefully as their loved ones served faithfully on the volatile tip of America's sword.

The Navy's légion étrangère was based in Yokosuka, Japan, twenty-eight miles south of Tokyo, and its flagship was USS Midway, a World War Two vintage aircraft carrier. Few Americans knew her name, but America's enemies certainly knew who she was — as did America's presidents. Upon initial notification of a crisis halfway around the world, the first question the White House always asked was, "Where's Midway?"

From its beginning, the Navy's foreign legion began patrolling the Western Pacific and Indian Ocean on a nearly continuous basis, remaining ever vigilant far from her home of birth. The ship's operating schedule was grueling; so grueling that her unofficial motto was Semper Separatus — Always Separated. It was a burdensome attribute for which foreign legions were known, and those who sailed on Midway embraced it as not only a personal badge of honor, but also one of privilege.

Midway was the perfect choice to plant the flag and carry the sword abroad. She was the oldest flattop in the Navy, yet the most operational. She was a flashback to the forties and a nation united behind its military, and then to the fifties and the Cold War. She played key roles into the sixties and early seventies and remained resolute through an unpopular war in Vietnam and a country divided.

During her service, Midway earned a reputation that magic ran from her bow to her stern. The aviators who flew from her deck and the sailors who kept the ship and aircraft operating believed it. Her operational schedule and performance was, many said, simply impossible for a ship of her age without a daily dose of divine intervention. Ultimately, Midway would serve her home country for forty-seven years, sailing in every ocean of the globe, and be forward deployed more than any aircraft carrier in America's history.

Those who had the privilege of calling Midway home learned quickly that membership in the Navy's foreign legion was never easy or safe, and the price tag was often perilously high. Most importantly, they learned that, in darkening storms or sunlight fair, Midway Magic would always be with them...somewhere over the horizon.

DEDICATION

Over The Horizon is dedicated to all those who sailed on the aircraft carrier USS Midway (CV-41) during her forty-seven years of operational service, and the families and friends who loyally supported them...you made the magic; and

Hal Fletcher, editor extraordinaire, accomplished actor, and dear friend; and

Eli, an exceptional husband, father, and Filipino caddy who may never see over his world's horizon, but whose heartwarming story is worthy of circling the globe.

CHAPTER ONE

Beneath The Southern Cross
Mid-Summer, 1980

In the wee hours of the morning that Willie was notified, a warm blanket of stars rested peacefully over the aircraft carrier Midway. A thousand miles of dark water separated the legendary ship and her crew from the nearest point of land as she glided effortlessly through the southern Indian Ocean.

Eight naval aviators, berthed in four sets of top-and-bottom bunks, were asleep in the cramped, but cozy, confines of Bunkroom Eight, called the Midway Oasis, when the telephone rang. As always, the man nearest it answered.

Lunker listened for several seconds, and then nodded. "Yes sir. I'll let him know." He turned slightly to his right and hung up the phone.

"Hey, Willie. It's the skipper. He wants to see you in the ready room." Willie was in a top bunk and rolled slightly to his left as he slowly opened his eyes. The small clock next to him indicated two-thirty. "This can't be good," he thought. *Strike one.*

Calls at that hour were rare. His still groggy mind was racing as he tried to make sense of why he would be called at such an hour, especially by his squadron's commanding officer. At sea, delivering good news at night could always wait until morning. Bad news was delivered immediately. Willie knew that to be true.

The Bunkroom Eight motto was *It only hurts when you're awake.* It was always said jokingly, but now it was likely to be painfully true. Still, he was an eternal optimist and refused to accept that tragic news awaited him.

Willie took a deep breath and could sense his heart beating faster as he eased himself down to the floor and walked the few feet to his locker. His body was becoming more tense with each breath as he quickly put on his green flight suit and black flight boots. As he did, the other men in the bunkroom either sat up in their bunks or left their beds and stood silently near him.

The air was saturated with compassion. All eight men knew the call would likely bring heartache. Seven knew the call could just as easily have been meant for them.

Willie didn't need to ask for their prayers. Their unconditional support was palpable, and the accompanying compassion radiated outward like the radars on Midway's island structure. That was the affirming essence that made the trusted bunkroom an oasis.

"Tie your boots, Willie," suggested Lunker. "You don't need to trip along the way." He, too, had experienced the indescribable stress of receiving an early morning phone call.

Willie nodded and knelt down. "Thanks, Lunker."

It took Willie just under one minute to quickly walk to Ready Room Five, the Attack Squadron One Hundred Fifteen Eagles' ready room located on the same level as Bunkroom Eight, which was one level below Midway's now-quiet flight deck. Along the way, he could feel and hear the mechanical humming of the carrier as she pushed her massive presence through the water. The majority of her crew was sleeping, but the ship remained alive. The mighty warship, launched in the closing days of World War Two, was a floating national asset with a never-ending mission.

Willie walked through the door and into the ready room, the place where pilots gathered to plan missions and relax after their flights. As he did, visions straight from the classic Hollywood movies he grew up watching flashed across his memory. Two men in khaki uniforms stood in front of him, less than thirty feet away.

Willie desperately wished this was a movie. "I hope this has a happy ending," he thought, but the dispirited look on the face of his commanding officer, standing to the right of the air wing's flight surgeon, indicated it wasn't likely. Their uncomfortably stiff body language spoke volumes.

In 1980, the only way that sailors and airmen on the ship could be notified of an emergency was with a Red Cross message, a form of communication begun thirty years earlier during the Korean Conflict. A small piece of paper in his skipper's left hand, upon which Willie's eyes momentarily focused, reconfirmed his worst fears. *Strike two.*

In the dozen steps it took him to reach his boss, he instinctively knew who it was likely to be and said a silent prayer. "Oh Lord, please don't let it be Archie. I never told him how much he meant to me; how I am becoming the man he always wanted me to be." Willie couldn't imagine anyone else he knew who was elderly and for whom his parents would send news this way. With each heavy step, he struggled emotionally at the thought of never again seeing or talking to his larger-than-life grandfather, a dear man who insisted on being called only by his first name.

His commanding officer was a fellow Naval Academy graduate, fourteen years before Willie. He was a wonderful boss and well liked by everyone, especially the junior officers. In the

3

first hours of this early morning, though, his unusually stiff posture confirmed the worst.

After saying "Good morning, Willie," but before any further words were spoken, his skipper put his right hand on Willie's left shoulder and handed him the piece of paper the size of a small envelope.

The movies had portrayed it accurately; this really was how it was done.

"I'm so sorry." His skipper's voice had a slight quiver as his shoulders noticeably sagged. *Strike three.*

Willie looked down at the Red Cross message in his hand, and his breathing noticeably deepened. "It has to be a mistake," he thought. "It just has to be." Two lines, seven short words. He read them once and then a second time, and took a deep breath. Desperately willing them to be different, he read them a third time, but the words never changed. Life, as he had known it since birth, was over.

Mother has metastatic cancer. Prognosis three weeks.

Willie stood paralyzed as he stared at the paper. His brain processed the words as his trembling soul strained to reject them. Already heartbroken at the answer he knew he would likely hear, Willie's eyes moved hesitantly from his hands up to the flight surgeon's eyes.

"Does this mean what I think it means?"

The flight surgeon remained quiet as he nodded slowly. His presence was required when one of the air wing's sailors or officers was notified. It was agonizing each and every time he had to confirm the unthinkable, but this time it was too personal. Twelve days earlier, he had flown in Willie's right seat in the two-seat A-6 Intruder, an all-weather attack jet, as the ship passed the northern tip of Indonesia. Life was good on that sunny South Pacific day; they were both living a dream.

Willie was almost halfway around the world from his hometown as his thoughts went to his mother. She had just turned fifty and was now facing death on the other side of the globe from her first-born son.

Midway's next port visit, scheduled for Perth, Australia, was over two months away. Even though fifty-two Americans held hostage by Iran had recently been released, the northern Arabian Sea remained a volatile area. Midway and her crew of five thousand, the tip of America's sword, were heading west-southwest, sailing further and further from their loved ones by the minute.

Leaving the ship wasn't a possibility, logistically or operationally. The realization that his mother and he would likely never again share a tender moment, see each other's faces, or hear each other speak hit him hard. This wasn't how it was supposed to end, and most certainly not this soon. He hadn't shed a tear in a very long time and, even now, although his soul was in tatters, his eyes remained dry as he stared again at the seven words that remained unchanged.

Willie took a deep breath as Commander Mason broke the silence. This was a first for him, too.

"I wish I had some good options for you, Willie, but we're a long way from nowhere and will be for a couple months, maybe more." His voice conveyed a tone of frustrated resignation that he couldn't help one of his men in a time of unfathomable distress.

Willie slowly looked up from the message in his hand and took another deep breath. He spoke in a calm voice. "Thank you, Skipper. I know you'd send me back if there was any way at all." His sad voice was distressing to the two officers standing in front of him. "I do appreciate it, but right now my best option is to go back to the bunkroom and try and get some sleep."

Willie's eyes looked once again at the message in his hand, whose seven words remained unchanged, and then returned to his boss.

"Skipper, I'm scheduled to fly later this morning, and I know you're supposed to ground me for a few days to let my head

5

clear, but I'll be fine. If I can't ever see or talk to my mother again, she'd hope I was doing something I love. I can compartmentalize; you know that. Put Doc or Lunker in my right seat. Let me fly. I'll be okay. I wouldn't ask if I thought I'd be a risk to anyone."

Commander Mason nodded. "Will do." The flight surgeon confidently agreed as well.

Willie didn't immediately return to Bunkroom Eight. Instead, he went up one level to Midway's dimly lit and mostly undisturbed flight deck. As she moved at fourteen knots through the ocean, waves rhythmically lapped against the sides of the illustrious carrier and propagated a slow, but steady, clip-clop sound eerily similar to that made by the caisson-pulling horses at Arlington Cemetery.

Willie looked through the black night to a barely visible horizon. He reminded himself that this magnificent ship had been steaming in foreign waters for over thirty-five years, beginning at the end of World War Two, eleven years before he was born. During that time, spirit-crushing news had been delivered to countless numbers of sailors and aviators far from home, far from those they missed and loved. No one promised that being part of a foreign legion would be easy or painless. On a dark morning over a vast ocean, Willie's broken heart had just become the newest addition to a long list.

Around him, over eighty aircraft sat parked, instruments of terrifying power majestically at peace. He walked slowly to a nearby A-6 Intruder parked at the edge of the ship with its tail sticking over the water.

His name was on the left side of the canopy by the pilot's seat in the side-by-side, two-seat attack jet. It was a mighty airplane at rest, waiting for its crew and a call to fly wherever it was needed.

Flying the Intruder was my first choice," he had told his mother, just a few days before he began his journey to Midway's homeport in Japan. "It's one-of-a-kind flying," he explained. "No other military jet in the world can do what we do. None. We're the only ones. It's why I asked to fly this jet as my first choice, and I'm glad I did."

Willie took his mother's hands in his. "We fly just hundreds of feet off the ground in good weather and in the worst weather, day or night; it doesn't matter to us. We fly in weather that other pilots and even birds won't attempt, and we do it at speeds of six, seven, and eight miles per minute. Sometimes we're the only jets that launch because of the weather." His pride overflowed as he spoke. "But we know how to do it safely. I promise you, mom, I promise." He couldn't stress the point enough. "I love flying the jet, but I'd never ever take off if I didn't think I'd return."

She listened intently as Willie excitedly shared his boundless joy at the profession he had chosen, even with its lengthy separations and inherent danger. He shared the unique thrill of launching from and landing on an aircraft carrier. He spoke of peeking behind a thunderstorm, of rolling the Intruder upside down simply to see the planet from a different perspective, and of circling a waterspout as it created a tornado of water that whirled and danced a random pattern across the ocean.

He was her little boy again, his mother thought, filled with the contagious excitement of a young child discovering the joys of climbing a tree, learning to ride a bicycle, and savoring, for the first time, the endearing feelings when a cute girl says she'll join him on the playground swings.

What he didn't elaborate on was that Intruder crews routinely flew low through mountainous areas invisible because of darkness or clouds, flying well below peaks they couldn't see but knew were so close — a black maze of granite lips that would, without any compassion, coldly kiss them goodbye in a final heartbeat.

Willie's mother listened with tears in her eyes as he said he was proud to be part of such a group of brave and selfless men who fixed and flew the Intruder, regardless of the weather or time of day. "The Intruder is one hundred percent American," he told her, smiling. "No foreign country will ever fly the jet, not even a single time. Many countries ask, especially our closest allies, but their request is always denied, even when they offer obscene amounts of money or blank checks."

She held her first son's hand and then pulled him close. Through soft tears flowing out of a mother's pure love, she begged him to be safe, admitting that she couldn't bear the thought of never seeing him again.

Two days later, as he prepared to board a commercial airliner for the long trip to Tokyo, Willie kissed her goodbye. That he may never see her again was a thought as far away as the other side of the world.

Soaring over horizons may have been her little boy's dream, but his mother dying somewhere over the line where the water met the sky wasn't a part of it. As he contemplated how he would confront and live with a dagger buried deep in his heart, Willie thought of Eli, a caddy in the Philippines. Eli had lost three of his five children, all of whom died before the age of seven. Yet Eli, a dear man of few means, had found a way to maintain a perpetually positive outlook. At the moment, his remedy eluded the young aviator.

Willie then thought of his grandfather, a man who had sacrificed so much for his family, and longed for the innocent days when, in the early morning hours of a new day, they would sit on the side of a hill in the North Carolina mountains, listening to moonshiners as they raced across winding roads without lights, driving solely by the shine of the moon over their heads. Life was good on those dark nights.

Now, he stood on the carrier's dark flight deck and leaned into a stiff warm breeze. The wind blew across Willie's light brown hair and his heart was beating to a sorrowful rhythm as he looked up at the black sky through grief-stricken blue eyes. Like his life in the past ten minutes, the stars carpeted across the great expanse were contentiously out of order, and he had trouble finding the easily recognized constellations he grew up memorizing.

Silently, he shouted to the heavens. "Where are they, Lord? Where's the Big Dipper? Where's Orion? Where's the North Star to guide my way?" He took a couple deep breaths as a warm ocean breeze wrapped around him. "Where are you, God?"

At this unfathomable moment in his relatively young life of twenty-five years, nothing but the steel flight deck upon which he stood and the black ocean surrounding him made sense.

Then, he remembered. Just a few days earlier, he and over a thousand other pollywogs had become shellbacks in an ageless naval ceremony on the flight deck as Midway crossed the equator and sailed alone into the southern hemisphere.

Willie was in a place, geographically and emotionally, in which he had never been before. If that latter place could be located on a nautical chart, it'd be the point where the latitude of a young man's dreams intersected the longitude of a parent's final days. Unfortunately, those two lines crossed in the middle of a dark ocean on the far side of Mother Earth.

He marveled at God's irony as he found the Southern Cross constellation. Willie was a fan of Victory at Sea, a popular television series, and he remembered one of its songs, *Beneath the Southern Cross*, which memorialized the loneliness of sailors in the South Pacific during World War Two.

Loneliness was such an understatement.

Willie wished he could sit next to his mother and be a comfort to her in her last days.

Sadly, a second Red Cross message was received nine days later. Like the first, it arrived as a demon in the dark.

CHAPTER TWO

Planes, Plans, And A Storm On The Move
Spring, 1980

Enveloped by a warm tropical sun, the short, thin man with brown weathered skin and jet-black hair focused his eyes on Subic Bay, an idyllic body of water surrounded by lush jungles in the Philippines. It was where, just eighty-three years earlier, the Spanish Empire ended and American influence began, courtesy of the United States Navy.

Visitors called the earth around him paradise, utopia, and the promised land. Many labeled it a pilgrimage; others said it was a rite of passage. To Eli, it was his home, the only land his eyes had ever seen and would likely ever see.

He was a caddy, a beloved caddy, at the golf course nestled within the Navy's sprawling base located fifty miles northwest of Manila. Eli related best to the golfers who took flight from the great flattops at sea. They ignored the law of gravity, laughed at the thought of growing older, and, most appealing to him, they could peek over the horizon in their jets with the ease of lassoing a sleeping water buffalo.

A few minutes later, Eli smiled broadly as he watched one of those fortunate aviators step from a taxi. He had a gleam in his eyes at the unexpected appearance of his favorite golfer, and turning his day immediately into one of immense joy.

"Good morning, my friend," said the tall man with an endearing smile. Lieutenant Carl Fishman, whose call sign was Lunker, was a naval flight officer assigned to a medium attack squadron onboard Midway. His squadron, VA-115 Eagles, flew the A-6 Intruder, a twin-engine, Vietnam-era jet that flew low and fast in any kind of weather or terrain, day or night, to deliver up to eighteen thousand pounds of ordnance as a lethal spanking to a deserving foe.

To make its high-risk missions relatively safe while remaining deadly precise, the Intruder was designed with a crew of two — a pilot and a bombardier/navigator, called a B/N — sitting side-by-side, just over a foot apart. Like trailblazers on a stagecoach, one man drove and the other did the navigating and shooting. They would live and die on the wild frontier together; one couldn't go over the cliff without the other. The arrangement fostered a mutual admiration society with few equals in aviation.

"Good see you, Lunker," said Eli, with an uptick in his voice. "No Midway in port. Where Midway?" His glee was palpable.

"Midway is somewhere at sea, south of Japan, Eli." Lunker smiled. "We flew here to escape a typhoon that's roaming around the western Pacific like a drunken sailor."

Eli laughed hard and loud. "Always better here, Lunker. What over horizon?" His joy was contagious. "What over horizon?" was a question he asked every time he saw his friend from the north Georgia mountains. Eli had an insatiable curiosity to see over the horizon, the mystical line where the water met the sky. His dream was in full view every day — less than twenty miles away if he climbed a nearby hill — yet out of reach for a lifetime, he had finally conceded.

"More water and land, Eli, but none as beautiful as right here. God made this the most special place under the sun and the moon, and you are the icing on the cake." Lunker responded emotionally and truthfully, the way he did each time he answered Eli's question.

Eli smiled and made a sign of the cross, just as he did every time he heard his friend's answer.

One day in the future, Lunker would leave for America and their unforgettable time together in the south Pacific would be over. Accepting that, Eli often reminded his tall friend that they could make a monkey meow before they could slow the passage of time, which is why on this day, like all their days together, they would simply and cheerfully celebrate their friendship in paradise...today.

Courtesy of the typhoon roaming around the western Pacific like a drunken sailor, three of Lunker's squadronmates — Rooster, Barkus and his commanding officer, traditionally called 'Skipper' — stood together with him on the first tee of the Binictican Golf Course. The course was meticulously carved out of an unforgiving jungle on the Subic Naval Base complex. Two of their four caddies had run ahead in the event any of the tee shots landed in the jungle rough.

Eli was the only caddy Lunker had used in over three dozen rounds played at the course during his time in the squadron. With a natural ease, the two had become dear friends. Eli sported a bony frame and flashed an oversized smile each time he hoisted a bag onto his shoulder. He walked slightly hunched over, a visual impact confirming nineteen years of carrying heavy golf bags up and down lush rolling hills.

Like time and tides, the views in Subic Bay were consistent and predictable. They were spectacular in weather good, bad, or treacherous. It was the only land Eli's eyes had ever seen, but he knew he was blessed to live among such natural beauty, even though it came at a high price — it was more likely that a child living in this lush paradise would die before the age of ten than live to see the age of sixty.

Despite outliving three precious children, and likely being denied the opportunity to ever see over the horizon, Eli would not argue with his Creator over the circumstances of his life on earth. He had many reasons to do so, but his principled ethics would never allow the economic disparity between his life and that of the men for whom he caddied to interrupt his faith in God, nor let it be a source of self-pity, nor justify actions he believed to be morally wrong. To live that way or teach his children that wrong was right when money was involved would betray every ounce of his character.

From their first round of golf together, Lunker recognized the uncompromising morals and principles that ruled Eli's world. It was those steadfast attributes that humbled the aviator from the north Georgia mountains each and every time he observed his caddy simply living his life. He also recognized Eli's determined efforts to elevate his self-taught literacy. Despite having very little formal education, he still became fluent in English and nearly fluent in Spanish and German.

"How many days here?" Eli's voice was emotionless, but he was praying the answer would be more than one.

"At least two, Eli. Probably three. A good time for you to make me a better golfer," Lunker answered hopefully.

"Impossible three days. Need three years." Eli laughed out loud; he was overjoyed. The God above who had taken three of his children home too early still loved him. Lunker always made his day brighter, and not just because he was a very generous tipper. Eli loved Lunker's irreverent attitude toward life and, equally, his unfailing reverence for the bountiful land on which they stood.

It was the same land, not too far away, where Eli had buried three of his five children, side by side, in graves he dug, and then refilled, himself. Two girls and a boy — Dalisay, Ligaya, and Nimuel — sweet children with silky brown skin who never lived long enough to celebrate their seventh birthdays. Their short lives and Christian names were now in the place God reserved for those who died too young, too often, and too easily in this tropical place that most called paradise.

By birth years, Eli was thirty-six, but on the back nine of middle age when compared to those where he lived. His parents had both died in their late forties. His older brother died at forty-three, and a younger sister at thirty-one. Two siblings, whom he never knew, died as infants. Only Eli was still walking the earth. He was grateful, and so was Lunker.

The skipper teed off first, followed by Rooster, Lunker and Barkus, most senior to most junior in rank. All four were on the green after two shots. Surprisingly, Barkus was closest, just fifteen feet away, but three putted. Rooster also had a bogey, and the skipper and Lunker made par.

"Number two can get interesting, Barkus," said his skipper. "The hole is famous for monkeys sitting at the edge of the green and stealing golf balls."

"Will the caddies chase them off?"

"Only if they become aggressive. They say the monkeys have as much right to be here as we do, and they're right."

As the group approached the tee box for the flat one-hundred sixty yard par three, two monkeys, each with a reddish-brown coat and a tail about two feet long, sauntered slowly from the edge of the jungle to within two feet of the left side of the green. A third monkey hung back about fifteen feet. They were the size of very large cats, lean, but muscular and powerful, maybe eighteen inches tall, although they looked much larger because of the way they sat, upright and sturdy, next to the green. Their eyes were focused like lasers on the men standing near the tee box.

"The mother, she has baby under her." Eli spoke like a protective father, and pointed toward the one furthest away. She was slightly hunched over, making it difficult to see the baby at a distance. However, as she eased closer to the green, the baby, dark brown, almost black, in color, could clearly be seen glued to her chest, facing inward, and looking from side to side, using its hands and feet to hang on.

The skipper walked up to the tee box and prepared to hit. He took just one practice swing. Two of the caddies had walked well over halfway to the second hole, one positioned on the right, and one on the left. They made no move to interfere with man's distant cousins.

As the monkeys watched like spectators in a small gallery, the skipper hit a beautiful shot. It started low and rose in a gentle arc, bending to the right to match the slight dogleg of the hole. The ball bounced a few times and rolled fifteen feet inside the fringe of the green.

"Nice shot, Skipper, but no gimme," reinforced Lunker, smiling. Still twenty feet to the hole."

As the skipper started to reply, his eyes locked on to one of the monkeys, the tallest and biggest of the three. The monkey slowly began walking toward his ball, daring anyone to challenge him. "Son of a bitch. That was a good shot," he remarked, and then added, "You see where it's located. I'll spot it there if he takes it."

"I don't know, Skipper, since we can't be sure where it really landed, you may have to hit another one if he decides he wants one of your balls as a souvenir," Lunker suggested, laughing. He loved improv comedy and this was as good as anywhere in the world.

"Get that monkey away from my ball," their skipper demanded, and then laughed. The caddies stayed silent, unmoving, not sure if the skipper was serious or not. They had no desire to tangle with a monkey; all four caddies had previously witnessed how fierce they could be. That was a lesson learned often by those who were indigenous neighbors with the monkeys, sharing the same jungle that fed them both.

The monkey walked directly to the skipper's ball and picked it up, keeping it in his right hand as he walked with a lazy swagger back to where he had previously been sitting, and resumed his squatting position.

"I hate and love those monkeys when they're a wise ass just like us," said the skipper to no one in particular. The other three Eagles were silent. "I'll hit a provisional," offered their skipper. His hair had a glisten of sweat as he leaned down and teed another ball.

His second shot looked like a copy of the first, but better, about six feet closer to the hole. "Take that, monkey butt." As he reached down to pick up his tee, the monkey by the green was on the move again, this time faster.

Seeing the monkey approaching his second ball, the skipper quickly teed a third ball. "He'll remember this round of golf," professed the skipper. He hit a powerful shot with a flat follow through. The ball had minimal arc; it was more of a low line drive than a typical golf shot, and it was rocketing toward the monkey that was now crossing the edge of the green with his second ball, near where the mother sat with her baby.

A sickening sense of dread briefly swept over the other golfers and caddies. Two of the caddies yelled toward the monkeys until they realized the skipper's shot was starting to elevate and turn right, high and away from the mother and her baby. The monkeys remained steadfast in their places.

The skipper's ball flew at least a hundred feet over the monkeys as it bent to the right, disappearing fast like a white dot deep into the jungle, well away from them. The monkey walking off the green looked toward the foursome and held the gaze, never slowing his deliberate stride as he retreated into the jungle with the skipper's balls in his right hand. The other two monkeys, one of whose very young passenger was staring at the men staring back at him, followed him.

I shall not be moved. The animal kingdom's silent and peaceful protest was indelibly powerful. No one said anything until their skipper turned toward them and laughed. "That friggin' monkey is squeezing my balls."

The two caddies nearby had remained silent, but now joined the Americans who were laughing out loud.

The skipper smiled and admitted, "Hell, he was just doing what I would have done if I was a monkey. Besides, I couldn't hurt a distant cousin." They all laughed as their skipper continued. "And don't ever forget that a scorned woman has nothing on a scorned monkey. A scorned monkey will try and bite your fucking leg off." He smiled. He had a scar to prove it.

The skipper smiled and handed his caddy a hundred pesos, about fourteen dollars, and asked him to run ahead to the snack hut and bring back four San Miguel beers for the golfers and four beverages of each caddy's choice. His caddy was happy to do so; he hadn't yet comprehended the skipper's sense of humor.

They finished playing the second hole as if nothing had happened. The comedy club had shut its doors. It was time for four competitive aviators to refocus on the game.

"Barkus, there's a real treat coming up. It's a steep climb up to the tee box for number three, but there's a creative solution that makes it easier," said the skipper as they walked off the green.

They reached the bottom of a steep hill, rising at least a hundred feet above them. Packed mud steps were carved into the side and partially reinforced with soft wood. To the immediate right of the steps was a rope tow, made of thick coarse hemp and powered by a rudimentary generator, dating back at least twenty-five or more years. One of the caddies pressed a green button, and the thick rope began moving slowly.

The panoramic view from the top was a two-page spread straight from National Geographic. The hole was at least two hundred feet below where the golfers stood, and the view across the top of the jungle encompassed Subic Bay's sparkling blue waters far to their right and the tall mountains beyond. To their left, a low canopy of palm trees framed a peek-a-boo view of blue South Pacific waters. They stood there for five or ten minutes, listening as the caddies described the plants around them, the birds that came into their view, and the various animal and bird sounds they heard.

The skipper's caddy arrived shortly with beer for the golfers and a soda for each of the caddies. He smiled and nodded his head in gratitude when the skipper told him to keep the change. "Salamat," he said, 'thank you' in Tagalog, an informal version of Filipino, the official language of the Philippines. The change alone would support his family for five days, maybe a week.

As they savored the view and chatted, Eli took a club from Lunker's bag and pointed to a small, harmless looking snake with alternating black and yellow stripes. It was resting lazily in standing water at the bottom of a tree, about twenty feet away.

Eli took a long sip of his Pepsi and said, in a soft voice, "This baby krait. Adult krait big." He held his hands about three feet apart. "If adult krait bite, will release venom it needs to kill. If get fast doctor, may live. Otherwise, die one day." He held up one finger, then a second finger. "Two lucky."

The four Eagles listened intently. Golf and beer were secondary for the moment. "Baby krait, like this," he kept the club pointed at the small snake, "release all venom when bite. All have in them. Die much quicker. Important get fast to doctor."

Each of the golfers contemplated this real life lesson on life in a jungle between holes of golf. It was a brief interlude that quickly became a father's heartbreak and an unfair chasm between two cultures.

Eli was silent for a moment. He retreated back to the group and stood next to Lunker. A few heartbeats later, his eyes looked toward the earth as he exposed a sad day in his heart. "My daughter Ligaya. She second baby. Her name mean happy." He paused, still looking down.

"Good name for her. She always smile, sing. She walk humming favorite song when step on baby krait by small river near house." He stopped speaking as his eyes looked at the snake near them and then skyward to the heavens. After a few moments, he looked at the four Americans in front of him.

"She die six seven hours later." He made a sign of the cross. "Fourth birthday."

Four men from across a wide ocean stood in numbed silence.

"Not right die young." Eli paused. "She better place. Always smile be happy. Place more far than all horizon."

What he didn't tell the group was that, after burying Ligaya, the third of his five children to die young, and after everyone else in his village had returned to their homes, Eli allowed himself a few moments to cry alone by the spot where his three babies were laid to rest. They were together, side by side, each in a small wooden coffin he built himself and in a grave he personally dug and, later, refilled with dirt.

Dalisay, meaning 'pure' in his Tagalog language, was Eli's first child and the first to die, succumbing to the painful wrath of a simple ear infection. Dalisay's name was perfect — pure love, he would say to strangers and friends alike. She was his first real love, he joked with his wife. He bragged to anyone who would pay attention that he would move the jungle and all its animals to protect his baby girl. Unfortunately, neither the jungle nor the wild animals could produce the antibiotics needed to keep her from dying from an illness easily cured in modern countries with a single trip to a pharmacy.

Slightly over twelve miles south of Eli's native village was a sprawling American naval base, where antibiotics and pain relievers were plentiful and free to the families based there. Two weeks later, Dalisay's suffering and diminishing cries ended along with her five years of life. She departed the jungle for whatever place God reserved for her and the other children who died too young, too frequently, and too easily in a land that, aesthetically, was a natural utopia.

Eli and his wife had picked their names at birth for what they represented: Dalisay — pure; Ligaya — happiness; and, for his only son, Nimuel, who fell prey to a minor respiratory

19

infection — peace. This is how they would always remember them.

The four American aviators and the four Filipino caddies occupied the same geographic plot of land, but the two groups were worlds apart. It was a thought the four aviators would have difficulty reconciling, no matter how many rounds of golf they played in this gorgeous land called Subic Bay.

The genesis of Eli's spirit was a dream, one that was unchanged since his youth. Maybe his dreams would never come true, but he could dream, couldn't he, he would joke with himself.

Since he was a young child, Eli wanted to take flight and see over the horizon, the mystical place where the ocean kissed the sky. He longed to dance among the clouds and rise above the dark ones that gave a daily soaking to the lush green carpet upon which he walked. He yearned to see behind a thunderstorm, to see the arrival of a distant typhoon, and to see dolphin and whales in the water. He ached to see the land his golfers called home, and from where the great ships sailed.

Most of the golfers he met told him he lived in paradise. Children wouldn't die so easily in paradise, he thought. Still, he never contradicted their statements, even though he couldn't understand why they complained about life in the Navy. They visited foreign lands, and they and their families were well fed, well paid, and had medical care any time of day. Many were aviators who tamed the untamable skies. To Eli, all of that sounded like a dream come true, but to contradict them fell into the category of trying to make a monkey meow or a dog quote Plato.

It was why he had grown close to Lunker. They made each other laugh, and both accepted that they could never win an argument with their creator over outcomes or circumstances, so they simply chose to turn their daily life into a day of living.

The rest of the round passed quickly. The caddies each had two hot dogs and another soda at the turn between holes nine and ten; the Eagles each had a single hot dog and another beer.

After the round of golf was completed and final scores tabulated, the group stood together enjoying a final round of sodas and beer. As always, Eli asked a question he always did when a new aviator joined the group of golfers. He was intrigued, if not amused, by the answers he heard.

"Barkus, how you get call sign?'

"Eli," Lunker interjected himself before Lieutenant junior grade Ted Snell could answer, "It isn't well known, but Barkus actually comes from royalty."

"Really?"

"Yes, really," Eli's dear friend answered. "Barkus is a direct descendant of King Daniel the Spaniel." Everyone howled as Barkus forced a half smile. He maintained it as Lunker continued and told Eli the real story behind Snell's call sign, which related to a dead dog named Spartacus.

In a moment of therapeutic and curiosity-driven clarity, Eli posed a question he had long pondered. "Is fly jets from carrier, fly over horizon up by clouds, high fast like great birds, see world upside down, all that better than sex?"

He watched as four heads nodded in unison. He listened with even greater curiosity when Lunker placed his right hand on his shoulder, and said slowly, "But Eli, is it better than really great sex that makes the toes curl and the whole body smile?"

Eli unconsciously leaned his body forward as he individually glanced at three aviators and, lastly, looked into the eyes of his dear friend next to him. "Never," was the simultaneous answer from four voices. Eli couldn't smile any broader. He and the aviators had something very dear and wonderful in common. It was truly a special day in Subic Bay, a spectacular place called paradise.

Nine hundred miles to the north of Subic Bay, shortly after noon, Lieutenant Willie McMahon's flight of three Intruders lifted off from Kadena Air Force base in Okinawa and made a turn to the northeast on a path that took them within twenty miles of Nagasaki, one of two cities that ushered in the atomic age. From there, they crossed the Sea of Japan and proceeded on a direct path to Osan Air Force Base in South Korea. They were running from the same typhoon that their squadronmates in Subic Bay had escaped.

Two hours later, the three jets were parked on Korean soil, and the six aviators gathered by Willie's airplane. "Here's my recommendation. Leave all your flight gear here at the airplane for now. Fish, how about sticking around to make sure the refueling guys know the fuel load we want. We'll see you inside in a few."

The five aviators had barely gotten inside the one-story brick operations building when an Air Force officer approached. "I'm Lieutenant Colonel Ed Carroll. Let's go to weather. We may have a problem."

Inside the weather office, they discovered the typhoon's track had dramatically changed. The base weather officer's words were foreboding. "The storm is heading almost due west again. Our best guess is it's going to slide across Hiroshima and then take a turn toward the northwest."

"Which puts it right where we're standing," Willie offered.

Lieutenant Colonel Carroll nodded. "And we don't have room inside the hangars for your jets." His terse statement was genuinely empathetic. He had been in their shoes before.

Willie stood in silence for several seconds, and then asked to use a telephone. Five minutes later, he had a plan. "We're heading to Misawa. They have good weather now, and the forecast is for more of the same over the next couple days. We'll stay there until Atsugi is open for business again."

Atsugi, Japan was home to Midway's air wing, formally named Carrier Air Wing Five, and abbreviated CVW-5, but most commonly called and written CAG Five. VA-115 was one of ten squadrons assigned to the air wing. Atsugi was located an hour away from the Japanese port city of Yokosuka, where Midway was based. Sailors pronounced Yokosuka as Yuh-Koos-Ka, with a slight emphasis on the middle syllable.

The base ops officer responded quickly. "We'll file a flight plan for you."

An hour later, Eagle 502, a flight of three jets with six tired and exasperated aviators, was airborne again. Misawa was still over two hours away.

By the time the three Intruders touched down at Naval Air Facility Misawa in northern Japan, the six occupants had spent nine of the past eleven hours strapped into ejection seats not designed for comfort. They were more than ready for hot food, cold beer, and, ultimately, a warm bed.

"Misawa ground, Eagle 502, three Intruders for taxi."

"Eagle 502, Misawa ground, hold your position. A follow-me truck will escort you to parking."

"Eagle 502, Wilco."

"This isn't good, Gully." Willie sounded concerned. "Three Champ A-7's are parked inside that hangar at our ten o'clock." The VA-56 Champs were one of two A-7 Corsair squadrons assigned to CAG-Five, Midway's air wing. He continued. "The hangar doors next to them are open, and there's nothing in there. I bet that's where we're headed."

Four minutes later, three tired airplanes and their crews were parked in front of the empty hangar. After flying for almost twenty-five hundred miles, they were just four hundred fifty miles north of their home base in central Japan.

Willie and his squadronmates walked into the air operations office.

"I'm Commander Tom Eller, air ops. I guess you haven't heard the latest about the typhoon."

"Nice to meet you, sir, and no, I can only imagine what it's doing now."

He laughed at Willie's comment. "I'm afraid we're stuck with each other, but I have some good news and two bits of bad news."

"Give it to us. Bad news first, please."

"The typhoon took a rather sharp turn north as it passed over the Hiroshima area and is now barreling up the Sea of Japan, picking up steam, and heading this way. Unfortunately, its massive size will affect Atsugi, so you're stuck here."

"What's the second bit of bad news," asked Willie.

"We have no room in the bachelor officer's quarters, the chief's quarters, or the enlisted barracks for you." After a short pause, he continued. "The good news is we did locate six rooms for you."

While it was good news, it wasn't worthy of any drama, the group of aviators thought. "They're in the dormitory where we exclusively house female teachers and nurses under a civilian contract with the base." There was a long pause as his words registered with the Eagles.

"This isn't a joke, is it?

"I just received approval from the base commander. By the way, the base mini-mart will be open for thirty more minutes."

There were high fives all around to celebrate their change of luck, although none would believe it until they arrived at their destination. The entire day had been surreal, and this was simply too surreal to be true.

Twenty-five hundred miles of flying to land in a women's dormitory. God bless stormy weather.

After buying a wide range of food and libations, they drove two miles before arriving at their destination, a medium size, two-story brick building. While unremarkable in appearance, it was what was on the inside that mattered to the men.

Their arrival was enveloped with a sense of predestined celebration. A welcoming party of eleven nurses and teachers greeted them, literally, with open arms and a choice of cold Sapporo or Kirin beer. Within ten minutes, typhoon party rations and the aviators' travel bags were unloaded, rooms assigned, introductions made, and the first of many toasts offered to a long, slow storm.

The wind was picking up, and a light drizzle had begun falling from the sky, but it was irrelevant. It could rain for forty days and nights and no one would mind. A splendidly long typhoon would simply be one more item to toast.

The women were intrigued by how the Eagle aviators' call signs originated. One of the nurses guessed Gully originated from Gulliver's Travels, to which Gully smiled. When Socks interjected that it was because he was "so damn gullible," Lauren Adams, a native of Ocala, Florida and a graduate of Northern Colorado University, quickly rose to Lieutenant junior grade Mitch See's defense. She was the high school's music director, and also taught guitar and voice in after-school lessons.

"Gully, the next time someone says they call you Gully because you're so gullible, you point out to them that gullible isn't actually a real word and can't be found in any dictionary."

"Really?" Even Gully was surprised at that information, but thrilled as Lauren looked at him and nodded. "Well, take that fellas. I guess it's time to come up with another call sign." He was smiling from ear to ear at the thought of being ordained Tiger or something similarly ferocious.

The laughter from Lauren and her roommates and his five fellow Eagles squelched his momentary elation.

"Damn it, I just can't win," he lamented out loud.

"You're a cutie, Gully. You just need a little extra instruction." The statement came from Sharon Navarra, a history teacher from Temple, Texas, and a graduate of Trinity College in Connecticut. She walked over and sat on the floor next to him. As Sharon put her arm across Gully's shoulders, Willie smiled at his B/N's good fortune.

The women unanimously agreed that the call signs for Mike 'Fish' Trout, Bobby 'Socks' Miller and John 'Doc' Holliday were as natural as green grass. When they asked about the origination of

25

Tonto's call sign, Lieutenant junior grade Dave Gregory remained silent, just long enough that Fish spoke up for him.

"I'll answer that with a question. Did the rock group Queen sing Bohemian Rhapsody or Mohican Rhapsody?" A few of the nurses and teachers quickly made the relevant connection and laughed. Tonto blushed slightly, but smiled.

Jackie Murphy, a pediatric nurse from Palo Alto, California, responded in an unexpected way. "That's one of my favorite songs, Tonto." The buxom brunette stared into his eyes. "And my call sign is Pocahontas," she said as she moved next to Tonto and put her right arm across his shoulders.

The typhoon party had officially started, and it didn't matter where the massive storm chose to go. If Misawa was a test, an A-plus answer was blowing in the wind.

Anticipating the imminent loss of electrical power, numerous pitchers of margaritas, pina coladas, and bushwackers were quickly made and placed in ice chests, coolers, and in the two refrigerators' freezers, one located on each floor.

Bushwackers, a creamy chocolate pina colada type drink, originated in its current form in 1975 at the Sandshaker Lounge located on Pensacola Beach, Florida. Enjoying a bushwacker was an unofficial curriculum requirement for both naval aviators and Navy nurses as they trained at the nearby naval air station and naval hospital in Pensacola.

Doc stood just inside the kitchen door, watching Lauren as she mixed a fresh batch of bushwackers in the blender. As a young child, her family relocated from Ocala to Lexington, Kentucky and then, a few years later, moved permanently to Manitou Springs, Colorado, a scenic mountain town seven miles west of Colorado Springs. The picturesque enclave was renowned for long hikes on trails where breathtaking vistas never failed to make her wish for just one more day on the continental divide. Misawa wasn't far from Japan's mountains, but Lauren's heart was firmly planted in the Rocky Mountains.

She was five-six, Doc guessed, or five-seven, with innocently sultry looks that were somewhere between perfect and ideal. As he surveyed her tantalizing features, he knew it'd be a challenge to a man who believed he could choose just one as a favorite. Lauren had the creamy olive skin of a European beauty, a sleek busty figure, small hips, and the strong but elegant legs of a dancer. Her alluring eyes resembled two radiant emeralds, and they easily penetrated right to the core of Doc's romantic soul. Medium brown hair, full-bodied and tied in a ponytail, fit her well, although Doc would learn that it could also be styled with randomly provocative locks that cascaded over her shoulders and a third of the way down her back. He would also learn that she sang with the voice of an angel. Without a doubt, this mountain-loving beauty was a teacher that the teenage boys in her classes would dream about for many years.

On this night, Lauren was wearing a pair of blue jean shorts and a black tank top, suitable for the steamy summer evening. She hadn't noticed Doc standing nearby, observing her movements.

"Need some instruction with that?" Doc spoke loudly over the noise of the blender.

Lauren turned and looked directly at Doc, surprised at seeing him there. She had noticed him earlier and loved the way he handled himself so easily around the group, but her cautionary nature had kept her from approaching him. She stopped the blender and smiled at him.

"I'm the teacher, you know."

"Did the Navy tell you that? The same Navy that trusts me with an expensive airplane?"

He walked toward her, mesmerized by the tantalizing smile in front of him, and stopped by the sink a few feet from where she stood.

"I was hoping you were making those for the two of us," he said in his most optimistic tone.

"I like that thought." She looked straight into his eyes and smiled, holding his attention. "So let's just call them ours."

"Allow me to formally introduce myself. I'm Doc Holliday, although my mother calls me John." He extended his hand.

"I'm Lauren Adams, and my students call me Miss Adams," she said, laughing as she shook his hand.

"Well, Miss Lauren Adams," he paused, "my grandmother would call you pretty as a fresh peach, but what if I call you the lovely Misawa bushwacker maker?"

She laughed as she turned the blender back on. "What did you just say?" she asked loudly, looking directly at him over the intruding whirring noise. "You want a peach bushwacker in a pretty cup?" She turned the blender off again.

Doc laughed. "Can I pour you a cup of Misawa's finest, Lauren," he asked as he reached for the blender. He was intrigued by her personality and quick witty replies as much as her beauty. It reminded him of how Willie, his best friend in the squadron, described his emotions when he first met Tosh, his girlfriend, in an unexpected encounter by a stairway leading to a beach in Japan. He could relate to that emotion.

"I'd like that." She smiled as Doc poured the smooth, luscious drink into her cup.

Just after midnight, the base's power finally succumbed to the storm. Like a well-rehearsed military operation, candles were lit and music shifted to battery-powered cassette players. No one missed a beat. Only the blenders were silenced as the party steadily matched the storm for intensity.

Doc and Lauren took their drinks and a small cooler with more Bushwackers, two large candles, a flashlight and a portable cassette player upstairs, and settled into the room Doc had selected. An oversized couch became their temporary home.

They shared stories of their pasts and their dreams for the future, places they'd visited and places they wanted to visit, and how they chose their current professions. They both loved to hike and hoped to visit the Caribbean. They compared their favorite movies, and Doc told her about Bunkroom Eight's Far East Film Society. For as long as anyone could remember, it had been the place to gather and watch movies, and rightfully earned the film society title.

Bunkroom Eight had two televisions; one was devoid of electronics, but housed at least eight or nine bottles of alcohol in the empty space. The Bunkroom Eight motto, *It only hurts when you're awake,* was a nod to Midway's extensive time at sea and justification for an inoperative television.

By the time the two fell asleep on the couch, Doc and Lauren had shared everything but their bodies. That was their mutual decision.

Two rooms away, the opposite was occurring. Gully and Sharon were like high school teenagers discovering the pleasure of touch for the very first time. She demonstrated the historical progression of passion and told him that she didn't want the night to end. Gully was a good student and believed her every word, every time.

In the room across from Gully and Sharon, Fish was demonstrating how to fly two-plane formation to Donna Ingalls, an elementary school teacher. She was a distant relative of David Ingalls, a Navy pilot who, in World War One, became the Navy's very first ace. They practiced tucking-it-in-tight until they were as smooth as the Blue Angels.

In the room above the downstairs living room, there was no doubt that Tonto and Jackie, whose nickname Pocahontas was affirmed by the aviators, were active as well.

Directly below them, though, Willie and Socks, both of whom had love interests of their own, were behaving in a manner that would please their women, both an ocean away, even though they were sitting with seven attractive women playing a drinking game called cardinal puff. It was a game that could be won, although few rarely maintained their concentration long enough to succeed. As drinking requirements increased, mistakes increased.

Incredibly, both Socks and Marti Williamson, a high school math teacher from Austin, Texas, prevailed over the mind-numbing effects and earned lifelong bragging rights that they overcame both alcohol and a typhoon to earn the drinking game's coveted title of cardinal. Had Socks and Marti not already had their own love interests, it's very likely they would have found a cozy corner in which to christen their achievement.

Mostly, though, the group downstairs shared stories from their varied backgrounds and their time living in Japan. It was a relaxing evening, intoxicating in so many ways, in spite of the maelstrom occurring just outside their walls.

By nine o'clock the next morning, the storm began to ebb as nurses, teachers, and aviators slowly stirred back to life. The wind and rain remained steady and strong but, fortunately, just remnants of the storm's earlier violence.

An hour later, a welcome breeze began flowing through the dormitory again. Life was slowly returning to normal, although the restoration of electrical power was an unanswered question. Around noon, a base security official requested that one of the Eagles' officers go with them to the hangar to ensure there was no damage to the airplanes. Willie volunteered; it would give him an opportunity to send a status report to the Eagles' squadron duty officer in Atsugi.

Not knowing when non-emergency power would be restored in Misawa, his message stated their intention to remain in place for at least one more night and that "aircraft and air crews are settled in and doing very well."

Doc and Lauren held hands as they walked in a light drizzle without an umbrella. It wasn't lost on either of them that they were in foreign territory, emotionally and geographically. Lauren was looking at him when he broke into a big smile.

"Are you smiling at something I just didn't say,' she asked, "or do funny jokes just randomly find their way into your mind?"

He looked at her and leaned in close, giving her a kiss on the lips that lingered a few emotions longer than casual affection. "I was thinking about the two of us. God used a typhoon to chase me across twenty-five hundred miles of western Pacific waters and two foreign countries just so I'd land right into your arms."

His unexpected kiss momentarily rendered her speechless, but she recovered quickly. "God is great, God is good. Let us thank him for our bushwackers and typhoon."

They both laughed and kissed again as rain dripped down their faces, cooling the skin but not their passion.

Doc was quiet for a few moments. "I'd like to see you again, Lauren. I hope you feel the same way."

"I do, Doc," she responded, glad that Doc had broached the issue and that their feelings were mutual. "I'll get the details on taking the train to Tokyo." She paused. "It'll be nice to see where this leads."

"That's a good plan, and I can bring probably bring a jet up here for a weekend or two before we deploy again."

The second night in Misawa was similar to the first night, except that electrical power was restored in the early evening, approximately twenty-two hours after it was initially lost.

Tonto and Pocahontas continued remodeling their wigwam, inch by lustful inch, while Fish and Donna perfected day and night formation flying. Sharon made Gully a tiger after all, and Doc and Lauren never broke their promise to each other.

Forty-six hours after arriving, six Eagle aviators and eleven residents of Misawa stood together by three Intruders, parked on the flight line like powerful statesmen. Saying goodbye to new friends met in foreign lands never grew easier.

As the Eagles made final preparations for flight, three single-seat A-7 Corsairs were being towed from their hangar to the flight line. Three VA-56 Champs pilots walked leisurely behind their jets, talking and laughing among themselves. The two groups of aviators smiled and waved to each other.

An hour later, three Intruders departed Misawa to begin the short journey south to Atsugi. Gully was quiet for the entire flight. He'd just had a heartbreaking introduction to the reality of life on Midway. The ship was known as the Navy's Foreign Legion for a reason — that exclusive badge of honor came with an unfairly heavy price tag.

A little over ninety minutes later, the three Intruders touched down on Atsugi's runway as the sun was starting to settle below the western horizon. As the crews walked into the hangar, Lieutenant Commander 'Cracker' Graham, the Eagles' maintenance officer, greeted them with somber news.

"The Champs lost a jet on the takeoff roll at Misawa."

"What?" Fish asked, incredulously. "Did the pilot get out?" That was always the first question.

Cracker shook his head.

"Have they released the name," inquired Tonto, with a sense of sadness in his voice.

It was sobering to think that they had been one of the last to see whoever had died, a selfless patriot smiling as the last minutes of his life ticked toward zero.

"Not officially, so don't repeat it, but it was Rita." Cracker delivered the stunning news. Jim 'Rita' Hayworth was a popular pilot in the air wing, and well respected as an officer.

"What happened?" Sock's question was asked quietly, his suddenly moist eyes looking at his feet and then back up. He and Rita had been in the same squadron in Beeville, Texas for almost a year during jet training. Rita was Socks' closest friend outside of the Eagles. They had dinner together less than a week earlier.

"Lots of speculation, but too early."

The middle-aged couple's home was situated directly on the Choptank River, one mile south of the quaint village of Oxford, on Maryland's eastern shore. They had picked the property because of the unobstructed views they had from their expansive back yard. With a slight adjustment of their Adirondack chairs, they could watch the sun rise in the east and, later, set in the west across the Chesapeake Bay.

They had two children. A daughter, their oldest child, lived ninety-minutes from Oxford. She was a new mother to a four-month-old baby boy, her first child.

Their son was a Navy pilot, living his lifelong dream of being a member of the elite fraternity that flew airplanes from the deck of a ship. He had recently returned from a five-month deployment on Midway and was planning a weeklong trip to Maryland in less than three weeks to see and hold his new nephew. Everyone was looking forward to the short but overdue reunion. Shortly after returning to Japan, he'd be deploying again for another lengthy cruise.

The couple was walking to their car when a black sedan pulled into their driveway. Two Navy officers in white uniforms stepped out of the car and began walking toward them. Their presence froze the couple with fear.

"Mr. and Mrs. Hayworth?" asked the Navy captain, wearing the gold wings of a naval aviator.

"Yes," the man answered, his voice fraught with the recognition of why the men were likely standing in front of him, "that's us."

Concern was etched into the father's face like chiseled valleys, wishing he could reach out and save his son, but knowing deep inside his aching soul that this chapter had already been decided, possibly finished.

"I'm Captain Tom Houston. This is Chaplain Jesse Pike. We're from the Department of the Navy." He paused for a second to compose himself at this incomprehensible moment. He spoke slowly and deliberately gentle. "I regret to inform you that your son, Jim, died in the crash of his aircraft yesterday while flying in northern Japan."

Jim was their only son, doing what he'd wanted to do since he was just a bright-eyed boy. He was still her little boy, a thought that made his mother collapse into the shaking arms of her despondent husband, both of them unable to comprehend the finality of his word "died."

"Oh No! No! Not My Baby! Oh God, Please, Please Don't Take My Baby!" She felt bile forming in her throat as her anguished screams shattered the peaceful morning along the tranquil bay, and added sound to the dagger penetrating deep inside her sobbing heart.

They had dreams of watching him grow older. He would become a husband and a father himself one day, and they would hold and spoil his children, but that dream died with him. Being handed a folded flag that would be draped over their son's coffin as it made the long flight from Japan to his beloved birthplace wasn't part of their plans for welcoming him home.

CHAPTER THREE

1-800-841-Priorities
Late Spring, 1980

"Attention on deck." All the officers in the Eagles' ready room stood as the squadron's skipper, wearing his short-sleeved khaki uniform, walked directly to a wooden podium in front of the group.

"Good morning, Eagles. Let's get right to business." Commander Singer was smiling. He had assumed command of the squadron just two weeks earlier. He looked around the room, thankful to have under his leadership such a fine group of relatively young men who unselfishly carried, on their shoulders, the preservation of peace for so many. Their average age was twenty-six and two months; he had done the math recently.

To those in the audience, especially the new aviators, the four rows of ribbons above his left pocket, most combat-related, gave them a sense of assurance that he knew exactly how to prepare them for any mission. In particular, the skipper wore the Silver Star, the third highest medal for bravery behind the

Medal of Honor and the Navy Cross. He was twenty-six when it was pinned on his chest.

"I know we've only been home for barely over a month, and the start of the next cruise is nine weeks from tomorrow, but we're going to have at least one at-sea period in the interim, probably at least a week long." He paused, ensuring the news resonated across the rows of seats. "The schedule was confirmed by Admiral McElroy this morning." He paused again. "Cruise will be five months and a week or two long, and we'll spend Thanksgiving and Christmas at sea, and then head back to Japan near the end of January. The long range schedule has us home for six weeks after cruise and then a scheduled deployment of four months, possibly five depending on world events."

As he made the sobering announcement, each person in the room silently heard a clock begin ticking. Even Lunker was silent. He knew the price some in the room would pay for their choice of profession. Living overseas and flying fast Navy jets from Midway was a one-of-a-kind thrill ride, but the extensive time at sea was accompanied by an above average divorce rate.

"You're in the foreign legion, guys. It's what you signed up for, which means you have a lot to take care of before cruise begins. First and foremost, make sure your personal affairs are in order, including updating your will. It's tragic enough if you buy the farm, but the aftermath is worse if your will isn't current." He paused to look at his officers.

"I'm not naming names, but one of the two who died in the Intruder crash back at Whidbey Island a couple months ago left a will that was last updated five years ago, when he was married to his previous wife." He paused to let that bit of information register with those sitting in front of him.

"Talk about dicking the donkey. I'd sure hate to be in his shoes right now."

A low level of laughter could be heard. 'Dicking the donkey' was the most infamous of Commander Singer's many

Singerisms, and he used it in a variety of ways. He sipped his coffee while many scenarios raced through his officers' minds.

"That goes for your troops, too, especially the ones who are married or have ex-wives. Do whatever you need to do to ensure they have time to get it done. If your guys or their families need anything that's getting stonewalled, I expect you to jump in and help them get it resolved long before we're underway."

He quickly scanned his notes. "From today until we leave on cruise, your priorities are your troops first, your wives and kids, if you have them, second, and yourself third." He paused again to let it sink in. "That may sound harsh, but that's our reality. They all have different needs, and you need to keep your priorities straight. You're a naval officer first and an aviator second. It's why you're paid the big bucks."

Lunker couldn't resist. "Do you have change for a nickel, skipper?" Everyone laughed, including the skipper.

"Thank you, Lunker, for reminding us that money certainly isn't why we do what we do."

Since arriving in Japan, Lunker had been away from his wife and daughter over eighty-five percent of the time, and Midway's last deployment, his third in a twenty-one month time span, had been the final nail in their marriage's coffin. His wife knew the next four years of their lives would be a busy schedule of very long days and time away from home. Life in the Navy wasn't the adventure that Lunker's wife anticipated or signed up for. She missed the stability of the mountains.

They had begun dating as juniors in high school in their hometown of Blue Ridge, Georgia, population one thousand twenty. They continued dating through college; both attended North Georgia College in the small, but quaint, mountain town of Dahlonega, Georgia, and married shortly after graduation in 1975.

By late 1976, Lunker and his wife had never traveled outside a one hundred mile radius of their hometown. One evening, while watching television in their small, one bedroom apartment, two newly released commercials caught their attention. One was thirty seconds of exciting flight deck footage and aircraft launches on an aircraft carrier. Another commercial showed sailors and officers in foreign ports, including Hong Kong and Japan.

Each commercial ended with "Navy. It's Not Just A Job, It's An Adventure. 800-841-8000."

Lunker's wife had always wanted to travel. Lunker wanted excitement and adventure. They looked at each other, nodded, and he picked up the phone.

Less than four years after that call, his wife and daughter returned to her hometown in the mountains of north Georgia. She filed for divorce a month after Willie's mother was diagnosed with terminal cancer. Lunker didn't fight it, and it was signed, sealed, and delivered from halfway around the world.

Willie and Lunker spent many hours during the last cruise walking together on Midway's flight deck after flight operations had ceased for the day. It was, most often, one or two in the morning, when the noise was at a minimum and so was any lighting. As they would walk and talk and their eyes became acclimated to the darkness, they saw a night sky reminding them both that, somewhere under those billions of stars, hearts were falling in love, and loving hearts were being broken.

If fate was a game of chance, their roll of the dice had come up snake eyes far earlier than they could ever have imagined. Death and divorce didn't discriminate; it followed in the foreign legion's wake halfway around the globe.

CHAPTER FOUR

Dreams and Demons
Late Spring, 1980

Caller ID was three years away from its first test market in America when the telephone rang in San Diego. "Hello."

"Is this the gorgeous tall blond who makes me smile?" The man's voice was the best alarm clock she could imagine.

"Oh my gosh! Willie, is this really you?" The connection wasn't as strong as those between American cities, but it was reasonably good. Any grogginess she had was rapidly overwhelmed by pure joy.

"I thought you might enjoy a personalized wake up call, Tosh."

"Oh, Willie, I miss you so much." She was fully awake and smiling, sitting against the headboard of her bed with her knees up and pulled in, wishing he was by her side and holding her close.

"It's nice to hear your voice, and I miss you, too."

"I heard you had a typhoon. I was worried about you."

"I flew one of the jets away and it worked out fine. You'll get a letter soon with the story. How are you doing? How's work?" He didn't want to spend time on too many details, especially since he was paying over two dollars a minute for the call. She'd be pleased to read about Doc and Lauren in his letter, but he really wanted to hear how she was doing.

"I'm fine, and work is good. I have lots of pictures from our time together, and they make me want to be back there with you when I look at them," said Tosh. She wished they could talk for hours, but she too had recently checked on the cost per minute to call Japan and knew it was prohibitive.

"I'm flying to the ship about seven o'clock your time tonight, out for about a week or so, and I'll call you when I get back, but I really did just want to hear your voice and tell you that you're always on my mind."

He'd like to have her in his room tonight, doing her own magic before he launched to a ship known for its magic. Government regulations required that he not share information about a ship's movement over a nonsecure telephone line, but he knew the reality was that wives, girlfriends, and bad guys knew the ship's schedule long before the sailors and aviators knew it. That was especially true in the Philippines.

"You be careful with your fast toy, flyboy. Oh, I love my flowers, Willie. They're just beautiful, and I cried when they arrived."

"Let them be a reminder that you are always on my mind, Tosh."

"You're always in my heart, Willie." She paused very briefly. "I'll be nervous knowing you're flying around the boat and all. I heard about the plane that crashed right after I left, the one that went into the water."

"I'll be careful Tosh. I always am." Willie wanted to change the subject and not dwell on the danger. "Oh, I have a new B/N. His call sign is Gully. I sent a letter telling you all about him.

Good guy. You'll like him. Doc and Lunker also asked me to tell you hello."

"Tell them hello back for me. I had one of the photos you hid in my luggage enlarged, the one of the two of us with Mount Fuji in the background, and it's in a frame on my desk at work. All my friends love it and want to meet you one day soon." What Tosh didn't say was that many of them also asked to meet Willie's bachelor friends.

"I miss you, Miss Collins. Every time I see Soupy, I'll think of you. His ready room is right next to mine, if you recall, so I'll see him often over the next week." John 'Soupy' Campbell was her brother-in-law, a naval flight officer on Midway.

"Please tell him I said hello, but don't give him a kiss for me." She laughed, making Willie miss her even more.

"Do you think a long passionate hug would be inappropriate?"

She laughed again. "Silly boy. Save all those for me."

"You know I will." He pictured her waking up; her slightly mussed blond hair and delicious morning smell a fond memory he savored as lonely shards of love penetrated his heart.

They chatted for ten more minutes before Willie succumbed to economic and scheduling realities and wrapped up the call. "I could talk with you forever, Tosh, and that still wouldn't be enough, but I have to be up in less than six hours, so I'd better say goodbye and get into bed."

"Is this goodbye or just sayonara, flyboy?"

"It's I love you past every horizon."

"Ah, I like that, mister pilot man. You make every part of me smile."

Willie was smiling. He'd give anything to be by her side. The separation was painful, and he knew it'd become more painful each time they spoke. "Feel my hugs, Tosh. I'll call you as soon as I'm back."

"Thank you, Willie. Sleep well and be careful. I look forward to hearing your voice soon."

"I love you, Tosh. Bye, bye."

"Bye, Willie. I love you, too." Tosh hung up as a few tears rolled slowly down her face. She wasn't sure if they were tears of joy or tears of fear, as Willie, far from her protective and loving embrace, prepared to do what he'd wanted to do since he was a young boy.

At the same moment as Willie and Tosh's telephone call was taking place, and as the former squadronmates of Lieutenant John 'Rita' Hayworth anxiously tried to sleep in preparation for returning to an aircraft carrier at sea, Rita's parents sat in the front row of graveside seats. Next to them were their daughter and her husband, who was cradling their son, born four months earlier, and named for the uncle he would never meet.

It was a spectacular morning in Oxford, Maryland, one befitting the life of a man who had brought so much light into those fortunate enough to know him during his short stay on earth.

Rita's final journey began as his flag-draped coffin was carefully removed from the hearse and carried by eight of his friends, all Navy pilots, to its resting place near where his parents sat. One of the eight was his fellow squadron pilot on Midway who never left his side as he escorted his friend's body from Japan.

Twenty minutes later, the service ended, and a military band played *Eternal Father, Strong to Save* as a military color guard meticulously folded the same flag that had been solemnly draped over his coffin since its departure from Yokota Air Force Base, just north of Naval Air Facility Atsugi, Japan, thirty-three hours earlier.

As the hymn ended, four A-7 Corsairs, based at Naval Air Station Cecil Field near Jacksonville, solemnly passed overhead in formation. As one of them pulled up and away, creating a missing-man formation, tears flowed like sad rivers down the cheeks of not only his parents, but most of those in attendance, including the two officers who had carried the burden of initially delivering the tragic news.

As the jets flew east toward the Chesapeake Bay, the officer in charge of the color guard approached Rita's family. Kneeling in front of his parents, he honored the ultimate sacrifice of their only son by presenting the grieving mother with the precisely folded flag, saying, "On behalf of a grateful nation." Those sitting close to Rita's parents could hear her softly saying, "My baby, oh my sweet baby," through her tears, as she held the flag tightly against her breasts like a small child.

For Midway's sailors, airmen, and aviators, Tuesday morning came quickly. The final group of Eagles flying to Midway completed their preflight brief at 0930, and had fifteen minutes before their path would end at the squadron's maintenance control office, where each pilot would sign for his jet. Each signature was, in the eyes of the Navy, the pilot's agreement to take ownership of anything and everything that happened to their Intruder until it was safely parked again.

As each of the aviators in CAG-Five crossed the coast of eastern Japan, they silently rejoiced that Midway would only be their home for seven to ten days, or maybe a few more. Soon, CAG-Five's airplanes would cross the coast again, heading east to the ship, but not return for at least five months, and likely longer.

Just after noon, the first Intruder crossed Midway's ramp. If all went well, in two hours Midway would again be fully operational and back to its role as the ultimate lethal weapon, ready to respond to any crisis or mission. The ship would continue to proceed south-southwest, conducting day and night flight operations, and then, in the wee hours of Wednesday morning, turn northwest at the southern tip of Japan to enter the southern boundary of the Sea of Japan. A few hours after that, Midway would make another starboard turn and proceed northeast to begin operations off the eastern coast of South Korea.

Ten minutes after saying sayonara to Atsugi, the final flight of three Intruders checked in with the ship. Gully's voice signaled the ship that a full complement of Intruders would bless the deck of Midway today. "Eagle 507, flight of three Intruders inbound, angels four." The term 'angels' represented the flight's altitude in thousands of feet.

"507, welcome back. Mother's heading one four zero." 'Mother' was the name used by the air controllers for Midway when she was underway.

Today, Midway was operating alone, at least above the water. Everyone on the ship assumed that there was at least one, maybe two, submarines gliding nearby as an underwater line of defense. Whether they were there or not was classified information.

As often as they flew to Midway's deck, it was always a thrill for naval aviators to see the aircraft carrier come into sight, majestically and easily slicing through the ocean, her wake stretching for miles behind her.

"Aviators have seen this view of Midway since long before we were born, Willie." Gully was expressing a sentiment every Midway sailor knew and felt. They were part of a proud history that predated them by over a lifetime.

Willie looked to his right at Gully and smiled as he gave him a thumbs up. Innocuous events such as this nurtured cockpit camaraderie that was memorialized long after the participants' careers were over.

After arriving overhead the carrier, Willie and Gully watched as jet after jet landed on Midway's flight deck. With a few exceptions, all the pilots proved that they hadn't missed a beat during the short time period since their last landings on the carrier. Soon, all aircraft were safely on deck, and Midway's full complement of officers, sailors, and marines were reacquiring their sea legs as the ship sliced through the water at nineteen knots.

Rooster and Preacher were the last to land, and the yellow shirts directed them to a parking spot next to Willie and Gully, who landed just before them. After the two crews each finished their post-flight walk-around and discussions with their jets' plane captains, they met in front of Intruder 516.

All four aviators looked across the flight deck to a seemingly endless sea. "Squeet?" asked Rooster.

Squeet was an abbreviated word created in Bunkroom Eight one evening when one of the pilots, after a long night trying to land on Midway months earlier, said he was too tired to ask, "Who wants to go eat?" Another way of asking was to say, "Who wants to take it in the face?" Although the line didn't work so well ashore, it certainly made perfect sense at sea.

"Sounds like a good plan," responded Willie. "Gully? Squeet?"

It was just another day filled with Midway Magic. In six hours, they'd find out if Midway Magic would overrule what would become a very frightful night, but not for a reason anyone imagined.

On a moonless, pitch-black night, their first at sea, fortune must surely have been favoring the fools. There was only one wave-off and five bolters and, in each of those cases, each pilot was successful on his next attempt. A bolter was a carrier landing where the tailhook failed to snag any of the wires.

The carrier was steaming almost two hundred miles from Atsugi, and everyone was breathing a big sigh of relief when Lunker's calm voice penetrated the silence.

"CATCC, 515. Request squadron rep." CATCC was pronounced "Cat-See."

During night launches and recoveries, each squadron provided a senior aviator to the carrier air traffic control center on the ship to offer specific assistance and guidance related to their respective aircraft.

45

"515, CATCC, roger." Squadron representatives were only requested when a jet had a problem to which the crew couldn't find a solution.

Less than ten seconds later, the Eagles' skipper was sitting next to the CATCC officer. "515, Skipper here."

"We have an unsafe gear indication, Skipper, and would like to get a visual."

"515, CATCC, climb to angels four and proceed overhead."

"515's climbing to angels four."

"514, CATCC."

"514, Go ahead."

"514, Proceed overhead mother at angels three until you have 515 in sight." CATCC was directing Intruder 514 to remain low so as not to create a potential midair collision. Besides Eagle 515, only Eagle 514 was still airborne. Every other aircraft had landed.

"514, Wilco."

"515, CATCC, say your state." CATCC was requesting 515's fuel state in thousands of pounds, the way that tactical jets reported it.

"Four point two."

"Roger. 514, say your state."

"Four point nine and we have a visual on 515."

"Roger, 514, you're cleared to angels four. Report when joined."

"514."

514 quickly rendezvoused on Lunker's airplane, whose pilot was Commander Rick Evans, call sign 'Badman,' who was the carrier air wing commander, commonly called CAG. 'CAG' is a throwback term that originated from Carrier Air Group.

CAG turned off his red anti-collision light so it wouldn't blind Fish as he flew next to him. Fish could see the nose gear and the left main gear extended. The right main gear was still inside the jet. "Your right main is up, CAG, and the gear door is closed." Fish's voice was calm.

On a morbidly black night, Eagle 515 was only being illuminated by 514's oscillating green light that, ironically, created the kind of ghoulish image seen at Disneyland's Haunted Mansion. Fortunately, the clear night made it relatively easy to see what was occurring as the two jets flew just fifteen to twenty feet apart in a circle overhead the ship.

A benefit of being an air wing commander was getting to fly all the aircraft assigned. However, Lunker had much more time and experience in the Intruder than CAG, who was an A-7 Corsair pilot throughout his career, and was providing him with critical recommendations. Lunker replied back to Fish a few seconds later. "Okay, we're going to cycle the gear."

For a safer margin of error, Fish eased his jet a little further away from CAG's jet as he and Birdie watched as 515's two gear raised upward and snuggled securely into the tanker as their landing gear doors closed. "You're clean," reported Fish.

"Roger. Coming down." 515's nose gear door and left main landing gear door opened, and the gear came down as expected, although the right main landing gear door didn't move at all.

"Your right main gear door didn't budge, CAG." Fish's response was clear and concise.

"Roger."

"I'm going to slide underneath and take a look." Fish was calmly and methodically going through each option available to try and provide CAG and Lunker with information to give them options that may work, although their options were very limited.

"Get your flashlight ready, Birdie. We'll take a look under here." Fish maneuvered under CAG's Intruder, flying within fifteen feet of his underbelly to see if anything appeared out of place, which it didn't.

"The jet looks fine except for the door, CAG. Have you tried positive and negative g's?" Fish eased his airplane back out to 515's starboard side at a respectable distance to give CAG plenty of room to try a new solution.

"Negative. We'll do that next." There was no angst in Lunker's voice. He was just a professional working through a problem on a moonless night. There were moonshiners in Lunker's hometown who, most likely, had been in his shoes before, but on the side of a mountain instead of four thousand feet in the air. He wasn't sure which was more precarious, but it didn't matter. They were there, and he was here. If Lunker used the language of his beloved mountains, he'd say this night was as black as a black horse's ass.

For the next fifteen minutes, CAG and Lunker tried every trick anyone could propose, including applying over six g's to the aircraft at high rates of speed.

Finally, with all other options exhausted, a decision was made to transfer fuel from 514 to 515 and for the two of them to fly back to Atsugi. Unfortunately, Murphy's Law predictably reared its poorly timed head, as landing ashore ceased to be an option. Atsugi had just closed due to a disabled Japanese anti-submarine airplane on the runway, and both Yokota Air Force Base and Iwakuni Marine Corps Air Station were outside of 515's available range, even with taking on what fuel the tanker next to them had available to give. Because Midway only had catapults on the bow, and the bow was crowded with airplanes, there was no time to launch a tanker before 515 would be out of fuel.

The situation was dire, and the clock was ticking. The ship had just launched a second helicopter in anticipation of 515's crew performing a controlled ejection at night.

Inside 515, CAG 'Badman' Evans privately confessed his trepidation to his B/N. "I had to eject at night once, Lunker, in the South China Sea during Vietnam, and I swore I would never do that again. I almost drowned that night, and it took the ship over two hours to find me." There was silence for about ten seconds, and then CAG continued. "And I'm even less thrilled about a night barricade with one main gear up."

"I have an idea, CAG." Lunker's voice sounded calm and reassuring, masking the angst raging throughout his body.

"I'm all ears."

"If we're going to dump this jet in the ocean or damage it when we effectively crash land into the barricade, let's try one more thing."

"Keep going."

Inside the cockpit, Lunker looked toward his pilot. "Let's raise the gear, jettison the drop tanks and climb as high as we can." He paused. "Then we nose this puppy over and let gravity and two Pratt and Whitney engines give us as many knots as we can get. When we hit ten thousand feet, you try and pull the wings off."

Lunker paused again, letting CAG absorb his suggestion, and then continued.

"We'll easily get well over seven g's. Hell, maybe eight or nine, and, as the g's peak, you throw the gear down."

Lunker continued after a short pause. "What's to lose? So we overstress the jet and the wings and it can't fly afterwards. Who cares? Right now there aren't any rules, CAG, so screw the jet. We're either going to dump it in the ocean or control crash it into the barricade. Maybe this'll work and we can stay safe and dry."

CAG was silent for about fifteen seconds. "CATCC, Badman."

"Go ahead, Badman." Skipper Singer answered the call.

"Hey Canyon, we're going to try one more thing. We'll let you know if it works." CAG explained their plan as they began a climb to over thirty thousand feet. Badman's reputation as an aviator was exceptional. If anyone was going to pull this off on a dark night over even darker water, he was the one.

At the start of the climb, to get rid of excess weight detrimental to the jet's climb rate, CAG pushed the emergency jettison button on the upper left side of the instrument panel and sent five empty drop tanks freefalling to the bottom of the Pacific Ocean.

A few minutes later came a call everyone was anticipating. "CATCC, 515, we're pushing over. Back to you in a minute." Inside Midway's air traffic control center, where everyone knew the two aviators who were in grave risk either personally or by call sign and voice, the silence on the radio seemed nightmarishly long. The radio calls were also being monitored in every ready room on Midway.

Inside 515, CAG had the engines at full power and rolled the aircraft into a sixty degree dive, flying solely on instruments, as there was no horizon or lights outside, the exception being a green twirling light moving through the darkness, far below them. The airspeed was reading 0.94 Mach as they approached ten thousand feet, and Badman, his focus never leaving his flight instruments, began pulling the Intruder's nose aggressively but smoothly toward the horizon. The moment of truth was approaching.

Lunker, monitoring the 'g' meter, said "gear" as the jet's accelerometer peaked at what appeared to be just over eight 'g's. With an arm that felt as if it weighed well over a hundred pounds, CAG lowered the landing gear handle as he continued the hard pull toward level flight, using only the artificial horizon on his vertical display indicator as a reference.

Inside the cockpit, the two aviators could hear the gear doors opening and focused their eyes on the landing gear indicator and an indication that all three landing gear doors had opened. Seconds later, to their great relief, they heard the 'ka-chunk' sound made when the gear are down and saw symbols that displayed all three landing gear as down and locked.

As CAG returned the Intruder back to level, stable flight, and stared several times at the landing gear indicator, he looked to his right at Lunker, took a deep breath, and offered his hand. "Thanks Lunker." He paused. "I owe you one."

Lunker shook his hand and nodded in the red glow of the instrument lights. It was just another day in the Navy's foreign legion, serving free Americans across a big ocean.

"CATCC, 515, three down and locked." Lunker's calm voice betrayed the notion that there was ever a problem.

"Excellent! Well done guys," was skipper Singer's reply, as he too took a deep breath, relieved that his jet and, most importantly, its crew were safe. "We'll have 514 take a look at you to be sure."

Fish, who had been monitoring 515's flight path from a mile away, was alongside within two minutes. "Hard to confirm in this bowl of black bean soup, but all three appear to be down and locked," reported Fish, as the two airplanes began a descent to enter the approach pattern for a night landing, which almost seemed benign compared to the tension of the past twenty minutes.

With great relief, CAG's Intruder slammed into the flight deck and the landing gear easily held their own.

Thirty minutes later, CAG and Lunker walked out of the Eagles' maintenance control office, both relieved to be in dry flight suits. CAG pulled Lunker aside and repeated his earlier promise. "I owe you one, Lunker. I'm serious. Your idea saved us."

"You did the flying CAG. I was just along for the ride, but there is one thing I could use your help on," admitted Lunker, who briefly gave him the details. CAG listened, nodded slowly, and said he'd see what he could do.

As CAG and Lunker proceeded to the wardroom for a late meal, several of the Eagles' maintenance petty officers and airmen thanked CAG for bringing himself and Lunker and their jet home. Their respect was the best reward Badman could receive.

Five minutes later, numerous Eagles were sitting in the dirty-shirt wardroom listening to the full description of the ordeal as CAG, Lunker, Fish, Birdie, and the others enjoyed late night cheeseburgers, french fries and bowls of soft-served ice cream. An hour later, the discussion relocated to Bunkroom Eight, where popcorn and medicinal alcohol of various types, stored in a faux-TV on top of a locker, were generously offered at a gathering of the Far East Film Society.

Playing on the actual television was the classic John Landis-directed movie, *National Lampoon's Animal House*. It had quickly become a bedrock film for the illustrious society located in the eight-man bunkroom just below the flight deck, and was played often.

Within minutes, the danger that had been so near was now far away. Cheating death was quickly forgotten as conversations in the bunkroom, appropriately known as the Midway Oasis, turned festive and reflected long ago days of few obligations or responsibilities, even as the movie continued to roll.

"I love flying off the carrier, but do you guys ever miss the good old days, when we were flight students in Pensacola, and all we really had to do was fly and drink and hang out?" Lunker smiled as he sipped a very tasty gin and tonic.

A long pause ensued before Doc spoke. "You mean, like what we're doing right now?" Everyone in attendance laughed.

"Exactly, and I think I have a low alcohol warning light." Lunker needed to be refueled; he had earned it. An inoperative television on top of a metal locker was never so inviting as the entire bunkroom continued laughing at the comedic irony of it all.

CHAPTER FIVE

Days To Remember
Late Spring, 1980

Bad guys didn't rest simply because Midway was nestled into Berth Twelve...Neither did the all weather attack component of the Navy's foreign legion.

The Eagles' skipper stood at the front of the ready room and addressed his aviators. "We've been invited to work with the South Korean Air Force in Kwangju for a six-day weapons detachment. The dates aren't firm, but we'll likely launch two weeks from tomorrow, so a weekend will be in the middle of the det. We'll send five jets and five crews. With transit time, it will be eight days away, possibly nine. Let the ops officer know if you want to go. We won't be swapping crews, so, if you volunteer, you're there for the duration."

Two weeks passed as quickly as a Japanese bullet train. Now, on a Wednesday morning at 0600, not long after the sun had made its daily presence known, four pilots and five B/N's sat in the Eagles' ready room in flight suits, anticipating the brief that would precede their flight to the southern tip of South Korea and Kwangju Air Base, one hundred fifty miles south of Seoul. They were waiting on Commander 'Spice' Curry, the Eagles' XO, who was currently sitting with CAG Evans and the Eagles' CO in his office. The two were on a telephone call with Rear Admiral Ken Sprouse, the commander of Naval Air Forces Pacific, located in San Diego, where the time was two p.m. on a clear and sunny Tuesday afternoon.

Ten minutes later, Commander Curry, wearing his green flight suit, joined the waiting aviators after stopping by the coffee pot in the back. As the XO was taking his seat in the front row, CAG 'Badman' Evans, always a welcome visitor to the Eagles' ready room, strolled in and headed toward the podium by the squadron duty officer's desk. He was wearing his summer khaki uniform. Lieutenant 'Fish' Trout, the offgoing duty officer, called "Attention on deck," as he entered.

"Good morning, everyone. Seats, please," said CAG. "I'm sorry we're late, but I didn't want to hang up on the admiral." Everyone smiled, understanding the delay. RADM Sprouse controlled their flight hours and operating schedule. CAG looked across the ten aviators sitting in front of him. Seven of them were twenty-six years old or younger. Their XO had just turned thirty-seven. CAG himself was only forty-one. He had the greatest respect for them, and envied their many years of flying yet to be flown. They would willingly give their last drop of energy and fly, run, or walk through fire if he asked. Danger was acknowledged, but irrelevant; in fact, he knew it only served to heighten their desire to excel.

If a disinterested outsider happened to enter the room, he'd sense a quiet enthusiasm, not unlike any gathering of professionals preparing for a significant undertaking. To a person, CAG-Five aviators, like all naval aviators, were outcome-driven, and they willingly accepted the burden that anything other than a successful outcome would come with a heavy price tag. Each of the Eagles' aviators loved flying the Intruder and any challenge associated with it, and they especially embraced an opportunity to take their show on the road to an opponent's backyard.

Badman continued. "Thanks for being patient. I know you're ready to head west. Knowing what I know," he paused to ensure they would digest and believe his sentiments, "I'm chomping at the bit to jump in one of your jets right now. Unfortunately, I can't because of pre-cruise obligations. But, if I could, I'd pull rank and kick one of you out of your seat in a heartbeat."

They all smiled and laughed at his comment. "I'm heading down to the hangar to personally brief your enlisted men who will be taking care of you. Like you, they're going to be part of an unprecedented, real-world exercise. It's the kind they'll tell their grandchildren about. Take good care of 'em while you're over there."

CAG hesitated, scanning the faces of the ten aviators who would represent his air wing in the skies over South Korea during the next week. Their unflappable devotion to duty was not only inspiring, but it was addictive. He wished all of America could know these men who served on their behalf.

"Eagles," he promised, smiling a smile that said he knew something they didn't, "this is going to be a detachment to remember. So, good luck and good flying. I'll be looking forward to your daily reports. I know you will represent us well." He nodded. "Carry on."

With those final words, CAG departed the ready room, thinking that for all the incredible moments in the air he had experienced in his career, he'd change places with any of these young warriors in a flash. The daily situation reports from South Korea would ultimately support his high expectations.

The XO took his place at the podium. "Life is more tense than normal in 'no man's land' these days." He was referring to Nightmare Range and the DMZ. "South Korean president Chun Doo-hwan is worried that the North could launch a limited hit-and-run attack at any time." The 'North' was North Korea. "He's personally asked our president for help in providing bad guys to ensure his new pilots and crews get up to speed quickly." He paused and smiled. "And we're the bad guys."

As his statement was absorbed by the assembled group, he took a couple sips of coffee. "You may wonder why we're dealing with the ROK air force on the southern end of the peninsula, instead of those in Osan or other northern bases closer to the DMZ." ROK, pronounced 'rock,' was an abbreviation for the Republic of Korea, more commonly known as South Korea.

"The ROK president is concerned that his air force units up north could be overrun quickly in a surprise attack. It will fall to the squadrons in southern Korea to stop the bleeding and turn the tables." The XO paused to let it sink in, and then dropped a bombshell fact of life on them. "South Korea's forces will not retreat from Seoul. South Korea will win or lose at Seoul. Seoul is their ground zero. This is why our role during the entire detachment is so critical to them. If the northern forces are overrun, then it is up to the air force units in the south to save their country."

The room was as silent as a packed morgue.

"This morning's flight is strictly a transit to Kwangju. While the jets are refueled and armed, we'll have a joint brief with the ROK units that we'll be flying against, as well as more thorough briefs on the targets and ROE." ROE, pronounced as the three letters in order, stood for rules of engagement.

Commander Curry continued with the brief. "We'll be launching high speed, low altitude attacks against Nightmare Range, Koon-ni, and a few other South Korean target ranges. If we're intercepted prior to reaching the target in the first phase, which will run for two days, we will discontinue the attack, and proceed to the next target with the same ROE in place. We will not engage in any defensive maneuvers, if engaged, during the first two days. The XO paused to jot down a note, and to take a sip of coffee, before continuing. "That's a hard rule, not up for discussion or breaking."

"If we reach our target, and prosecute an attack without being intercepted, we will reattack the same target after pulling off and proceeding outbound for five miles. After the second run, whether we're engaged or not, we'll proceed to the next target. We'll attack as many targets as our fuel will allow, and bring back any unexpended ordnance." The XO paused. 'Any questions?"

There were none. "In days three through five, if we're engaged prior to reaching the target, we'll go into an air combat mode. That's two defensive turns and then bug out to the next target. If you become offensive and have a simulated Sidewinder shot, call 'Fox Two,' and proceed to the next target." During air combat maneuvering, commonly called dogfighting, "Fox Two" was a call that a pilot had acquired a launch solution for his heat-seeking missile, and was simulating firing it at an opposing aircraft.

"If a ROK pilot calls a shot, break off the fight, rock your wings, and proceed to the next target. Hard deck, for any air-to-air maneuvering, will be five hundred feet." The hard deck was an altitude designated to simulate ground level. Its purpose was to provide a buffer for pilots who pressed an attack a little too aggressively.

As he ended the last comment, a few of the Eagles replied with comments like "sure thing" and "yeah, right," all loud enough to elicit laughs from the group. Lunker made a verbal suggestion that everyone was thinking. "If they want realistic training, XO, let's make the hard deck two hundred feet."

Commander Curry instantly responded. "That came up in the call with AirPac. His staff wanted a thousand feet; Badman made a case for two hundred feet, based on our operational status and ongoing training. Admiral Sprouse bought off on five hundred feet." He paused to sip his coffee, and ended any further debate on the issue. "On days four and five, we'll start later in the day because night attacks will be integrated into the schedule, including at Nightmare, and then day six is where it gets really interesting."

Everyone in the room perked up. Whatever it was that was going to be revealed was likely to be sweet music to their ears. As the XO described the proposed scenario for day six, and the final flight of the detachment, teenage-like giddiness swept the ready room.

What they didn't know, and neither did the XO, was that General Jeong, the ROK Air Force general in charge of the base, was planning a party of monumental proportions on the last night of the joint exercise. More than just a party, it was a planned event that would have ROK aviators testing the ten Eagles one final time.

As Commander Curry was wrapping up the final few items, he did what Commander Singer often did with both officers and enlisted men, which was to put their place in the world in perspective, especially when the hardships that accompanied deployments and detachments were staring them in the face.

"It isn't lost on anyone that we're leaving on cruise again soon. Some of you sitting here are married; it's a big commitment you're making, and the skipper and I appreciate it. What you will be doing is unique in all the world. These will be stories that you'll never forget, and one day your kids and grandkids will ask you to retell them over and over." He paused, taking stock of the fine officers in front of him.

"This can be life or death, guys, especially for those of you flying nightmare range for the first time. You can't go up there thinking you can dick the donkey and get away with it, because they'll take a shot at you without blinking." He looked at the aviators in front of him. "That is why you have to fly smart but very aggressively, like you're the third donkey to arrive at Noah's ark."

The skipper paused, glancing at his flight crews. He could see a slight change in their facial expressions as they absorbed his 'third donkey to the ark' comment. No one asked if the donkey-at-the-ark's name was Dick; that saddened him a bit. He was sure Lunker or one of the junior officers would have spoken up. Regardless, he knew that was how they'd fight.

"Okay, brief as a crew, and then with your section lead. Magic and I are going to depart twenty minutes earlier than scheduled so we can meet with the ROK air operations officer. We'll see you on deck in Kwangju."

The first section of Eagle A-6's, with Willie and Lunker in the lead, and Flood and Jackal flying wing, released their brakes at 0755 to begin their journey of 630 nautical miles, or 725 statute miles, from Atsugi, located in a country America once fought against, to Kwangju, located in a country America once defended and fought alongside. They would fly from the east coast of Japan on a heading of almost due west, passing just north of Hiroshima, and then across the Sea of Japan, near its southern boundary, where it blends with the East China Sea and Yellow Sea. Finally, they would cross the South Korea's eastern coast and fly direct to Kwangju, their destination, located twenty miles from the country's western coast and a hundred fifty miles south of Seoul.

Ten minutes later, the second section of Intruders, with Fish and Moliver in the lead, and Frank Endacott, still without an Eagle-approved call sign, and Preacher flying wing, rolled down Atsugi's southerly runway and made a right hand turn to a westerly heading. Little could Lieutenant Endacott have guessed that he'd have a call sign, blessed by the XO, eight other Eagles, and several South Koreans, by the time his flight boots touched Japanese soil again.

During their trip, somewhere high over the Sea of Japan, Lunker shared a piece of trivia with his pilot. "Did you know that Atsugi, Kwangju, and your hometown of Concord, North Carolina are essentially on the same line of latitude?"

Willie, whose mask was hanging from its fitting on the left side of his helmet, looked to his right and smiled as he shook his head. He placed his mask against his face to respond. "If my mom were alive, she'd probably find some kind of comfort in that, Lunker." As Willie let his mask hang down again, Lunker could see and hear him laughing.

"Just trying to keep you awake and entertained, Willie," Lunker said, smiling. "I know how tough it is being a bus driver over there when you have the autopilot engaged."

"Since Gully and I will be flying together on the next cruise, perhaps you should train him in the art of feeding, entertaining, and watching out for his bus driver," Willie suggested with a grin on his face. "You're certainly a star at it, or at least that's what CAG told me about the night you had the landing gear problem."

After a long delay, Lunker nodded. "Yeah, that was some night, Willie. I'm glad it worked out."

"You must have earned a favor or two after that," inferred Willie.

Lunker debated telling Willie the favor he had, in fact, asked of CAG, but decided not to, since it was highly unlikely that even CAG could pull it off. "I'm just glad we didn't go swimming that night," replied Lunker, truthfully.

"I'm glad you didn't either, Lunker," agreed Willie. They were silent for a minute or two, both of them looking outside the airplane at nothing but the water below, a distant horizon that didn't seem to move, and a bright sun warmly nestled in the clear skies above.

"I'm still in disbelief that Rita is gone," admitted Willie. In his peripheral vision, he saw Lunker nodding in agreement. The two of them sat in silence, both thinking that only God knew how many heartbeats were left on their personal countdown timers. Certainly, Rita would have laughed at the thought that his days were numbered in minutes as he walked to his airplane in Misawa on the sunny day he bought the farm.

"I'm not sure I could have handled it if you didn't come back to the ship that night," Willie confessed. The two friends sat in silence for a couple minutes.

Willie then continued his thoughts. "We're in the middle of it all, not thinking about the 'what if,' but I don't know how my dad or Tosh deal with it." He paused. "I don't know how any of our loved ones handle it."

Lunker responded a minute later. "That's the real reason my Susan left." He paused. "It was tough enough to be alone and a single parent, but adding the not knowing what was happening at any moment, fearing the knock on the door, was just too much for her."

"That's why I call Tosh twice a week, even at the steep cost," said Willie. "I called her this morning, before we briefed, just to ease the angst and pressure on both of us, I suppose, and to let her know I appreciate what she's undertaking." He paused. The two aviators could feel the silence in the cockpit racing along with them at a groundspeed of just over four hundred statute miles per hour. "I hope she'll hang in there, but I'll understand if she doesn't. It's an awful lot to ask of a woman."

He looked to his right at Lunker, who was staring out the right side of the cockpit, looking north across a distant horizon.

"Somewhere out there, Willie, across the north pole and a jink to the right, is the wife and daughter I lost." Lunker's wistful voice carried the full weight of a sad heart. "Our great family adventure was never supposed to end this way."

An hour later, all five Intruder crews were gathered in the air operations building at Kwangju air base. A few minutes earlier, as they were walking from their jets to the building, they stared across the ramp at the seven ROK F-4E Phantom and five F-5 Tiger II aircraft they'd be tangling with in airspace just above the South Korean treetops. Seeing them, the reality of what the next six days would bring began to register with the Eagle aviators. CAG was correct. This was likely to be a detachment to remember.

The generosity of their hosts was aromatically evident as they entered the air operations building. A long table of delicious Korean breakfast and lunch dishes, freshly squeezed juices, coffee, and sodas were waiting for the ten Eagles, as well as the thirty-eight ROK aviators that they would be trying to evade or defeat. Twenty-eight would, alternately, be flying in the two-seat Phantoms, and ten would share duties flying the single seat Tiger II's — twelve ROK aircraft against five Eagle Intruders. The Eagles, to a person, believed that to be a very unfair advantage. Three or four more ROK aircraft, they thought, would even the odds.

Soon, all the participants were seated in a large room, where they received a mandatory operations and safety brief. Ninety minutes later, the American and ROK flight crews were walking to their assigned aircraft. It was time for the games to begin.

For the Eagles, day one's plan was simple and safe. Each of the five Intruders would take off individually, five minutes apart, climb to an altitude of two hundred feet above ground level, and proceed to the six targets in an order each of the B/N's decided would conserve fuel, while still confusing the ROK controllers with their nontraditional choices for a navigational route to the target.

Two hundred feet above the ground was an altitude that optimized tactical surprise while maintaining an acceptable peacetime safety margin. The Eagles would fly their routes at a ground speed of four hundred twenty knots, over four hundred eighty-three miles per hour. At that speed, the Intruders were covering two statute miles every fifteen seconds. The Eagles launched, using visual flight plans, which did not require the use of the South Korean civilian air traffic control system. This minimized the opportunity for the ROK Air Force to get an unfair advantage as to the Eagles' plans.

After the first day's single flight was complete, the Eagles hosted a group debrief at the Kwangju officers club, which included U.S. Air Force and ROK officers who were monitoring the flights. The traditional Korean appetizers were tasty, and the beer was cold. The camaraderie between American and ROK aviators was professional, friendly, and full of "wait until tomorrow" promises emanating from both sides.

There were friendly disputes on whether the South Korean pilots could have gotten legitimate firing solutions on the eight intercepts they made against their American adversaries. For the fifty-two attacks that were, ultimately, flown all the way to weapons release, the Eagles had an overall circular error of probability, called CEP, of seventy-two feet, meaning that fifty percent of the inert practice bombs dropped landed within seventy-two feet of their intended target. It was a still a lethal CEP: the 'hard kill' radius of the bomb they were simulating dropping was just over one hundred feet.

One area where both sides had no disagreement was that Hite's Prime Max Lager, brewed in Seoul, was a mighty fine beer. During a reception and dinner on their first evening together, the ROK leadership team, which included General Jeong, ensured that a wide range of traditional Korean dishes and delicacies were kept in front of the Eagles. Being officers and gentleman, the Eagles sampled them all and smiled, even though they had difficulty determining the origin of at least half the dishes.

As the evening was concluding, and the American and ROK officers were starting to say their goodbyes, Frank Endacott, the newest Eagle, and the Eagle who seemingly consumed the largest quantity of food and Prime Max among all the aviators present, was having great difficulty getting a question answered.

"Does anyone have any chicken lips?" He was having trouble standing as he tried to get anyone who would listen to answer his question.

Several aviators from both sides asked him to clarify his request, which he tried to do, but failed.

"You know, chicken lips. I need some damn chicken lips." He leaned against Lunker, who was just slightly taller and gladly provided support. "Help me, Lunker," he pleaded. "Find me some chicken lips." Lunker laughed.

"But what are chicken lips," asked Lunker, who, fortunately, had mostly consumed soft drinks during the evening.

"You know, chicken lips. I put one in my mouth and chew it so my mouth doesn't taste like a dog's ass."

"Do you mean Chiclets, Frank? Gum?"

"Yeah, chicklips, that's it. What's so damn hard about chicklips?"

Lunker turned to his right, and looked toward almost four dozen aviators from two countries. Laughing along with them, even as he supported his fellow Eagle, Lunker offered the ROK officers a tidbit of naval aviation.

"And this, my new and dear friends from South Korea, is how we, in naval aviation, earn a call sign." He smiled and looked at his old and new friends.

"Allow me to introduce you to our newest Eagle, Lieutenant Frank 'Chicklips' Endacott."

Chicklips had a big smile. Because his brain was moving at a pace slower than Lunker was speaking, he didn't quite understand what Lunker had said, but he knew it must have been very good. All the ROK pilots and his fellow Eagles laughed and clapped and most shook his hand, even the Korean general.

Day two was originally planned with a first launch at 1100. However, to respect and give wide berth to the Navy's twelve-hour 'bottle-to-throttle' rule, Commander Curry requested and received approval to slide the first launch to noon.

For the second day, the Eagles changed their tactics, from five individual flights to two distinct 'two-plane' sections, with the two aircraft in each section flying five hundred feet apart in a modified spread formation.

The fifth Eagle Intruder crew filed an instrument flight plan from Kwangju to Atsugi after Commander Curry notified the ROK general that the Eagles needed to swap out a pilot. He was, the XO said, under the weather from the previous evening's activities. General Jeong understood; he had been there a few times before, he told the XO as they both laughed.

What the ROK general failed to remember was that the first rule in combat was that there are no rules. The second rule was that if you ain't cheating, you ain't trying.

At 1045, an Intruder manned by the XO and Magic was rolling down Kwangju's active runway. To the air traffic control system and the Kwangju Air Base's tactical control center, an instrument flight plan filed earlier that morning indicated Eagle One's destination was Atsugi, Japan.

At 1100, the first Eagle flight of two Intruders, their takeoff checklist complete, were cleared to position themselves on the runway, so that each was in the center of their half of the runway. After less than twenty seconds on the runway, the tower controller's voice pierced the airwaves.

"Eagle Two, Kwangju tower, wind zero-six-zero at nine knots, switch to tactical frequency, cleared for VFR takeoff."

Willie and Flood pushed their throttles as far forward as they would go, each using brakes on top of their rudder pedals to keep the vibrating, forty-nine thousand pound aerodynamic instrument of peace in place.

Via their internal communication system, ICS for short, Lunker reported to Willie, "Thumbs up from Flood."

"Okay, let's go." With those words, Lunker put his right forearm and hand, both vertical, against the right side of the canopy for a couple seconds and then dropped it. As both pilots saw his arm disappear, they released their brakes, and the jets began moving together as one.

After takeoff, the two aircraft climbed to two hundred feet and accelerated to three hundred seventy-five knots. "Push him out," said Willie.

With that command, Lunker showed Flood the palm of his right hand and made a motion as if he was pushing Flood's Intruder away. Flood's only acknowledgement was to start moving away from Willie into the prebriefed position, which placed Flood's Intruder in a position about thirty degrees behind Willie's jet and five hundred feet away.

Their route first took them north, along South Korea's east coast, where Willie remained over the water, hugging the coastline at just over one hundred feet off the water, with the other Intruder a thousand feet inland. Both aircraft were flying at two hundred feet above the ground.

At 1102, the second Eagle flight of two lifted free of the earth and turned left to proceed to Korea's west coast. Like Willie before him, Fish leveled off at two hundred feet and Chicklips, armed with a new legitimately earned call sign he didn't mind, mimicked the position that Flood was taking as the wingman in his own flight. Ironically, Fish and Chicklips had met as flight students at Training Squadron Four in Pensacola and became close friends, although they were six months apart in the training pipeline. Like Willie and Doc, they were pleased to be assigned together to the Eagles.

While the two sections of Eagles were racing north on opposing coasts over two separate seas, the Yellow Sea to the west and the Sea of Japan to the east, the XO and Magic cancelled their flight clearance to Atsugi. Immediately, they made a descending turn to fly southwest under visual flight rules, back toward Kwangju and the southern targets, having received approval from Korea Area Control Center.

The XO's expectation was that the ROK pilots and tactical control center would focus on the four Intruders flying north, and not look for the fifth Intruder that had earlier departed Korean airspace on a flight back to Japan with, they assumed, Chicklips at the controls.

The 'any weather, any time' capability was on full display on both coasts of the Korean peninsula, as the four Intruders approached their first targets. All four aircraft were utilizing an automatic system attack mode in which the Intruder's attack/nav system would release the bomb at the precise moment, as opposed to a traditional visual attack, where the pilot looked through a gunsight and manually 'pickled' the bomb.

As Fish and Chicklips approached Koon-ni, two ROK Phantoms engaged Fish about three miles from the target, but didn't see Chicklips, who was hugging the treetops until he was two miles from the target. At that time, he eased over toward the water and pointed the jet at their target, located on a very small peninsula.

Hugging the treetops was an understatement. The Intruder became inherently more stable the lower to the ground it flew. Every Intruder pilot experienced it — felt it, actually, as his jet and the ground grew closer — and benefited from the rare characteristic of a tactical jet.

While the four Intruders were keeping the ROK Air Force occupied in the airspace over the northern part of South Korea, the Eagles' XO and Magic were enjoying unopposed attacks at the other five South Korean targets, recording each attack on their Intruder's FLIR system, which resembled a live action, black-and-white television, so they could play it back to the ROK aviators.

Two hours and twenty minutes after takeoff, five Eagles' Intruders were parked back in Kwangju, preparing for their second flight of the day. The tactic for the second flight was back to single ship attacks, except that each Eagle Intruder took off two minutes apart and proceeded toward the same target. By the time the Eagles approached Nightmare Range, their final target, most of the ROK aircraft that were protecting the area had returned to base because of low fuel. Overall, though, the ROK defenders had engaged the Eagle attackers sixty-five percent of the time.

At the debrief for day-two's flights, held at the Kwangju officers club, the ROK general said he was impressed by the Eagles' bombing accuracy, which averaged just under forty feet. He followed that by expressing his surprise at the tactic used during the first flight of the day, that being the bluff of an Intruder flying to Japan. He was mostly impressed, he said, at the

Eagles' creativity, although he pointed out that it violated the agreed upon rules of engagement.

Commander Curry's response was short and sweet. "Well, general, you should know that in combat, rules don't apply." He smiled and continued. "As we say in naval aviation, if you aren't cheating, you aren't trying."

The general smiled and laughed, as did his fellow ROK airmen. "You are correct, Commander Curry. Well done."

Days three, four, and five were very similar to the first two days of the detachment, except that the Eagles made defensive turns against the ROK aircraft when engaged, enroute to, or in the target area, and became more creative in their strike tactics. Both sides were impressed at each other's willingness to engage at low altitudes, often resulting in 'relatively flat dogfights' that often stayed below fifteen hundred feet above the ground. More than trying to obtain an offensive shot, the fight generally turned into a dogfight in which success, for both sets of pilots, was to create an opportunity to "bug out" and live to fight another day.

During every flight, the Americans flew over South Korean highways with two-mile long sections of the road, deliberately modified, to be used as 'highway runways', if needed. Each section was protected by four sets of military anti-aircraft guns or missiles. It was sobering to see them, not only for the first time, but every time, especially north of Seoul, although they were prevalent throughout the country.

The simplest description of the detachment through five days of American and South Korean interaction was days of aerial engagement, followed by late nights of enjoyable social engagement. There was great camaraderie between two countries that had, once upon a time, fought alongside each other in a real conflict, and were committed to doing it again, if necessary.

However, the evening before the final flying day was relatively low key; the Eagles' crews were knee deep in strike planning. Earlier in the afternoon, the second flight of the day was unexpectedly cancelled. A Navy rear admiral, assigned to the U.S. Pacific Fleet staff in Pearl Harbor, and General Jeong met with the five VA-115 flight crews who would be participating in the final 'fly day' of the detachment.

The American admiral spoke first. His tone was deadly serious. "The distance from Seoul to the North Korean border is thirty-five miles. To put that in perspective, it's about the same distance as Washington, DC to Baltimore, or Miami to Fort Lauderdale." He paused to let the information register with the Navy fliers. "You can understand why there is angst in the capital."

"North Korea has deployed about half of its fighters in their southern front area, which makes a short-warning attack against all areas of South Korea a significant and considerable threat. In addition, North Korea has built dozens of reserve airstrips for emergency use for their fighters along highways and ordinary roads across the country. You've seen similar highway runways in South Korea — Imagine that number times eight to ten."

The Eagles' aviators didn't require much imagination to grasp the grave consequences of such a capability, or the difficulty in defending attacks from so many locations. They had flown over such impromptu runways in South Korea often during each day of the detachment.

The admiral continued. "General Jeong has asked our Pacific Fleet commander for assistance in creating a realistic scenario, in which the North Korean air force launches a daytime, unprovoked attack against Seoul." The admiral looked toward the ROK general, who nodded back at him. "We have picked nine high-priority targets in or immediately around Seoul. The tenth target was selected by the general." General Jeong smiled, and the admiral continued.

"Each of you will be assigned a primary and secondary target. Once this brief is complete, we will have senior analysts from my staff in Pearl Harbor work with you in the same manner that Midway's intelligence officers work with you

69

preparing target packages before and during cruise." He paused to take a sip of water.

"The advantage, to each of you, is that you will be planning and flying a strike against a real city and complex targets you have never seen before. The advantage to the Republic of Korea is to test their alert and response systems, as well as to give their pilots a real world, surprise attack scenario to respond to. I'm sure you're curious as to weapons loadouts. The answer is that neither side will be carrying weapons of any type. Our risk factor is high enough without an unintended air-to-air gun or missile firing."

The admiral was correct. Each of the Eagles held silent concerns about an inadvertent weapons release, especially the XO, who knew that his flying career would likely come to an immediate end if any of the Eagles dicked this donkey.

"For added realism, an hour ago the ROK pilots and radar intercept officers who will be responding were sequestered, and will remain sequestered, inside the Kwangju alert building until receiving an alert launch signal tomorrow. The scenario they are currently being presented, and planning for, is a response against targets in North Korea, utilizing Koon-ni and Nightmare as surrogate targets. They will be given the impression that you will be defending Koon-ni, simulating a North Korean city, and engaging them as North Korean fighters from very low altitudes at random times and directions." That was a plausible misinformation strategy. Had it been fighters from high altitude, there were plenty of U.S. Air Force fighters based in South Korea that could fill such a role.

"Another reason the ROK crews are being sequestered is to keep them unaware of an intensive mass-media campaign already underway in Seoul and surrounding areas. To keep potential hysteria to a minimum, citizens are being made aware that a preplanned, peacetime exercise between ROK and U.S. Navy aircraft will be taking place over Seoul around noon tomorrow. The notifications will continue from now until two hours after you have departed the area tomorrow."

"I'm sure many of you, if not all of you, have wondered about airline traffic into or out of Kimpo, the international airport nine miles west of Seoul, as well as other air traffic. Over the past month, our Department of Defense has been coordinating with our own FAA and its South Korean counterpart, the Korean Office of Civil Aviation. A plausible scenario has been disseminated that will keep all civilian air traffic clear of Seoul's airspace for a two-hour window, beginning thirty minutes prior to your planned arrival time. Let me repeat that. There will be no civilian air traffic allowed in Seoul's airspace for a two-hour window. That alone should indicate the priority this mission has in the American and South Korean capitals."

After another sip of water, the admiral continued. "The threat to South Korea is real and constant. I am here, on behalf of the President, to let the people of South Korea know that the United States stands behind them. There is no debate."

"The United States is serious about defending peace and we will not be intimidated. We will defend peace, and we will help our allies defend peace. Hopefully, the leadership in Moscow will recognize our commitment on this peninsula's soil. I wish each of you safe flying. At this time, I am going to turn the briefing over to General Jeong."

The Eagles' ten aviators watched as a grim-faced General Jeong walked smartly to a position in front of the gathered aviators. He spoke slowly and passionately. "Twenty-five minutes before your time on target, when you are already airborne, my crews will be told to scramble to face a threat coming from the north. That burden will weigh heavily on them, as I imagine it would on you if you were defending Midway." To a person, the ten American aviators nodded, either noticeably or tacitly. They could relate to that emotional burden. "The air controllers who will be manning the ground control radar stations will also be informed of the inbound threat."

"Our pilots will not know that the enemy they are facing is you until they arrive at their aircraft. This real world opportunity will not only give my aviators and me an accurate measurement of our real-world response capabilities, but it will also challenge the radar controllers who have the responsibility to get my aircraft optimally engaged against a surprise low-altitude, high-speed attack in a densely populated area." He paused to let the message sink in.

"It should not be lost on anyone, in the air or on the ground, that the densely populated area you will be attacking is our capital." He paused for a brief second. "Seoul."

General Jeong noticeably stiffened as he spoke the name of his capital city. The mere thought of defending the city went right to his core. "My country's strategy, which I strongly support, is to draw a line at Seoul in the event of an attack from the north. We will not fall back or retreat from Seoul."

The general paused before continuing. "Our pilots, soldiers, sailors, and those who support us, including the controllers on the ground, understand this. Our ultimate fate will be determined in the air above and on the sacred land of our capital." The room was morbidly quiet as he restated the ROK policy more clearly.

"We will live or die in Seoul."

He paused as he surveyed the aviators sitting in front of him, grateful for their presence. "I ask you to make safety your highest priority. Tomorrow is not a day to die. Tomorrow is a day to train and learn. I thank each of you for your commitment so far from your own homeland, and I look forward to seeing you upon your return." General Jeong bowed lower than what the Americans had previously observed and held it for several seconds, the traditional Korean sign of a person's deepest respect.

After General Jeong and the admiral departed, the list of the ten targets within the Seoul metropolitan area was distributed. Commander Curry allowed his crews to submit their first choices from both the primary and secondary lists. The primary list contained five South Korean governmental and critical infrastructure targets, including their capital building. The secondary list included popular cultural and commercial targets. "Targets just to be funny or mean," is how one of the Eagles described them.

The most popular choice from the secondary list was the Hite Brewing Company, and each of the crews wanted the bragging rights of saying they'd flown over it up close and personal, pretending to blow it up. Ultimately, Moliver won the 'rock, paper, and scissors' competition that determined the winning crew. His pilot, Fish, was pleased with his B/N's performance. They hadn't launched yet, and he had already scored a bullseye.

All but two of the targets sat along, or close to, the Han river, a half-mile wide river that flowed through Seoul's metropolitan area in the shape of the letter 'W.' Visions of flying low and fast, no higher than two hundred feet off the water at most, energized and heightened the Eagle crews' enthusiasm for this mission. Equally exhilarating, they would be guiding their jet as they skimmed over a number of the twenty-three bridges that crossed the river, as it wound through the city, and well below the top of many of the city's buildings.

On this once-in-a-lifetime mission, the Eagles would be engaged in complex bombing, which is a fancy two-word way to say they'd be trying to pick out, and attack, a single building from among hundreds clustered tightly in an expansive metropolitan area, and have only one chance to get it right. They'd be traveling at close to eight miles per minute and evading ROK pilots in pursuit of a bullseye on each target.

In an era long before GPS bombing, the Eagle B/Ns utilized highly reliable inertial navigation systems, although the acceptable drift rate was one mile per hour. They'd be performing constant radar updates on known fixed points during the circuitous, one-hour transit from Kwangju to Seoul, in order to minimize the system's drift rate and to maximize their likelihood of locating the target and scoring a direct hit.

Sodas and coffee replaced Hite's Prime Max lager through a long evening and early morning of target planning. Such a schedule was routine to the Eagles. It was no different from the endless days of flying and target planning when underway on Midway. Just like being on the boat, it was easy for the Eagles to sleep soundly prior to their 0730 wake up call for a 0830 brief. It was also easy for the five crews to wake up with a full tank of enthusiasm and make final preparations for the much-anticipated flight.

Overnight, the Eagles' enlisted maintenance personnel, who had been nothing short of heroic themselves during the five previous days, had reconfigured the five Intruders so that each jet carried only a single drop tank on the centerline station underneath the aircraft's fuselage. Although it meant four thousand pounds less in fuel than the Eagles had been carrying throughout the detachment, the lighter weight and slick wing would enhance each Intruder's maneuverability and help with fuel efficiency.

As the Eagles sat in their jets, waiting to start their engines and eager to get airborne on the final, and most anticipated, operational flight of the detachment, petty officer Buzz Tessaro climbed up the right side of Willie and Lunker's Intruder. "How's your system, lieutenant?" asked the Eagles' petty officer of the year.

"Looks tight so far, petty officer Tessaro," replied Lunker. "I need it to be tight. We're going downtown."

"Downtown? Which downtown is that, sir," asked Buzz, silently guessing at the city.

"Seoul."

"Holy shit! Seriously?"

"Seriously. Bombing right smack downtown. We'll be trying to find our two targets while being harassed by ROK fighters. That's why I need a tight system to get my mozo bombs on target." Lunker laughed.

Buzz laughed as well. "Bring me some good video back of those thousand pound mozo bombs hitting the target, sir."

"Good video of mozo hits; you got it." He laughed as he gave Buzz a thumbs up.

Two cruises earlier, Lunker had launched on a flight with twelve practice bombs. Inadvertently, he selected a wrong setting and, instead of dropping just one bomb on the first pass at the target, dropped all twelve of the practice bombs. Embarrassed at his mistake, which he admitted to his pilot, he told the pilot he would log twelve separate hits, all good, as if nothing amiss happened, which is what he did.

Later that day, his pilot, feeling guilty, told Buzz what actually happened, since Buzz, as a collateral duty, was assigned to log the bomb scores in order to track individual armament control units for accuracy. The next time Lunker was in the cockpit, readying himself and his system for flight, Buzz climbed up the right side of the Intruder and asked Lunker if he was dropping real bombs, or 'mozo' bombs, for hits two through twelve. The word got around the ready room, and 'mozo bombs' became an accepted term, when appropriate, in the Eagles' attack vocabulary.

Buzz smiled as he climbed down from the jet. He knew he'd miss these interactions when his days in the Navy ended sooner than anyone imagined, and he returned home to southern California. He'd miss it a lot more than he probably knew, he thought, as a melancholy sense of duty overwhelmed him. He knew he had served faithfully and honorably, but he still felt guilty at the thought of leaving while his friends continued to serve on the tip of the sword.

At 1110, the first Eagle Intruder, flown by the XO and Magic, released their brakes and rolled down Kwangju's southwesterly runway, leveling off at five hundred feet and turning east toward Busan on South Korea's southeast coast. At ten second intervals, the remaining four Eagles, in order, Fish and Moliver, Chicklips and Preacher, Willie and Lunker, and Flood and Jackal followed the XO's flight path, remaining approximately a mile apart as they flew east.

At Busan, they turned right and made a southeast to northwest diagonal across South Korea, on a direct route to Inchon on the northwest coast. Almost thirty-one years earlier, in September, 1950, General Douglas MacArthur commanded a multinational force that made an amphibious invasion at Inchon, leading ultimately to the recapture of Seoul two weeks later, and a marked reversal in favor of the United Nations.

Approaching Inchon, the Intruders closed to within one hundred feet of each other as the XO turned toward the north-northeast, as if they were flying directly to Nightmare Range. Twenty-eight miles north of Seoul, the Eagles began a turn south on a course directly toward the capital city at an altitude of two hundred feet above the ground.

At that time, five aircraft became three distinct units. The XO remained a single entity, while Willie and Flood joined as a section on the XO's starboard side as Fish and Chicklips followed suit on the lead aircraft's port side. The two sections of Intruders and the XO's single Intruder, flying two hundred feet from each other, accelerated to an airspeed of approximately five hundred knots, a skooch over five hundred seventy-five miles per hour.

Additionally, the two aircraft in each section flew 'welded wing', which meant to fly as close as they felt comfortable in order to appear, to controllers, as three aircraft instead of five, which, it turned out, they did.

The Eagles had chosen to approach the city from the north, using the many tall mountains and rolling hills between their position and the city as a tactical advantage by masking their approach from radars.

At the same time, ten ROK aircraft, six F-4 Phantoms and four F-5 Tiger IIs, were racing northward toward Seoul at an altitude of five thousand feet, and at an airspeed close to mach 1, the speed of sound, in a desperate attempt to save their capital city. The South Koreans had a two-to-one advantage in aircraft. The Intruder's advantage was that it was designed specifically to fly, attack, and maneuver at high speeds and very low altitudes. The Phantoms and Tiger IIs could also fly and maneuver at high speeds; however, they weren't designed for aggressive maneuvering at very low altitudes.

As the battle was nearing its climax over Seoul, Korean generals and senior U.S. Navy officers, including two admirals, stared as the situation unfolded on oversized, wall-mounted status boards in a secret South Korean military operations center. The two groups of allies, one much more tense than the other, stared as two distinct groups of radar blips converged toward a single piece of South Korean real estate.

Forty-five miles south of the city, the ROK aircraft received a call from their controller. "Three unknown aircraft bearing zero-one-zero for seventy-two miles, heading one-seven-zero, altitude two hundred feet, airspeed five-zero-zero." The message sent a chill through each of the ROK pilots.

The American and ROK aircraft were closing on each other at over twenty miles per minute, destined to meet approximately one-half mile north of downtown Seoul in less than three minutes. The ROK pilots were transonic, flying just below Mach 1, and descending to a lower altitude. Because of the extensive damage to windows that would likely occur if the ROK aircraft broke the sound barrier, they were limited to less than Mach 1 throughout the realistic scenario.

Inside the ROK jets, the Eagles' extremely low altitude was playing havoc with the aviators' ability to discern the American jets from amidst the ground clutter of the city's buildings and houses. The same situation was frustrating the ground controllers as well.

At twelve miles from their targets, each Intruder pilot pressed a button on his control stick that shifted his jet's weapons and navigation system into a system attack mode. "Stepping into attack," said Willie to Lunker.

"Roger. In attack. Good lights." Lunker remained fixated on his radar and infrared displays.

"Good symbology," reported Willie. The Intruder's computer was calculating a precise release point in the sky; steering commands on two of Willie's instruments were guiding him to that specific spot.

The Intruders had just passed over the last significant mountain that would hide their presence, and were now heading directly toward a predesignated point, approximately ten miles north-northwest of Seoul's city center, accelerating slightly while traveling over Seoul's crowded hillside suburbs. Each Intruder remained at two hundred feet above the ground.

In the distance, the taller buildings in the city were coming into focus as they rose above the horizon. It was a beautiful but surreal sight to each of the pilots as they raced to simulate destroying them. While their focus remained on flying precise formation, each pilot couldn't help but observe densely packed neighborhoods that blended centuries-old homes with modern slums.

Inside the cockpit, all five B/N's were singularly focused on their radar and infrared systems, tweaking their primary target placement while trusting their pilots to keep them away from the ground.

Inside the ROK aircraft, the pilots were given vectors to the three contacts approaching from the north. The merger point for the good guys and the bad guys was shaping up to be approximately a quarter-mile to a half-mile northwest of the city center, exactly where General Jeong wanted it to be. To the ROK pilots, though, they were willing every subsonic knot from their aircraft they could get; they wanted to merge as far north of Seoul as possible.

With their oxygen masks on and dark visors down, the pilots and flight officers were faceless, unidentifiable warriors, medieval knights of old, with jets instead of stallions. The key to life wasn't personality, but performance.

At seven miles, all five Intruder pilots could see the Han River, ahead and to the right of them as it flowed to the northwest out of the city toward the Yellow Sea. Six miles away, the Intruder pilots each visually acquired their primary target, which they reported to their B/Ns. By pressing a trigger on their control stick to its first position, the crosshairs in the pilot's gunsight moved to display outside what the B/N's radar crosshair placement showed on the radar. In addition, each B/N had an infrared video display of what his radar's crosshairs were targeting.

Seconds later, the Intruders accelerated very slightly and the XO passed a signal to detach to the two section leaders. "Detach Flood," said Willie to Lunker, who then quickly detached their wingman. Willie watched as Flood banked significantly to his right and took direct aim at his primary target.

All five Intruders were now in control of their own destiny. Each lethal flying machine was closing on their primary target in downtown Seoul, one of the world's most densely populated cities, at a speed of a statute mile every six seconds.

"At least three black contrails on the nose, Willie." Lunker could see their heat signature on his infrared display.

"Roger. Got 'em in sight." They both knew those were telltale exhaust signatures from the ROK Phantoms.

To the pilots, the downtown buildings seemed much closer than just under four miles, less than twenty-six seconds away. Two hundred feet below them, densely populated neighborhoods where, too often, poor met poorer, passed by in a flash. Ahead of them, in the heart of Seoul, the Han River, and at least eight or ten newer tall buildings, rising much higher above the ground than their jets' current altitude, towered over predominantly two and three story buildings.

It was a surreal scene, Willie thought, as they passed several groups of children looking up at them from where they stood in a large park, some of them waving, as the jet transited the area in a matter of seconds. It reminded him of seeing the sweet smile of the young girl standing by the water buffalo in the Philippines. "What warped irony in the Intruder and its mission," he thought. "Killing in the name of peace by unceremoniously attacking another country with an aesthetically unattractive jet."

At the same time that innocent children in a peaceful park were waving at the Intruders speeding by, the ROK controller advised the ROK aircraft that the three contacts were now five distinct targets, and passed them corresponding vector information.

Inside his aircraft, Willie could see his primary target clearly, a three-story government building housing key treasury and finance offices, which was located just off the Han River, to the south. The XO's primary target was, effectively, the country's capital building. The Eagles' other three primary targets were an electric power plant, a prominent broadcasting center, and Gyeongseong Station, more commonly called Seoul Station, the city's main railway station.

As they raced to simulate destroying Seoul, it was hard not to admire the beauty of the city and its outlying suburbs, a few situated on low rolling hills nestled near taller mountains. The river was approximately a half-mile wide, maybe a little more in places, as it weaved its 'W' symbol through the city. They could see the area of the river in the heart of downtown where a single small island acted like a lone sentry.

Construction of new buildings was evident everywhere, as they closed toward the geographic center of Seoul's cultural, business, and government activities. They could see more parks, gardens, and thousands of people staring up at them, many pointing, and some waving, from densely packed neighborhoods.

"Hey Lunker, take a peek," said Willie.

Lunker, bent over as he looked into the boot, sat straight up and was stunned at what he saw — a massive city where old and ancient was being slowly encroached by new and modern. "Surreal," he thought, "I'm a long way from Blue Ridge, Georgia." The view could easily be paralyzing; they were part of an action movie that was taking place in a modernizing country, halfway around the world from where the Intruder was built. However, the reality of their mission quickly returned as Lunker's first priority.

The Intruders were simulating dropping two Mk-84 two thousand pound bombs, with high-drag snake-eye retarder tailfins, on each target in a high speed, low altitude delivery for the first target. The choice of ordnance maximized their aircraft's distance from the target at the moment of the bombs' impact. Being shot down by the fragmentation pattern of their own bombs was not part of their attack plan.

Willie and Lunker were less than three miles from their target. "Two and a half miles. Pipper's centered on the target," Willie transmitted to Lunker. The pipper was a symbol on Willie's gunsight that showed him where their two bombs, four thousand pounds of high explosives, were destined to hit.

"FLIR's holding on the front door. Oh man, the AQs and ordies are gonna love this video," said Lunker. AQs were airmen who maintained the navigation and attack capability of the Intruder, including the forward-looking infrared system. Ordies were ordnancemen.

They were less than a mile from the target. Looking over the nose, Willie saw a visual indication on one of his instruments at the same time that the Han River, and then the target, disappeared under the Intruder's nose. As Willie pulled off target with six times the force of gravity, he saw two Phantoms closing from their left side.

'Bogeys, one mile, left eight o'clock, slightly high," he said to Lunker. Willie remained at two hundred feet and pulled the Intruder into a hard, six 'g' left-hand turn, flying the Intruder between two tall buildings under construction as they turned back north over the Han River.

"Yep, and steering's good to the museum." Lunker's voice was straining against the heavy gravitational forces. The simple act of pressing a single button took a monumental effort as his hand felt as if it weighed almost eleven pounds.

Willie pulled hard to a heading of northeast and dropped down to an altitude best described as just barely over the river. His flight path was direct to their secondary target, two and three-quarters miles away. The front of their windscreen was seemingly filled with water as Willie pulled up twice in the cross-river journey to avoid hitting a bridge. As he approached the far river bank, Willie saw two other Intruders, both at a very low altitude; one was passing over the river, heading north, and the other was flying west on the opposite side of the river.

"Popping," said Willie. "In attack." Based on the distance to the target that Lunker's computer was indicating, Willie pulled hard up and to the right, over four times the force of gravity, for about four seconds. He then rolled to the left, almost inverted, and pulled his nose hard down toward the target in a maneuver called an offset pop-up attack.

"Committing." Willie was indicating to Lunker that he had handed off the responsibility of determining the optimum bomb release point to the Intruder's weapons system. Willie flew the jet the few seconds to the simulated release point of two Mk-84 two thousand pound retarded bombs, and immediately pulled six 'g's hard to the right, just above the building tops, to get back to the river.

As his Intruder was passing over the museum, a momentary thought flashed into Willie's brain. If Tosh asked about the museum, all he could say was he had about six or seven seconds of viewing time, of which half was upside down, and then his pretend bombs blew it up.

As Willie and Lunker raced toward the river, two ROK Phantoms maneuvered to try and get a shot on their jet. As they tried to keep sight of the ROK Phantoms, who were their foes, Willie and Lunker saw another Intruder to their right, flying in the opposite direction at their altitude, more accurately called 'bridge level, about a half mile away, heading toward a target on Seoul's north side.

As they crossed the river, Willie executed a starboard turn to the west, using the city's buildings as shields. They also observed that the government's awareness campaign had an unintended consequence. A large number of people turned out to watch the impromptu air show taking place over their city.

"Stay on the buildings, Willie. They can't get a clean shot right now." Lunker's voice was strained.

Willie continued jinking among the buildings and, ultimately, found his way back to where he could hug the Han River's southern bank, seemingly feet away from commercial buildings. He was hoping the midday sun's heat off the buildings wouldn't allow the ROK Phantoms to get a good tone on their heat-seeking Sidewinder missiles, if they would even simulate shooting with so much real estate in their missile's path. A good tone from the ROK Phantoms missiles would be bad news for Willie and Lunker in an actual fight.

As Willie continued to fly low over several bridges, Lunker's very labored voice made him smile in the middle of a hard six 'g' turn into one of the Phantoms. "I think we just flew over the Seoul high school cheerleaders, pom-poms and all, about fifty of them on that bridge, waving and shaking."

"I guess we know who they're rooting for," replied Willie. His semi-laughing voice was also strained by the heavy g-forces on their Intruder as he continued to focus on keeping the jet close to the buildings and bridges in order to keep the Phantoms from acquiring a valid firing solution.

"Amen," said Lunker, "but shit..." His voice was half-grunting, half-straining. "...I'm sweating so much..." Lunker was grunting even more under the increasing g-forces. "...I think I can smell the sweat on my flight suit, Willie."

"They're fighting for their capital, Lunker." Willie was grunting as he contorted his body to look behind him. "I bet they smell the sweat on the sweat on their flight suits."

Behind his oxygen mask, Lunker smiled. "Bingo," he said, glancing quickly at Willie.

As he did constantly over a six minute period, Willie kept his flight path unpredictable in three dimensions, pulling toward the vertical, always topping out at barely a thousand feet, and trying to keep the Phantoms at a fifty to ninety degree offset angle during the pull, to minimize their capability of acquiring a firing solution. He then rolled the Intruder inverted to a hundred thirty-five degrees and pulled back down, at various dive angles, toward the safety of the river, buildings, and other obstacles.

"Keep me out of the dirt, Lunker. These guys are good." Willie's voice was stressed by a force that made the two of them feel as if they each weighed a thousand pounds. Both of the aviators were twisting their bodies, left and right, trying to keep sight of the ROK aircraft desperately trying to get a clean shot on their jet.

"That's what I'm here for." Lunker had twisted his body such that he could almost see directly behind them. "I'm beside you all the way, Willie. I'm not going anywhere you don't go." Even in the stress of very low altitude air combat, Lunker could find a way to slip in a memorable quote.

"That's...reassuring...Lunker." Willie spoke in the strained language of six times the force of gravity.

Although the Intruder had great air conditioning, Willie and Lunker, like all the Eagles, were drenched. Their flights suits, flight gear, and bodies were soaked. In addition, each of the four, five, and six 'g' pulls caused beads of stinging sweat to roll unabated into their eyes.

Taking advantage of the Intruder's better turning capability at low altitude than the Phantom's, Willie's goal was to remain neutral until the Phantoms reached a low fuel state, while hoping no other ROK jet would enter the fight. However, the

ROK fighters were fierce competitors, and remaining neutral was getting tougher, as they were engaged in a high-speed, low-altitude scissors maneuver, constantly utilizing all three dimensions, in an attempt to remain neutral over the city center.

Two minutes later, the Phantoms broke away, which was good for Willie, but not for Fish. Fish made a great move to neutralize an F-5 Tiger II, but he unknowingly flew right into the sweet spot of the two Phantoms who were engaged with Willie's jet.

"Bug out southwest, Willie! Unload! Unload!" Lunker's urgent command was timely; they were getting low on fuel, and Willie made a hard turn to the southwest, pushing the nose of the Intruder over slightly to get 'zero g' for optimum acceleration — unloading, it was called — as they made a run for home. They would live to fight another day, while four of the Eagle Intruders and six ROK fighters remained engaged in a massive, low-altitude furball over the skies of Seoul.

A furball was another name for a tight and crowded aerial engagement of numerous combatants that, by its intrinsic three-dimensional nature, could easily become a very confusing and potentially dangerous place in which to fly and fight. In a furball, success was, for all practical purposes, simply surviving without an aviator seeing his life flash in front of his eyes....or worse.

They were the first ones back. After they parked and shut down their Intruder back in Kwangju, Willie and Lunker remained sitting in the jet for a couple minutes with their helmets off. It was quiet. The western landscape of the air base was one of agricultural fields. A few workers could be seen bent over, either fertilizing or harvesting, depending on the crop. The concrete tarmac, partially filled with jets at rest, and the fields of green blended in tranquil and perfect harmony – one of them nourished; one protected.

The two friends were mentally and physically exhausted. Any reservoir of focus they may have had was depleted. Their flight suits were not only soaked with sweat, they looked as if they'd been dipped in water. Sweat had even soaked the flight gear the aviators wore over their flight suits. Flying so low and fast in formation for as long as they did, and then transitioning to a high speed, low-altitude hostile environment over a city in which an accident would be catastrophic to more than themselves, had brought the two friends and aviators to a point where they were simply exhausted.

"I'm too tired to move right now," said Lunker. "

"Me, too, my friend. I'm too tired to think," admitted Willie. "I could take a combat nap right here, right now."

Lunker laughed. "I'm with you on that, and I bet Seoul sure seems really quiet right about now."

"Maybe the cheerleaders are still at it," said Willie, smiling.

Lunker agreed. "Not sure how I'm going to explain all this to Eli. Instead of what over horizon, he may want to know what over building." Lunker missed his friend, but mostly he wished he could strap Eli into an Intruder just once — just one time to quench his lifelong curiosity of crossing an elusive horizon. He'd give up his seat in a heartbeat if there was a way to pull it off.

"Maybe you should just regale him with Seoul high school cheerleader stories."

"Yeah, then he'd want to know, how high girl jump, higher than scorned monkey?" They both laughed as they saw two Intruders over Kwangju's runway turning downwind for landing.

"That was something, Lunker. What an experience," said Willie. "I wish the troops could have been riding with us to see it all." Willie would also have loved for Tosh to have experienced it.

A moment later, petty officer Tessaro appeared next to Lunker's seat, standing on the boarding ladder. "What did I miss?"

"Mozo bombs and mozo explosions, followed by dogfights down in the weeds and over the river that runs through Seoul," said Lunker, "but we have the FLIR video." He smiled.

"Dang, fellas, sounds like a new thrill ride for Disneyland."

"Maybe you can propose it to the folks at Disney when you're back home in southern California next time," suggested Willie.

Buzz was noticeably quiet, his grin now a forced half-smile, and his eyes looked down, as if he had something to say. "A penny for your thoughts, Buzz," said Lunker.

Petty Officer Tessaro looked at them both. They, like so many others, made his decision painful. "I've decided to leave the Navy at the end of cruise." His eyes dropped, and his lip quivered very slightly.

Lunker put his hand on Tessaro's shoulder. His decision wasn't unexpected. "You've done your duty, Buzz, better than anyone, and you chose to serve the country when, probably, ninety-five percent of our generation chose not to and never will. We'll all leave the Navy one day. You have no reason to feel bad."

"Lunker's right, Buzz. The Eagles will survive just fine long after we're all gone. Time for you to do what you want to do," said Willie. "You owe nothing more, but you can't leave without letting us buy you dinner to say thanks. Deal?"

"Deal, sir." Buzz smiled. "Deal."

"Good. Now go pull the video and enjoy the thrill ride." Lunker smiled. "Oh, our system was deadly accurate. We owe you."

Buzz smiled as he climbed down the boarding ladder, eager to watch and share the video with his fellow fire control techs and ordnancemen. As they watched petty officer Tessaro walk away from the jet, with the video in his hand, the two aviators sat in sad silence. Life was unfair when unheralded sailors and airmen, like Buzz and all the others, toiled so loyally in harsh conditions, far from home, to get their jets airborne, but got no closer to the indescribable thrill of it all than viewing an infrared video.

In the early evening, at the officers club, a joint ROK/U.S. debrief was ending, and dinner was being served. The Eagles were wearing clean flight suits; the ones used in the raid were hanging up, still wet.

Nine ROK pilots who had flown in the final raid were in attendance, and they had changed into a short sleeve, olive drab uniform, with their nametag and wings, but no ribbons. Even though the ROK pilots occasionally held such exercises around Seoul, it was the first 'downtown' exercise with non-ROK pilots and aircraft. There was unanimous agreement that it was beneficial to both sides, although whether the risk was worth the gain would have to be decided at levels well above those in the room.

If a scorecard was kept, three Navy Intruders successfully attacked their primary and secondary targets and returned to Kwangju without being shot down. The other two Intruders successfully attacked their primary targets, but were engaged and 'eliminated' by ROK fighters enroute to their secondary targets.

As a sign of appreciation, General Jeong proposed one final competition before the Eagles returned to Atsugi the following morning. "It was an honor to compete with each of you these past six days. I am glad we are on the same side." He began clapping, and was quickly joined by everyone in attendance.

"Here in Korea, I am called the Scotch General because of my love for the sweet nectar. Based on my interaction with naval aviators, I know you all enjoy the nectar as well." He smiled as he looked at his aviators and then the American fliers.

"Commander Curry, will you please join me?" As he asked the question, eight very attractive Korean women, in traditional long dresses, wheeled two long tables into the room. The first table was covered in exquisite looking food befitting a royal coronation. The second table contained at least twenty bottles of the highest quality Chivas Regal Scotch, next to which were placed glasses that were a cross between a shot glass and a tumbler. At the same time, several Korean men quickly stacked two dozen additional cases of the smooth liquid, two high, off to the side.

"Chivas Regal is the scotch that your Frank Sinatra and his Rat Pack drinks. It is the only scotch that I drink." He paused, beaming at his self-comparison with Frank and his friends. The Eagles glanced at each other. An evening like this could end up with them acting more like the Little Rascals, and they were being set up to be Spanky, Alfalfa and the gang.

"All my pilots and I admire you who land on ships. You stand alone, as aviators, because of that." He paused again, looking across the gathered group. Like his aviators, Commander Curry had a niggling feeling the general was buttering them up for something where he already had or would quickly gain an advantage.

The general continued. "There are ten of you. I have invited nine of my finest pilots to join you, and myself, for dinner of the finest dishes and delicacies in Korea and America."

He paused again as the scene unfolded. Two tables of the best were displayed behind him; two groups of the best were standing in front of him. He then continued, "During and after dinner, I propose we have rounds of toasts with Chivas Regal to see who stands alone in drinking the scotch of Frank Sinatra." He turned toward Commander Curry. "XO, are your aviators up to this challenge?" He smiled.

The Eagles XO smiled and nodded. It was a set-up, he was sure of that, but at least it looked like a fair fight. "We're Eagles, the best in WestPac. We're up for any challenge." The nine Eagles joining the XO on the detachment were volunteers, but, fortunately, they were nine volunteers who he knew could be competitive in any arena, and would certainly never be confused with tee-totaling choirboys.

"Excellent," said the scotch general. "Let us begin. I have beautiful women to serve our drinks and assist with the feast."

The dinner was world class. There were fine cuts of prime rib and filet mignon, salmon that melted in one's mouth, spicy chicken, a wide range of vegetables and fruits, and many rice dishes. While there were places to sit, everyone chose to stand and mingle.

Fortunately, there were only two toasts; one at the beginning of the meal, and one about thirty minutes later. After the table with the food was wheeled away, a smaller table with finger foods and small desserts, all delicious, replaced it. At that point, toasts became more frequent, about every ten to fifteen minutes.

The glasses of the Koreans and the Eagles were filled from the same bottle, the XO and other Eagles noted. They certainly weren't trying to cheat there.

At the end of the first hour, the Eagles, to a person, were starting to feel the effects of the alcohol, a little more, it appeared, than their Korean counterparts. Still, the mood was one of fun, as they relived various encounters in the air. Both groups were doing what they did very well, which was to use their hands to recreate air-to-air combat.

An hour later, the Eagles, to a person, were beginning to fade. Several of the Eagles' commented that, "These guys are good; they know how to hold their liquor." Chicklips and Moliver were the first to call it a night. The scotch general also called it a night. The Koreans were clearly feeling the effects, but not nearly to the level of the Eagles.

Many of the Eagles justified the reason for the disparity by noting that beer had been widely consumed throughout the previous days by the Eagles, much more than hard liquor. On this night, unfortunately for the Americans, there was no Hite beer, but there was unlimited scotch.

Forty-five minutes and six or seven more toasts later, only four of the ten Eagles remained, although three of the ROK pilots had recently dropped out. The XO, Lunker, Willie, and Jackal were left to salvage the Eagles' pride.

"It's up to us, boys," said the XO. "This is for the U.S.A....we're drinking heavily in the pursuit of foreign relations."

Soon thereafter, during a discussion he was having with a ROK F-5 Tiger II pilot named Kwan Lee, Lunker thought he was really losing it. "Kwan, am I getting taller or are you getting shorter?"

Kwan laughed and pointed toward his feet. "I exchanged flight boots for loafers. Feet hurt."

Lunker smiled and looked down. His eyes weren't focusing; all he knew was that Kwan wasn't in his bare feet. "That's good. I was getting worried." Both aviators laughed together.

Thirty minutes later, the Eagles' XO waved the white flag. He and Lunker, the last Eagles standing, stumbled their way to the BOQ. The Eagles' night was over. They had lost the final battle, and it was still an hour before midnight. World peace had fallen victim to Frank Sinatra's scotch of choice.

The next morning, at ten a.m., the ROK general hosted a farewell breakfast for the Eagles at the officers club. Although several of the Eagles weren't sure they had an appetite, all of them were on time and were wearing clean flight suits. Their departure time for returning to Atsugi was noon.

When the Eagles arrived at the club, only the scotch general was there, along with the cases of scotch that had been placed to the side of the food and drink tables the night before. "Please, have a seat. Your competitors from last night will be here shortly."

The general paused. "As a way of saying thank you, these cases of Chivas Regal will be shipped to you in Atsugi. I hope you will share them with your entire squadron. It is our way of saying thank you and to wish you nothing but safe skies and calm waters as you deploy on Midway in the future. We will miss you."

Each of the Eagles was touched by the gesture from an officer they would all miss as well.

Suddenly appearing, thirty-eight ROK aviators entered the room, all within an inch or two in height and, at least to the American aviators, somewhat similar in appearance. The Eagles looked at the group from where they sat. These were the pilots they had flown against throughout the detachment. The scotch general cleared such confusion as he made an introduction, sweeping his hand toward the large group of aviators from his country.

"Commander Curry, you told me that if you aren't cheating, you aren't trying." He laughed a genuine laugh that, in turn, made everyone laugh. "We hoped that, as you drank more and more last evening, you wouldn't notice that we made replacements, even swapping name tags to keep our original nine pilots in the room. I guess it worked."

Commander Curry stood and started clapping, followed quickly by the other Eagles. He walked to the ROK general and shook his hand. As he did, he said to the general, "You won fair and square, General, even if you did cheat. It's nice to know we are allies who think the same way." They both laughed.

"Lieutenant Lunker," the general said, "you almost caught us. Good thing my pilot, Kwan Lee, thinks fast." Everyone laughed harder, especially Lunker. He was a long way from Blue Ridge, Georgia, but felt right at home.

The breakfast was as friendly as the previous evening, although both sides were subdued. At 1100, the scotch general, several of his aviators, and five Korean women who presented flowers to each crew, gathered for a group photo by an Eagle Intruder before saying their final goodbyes.

At noon, as the first of five Eagles lifted off, one minute apart, from Kwangju's runway for the final time, little did any of the Eagles know that the scotch general was standing alone outside one of the ROK hangars near the runway's departure end. As each Intruder passed by where he stood, he solemnly bowed and said a prayer for their safe journey home.

Thirty minutes later, as the Eagles flew east over the Sea of Japan, a familiar voice penetrated the silence.

"Eagle one, Badman on eagle common."

"Go ahead, Badman," responded Magic.

"Heading to Osan, but looking forward to hearing about your trip to Seoul when I return." He paused for a second. "Is Lunker in your flight?"

"Yes, sir. He sure is," replied Magic.

"Hey, Lunker, who are you flying with?" asked CAG.

"Willie, sir." Lunker's voice was as easily recognizable as Badman's.

CAG smiled under his oxygen mask. "You may want to pay extra close attention to what Willie's doing today," suggested Badman, a hint of laughter in his remark. He paused, waiting for Lunker's reply.

The odd comment took Lunker and all the Eagles by surprise, but most especially Willie. "Why is that, Badman?" queried Lunker.

"I was on a telephone call with Washington this morning." CAG paused several long seconds for effect. "BuPers is rolling you out of the squadron this December. They're sending you back to Pensacola to be a pilot."

Lunker was stunned. The Navy's Bureau of Personnel, BuPers for short, had twice previously turned down his request for a pilot transition. Yet, CAG had taken his request after their long night flying a jet over a dark ocean with a landing gear that wasn't functioning properly and somehow had gotten it approved. Lunker was so overwhelmed that he didn't know what to say, although his heart felt like it was thumping its way out of his chest.

"Thank you, CAG. I appreciate it," he said, humbled as numerous whoops and yells and congratulations from the XO and his fellow Eagles bombarded the frequency. Lunker's dark visor was down; Willie couldn't see the tears that appeared on his cheeks.

"You earned it, Lunker." CAG had been thrilled to receive the news from Washington.

By early afternoon, all the Eagles' Intruders were securely parked in Atsugi. As CAG had predicted a week earlier, these had been, yes and amen, days to remember.

CHAPTER SIX

International Affairs
Mid-Summer 1980

From a leading Tokyo newspaper:

In less than twelve hours, on what is forecast to be a morning of perfect weather, the American carrier USS Midway will bid sayonara to our country, her host country, as she eases out of Berth Twelve at the U.S. Navy's base in Yokosuka. That berth has been her only home since arriving in Japan in October 1973 to serve as the flagship of the Navy's 'foreign legion', a title bestowed by her crew and officers. The skies are forecast to be clear and the winds calm as the legendary ship begins her return to the South Pacific and Indian Ocean waters it dutifully patrols in modest but powerful anonymity.

A new year will be dawning before Midway and her crew return to Japan. Everyone who sails with the foreign legion recognizes that their lives, like on every other cruise, will likely be forever impacted; the great unknown will be how or to what degree, but none will be untouched. Events and emotions that can never be accurately conveyed, except to those who experienced them, will be logged in the memories of those who sail on the warship known here in Japan as Kubo Midway.

Unspoken among the crew is that, historically, not everyone who departs will return.

A month shy of her thirty-fifth birthday, Midway will glide past families waving farewell from her dock as news helicopters documenting her deployment hover overhead. Even in their opposition, Japanese citizens, our people, including some in small boats protesting America's nuclear arsenal, will politely bow as the ageless carrier passes and sails north out of Yokosuka's protected harbor. Respect for her mission will always supersede any individual emotions.

Minutes later, she will turn south toward an endless horizon. As on thirty-four other at-sea periods in her history, Midway will silently say sayonara and become a bustling city at sea, returning to the Pacific waters that would bring the warship to life and enables the Navy's foreign legion to become a deadly instrument of peace for all mankind.

Until then, the beloved ship will float at rest, even though a constant flurry of activity is underway from the carrier's bow to her stern, from the top of her island to the deepest bowels below decks. It is a labor of love for which this newspaper, like all peace-loving citizens, is grateful.

To those who unselfishly sail across the seas in the name of peace for all citizens of the world, we say, "Watashitachiha, anata no kokoronosokokara arigatō. Thank you from the bottom of our hearts."

With the previous at-sea period behind them, the relatively short inport period flew by like a Japanese bullet train. Sooner than anyone would like, the countdown clock to Midway's departure on at least a five month cruise hit zero. Had they known the cruise would ultimately be extended, and that a new year and a new president would be in place before Midway and her crew would return to Japan, the inport period would have suddenly seemed even shorter. On a perfect weather morning,

96

and sooner than anyone would like, Midway eased out of Berth Twelve at the Navy's base in central Japan and bid her host country sayonara. The skies were indeed clear and the winds were calm as the Navy's foreign legion began its return to the south Pacific and Indian Ocean waters it dutifully patrolled in modest but powerful anonymity.

The Tokyo newspaper was accurate. Everyone who sailed with the foreign legion knew that their lives, like on every other cruise, would be forever impacted if they returned home safely.

At 0945, the crews began donning their flight gear after signing for their jet and making a final visit to the men's head, or restroom. By 1020, they had each finished preflighting their Intruder and were saying their last goodbyes. Each time one of the Eagles took a moment to thank Hanako for being there, a tear and a traditional bow acknowledged her emotions. It was especially hard when Willie said his final goodbyes to her.

Tears were streaming down her face as she hugged him and said, "I'll have sake and manju waiting for you, Willie-san."It was all she could get out.

"I'll look forward to that, Hanako. Nothing compares." Willie had a few tears too. "Sayonara, my sweet friend."

Willie turned back to Tosh, who had her own tears. "Thank you for making the long trip to see me, Tosh. You'll never know how much you being here means to me."

"I love you, Willie, I wouldn't have missed it for the world."

"I love you too, Tosh. My heart is yours." He didn't need to say a lot to her. She'd find lots of hidden notes over the next few hours and days, as well as receiving flowers at her sister's home in Nagai and at her office in San Diego after she returned.

"You know you have mine too, Willie." Tosh didn't feel the need to say much more either. She'd hidden several notes and a photo in Willie's bags, plus a few dated envelopes of love letters she gave Gully to pass to Willie over the next several weeks. Two of them included recent photos of her taken in San Diego during the past month.

"Don't forget to wear your hearing protection, Tosh. I want you to be able to hear me tell you I love you when we're old and gray."

She smiled and nodded as more warm tears streamed down both of her cheeks.

Nearby, Gully and Sharon, Doc and Lauren, and Socks and Marti, were going through similar discussions. The countdown timer to the start of cruise was at zero. There wasn't enough time or enough words to compress five months away into a few sentences that would carry a person through good and bad, happy and sad, and so many nights alone. Eyes strained to remember every smile, ears every word, hands every touch, and hearts every emotion. They exchanged a few more hugs and kisses, and then a final one, which was always the hardest. More than anyone, having experienced it during the last cruise, Willie and his mother in heaven knew that a final embrace could actually be a final embrace.

Immediately after hearing Tosh say, 'Sayonara, Mister Bond," Willie climbed the boarding ladder to his seat, as Gully did the same on the other side. Like the smile and touch of Tosh, Willie found great comfort and security as he strapped himself into the Intruder's ejection seat. He instinctively placed his right hand on the control stick and his left hand on the throttles, and then took a deep breath.

His reality, like many of the others, was both fun and painful at this moment. He was doing what he'd wanted to do since he was just a small boy, but that was before he and his heart met and embraced Tosh Collins. Though he hadn't quite let go of the woman standing on the tarmac nearby, his brain overrode his lustful desire to say, 'I quit,' and climb out of the cockpit. It'd do him, Tosh, his dad or other loved ones little good if he diverted his concentration at any time and didn't return.

As he began running through checklists and performing countless other 'housekeeping' items on his side of the cockpit, Willie's mind made the rapid transition to being focused and compartmentalized on the task at hand. Everything he needed in the world, in reality, was close at hand, right where it should be, at least for a few more moments.

Two weeks later, just three days before arriving at Subic Bay, Philippines, for the first port visit of the cruise, Lunker was in Bunkroom Eight, packing a hanging bag. He and another aviator were being flown to Manila, where they'd represent CAG-Five at a planning conference for a joint exercise that would take place later in the cruise. Following that, Lunker would attend a two-day foreign affairs conference and dinner that had requested the presence of two naval officers, one from the air wing and one from among Midway's complement of officers.

"How did you get this good deal?" asked Jackal, as he sat in Bunkroom Eight chatting with Lunker, Willie, Socks, and Gully. The rumor was that the foreign affairs conference was packed with beautiful women from Europe and Asia.

"Little did you college boys know that since I've been in the Navy I've been taking correspondence courses to get a masters in international affairs. You know, just one more way to sample what the world offers outside of the north Georgia mountains."

As his friend finished his answer, Doc entered the bunkroom as Lunker continued to pack his bag, which included his white mess dress uniform, the Navy's equivalent of a tuxedo. "Where are you off to, Prince Charming?" inquired Doc.

"Lunker's getting a masters degree in international affairs, and is representing the air wing in Manila," answered Socks.

"Our Lunker? Seriously?" Doc turned toward his friend from Georgia, laughing. "Seriously? You're not shitting me, are you? Who's sponsoring this masters' program of yours...Captain Kangaroo?"

"As a cosmopolitan ambassador from the north Georgia mountains, am I the breathing definition of oxymoron or what?" he said, smiling as he packed his black dress shoes.

"You have the second half of that right, you moron." They all laughed, but it was laughter soaked with pride at their friend's achievement.

On the third afternoon of the first Subic Bay inport period, Lunker left a message for Willie and Doc to meet him at the upstairs dining room in the Cubi Point Officer's Club at eight o'clock. Upon arriving, their eyes were treated to a ravishingly gorgeous woman standing next to their friend. Nearby, a perfectly positioned light spotlighted her many beautiful features, which easily convinced them that she likely had few equals among females.

She was five feet five inches tall, but her height was irrelevant. Her dark brown eyes spoke straight to a person's innermost desires and unfulfilled fantasies. Equally inviting was her dark brown hair, filled with wild but meticulously placed curls. It was just long enough to teasingly touch the bottom of her voluptuous breasts, which rested perfectly below her smooth neck and lips as luscious as a succulent red plum. Her taut waist was an entry point for two sculpted legs beneath her mid-length skirt. All her features were enhanced by slightly tanned, olive colored skin that stretched unblemished from her head to her toes.

"My dear friends," said Lunker, "I'd like you to meet Mirela Salai, from Cluj, Romania, who now lives in Hong Kong. We met at the foreign affairs conference in Manila." Her name was pronounced as 'Me-rel-la,' with the 'R' sounding like a soft rolling of the tongue.

Her birth city, considered the unofficial capital of the Transylvania province, was founded three hundred years before Christopher Columbus discovered America. It was located in northwestern Romania, and was the second most populous city in the country. It had a continental climate, typically producing dry, warm summers and very cold winters.

Geography and history, at this moment, meant little to Lunker's friends, whose mouths barely managed to say, 'It's nice

100

to meet you, Mirela,' as she extended her hand, first to Doc, and then to Willie.

"It is my pleasure as well," she said, "Lunker has spoken so highly of both of you."

Her command of the English language was superb, and her noticeable but delicate European accent, flowing like honey across her tongue and lips, enhanced her overall sex appeal. Her family, except for her father, had received permission to emigrate to the United States when she was fourteen years old. Now almost twenty-four, she was currently employed in Hong Kong, where she worked for an international public relations firm based in Chicago.

"These are my two favorite servants I told you about," said Lunker. "Doc cooks, Willie cleans, and I let them fight over who polishes my boots," he said, grinning at his two dearest friends in the squadron.

"He's right, Mirela, and we flip a coin to see who gets the dime the cheap aviator pays us." They all laughed, and then Willie continued. "Eli asked about you yesterday, Lunker. He was quite concerned that Midway was in port, but the cosmopolitan man was nowhere to be seen."

"I'm sure that's just exactly what he said," Lunker responded, laughing, "although I wouldn't be surprised. He is such a kind man. In fact, I promised Mirela she could go with me tomorrow and walk the course. You guys want to join us?"

"Sure, that sounds good," said Doc, as Willie nodded. "What time?"

"Let's meet at the Chuckwagon at nine, and we'll be on the first tee by ten."

"That works, but enough about golf. Golf can wait."

Lunker's two closest friends were trying their best to be quintessential naval officers, as articulated by John Paul Jones, father of the United States Navy — gentlemen with refined manners, punctilious courtesy, the soul of tact, and the nicest sense of personal honor. However, within thirty minutes all four of them were chatting in the irreverent way that aviators preferred to converse, including some very colorful words they learned to say in Romanian as the evening progressed.

As the clock ticked past eleven o'clock, the crowd at the officer's club had dwindled to just a few. Lunker ordered coffee and water for each of them, and the discussion sharply changed course to Mirela's journey out of Romania, a communist country where people lived under the repressive and cruel Ceausescu regime. Her family's story was nothing short of a riveting testimony to a mother and father's unquenchable desire to raise their family under the banner of freedom.

"We lived about a half mile from the city center, in one of six two-room, one-story apartments, clustered closely together around a small courtyard in the very back of a wide, but cramped, alley. At the front of the alley was a group of stores, about four deep. None of our tiny apartments had a bathroom, just a single communal outhouse for, well, number two, as you say. We kept a bedpan in our apartment when we needed to pee, and then emptied it at a place at the edge of our little housing area. Because we were all Christians and, worse, Romanian Baptists, in our little cluster of homes, it was the best my family and the families around us were allowed to have. If Romanian citizens were a ladder, we were the next to bottom rung. The only people considered lower were the Romanian Pentecostals; they really were at the end of the alley."

"Our door opened to the back of a meat store, an area that was always overrun by trash. One of our two rooms was a small windowless bedroom, and the other room was a combination kitchen and living room, with a double bed off to the side. We felt lucky that we had our one window, although it was small and didn't let much light in, especially since we were packed so closely together. At night, though, it wasn't bright in any of our homes, because the government limited people who weren't party elitists to nothing more than twenty-five watt light bulbs."

She paused, seemingly reflective.

"I remember us being happy, though, even in the bleak darkness of winter, when we would huddle around our little gas-lit stove to stay warm. My parents would tell us stories of their childhood and read fairy tales to us, often exaggerating and making us laugh." She paused and smiled, her mind revisiting the past, and then her smile faded away.

"Teachers were so harsh on me from my very first day at school. I was left-handed, but they told me in Romania we could only write with our right hand, so I was punished when they caught me using my left hand, and then they would make fun of me in front of the class." Her eyes looked toward her lap as she momentarily remembered the exasperation and humiliation. "Often my teachers used a long, thin piece of leather to strap my left arm to my side so I couldn't use it at all. It was so frustrating, and so hard, but I ultimately learned to write with my right hand," she said, taking Lunker's hand into her own, "which is why I am ambidextrous today." She smiled and laughed.

"How about that?"

Mirela's relaxed posture stiffened again, and her twinkling eyes grew distant, but her voice remained upbeat. "My daddy worked in a small factory with some of the other men in our area. A truck came every morning and took them to work and then brought them back in the evening. It was hard work and the hours were long, so the burden of everything but a paycheck fell to my mom. I adored my daddy. He had very thick, but soft, dark brown hair, and I loved running my hands through it. I would tell him endlessly that one day I would style his hair for him, which would always bring a big smile to his face." Mirela paused as memories and emotions stirred deep within her.

"My mom was a hard worker, too, raising my younger brother and me and keeping our little apartment clean, and making it as much of a home as she could for us. Like most Romanians, we didn't have much, so we took care of everything we had, like shoes and clothes, and didn't waste anything. My mom was also relentless in writing letters to my country's emigration department in Bucharest. Several times a year she would send in a request in hopes of receiving one of the thousand or so slots available each year for Romanians to emigrate to the United States."

She paused, and her face noticeably tightened as she crossed her arms in front of her.

"As our hope for an official exit waned, my parents decided to make their way to the border and escape to Vidin, Bulgaria, which is on the banks of the Danube River, about two hundred miles south of Cluj, where they knew someone who could help them get to America. They decided to leave my younger brother and me with my grandparents, because it'd be less risky for them without two young children. I was four at the time, and my brother was two. Once they were safely in America, it'd mostly be a matter of paperwork for them to get permission for us to join them."

She paused for a few sobering moments. "Unfortunately, they were caught about two miles from the border."

Mirela took a deep breath before she continued. The three men were anxious to hear the outcome, even though Lunker had previously heard the story. "My mother was taken away with the other women and kept in a holding area for two months before she returned home. She said the conditions were fair, although the food was barely adequate. I was overjoyed when she came home and held my brother and me in her arms, but I was so worried about my daddy, especially after I heard my mother tell my grandparents that she had no idea what happened to him after he was taken away."

Mirela's body was a long way from Romania, but her mind was not; neither were the nightmares. The three men noticed her eyes begin to moisten. From where the group sat, she was detouring into a moment that she rarely shared, simply because it was so painful to relive. Whether it was due to the effects of the alcohol, or just a matter of unconditional trust in Lunker and, by extension, his trusted friends didn't matter.

"My poor daddy," she said, as she wiped tears from her eyes. "I remember the day he came home, because I barely recognized him." As tears began to roll unabated down her cheeks, the anguish of a young child revisited a tender, but lacerated, crevice hidden deep within the roots of her soul. The despair of that moment flowed into her voice as she relived her heartsick emotions.

"My daddy looked like a holocaust survivor." She paused and took a couple long breaths. "He had been gone for barely five months and his ribs were sticking out. His shoulders and arms and legs were so bony, and I could see scars and marks on his body." She took another deep breath. "His beautiful brown hair that I just adored, that I was going to style one day, had been cut short, like a crew cut, and I didn't know if it'd ever grow back."

After a brief but quiet delay, she continued. "I learned later that my daddy, when he was caught, was told by a young soldier, who didn't even look old enough to be in the army, to lie down on the ground. When my daddy refused, the soldier hit him in the kidney area with a rubber mallet, but he remained standing. Twice more this happened, but my daddy was too proud to go to the ground, even when the soldier pleaded with him to just kneel down so he wouldn't have to hurt him again. He would die on his feet, but not on his knees or his belly, he confessed to me a few years ago. My daddy was hit with the mallet in his back and kidneys three more times before they finally dragged him and the others away, but he never laid down on the ground."

The three men with Mirela sat in stunned silence, even Lunker, who already knew what happened. It was a formidable challenge for them to keep their own emotions in check as they watched tears stream down her face.

After pausing and reflecting on what to say next, she continued. "Romanians are proud people, close knit and hard workers. I knew that even at my young age, which is why I couldn't believe other Romanians would do that to my daddy."

Mirela's head tilted to the right and settled onto her hand, which was anchored by her elbow resting on her chair's armrest. Lunker, sitting to her right, placed his left hand on her upper back. "I couldn't rationalize it then, but now I know that the innocence and goodness that God places inside of children was taken away from me that day by my own country." She paused again for several seconds.

"My parents decided to try to escape again three years later, when I was ten. My dad's health had recovered along with his beautiful brown hair." She turned to smile at Lunker, taking his left hand into her right hand. "This time, my brother, who was almost six, and I would join them."

Lunker and his two friends were spellbound, just passengers along for a ride, sitting in the middle of an intriguing book as it was being penned by its author.

"Before we began our trek toward the border with Bulgaria, and numerous times along the way, my mom stressed that we'd be crawling through a field of tall grass and weeds the last mile or so to the border. She said it wasn't enough to stay low and remain unseen as we crawled on our hands and knees below the top of the weeds. Over and over, she stressed that I had to be constantly alert for very thin wires that zigzagged low across the ground as we neared the border. If we tripped any of them, it would alert the soldiers, and we'd be quickly captured. It was how they were caught the first time."

Her eyes again seemed distant, revisiting the past, as she crossed her arms over her waist, each hand firmly holding the opposite elbow.

"Finally, the day came for us to try to reach Bulgaria and our freedom. After several long hours of walking and then crawling, I heard my mother's voice whisper that we were very close to the border and to watch for the wires. It was then that I realized I had lost sight of her. I could hear someone crawling slowly near me, and I remember looking to my right to see if it was her."

"As I did, I felt my left hand push a thin wire." Mirela looked down at her arms, still crossed, then over to her left hand and, finally, up at the three men. "I knew instinctively I had just cost us our freedom."

She sat motionless for at least thirty seconds, her eyes and mind traveling to a painful memory permanently etched into another heartbreaking crevice of her very essence. "I didn't want to think what price we would all pay for my mistake. All I wanted to do was cry."

No one spoke for several seconds as each of the aviators felt his pulse quickening and his heart breaking for a child's innocent mistake.

"I heard a loud alarm sound in the distance and, within a couple minutes, I could hear a truck approaching and then soldiers yelling for us to stand up. 'Get up, get up, stand up', so much yelling over and over, and they were angry and mean. Counting the children, there were probably twenty, maybe twenty-five, of us. My brother and I were holding on to my mom. I'm not sure he was old enough to really know what was happening, but I was, and I was so scared, especially when the soldiers started rounding up the men, pushing them into a small circle." She took a few deep breaths.

"I remember hearing the sound of a second truck and then seeing it, rumbling fast across the field behind us, as a few more soldiers appeared, each holding a rifle. It looked like an oversized pickup truck, and I saw my daddy look back toward us as he was being forced up and on to the bed of the first truck, and there was still so much yelling. I remember his beautiful brown hair, and then he disappeared from my sight as the soldiers got on the truck and surrounded the men, and suddenly they were all gone, driving away fast. It seemed deathly quiet as the truck drove out of sight and its noise faded away."

She unfolded her arms and took a single sip of water from a glass next to her.

"After a minute or so, the soldiers separated the women from the children and placed us in two lines, facing each other, about thirty or forty feet apart. It's hard to estimate, me being so small at the time. One of the lines was for the women and the other for the children. I remember holding my little brother's hand and looking across at my mother, a little to the left of me. As I stared at her, a young soldier, with a rifle in his right hand, walked between the two lines and turned sharply toward the women."

Mirela paused, reliving the fearful moment. "I was close enough to see that his rifle was pointed at my mother. I had just seen my daddy being driven away and I was convinced this young soldier was going to shoot her." Her voice didn't reflect fear; just a loving woman's unconditional love and concern for a parent.

"I broke from the line and ran to the soldier, wrapping myself around his right leg, pulling at him, crying, and begging him not to shoot my mother." The emotions in her description sounded as fresh as if the event had happened just minutes earlier.

"He looked at me and said, 'I'm not going to shoot anyone,' and I asked why he was pointing his rifle at my mother. He told me to point to her, which I did. She was standing right in front of us, and then he looked at his rifle, which was actually pointed toward the ground at about a forty-five degree angle, maybe more. He told me that his rifle was pointed at the ground because he didn't want to shoot anyone, especially my mother, and then he told me to go get back in line with the other children."

Mirela was silent for a minute, during which time no one spoke.

Willie and Doc were stunned at her story, not saying anything, and her depth of despair reminded them of the first time Eli described burying his three children. It was one more story of heartache from a foreign piece of soil that few Americans could likely find in an atlas.

"After a few more minutes, a truck arrived and took all of us to a concentration camp that looked more like a primitive prison, consisting of four stone buildings, each about the size of a small home. A crude wire fence, about eight feet tall and topped with coiled barbed wire, surrounded the area. I remember it well. The children were taken to one building and the women to another. Inside our building was an open courtyard that became our play area."

"We adapted; I guess children do. We didn't know anything but hope, although we missed our parents and were afraid we would never see them again. I had my brother, and for that I was grateful. I spent most of my time trying to comfort him and ensuring he was okay. I played games with him and told him stories and kept reassuring him we'd be fine."

Her description was simple and straightforward, but the mental image in the minds of the three aviators was both numbing and heartbreaking as they tried to imagine being a young child in that predicament. Mirela continued. "We were kept in that camp for over seven weeks before we were reunited with our mothers." She then took two deep breaths, seemingly lost in another place or time. "We spent almost four more months in the compound before they released us and took us back to my home in Cluj."

"My mother began writing the emigration department again. She was so persistent, writing them again each time she received a rejection letter. Over and over she wrote letters, year after year, even sending one to a relative she had in Chicago, hoping that she could persuade the American government to intervene. In that time period, we had no word on whether my daddy was alive or not."

Mirela paused, her eyes suddenly far away, and then she continued in a voice that reflected memories both joyful and sad.

"One day, almost five years after we were released, my daddy walked through our door." Those were Mirela's only words before tears began forming again and her head dropped. "And I barely recognized him." Her body language screamed revulsion toward her native country, although her lips were silent for several long seconds.

"He was emaciated as before, but his hair was all white and cut down to nothing. I just started crying as I hugged him. If his eyes weren't so recognizable and still so beautiful, I would have believed he was a holocaust victim who was an old man, certainly not my thirty-seven year old daddy."

Even now, so many years later, the silent rage that was part of an almost twelve-year-old daughter's reaction was rising in her voice as she spoke. "I was so happy to have him home, back with us, making our family whole again, but then I learned he had been beaten, like during his first escape attempt, with a mallet, hit in his kidneys when they told him to get down on the ground, but he never did. I hated my country for what they had done to him. I could feel throughout my soul that the innocence of my childhood was stripped away as I looked at my daddy. He had a big smile as I hugged him, but feeling his bony body that used to be so muscular and strong just crushed my heart. He was still the strongest man I ever knew, but all I could think about was how my country treated him."

She paused for a moment, looking at each of the three men for several seconds each, although it was obvious that her focus was somewhere else. "And his hair, cut so short, not evenly cut, just white stubs sticking up. I knew at that moment that my family would never be the same again." More tears made their way down her cheeks as her head dropped and her eyes focused on the ground.

"A little over three years passed, and my family grew by two with a sister and baby brother, and then one day my mother received a letter from the Romanian emigration department. We could leave; it was approved, but not with my daddy. He had to remain in Romania. It wasn't fair, but my daddy was adamant that we go without him. He wanted us to be free more than he wanted us to stay together." She sat in silence for a few moments as a few more tears made an appearance.

"Less than two months later, we were on our way to Chicago and taking our first steps toward becoming American citizens." She took a deep breath. Lunker knew what was next; his friends didn't, but they could tell the story wasn't finished.

"I had just turned fifteen and only knew a few words in English. In Romania, we began learning English in the fourth grade but, like most of my classmates, I didn't care whether I learned any or not. When we arrived in Chicago, we lived with my mom's distant cousin and her family in a small but upscale ethnic suburb, comprised mostly of eastern Europeans. Since my siblings and I understood very little English, it wasn't surprising that most of the first words we learned in school were bad words, which was typical, I suppose. Our school was populated with children from well-educated, middle and upper income families. It was a nightmare, as we received no breaks from our teachers or classmates regarding the circumstances that led to our difficulty in understanding or speaking English."

She paused for a moment, thinking.

"We were smart, reading and writing and doing math at our grade level or higher. My mom made sure of that, but that was in our native language." She looked at the three men staring at her. "Want to go to Romania or Russia and sit in on a college class and try to learn something new?" she asked, looking at each of them as she smiled and softly laughed. "I don't think I need to say much more about our introduction to the Chicago school system and our chance of fitting in." She paused, after which a sense of despondency returned that saturated the air around them.

Willie and Doc had no idea what they would hear, but they knew it was probably quite far from Walt Disney's idea of the most magical place on earth.

"We were driven to school by my mom's cousin, but we had to walk home." She sat silently for almost a minute; none of the men said a word.

"We were taunted and picked on by our classmates as we walked home, so every day I told my siblings to run to the small park that was along our path, just a few blocks from our home, and to get on the swings and just start swinging hard and keep swinging, higher and higher, not stopping. I lagged behind to try and keep these mean kids, these bullies, from my brothers and sister. Then I'd get on a swing and tell my siblings to hit the kids with their feet if they tried to touch them. We did that every day for almost a month before they finally stopped. 'Get to the swings and swing hard,' I'd tell them over and over, even my baby brother."

Mirela's eyes reflected the memories of an oldest sibling born with strong maternal instincts. Each memory clung to her soul like the teardrops flowing from her eyes.

"After a couple months, we were taken from the school and put into classes in our village to learn English from a government-paid tutor. We spent every day there until the end of the school year. Even after that, it was deemed impossible for me to ever catch up to my peers. The high school counselor's projection was that it'd take me until my early twenties to graduate from high school." She looked toward her feet for a few moments, then toward Lunker, taking his hand in hers.

"When I was seventeen, I dropped out of school, and learned how to style hair and do nails so that I could work and make money, which I did, and I became very good at it." She paused again. "My choices were very few, but my artistic sense found a home and I became the most sought after hair stylist in my little area of Chicago very quickly," she said smiling. "My English skills improved, although many of the salon's customers were from Eastern Europe, and I was able to speak with them in Romanian as well as English."

She looked at Lunker and gave him a half-smile. "When I was nineteen, I earned a GED at the suggestion of one of my hair clients. It was the same year my daddy was finally allowed to travel outside of Romania." Mirela paused, but she wasn't finished with her riveting story of a journey from the depths of human indignity and survival, to unqualified self-worth and pride.

"Not long after that, a client, whose hair I had been cutting for almost a year, and with whom I had developed a warm friendship, was sitting in my salon waiting for me to finish with an appointment. In   the fifteen minutes she waited, she heard me telling my story of the failed escape in Romania to a lady from Germany who was in my chair and had asked about my emigration from Cluj to Chicago." She paused.

"When it was my next client's turn to have her hair styled, she instead invited me to an early lunch."

Mirela was at ease again, returning from an emotionally draining period in her life to the present. "Over lunch, she wanted to know my full story, so I told her what I just told you. She told me her son was in the Army, serving in Berlin." She paused and then continued.

"I told her that he and the Americans and our NATO allies, those who serve in the name of those who aren't free, would never know me or my family or people like us — people trapped and treated like caged animals under horrible regimes. Yet, the sweat on her son's uniform, like the sweat on your flight suits, linked directly to the tears my mother and father cried while we suffered in Romania. His sweat, your sweat, the sacrifices all of you have made and are still making. You freed us."

She looked at each of them. "That same sweat linked to the tears we cried when our family finally stepped off the airplane in America." Mirela paused for a moment, and then took a noticeably deep breath.

"I said her son, and maybe each of you," Mirela looked at each of the three men sitting with her, "may wonder if your time serving actually matters. Only time will tell about your personal journey, but it's already mattered, or I wouldn't be sitting here this evening." She paused.

"Today was probably the first day of freedom for someone in Romania, or another country that isn't free, and your sweat, her son's sweat, it matters to them, it links to their dreams and their pain. That's essentially what I stressed over and over to her."

Mirela took only the second sip of water since she had begun describing her family's fateful journey.

"She surprised me. Without any hesitation, she told me she wanted me to come work for her, to tell my story. She's the international director for a public relations firm that is headquartered in Chicago and represents a group of organizations around the world pursuing freedom for people trapped behind the Iron Curtain, people like my family and our friends. Their Asian branch is in Hong Kong, which is where I am based. That's how I wound up at the conference in Manila and how I met my sweet Lunker."

As she finished, she leaned over and kissed the aviator next to her, causing him to blush.

"Our goal is to provide a formal structure to interact with and connect organizations, individuals, and government agencies that lift up and support those who desire freedom, as well as those working on their behalf. My message to audiences is what I just said to you. The sweat on your flight suits, on the uniforms of everyone who serves, relates directly to the tears of despair that enslaved people shed while being held captive by their own country and, subsequently, the tears of joy when people can finally taste freedom. Maintain the good fight, I tell them. My family is proof that those who serve on behalf of others do make a difference. That's my message."

Doc and Willie were stunned. "That's an incredible story, Mirela," said Doc.

"I'm not speechless often, but I'm speechless now," added Willie.

"So how did you and Lunker actually meet?" asked Doc. "That has to be a good story too."

She smiled and took Lunker's hand again. "Lunker approached me on a break and offered to pour my coffee. I couldn't turn down an offer from a tall, handsome man in uniform, so I asked him about it. He said he was in the United States Navy, and then he asked about my accent."

The three men laughed, Doc and Willie the hardest. "I think that line about coffee is on page twelve of the naval aviators' handbook of great pickup lines when encountering beautiful women," said Doc.

"I'm glad he asked, no matter his reason." Mirela, with a soft smile that continued to capture Lunker's heart, squeezed his hand.

"Mirela, I'm sure I'm speaking for Willie as well when I say that it has been wonderful to have met you, and so humbling to hear your family's story. I can't wait until Lauren and Tosh join us and can get to know you, too."

Doc was sincere, an emotion seconded by Willie, who was nodding in agreement. The two friends knew that Lunker, although he wouldn't say it openly, really wanted an opportunity to spend more private time with his date; he'd spend plenty of time with his two friends during the next three to four months.

"We're going to say goodbye and head back to the ship and give you two a little time alone."

"It was nice to finally meet you both, and, yes, Lunker should be looking forward to our time alone," she said, laughing as she patted her blushing date's knee.

Willie laughed and said, "I must warn you, Mirela. I think you'll find that Eli will love you more than he loves Lunker, and that's saying a lot." He was sincere, even as he was laughing. Moments later, Doc and he stood and said goodbye.

The next morning, after the three men each enjoyed an overstuffed breakfast burrito and Mirela had oatmeal with fresh fruit at the Chuckwagon grill on the Subic side, they took a base taxi to the Binictican Golf Course. Lunker had called the course manager earlier, asking him to let Eli know they would be arriving sharply at ten o'clock.

As their white taxi pulled up to the circle in front of the facility, Eli was already waiting. He beamed when he saw Lunker, although his big smile became even larger when he saw Lunker holding hands with Mirela. Eli was faithful to a fault regarding his own wife, but he was immediately drawn to the European beauty's charm and was overjoyed that she'd be joining them.

The front nine was characterized less by their attention to golf and more to new and old friends renewing fresh memories between them. At the turn between number nine and number ten, the golfers and Mirela ordered a hot dog and a San Miguel beer for themselves, and two hot dogs and a Pepsi for their caddies. The group sat near the small food stand on park-like benches under a makeshift open-air gazebo. The discolored wood structure had no floor — the dirt of the Philippines was more than sufficient. The roof of the structure and the posts that supported it, well weathered from frequent storms, had been stained and cleansed by tears and laughter and stories of happiness and sadness since the Korean war.

As an earlier discussion was finished, Lunker asked his beloved caddy about his family, a question that generated subtle but noticeable lines of concern across Eli's forehead as his head dropped and his eyes looked down — two uncharacteristic facial expressions that Lunker noticed immediately.

He spoke before Eli could respond. "What's wrong, Eli? I can tell something is wrong." Lines of concern were written across Lunker's face as well.

There was silence among the three Americans and two Filipinos watching the conversation unfold between the two

116

men. They could see shards of anguish spreading across Eli's entire body.

Lunker treasured the man sitting next to Mirela, and became more adamant when he noticed his friend's eyes begin to moisten and his shoulders droop. He had seen that only once before, and that was when Eli first described the death of Ligaya, who had stepped on a baby Krait. "Eli, we're friends. Let me help you. You don't need any more heartache. Tell me what's wrong." He moved and sat against the man who was more than a caddy to him.

The thirty-two year old Filipino, suddenly looking unusually tired and far older than his age, collapsed wearily into Lunker, his head falling against the tall aviator's upper left arm. Lunker could sense barely perceptible convulsions radiating from Eli's body, as if his dear friend was weeping silent tears from the heart.

"My daughter, Diwata, she my baby, have rash on neck spreading and fever. Cough all time. Have what make children die in villages." Eli's heartsick voice flowed straight from a father's terrified heart. "Don't think can dig grave for my baby. Already dig three."

Lunker placed his arm across his friend's shoulders and responded immediately.

"I bet it's measles," he said, turning to his friends. "There was an outbreak of it here during my very first cruise, and it killed a lot of kids." He paused and continued. "It still does. One of us needs to go back to the ship and talk to Doc Wilde. He can help."

Before he had barely finished his sentence, Willie stood and gave his young caddy a handful of pesos equivalent to twenty dollars, slightly over what he typically earned in a week lugging a golf bag for American sailors.

"I have the phone number to the pro shop. I'll call and leave a message for you."

Twenty minutes later, in between patients, Doc Wilde responded to Willie's description of Diwata's symptoms. "It's most likely measles," he said, echoing Lunker's thoughts. "I was briefed on it in San Diego a couple days before I came over."

"What's the protocol to help her?" asked Willie. He wasn't smiling. He was focused on measles and no other disease.

"I need to get the approval of Midway's senior medical officer, which I think I can do before this time tomorrow. He's off the boat this afternoon."

"C'mon Doc, she may not have time if it's spreading. Eli's already lost three of his five children. How much more could you or I take if we were in his shoes?" Willie laid bare a core emotion in front of the man who, himself, was the father of a daughter. "What medicine does she need?" he asked.

"She needs fluids and a vitamin A supplement."

"Do we have it here on the ship? Right now?"

"Well, yes." He was silent for a couple moments. "I'm sure we do."

Willie had a momentary flashback to his grandfather's exhortation on the night he became aware of a moonshiner, his namesake, known as Mister Willie. "I know we're walking on the wrong side of a fine line, Doc, but we're talking about a child's life here, a father's baby daughter. We have to do what no one else is willing to do."

Willie paused, not willing to leave the ship empty handed. "Why don't you get what she needs, lay it out on the treatment table, and turn your head for thirty seconds. I'll take care of the rest. If you have to, ground me from flying after diagnosing me with whatever this would treat me for."

There was silence between them for several seconds until a final plea broke the stalemate. "Giving me what she needs right now won't hurt anyone else, Doc, but it may save his daughter's life. Eli's already lost three children. He shouldn't have to lose his baby."

Willie's resolve was convincing. Doc Wilde knew there was no national health insurance in the Philippines and that, for fathers like Eli who earned, on average, less than one thousand U.S. dollars per year, there was no way to pay for the medicine that would help.

Doc Wilde nodded. "Okay, consider yourself grounded until we go back to sea and start flying again." He patted Willie on the shoulder and smiled. "Tell Eli I'll do whatever is necessary."

Thirty minutes later, after calling the pro shop, and while Doc Wilde continued to see patients, mostly sailors who complained that they were pissing razor blades, Willie was in the back seat of a taxi. He returned quickly to the golf course, armed with supplies for Diwata and a preventative supplement for Eli's other daughter, Macaalay. Rejoining the group, Willie explained the steps Eli needed to take. The ship would depart in slightly less than four days.

Ten minutes later, and for the first time ever while playing on the course, Lunker walked alongside a caddy other than Eli. After giving Willie, Doc, Mirela, and Lunker quick but warm hugs, Eli had swiftly walked away from the group, heading for the village that he had called home since his birth, racing against time in a desperate bid to save Diwata.

As he departed, tears began to flow from Eli's eyes like a warm tropical rain. He wasn't sure he could find the strength to shovel dirt from the earth one more time, and then refill the space that would be the final resting place of his baby daughter.

The day before the ship departed Subic Bay for its next at-sea period, Eli was again hoisting Lunker's bag on his shoulder. Diwata was fine, as was Macaalay. A smile was frozen on his brown, weathered face, and the unselfish efforts of his American friends were permanently written on his heart.

Lunker, Willie, and Doc collectively gave him thirty-six hundred pesos, about four hundred sixty dollars, an amount that normally took him over three months to earn. Eli refused it initially, but the three men, who cared so deeply for him, were adamant. It was for his two remaining children, and their continued health and wellbeing, they stressed. Lunker told his friend that, while they couldn't save every child who needed medical attention in this beautiful and lush country, they would do everything possible to save his children.

Eli was still reluctant until Mirela, walking with the group on the final day, added her thoughts.

"What is your wife's name, Eli?"

"Violetta," he answered.

"That's a beautiful name, Eli. I'm sure her name fits her perfectly." Eli nodded and smiled as Mirela continued. "Violetta has suffered the loss of three children that came from inside her body. This money will give her the peace of mind that every mother deserves. Please accept it and give your wife that peace."

Her simple maternal persuasion closed the deal. Eli humbly accepted their gift.

Later, Commander Singer, the Eagles' skipper, who was also playing in the final day's foursome, privately gave him six thousand pesos, along with additional medical supplies. It was to thank him for all the years of joy he'd brought the Eagles' golfers and himself. With that kind gesture, Eli was unable to restrain his emotions any longer, and tears flooded his cheeks. The God to whom he prayed daily, and who held his two daughters — Dalisay and Ligaya — and Nimuel, his only son, in the palm of His hands, had heard and listened to his prayers.

During that same final round of golf, Lunker announced that Mirela was going to meet the ship in Singapore. The skipper responded by sharing with his three junior officers the relationship he had with Connie, one he kept secret for almost two years but could finally divulge now that her divorce was final. During that time, he had been loyal and faithful to her even though her divorce had lingered for over a year longer than it should have.

As the last hole of the last round of golf for the port visit was completed, drinks among old and new friends were ordered, although the skipper departed after one round, as did all the caddies except Eli. They sat together around a large picnic table under an open-air gazebo, its paint faded and worn from years of late afternoon showers and harsh seasonal monsoons. The backdrop of a beautifully lush, although unforgiving, jungle reminded them of their intoxicating place on the planet.

Three aviators, Mirela, and Eli each enjoyed three rounds of San Miguel beer, savoring every drop of the smooth liquid. As another countdown timer ticked toward zero, Eli asked, as he did every time, "So what over horizon, Lunker?"

"Oh, Eli," said Lunker, smiling, "everything's over the horizon, but sometimes it's enough to just take a jet up on a beautiful day and make it dance with the clouds." Typical of aviators, Lunker artistically used his hands to help a smiling Eli visualize the airborne waltz between man's creation and God's creation.

As Eli grinned from ear to ear, Mirela, elegantly casual but so alluring in white Capri pants and a fuchsia tank top, both of which complemented her warm olive skin, dark brown hair, and hourglass figure, innocently but genuinely asked, "So what kind of dancing do you do up in the sky, Lunker? Twirls? Curls? Pirouettes?"

Everyone laughed, and Lunker put his right arm around his Romanian companion's bare shoulders and pulled her close, softly kissing her left cheek. "This is what makes you so adorable, my sweet Mirela. You ask the questions that put color into our stories."

Fifteen minutes later, five friends, born in three different countries, bid each other an 'until our next visit' farewell. What was left hanging in the air, like a dark rain cloud on a distant horizon, was the realization that within the next year or two there would be sad, and final, farewells between Eli and each of the American aviators to whom he had grown so close. For now, though, the present was perfect — the future was somewhere over the line between the sky and water.

Sixteen hours later, one more visit to the Philippines was over. As Midway eased away from its berth at Naval Station Subic Bay just after nine a.m., the level of activity on the ship steadily increased. A larger than normal number of sailors stood on the flight deck or by one of the cavernous openings on the hangar bay to watch Olongapo become a memory. Many memories were etched into granite; they'd never change. Others were written into soft sand at low tide, and would be selectively modified or embellished to best fit a boast or bragging rights that began with, "So there I was, crossing the shit river bridge..."

Eight sailors, two of whom were in air wing squadrons, missed the required 0730 muster on the morning the ship departed for yet another horizon. Their lapse in judgment would mean they'd be restricted to the ship during Midway's visit to Singapore. They likely overslept in the arms of a new or old lover and would be panicked when they awoke to see the great carrier heading west toward Hoover Mountain, the informally named peak that majestically guarded the entrance to Subic Bay.

CHAPTER SEVEN

A Night To Remember
Mid-to-Late Summer, 1980

Five days before arriving in Singapore, a C-2 Greyhound, a twin-engine, propeller-driven aircraft used to carry passengers and supplies, transported five officers and eight enlisted men from Midway to Singapore to coordinate the carrier's visit. Unlike Subic Bay, which was a U.S. Navy base well versed in receiving aircraft carriers and their crews, ports of call in Singapore, Hong Kong, Thailand, Australia, and other places required extensive assistance, planning, and coordination prior to the ship arriving with five thousand men ready to play on dry land again.

Although predominantly consisting of aviators from the ten squadrons in the air wing, several ad-hoc groups among the men on Midway had reserved large suites at the more prominent hotels in Singapore. One of the officers among the pre-arrival group would, among his duties, ensure the rooms were confirmed and ready.

The Eagles' wives and girlfriends, including Tosh, Lauren, Sharon, and Mirela, would arrive the day prior to the ship's arrival in Singapore. With the exception of the skipper's friend, Connie, they had all booked rooms at the Grand Hyatt Singapore, a luxurious hotel located near the city's renowned botanical gardens.

The wives didn't select it for the gardens, though. Those who had visited the city-state and island country eighteen months earlier, when Midway made a port call there, pointed out that it had a world-class spa, and that it sat at the start of Orchard Road, the hub of Singapore's shopping, dining, and entertainment district. It was everything they needed and desired besides their lovers. As a result, the Singapore countdown timer was cheerfully ticking toward zero.

Two days before arriving in Singapore, and thirty minutes before the first flight brief of the day, the Eagles' skipper scheduled an all-officers-meeting in Ready Room Five to discuss the basic rules of engagement for thriving and surviving in Singapore. This would be Commander Singer's fourth trip to Singapore, having first visited while flying Intruders from an aircraft carrier during the Vietnam War. Strolling up to the podium, he was firm in his message.

"Listen up, guys. What I'm going to say is short and sweet but very serious, and I expect you to drill it into the hearts and minds of your sailors." As he typically did, he paused and took a sip of freshly poured black coffee, and then leaned against the wooden podium.

"Singapore is not Subic Bay. They're as far apart as the North Pole is from the South Pole. It's a city that is brutally tough on littering and crime. If one of your troops decides to steal a purse from an old lady, he'd better remember that cops are everywhere, often hiding and waiting for such a moment, and they'll step out from the shadows and shoot you. If they don't shoot you, they'll beat you and then make you pay for their broken nightstick, and then beat you again if you complain." He paused to let his last remark sink in.

"Throwing a McDonalds' wrapper or a piece of trash on the ground won't get you shot, but it will garner a massive beating if you don't pick it up right away when a cop tells you to, and then you will likely be buying a new nightstick for the cop as well."

The skipper took a sip his coffee, but he wasn't done. "I want each of you in your shops multiple times between now and when we arrive, hammering home the message to the troops that Singapore is no place to bend or break any rules."

He looked across the ready room at his officers with a hint of a smile on his face. "One last thing for you single guys. Dust up on some sweet things to say in Dutch. Singapore is crawling with KLM stewardesses and, although most of them speak English, they love it when you try and say a few words in their language." He paused.

"Jij bent mooi is one you may want to try." The skipper took a sip of coffee. "Good luck with that," he said with a grin that suggested a positive experience telling a KLM flight attendant that she was beautiful. After taking another sip of coffee and letting his last message sink in, the skipper ended his time in front of his officers. "That's all I have. Any questions or comments before we adjourn?"

"Uh, skipper, one more point, if I may." The sound of Lunker's voice was a surprise only in that it was softly spoken and polite, almost meditative.

"The floor is all yours, Lunker." The already silent ready room grew even quieter.

"All I want to add is a simple reminder to my fellow Eagles that," Lunker paused for a few seconds before continuing in an uncharacteristically somber voice, "a good wingman joins up and shuts up. We all know that." He was silent for a moment. "But a truly outstanding wingman," he held their attention for a few seconds, "will buy the first round and also take the overweight flight attendant."

Even the skipper couldn't keep from howling along with the rest of the ready room. Everyone was more than ready to walk the streets and enjoy a cosmopolitan city known as the lion city, although lions never lived there. Not even the most imaginative pilots could figure out how that call sign came about.

On the day before Midway would anchor in Singapore's harbor, and ferries would begin shuttling officers and sailors to and from the city, the ship's air plan scheduled the first launch of the day at 1030 and the last plane on deck at 2030. However, at 0730, the voice of Midway's popular and highly respected captain resonated from the internal intercom throughout the carrier. "Good morning Midway, this is the captain. After consulting with the admiral and his staff, we're going to make a few changes to our operations plan today." He paused briefly.

"We are going to fly four events instead of five. The first launch this morning will be at ten hundred, thirty minutes earlier than the original air plan. The last plane on deck will be at approximately eighteen hundred, a few minutes after sunset."

"At that time, we will take advantage of the ship's position and begin a night exercise in which EMCON Alpha will be set throughout the ship. The ship's lighting will be set to simulate that of a merchant ship as we sail through the waters between the northern coast of Borneo and Palawan Island at the southern tip of the Philippines. During that time, we will double the number of lookouts until we are back in open waters and on a direct course for Singapore. The exercise will not involve the air wing. That is all."

EMCON Alpha was the Navy's most restrictive form of emissions control, and was used when it wants a ship at sea to disappear. During EMCON Alpha, no emissions were permitted at all; no use of radars, external radio communications, or even the Identification, Friend or Foe (IFF) system that enabled Midway to identify inbound aircraft as either friendly or as a possible threat.

From the perspective of the ship, airwing, and aviators, the four events were uneventful. The launches were conducted seamlessly, and, among all the landings attempted through the four events, there was only one foul deck waveoff and one bolter. Otherwise, every pilot was safely on board in his final look at the deck prior to the welcome break of relaxation in Singapore.

Both of Midway's officers' wardrooms and all the enlisted mess decks were packed at 1800 and remained so for a few hours. Between bites of food, conversations were dominated with plans for Singapore, mostly catching up on sleep or simply spending time in the sunshine away from five thousand smelly guys. With the exception of the night navigation exercise being conducted by the ship, and some of the ship's spaces being cleaned before anchoring in a little over seventeen hours, the mood throughout the ship was very relaxed and upbeat. Among those who called the legendary carrier home, including air wing personnel, less than fifteen percent had been to Singapore, which heightened their anticipation of seeing the sun shining over a new destination.

Shortly before Midway entered the narrow straits between the southernmost point of Palawan Island in the Philippines and the northern tip of Borneo, a test of the ship's alarms was conducted, as was customary at 0630 and 1830 every day. Bellowing loudly from every speaker on the ship, such tests became one more memory that sailors would recall long after stepping away from a gray Navy ship for the very last time.

"The following is a test of the ship's alarms. This is only a test. General Quarters alarm." The GQ alarm sound was that of a klaxon, ringing once a second. "Chemical alarm." The sound of the chemical alarm was a continuous medium-to-high pitched tone. "Collision alarm." The collision alarm was three rapid high-pitched notes, repeated once a second, sounding like 'deet-deet-deet, deet-deet-deet.'

Whether in port, at anchor, or underway, any activity related to safety or security on the ship would continue without interruption. Accordingly, during the ship's time in Singapore, one of four duty sections, each consisting of twenty-five percent of Midway's complement of officers and sailors, would always be onboard the ship to immediately get her underway or to react to any shipboard emergency or contingency. Even when she was placidly resting at anchor, the carrier remained a vibrant and active city at sea, inclusive of issues that occur in any large city, as she maintained her role as the flagship of the Navy's foreign legion, a formidable American instrument of peace.

By 2000, or eight o'clock in the evening, most of the Eagles' officers and sailors were relaxing in their living spaces, or catching up on paperwork or other tasks in their work spaces. Like the impact on a child on Christmas Eve, time seemed to slow down the night before a port visit. Also like a child, everyone sought some form of escape in the hope of making time accelerate.

In Bunkroom Eight, at a gathering of the Far East Film Society, a new Mel Brooks movie, Blazing Saddles, had recently been placed into the VCR. It was the third showing so far during the cruise, and would be on their 'watch often' list. Years into the future, the informal society's taste would be justified when the movie was deemed *culturally, historically, or aesthetically significant* by the U.S. Library of Congress. For this showing, twelve aviators, including five for the first time, were crammed into an area more suited for eight people. As they eagerly awaited the second round of popcorn that would be ready in just over a minute, the bunkroom was filled with laughter and good cheer.

Willie and Chicklips, however, were absent. They were camped out in the Eagles' administrative office, which was located one level below the carrier's flight deck and positioned about one hundred feet aft of the end of the angled deck. The two of them were combing through the records of the men assigned to the line division in preparation for evaluations that would be due a few weeks after the visit to Singapore concluded. They were also discussing who among the sailors qualified would replace Buzz on the flight deck when he left the Navy at the end of the cruise.

On Midway's bridge, as the carrier cruised in radio silence with EMCON Alpha still set, the officer of the deck and the junior officer of the deck were engaged in lively discussions about the unexpected emergence of clouds slowly edging down to the ocean's surface, lowering the visibility on the bridge to under five hundred feet. There wasn't a sense of urgency among the two as, just several minutes earlier, all the lookouts reported negative contacts. Midway's captain, who would commonly and often say that there is nothing scarier to a mariner than fog, was comfortable as he went to his underway cabin, located adjacent to the bridge, to take a private call from the embarked admiral.

On the flag bridge, the Admiral's underway watch standers were engaged in similar discussions regarding the clouds. A few wanted to break EMCON Alpha. Those who objected made the argument that the current weather conditions created a real-world training environment, especially since EMCON Alpha would be used for the vast majority of the time that the carrier was in the Indian Ocean following the visit to Singapore.

Three minutes later, a senior member of the admiral's staff rushed onto the bridge. "Turn the damn radar and lights on now!" he thundered. Midway's surface search radar and ship's lights were brought back to life in a matter of a few seconds.

With the first sweep, a blip appeared on the radar's screen, less than two hundred yards from the carrier and closing. On a pitch-black night on an even darker sea, upon which the blanket of descending clouds created a milky perspective of each other's relative motion that was suspect at best, two vessels appeared out of the darkness to each other, and both took drastic evasive actions.

In the Eagles' administrative office, Willie and Chicklips had just closed one file and opened another when they heard a familiar but unexpected sound coming from Midway's shipwide intercom system.

'Deet-Deet-Deet…Deet-Deet-Deet…Deet-Deet-Deet…'

Chicklips turned to Willie and asked, "Didn't they just test the ship's alarms?"

Before anyone could answer, a seemingly invisible hand of a very angry God swung a giant sledgehammer and hit the ageless carrier about seventy feet forward of where the three men stood. Everyone in the Eagles' administrative office was immediately knocked to the floor by the massive concussion as they heard the surreal but horrifying sound of ripping metal just above their heads.

Instinctively, Willie yelled, "Put on your float coats now!" to the five enlisted men in the office, and then turned to Chicklips. "Get your SV-2 and get to the ready room!" Willie remained in place until he had ensured that no one was injured among those in the office, and then proceeded to the Eagles' flight gear locker, where he grabbed his own SV-2 life preserver and headed toward the Eagles' ready room.

On Midway's bridge, the officer of the deck had taken evasive action, but it was too late. The dim lights of the freighter that appeared out of the cloud slid underneath the end of Midway's angled deck, slamming into a spot in the ship's hull that housed the carrier's fuel farm and its liquid oxygen compartment, located side-by-side. As it did, the Panamanian-registered ship's superstructure, towering above its decks packed with wooden pilings and lumber, raked the edge of Midway's flight deck, completely destroying the tail sections of three F-4 Phantoms and damaging four additional Phantoms, one of which was ripped from the chains that held it to the deck and was pushed into a nearby A-7 Corsair.

Within seconds, the general quarters alarm's klaxon sound wailed throughout the carrier, followed by a man's voice. "General quarters! General quarters! This is not a drill! All hands man your battle stations!"

In Bunkroom Eight, the response to hearing the collision alarm was similar to that in the Eagles' administrative office,

130

only the twelve men glanced at each other with puzzled looks. "Is that for real?" asked Gully.

Five seconds later, the men felt the titanic concussion aft of where they sat, and realized that they were suddenly in the middle of the sea on a vessel that had just been struck by another ship or a missile. That they heard no massive explosion was the only peace of mind that took root. However, the "this is not a drill" announcement quickly superseded the unimaginable realization that the ship was actually in distress, and the twelve men left Bunkroom Eight for the Eagles' ready room. In a moment of intelligent clarity, Lunker unplugged the popcorn popper before he left the Midway Oasis.

At the point of impact, two men performing routine checks on their assigned equipment, one in the liquid oxygen (LOX) plant and one in the fuel farm, were killed instantly. Neither would know that the various pieces of equipment they so meticulously maintained were ripped from their foundations, resulting in leaking jet fuel and supercold liquid gasses, including both oxygen and nitrogen, being sprayed wildly about the two spaces.

The two men were the newest victims of a cold war between the United States and the Soviet Bloc, as American agents later determined that a significant component of the freighter's officers was composed entirely of Russian sailors and officers.

A minute later, in Ready Room Five, their battle station, the Eagles' officers were intently focused on Midway's black-and-white closed circuit television system, whose camera was positioned high on the carrier's island. It was broadcasting the orderly response along the carrier's angled deck and deck edge. They could hear the men yelling and shouting on the flight deck above them. That much of the activity on the screen was taking place almost directly above where they sat, with just a few feet of metal separating them, created a surreal moment as the sounds of the response seemingly fell right into their laps.

"One, two...three Phantoms are missing their tails," stated the XO, very matter-of-factly.

"Looks like a Phantom is resting against the aft part of an A-7," said 'Rock' Pyle.

"The Fresnel lens is gone," observed Gully. The 'meatball' that guided pilots on the glideslope to touchdown was just aft of the damaged A-7 and was indeed missing or severely damaged enough to be unrecognizable.

The aviators counted four additional Phantoms that appeared to have damage to their tails or wings. They also noticed a great deal of commotion around one of the severely damaged Phantom's front cockpit. As they would later learn, a pilot strapped into the cockpit, dutifully fulfilling his turn as the air wing's "alert five" fighter, was injured when his open canopy was dislodged and collapsed on one of his hands. Two petty officers working under the jet were also injured, although neither seriously.

Midway's captain, working in his at-sea cabin less than fifteen feet from the bridge, had reached the bridge within five seconds of hearing the collision alarm, arriving just in time to see the freighter disappear under the landing area's overhang. The Carrier Group Five commander, a rear admiral, joined Midway's captain on the ship's bridge within twenty seconds.

"What's the latest?" asked the admiral.

Midway's captain responded very matter-of-factly. "The LOX plant and the fuel lines are compromised and have major damage. Both are leaking heavily, and the damage control team is trying to get a barrier of light foam between them. The only good news so far is that a Phantom doing a low power turn on the flight deck right above the impact point was hit, but the pilot immediately shut both engines down."

The two men moved to the side of the bridge as the admiral's chief of staff joined them seconds later. "Well, that's one bullet we dodged. How many gallons of LOX are at risk?" asked the admiral.

"Five thousand," stated Midway's captain. "But the critical issue is that the ship's expansion joint is right at the impact point." The three men looked at each other in silence for several seconds; they each understood the implication.

"The ship could break in half..." said the captain.

The admiral finished the sentence. "We're in a black sea, filled with the deadliest sharks in the world, and the nearest response ships are probably five or six hours away. We could lose twice as many men right here than were lost in total at Pearl Harbor." He paused.

"It'll be the greatest tragedy in the Navy's history."

If Midway ever needed a real dose of magic, this was the moment. The fuel and liquid oxygen were clearly in undeniable danger of being mixed, and if so, would instantly trigger a massive conflagration with the slightest spark and do irreparable damage to the carrier's hull along the expansion joint. It would surely kill hundreds, if not all of the crew of almost five thousand, and send the ageless carrier to the bottom of the dark Pacific waters that had been her home for so long.

"My men won't let us down, admiral. Our damage control team is the best in the fleet. They win awards for a reason, and they're one of the reasons this ship has magic. These men will ensure we see the light of a new day. They'll get us through this."

The admiral nodded. The captain's confidence was believable as he shifted his immediate focus on the safety of his ship's men. "Let's get the entire crew on the hangar deck, except for those directly involved in the response, and have the life boat captains standing by. It's the only chance the men will have, Admiral, if the unthinkable happens."

Although abandoning ship could still become the best option remaining to ensure the survival of the crew, Midway's captain was accurate about his men. The carrier's response team had, just a few months earlier, earned a score during a damage control evaluation that was the highest in the Navy for the third year in a row.

"Midway, this is the captain. I want everyone not directly involved in the response to immediately gather on the hangar deck wearing your general quarters gear."

No one in Ready Room Five had yet said it, but all the Eagles' aviators were thankful that none of the Intruders appeared to have been affected. What was audibly shared among the Eagles' officers during their walk to the hangar bay was that the visit to Singapore was surely cancelled and the ship would be back in Subic Bay by the next afternoon.

A flood of men flowed quickly, but orderly, through Midway's passageways toward the hangar bay. There was no panic; the self-confident men were well-trained professionals. As they moved into the hangar bay, they could see a dark night consumed by a low fog as the ship continued to slice steadily through the water. She was moving at a speed fast enough to maintain steerageway and keep the prevailing wind in a direction that would not endanger the responders in their precarious positions.

On Midway's flight deck, the response team was immediately in action. Seven damage control petty officers had quickly, and ingeniously, turned fuel hoses mounted at the side of the ship into harnesses, enabling two experienced men to hang precipitously over the side of the ship. In the black of the night, and above turbulent and foreboding waters churning below, the two brave men sprayed water continuously from fire hoses into the fuel farm to dilute the spraying fuel.

At the same time, another team of young damage control petty officers courageously entered the severely damaged liquid oxygen compartment and sprayed liquid foam into the space in a valiant effort to confine the supercold gasses to their current location.

If the efforts of the two groups failed, they would likely never know it. They, like most, if not all of their shipmates, would perish in an explosion that would, for a split second, feel like the heat of ten thousand suns as it sent the carrier and its crew to a black and watery grave.

Less than three minutes after impact, the first urgent messages arrived at the Pentagon, where it was just after eight-thirty in the morning. Less than a minute later, the White House was notified that one of its aircraft carriers was in distress in a remote part of the world and at legitimate risk of sinking with all hands in a dark and very inhospitable sea.

The carrier was in grave danger, and the angst and trepidation among the almost forty-eight hundred men on the hangar bay was palpable. They stood helpless, well aware that the fate of Midway was in the hands of a small group of courageous sailors wrestling with the ship's destiny. It was impossible not to hear the clamorous commotion — the sound of unbounded bravery — resonating from the port side of the flight deck, less than thirty feet above their heads.

Unseen were men who would have no chance of escape as they remained at their posts. They were in the engineering spaces deep in the bowels of Midway, a core team of silently heroic and supremely dedicated men who ensured the carrier would continue functioning with whatever mechanical, electrical, or propulsion power was required during the crisis. If the unimaginable happened, they would never see the low fog on the dark water before they perished.

The low buzz of tense conversations echoed throughout the somber cavernous area, filled with highly trained men. Many discussed what it would be like to abandon ship, to jump from one of the hangar bay elevators into a black abyss. For each man who verbalized it, dozens more were thinking the unthinkable.

Many of those gathered walked to the giant elevators at the side of the ship. The large platforms, designed to move airplanes up to and down from the flight deck, reached out into the darkness. It was unfathomable to consider, but if the order to abandon ship was given, the elevators would be the last contact the men would ever have with their legendary ship before they jumped into an unforgiving sea.

Low hovering clouds were still present; not even the stars above would see them in the water. Only the sea creatures below would know they were there if the sea became their new home.

At the very same time in Singapore, wives and girlfriends were enjoying a warm and delightful evening strolling along Orchard Road; most had plans to finish the evening by lounging with glasses of wine by the Grand Hyatt's pool. Earlier, several had eaten dinner at Newton's Car Park, a parking lot that was emptied of cars by six o'clock, and then repopulated by a wide range of food vendors.

Barely an hour after the impact, the captain of the ship spoke to the crew over the ship's intercom.

"Midway, this is the captain." The strain in his voice was evident. "The response to the collision was successful, and the ship is stable and able to steam safely on her own. It is my sad duty to report that we lost two of our shipmates at the point of impact. I'd like to take a moment of silence to honor their sacrifice."

The men gathered on the hangar bay stood in respectful silence. Some had their heads bowed, but most continued to stare into the black abyss. After a brief period, the carrier's commanding officer continued.

"We have reversed our course and will arrive back in Subic Bay tomorrow morning to immediately assess and begin whatever repairs are required. We offered assistance to the ship that collided with us, but our offer was turned away. That ship is now proceeding on its own power to an unknown port. Once we arrive in Subic, I will address you on the flight deck with an update to our plans and schedule."

There was a short pause as he harnessed his composure. He loved all these men and always would. They were the beating heart and incandescent soul of Midway's magic.

"You are all to be commended. In a moment of extreme danger, there was no panic. You remained calm and responded as the professionals you are. I am grateful to each of you." He paused. "I wish every American could know you. They would sleep better knowing that you are on the tip of the sword." He paused again. "That is all."

On Midway, the crew could sense and, if they wandered out on a weather deck to check for themselves, visually see that their beloved carrier still had magic in her as she steamed toward Subic Bay at a speed of twenty knots. It was a remarkable ship, they thought. No one wanted to believe that the tragedy that was so close at hand would have actually occurred. That the ship escaped an explosion of cataclysmic proportions was proof of Midway magic, many said.

Unfortunately for the families of the two dedicated petty officers who perished, the magic ended far too soon.

July 1980....USS Midway's commanding officer addressing Midway's officers and crew on the morning after the collision with Cactus

USS Midway enroute to Naval Station Subic Bay, Philippines following collision with Cactus...July 1980

VA-115 A-6E Intruder launching from USS Midway (CV-41) in the western Pacific, circa 1980-81

VA-115 aircrews with the 'Scotch General,' his aviators, and five Korean women who presented flowers to each VA-115 crew; early Spring, 1982. (Author bottom row; far right next to women presenting flowers)

VA-115 KA-6D tanker being prepared for launch 1981

VA-115 A-6E Intruders bombing in the South China Sea 1981

The Intruder Mission: Attack

Somewhere Over A South Pacific Horizon

Naval Air Station Cubi Point, Philippines circa 1980

Shit River Bridge; Olongapo, Philippines circa 1980

Bunkroom 8.......Far East Film Society

Bunkroom 8.......The Midway Oasis

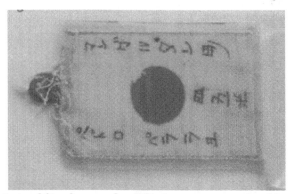

Actual 'tag' worn by Filipinos, as required by
the Japanese Army during World War II

CHAPTER EIGHT

One Place; Two Worlds
Mid-to-Late Summer, 1980

The morning after the collision, not knowing how many days would actually be required to make the necessary repairs to the ship, a decision was made to launch four jets each from the Intruder, Corsair, and Phantom squadrons to Cubi Point. The relocation would ensure that the air wing's pilots could remain in compliance with day and night landing requirements. Also launched were two EA-6B Prowlers, one Marine RF-4 Phantom and one E-2 Hawkeye.

Fortunately, all the jets had been refueled between the end of flight operations and the collision. Like clockwork, just after eight in the morning, the launches were seamlessly accomplished in a short period of time, and all planes were safely on deck in the Philippines less than an hour later.

In Singapore, Midway's shore detachment was notified just before midnight that the ship's visit was cancelled. Already, a plethora of food, trinket and souvenir vendors, taxis drivers, panhandlers, and many more were jockeying for prime positions near the ferry landing where sailors were scheduled to arrive. The detachment's senior officer quietly notified Singapore's disappointed liaison official of the change in plans without giving any details except that "Midway has an operational reason to return to the Philippines operating area." Local citizens, who were actually Soviet agents, were planted among those eager to take money from arriving sailors. They would be plying for sensitive information that the loose lips of a sailor, especially a drunken sailor, would reveal. They, too, were disappointed.

Midway's officer-in-charge of the Singapore shore detachment left messages for each of the wives and girlfriends who were in Singapore, having received their lodging information the day before he left the ship. What they did next was up to them. As it turned out, a significant majority chose to remain in Singapore to enjoy the sights and sounds there, and then return to Japan as planned.

The remainder chose to fly to the Philippines. Among the latter group were Tosh, Lauren, Sharon, Mirela, and Connie. Although Singapore was exciting, their new loves were far more enticing. The liaison officer would coordinate delivering messages to the affected officers on the ship regarding the individual decisions of the ones they held dear.

For security reasons, predominantly because of two attacks in the past year on vans carrying sailors or their dependents enroute from Manila's airport to Subic Bay, Navy officials made an unusual, but prudent, decision to ensure safe travel for those leaving Singapore. They would utilize a military version of a DC-9 passenger jet that was already in Singapore to fly the group of women, who had chosen to leave, directly to Cubi Point, a three hour flight away. Waivers were quickly obtained to also transport non-spouses. Because they weren't official Navy dependents, these were the girlfriends who would otherwise have to use civilian airlines and buses.

A few minutes before eleven in the morning, Midway steamed past Hoover Mountain and entered her berth at Subic Bay. From her starboard side she looked no different from her just completed visit. Even from her port side, except for the damaged Phantoms, a very quick glance wouldn't yield a mental snapshot that suggested anything was seriously amiss, and certainly would not give any indication of the massive calamity that was narrowly avoided barely thirteen hours earlier in the black of night. A team of ship inspectors based at Subic Bay had been flown by helicopter to the carrier's flight deck three hours earlier, landing just after sunrise. In addition, a team of Navy ship inspectors from Pearl Harbor was less than thirty minutes from landing at Cubi Point's runway, just a ten-minute drive to the dock that Midway would occupy. A similar team from San Diego was scheduled to arrive later in the day.

Onboard Midway, the ship's executive officer announced that liberty call would begin at 1300, or one p.m., for those not in the day's duty section. During the inport period, the carrier would maintain a four duty section rotation, much to the delight of all those who were eager to cross the shit river bridge once again, and seek pleasure, libations, entertainment, or whatever forms of self-indulgence were on their minds. He also announced that Midway's commanding officer would make remarks to the crew at noon on the carrier's flight deck. The assumption, among the officers and enlisted men assigned to the ship and air wing, was that he'd be relieved of his duties, as was customary after any significant mishap, and that these would be his farewell remarks to the officers and crew.

At noon, precisely on time, and a little over eight hundred miles north of the equator with a blazing sun overhead, Midway's popular and well respected captain stepped out onto the catwalk on the port side of the ship's bridge, about twenty-five feet above the flight deck. The stress in his face was visibly apparent as he held a small notepad in his left hand. Except for a

Navy photographer standing fifteen feet to his left, he was alone, visibly bearing the burden of command.

Wearing a short sleeve, summer khaki uniform and one of Midway's navy blue ball caps with 'scrambled eggs' on the bill, he looked across a human sea of incredibly talented men standing on the flight deck, over four thousand strong, as they looked back at him. A significant number were under the age of nineteen; the majority were under the age of twenty-six. If mutual respect was rain, they'd be standing in the middle of a tropical typhoon.

"Good afternoon, Midway," he began. "Before I make my remarks, which will be short, I'd like for everyone to take a moment of silence out of respect for our two shipmates who were killed last evening." He paused for ten or fifteen seconds, and the silence across the flight deck was emotionally palpable. "I'd also ask you to say a prayer for the families of our deceased shipmates and a quick recovery for those who were injured." The captain paused again, and then continued in an upbeat voice.

"Among you, here in the waters of our home away from home, are men who saved this great ship last night and to whom a great debt is owed. To each of you, last night was a night to remember and not just for the collision. You can be proud that in that moment of crisis and calamity, each of you responded as you were trained. You didn't panic; you were brave, and responded as the professionals you are. You did as I asked, and for that I will always admire and love each of you. Because of you, Midway magic is alive and well."

"I just received the first assessment of the damage to the ship and what repairs will be required. The initial estimate is that we will be underway again in five or six days, seven at most. After that, the ship will operate for seven to ten days in the local area with a full schedule of day and night flight operations, as well as two underway replenishments, and then proceed into the eastern Indian Ocean as previously planned."

"Most likely, this is my last time addressing you." He paused, surveying the men who had served him, the ship, and their country so well. He wished he knew each of them personally; they were such talented and dedicated men. "In a few minutes, I will shoulder the burden of command that is mine and only mine," he said, pausing again for a moment before continuing, "and I will likely be required to relinquish what has been the greatest honor of my life, which is the opportunity to serve alongside each of you as the commanding officer of this remarkable ship named Midway."

"Last night, you stood together on the hangar bay on a very dark night. This morning, you continue to stand faithfully and dutifully together by foreign shores in the warmth of this beautiful and sunny day. Regardless of my fate, I know you will continue to stand together in the future. You and you alone are the essence of Midway magic. It preceded me; it will survive me." He paused for a few quiet moments. 'I wish each of you the very best in your career and in your life." The captain paused again. "Please accept my deepest gratitude for your loyal and dedicated service during my time in command. All I will ask, in closing, is that you give Midway's next captain the same devotion to duty you gave me."

He was silent for a final reflective moment. "I will never forget you." He looked across the flight deck at the brave and remarkable men in front of him, and then across Subic Bay to the opening that led to the Pacific Ocean. He'd miss taking the ship and these men, the Navy's foreign legion, back through that watery passage to where they performed their magic so admirably and professionally, so far from home, night and day, over and over.

"That is all." The photographer snapped one final shot as Midway's captain turned and walked back into Midway's bridge.

Twenty minutes before the Navy C-9 Skytrain, a military version of the DC-9 civilian aircraft, was scheduled to land, the first of nineteen men who were eagerly awaiting wives or girlfriends stood in the shade of Cubi Point's air terminal building and gazed across Subic Bay, to where the injured carrier was being swarmed by inspectors, technicians, and repair personnel. Not seen was the intense grilling that Midway's commanding officer was undergoing in the admiral's conference room onboard the carrier as the formal investigation into the accident was entering its second hour.

The essence of command in the Navy, most especially command at sea, has always been defined by the highest sense of personal integrity and an ultimate accountability that rests solely on the person at the top. Since the days of John Paul Jones, being in command in the Navy has carried with it both a great burden and a special privilege to those selected. Every outcome, good and bad, belongs to the commanding officer. Delegating responsibility is not an option.

Right on time, the C-9 from Singapore landed in the early afternoon. During their airplane's rollout on Cubi Point's runway and subsequent path as it taxied to its parking spot, each passenger could see Midway across the bay, surrounded by numerous boats and barges at its berth at Naval Base Subic Bay.

As they disembarked from their airplane and began walking toward the terminal building a few hundred feet away, each of them glanced at a barge, about a quarter mile offshore and slightly behind their left shoulders, making its way slowly across the bay toward an aircraft repair facility on the Cubi side. On the barge was one of the damaged Phantoms whose tail had been ripped apart, with most of its pieces now settled in the deep waters of the South China Sea. The viciousness of the collision was very apparent and immediately imparted a realistic and sobering impact on the women, bringing the danger of their loved ones' occupation closer to reality than they ever wanted to see.

For Connie, the Eagles skipper's new love, such events had been part of her life for over seventeen years. Her former husband had been in three Intruder squadrons that collectively lost seven Intruders, three during the Vietnam War and four during peacetime. Of the fourteen aviators involved, five were killed, two became prisoners of war, one sustained permanent injuries that ended his flying career, and, of the six remaining, only half sustained no substantial injuries. She knew the reality of naval aviation and accepted the good, the bad, and the tragic that accompanied it, which is why she prayed daily that she would never be the one answering a knock at the door from a man in uniform.

For Tosh, Lauren, and Sharon, the sight of the Phantom on the barge against a backdrop of Midway, tied up to its dock across the bay, had a sobering effect. They had each seen Midway before, but never with its full complement of combat aircraft, altering what had previously been a sterile, almost tranquil, exhibit of America's military strength. They were all acutely aware of the dangers of naval aviation; however, seeing the risk stare defiantly back at them, seemingly taunting them as a crane lifted another damaged Phantom from the carrier's flight deck packed with aircraft, was a pungent dose of a brutal reality. It was especially terrifying that, less than eighteen hours earlier, the ship and a dark sea could have been the final resting place for thousands of men, including the men they loved.

For Mirela, taking great risks was a very natural part of her path to being a free citizen. She knew from personal experience that blood, sweat, and tears were three of the elements required to break the chains that bound enslaved people everywhere.

Under an intense south Pacific sun that made the already humid air feel like they were wearing damp wool overcoats, nineteen men and nineteen women walked quickly across the concrete tarmac with a laser-like focus toward those they adored, although with different mindsets. To the men, casually attired in jeans or slacks, it was a planned reunion in an unplanned spot on the planet, a memorable moment to be savored due to a tragic twist of fate on the high seas. To the women, it was a brutal reminder that tragic twists of fate occur on the high seas, most predominantly to men who strap themselves into ejection seats of high-performance aircraft and operate in the most demanding and dangerous flying environment ever conceived.

At the moment of first touch, though, such thoughts were pushed aside, creating an unobstructed path for rapturous waves of blended emotions that reflected joy and relief. Very little was spoken that referenced the actual collision; those words would come later. All the tears and words and hugs and kisses that flowed now quickly morphed into the anticipation of being reacquainted in a tropical paradise.

As the large group began to walk toward Cubi's small passenger terminal, one of the wives made a timely suggestion. "Let's get a group photo so we can forever remind our husbands of the day we chose to leave what would be a ladies-only week of unencumbered shopping, dining and relaxing in a five star hotel in a cosmopolitan city to fly to the Philippines for a BOQ room on a Navy base just to prove we really do put them first."

Everyone laughed as several women handed their cameras to the air operations petty officer escorting them. With the carrier Midway in the background across the bay, nineteen couples smiled under a tropical sky for photographic evidence of a remarkable story to explain how the moment all came to pass.

After the photos were completed, the Eagles' skipper and Connie, along with the other four VA-115 couples, each of them holding hands, walked across the tarmac and stood just inside one of Cubi's large hangars to escape the sun's relentless rays and the humidity piling on like wet blankets.

"Connie and I have been invited to use Admiral Seipel's guest quarters while we're in port," said the skipper. "He and I were in two squadrons together. I asked him if I could get VIP rooms at the Cubi BOQ for you four, and he agreed."

He looked at his junior officers and smiled. These were the actions he could take on their behalf that would pay dividends, he hoped, when their initial obligations to the Navy ended and they had to decide whether to stay in or leave the sea service.

"They're under your individual names and should be ready now. If you have any issues, call the admiral's secretary, and she'll straighten it out. Anything you need, just ask. I'm calling in a few blue chips, so take advantage of it." He paused as they all smiled and thanked him.

The skipper knew his officers would likely ask him, when they were on the ship again, what he had done to earn the favors. He looked forward to sharing it; it was part of educating his officers. He had also called in favors with the admiral on behalf of several of the squadron's enlisted men. Taking care of them was always included in the education of his officers. To the skipper, taking care of the troops was, in fact, far more important than flying the jets. The reliability and performance of one depended entirely on the care and feeding of the other; it made setting his priorities easy.

The skipper continued, "Connie and I are heading to Baguio for a couple days. It's nice and cool up there, like the weather at Whidbey right now." He paused. "And very private," he said, smiling. "The XO knows how to reach me if he needs me for what better be a very dire emergency." He smiled.

"Have fun, skipper," said Lunker, "and you can go ahead and pay me now for the money I'd take off you on the golf course since you're weaseling out with this Baguio excuse." The entire group laughed and looked forward to their own private moments, which couldn't begin soon enough.

"I hope you all have a wonderful time," said the skipper. "And Lunker, I'm glad you're still a dreamer." He smiled and shook hands with each of them before Connie and he walked to where a sedan was waiting.

Baguio was a city nestled at an elevation of just over five thousand feet above sea level in the mountains of northern Luzon, one hundred eight miles north of Olongapo and Subic Bay. In the early eighties, roughly half of its population comprised students at one of eight local colleges and universities. Baguio's cool climate and summertime temperatures that generally peaked in the seventies resembled, in many ways except for the jungle flora, a town in Washington State's Olympic peninsula.

Baguio occupied a unique place in the history of the Philippines. It was the first place in the island nation to be bombed by the Japanese in World War Two, just hours after the attack on Pearl Harbor.

The Eagles' skipper and his date had lodging reservations at Camp John Hay, a military reservation in Baguio used for rest and recreation, 'R & R,' for American armed forces personnel and their families since its establishment just after the turn of the twentieth century. Commander Singer knew that Connie, as a long time resident of northwest Washington State, would struggle with the heat and humidity of Subic Bay, so he decided the Whidbey Island-like temperatures in Baguio would be a perfect start to launch their long awaited romance. Both were avid golfers, so the legendary course at the base was also a perfect place to enjoy a long, scenic stroll and intimate discussions, unencumbered by stifling temperatures and an ever present aircraft carrier reminding them of the perils always just one tragic moment away.

As their skipper and Connie drove away, the remaining four couples took taxis to the BOQ, where they spent thirty minutes unpacking, settling in, and reacquainting. Before leaving their rooms, they left all their valuables in the safes provided, including watches, bracelets, rings, and necklaces. The men carried only their military identification cards and more than enough pesos for lunch and cold beverages and anything their dates may want to buy.

The four couples stood together in front of the Cubi BOQ, each with a cold San Miguel beer, waiting for the two taxis that would drive them to lunch at the Chuckwagon grill on the Subic side. As they did, the sight from the building's hilltop location, a few hundred feet above all that was in front of them, was paralyzing to the four women; even Mirela, who herself had stood in this very spot, frozen in place by the view, less than two weeks earlier.

The spectacular postcard-like panorama, tinted by myriad shades of green, included a large deep-blue bay fronting a backdrop of lush foliage, untamed jungles, and tall mountains rising from the sea, beginning from their far left and sweeping to their right toward a distant horizon. On this day, the view was anchored by a World War Two vintage aircraft carrier, and the sights, sounds, and smells from Navy jets below them.

In front of them, slightly below the horizon from their vantage point, was a trinity of diverse destinations — Cubi Point, Subic Bay, and Olongapo. The three were nestled reverently together around the beautiful blue waters of the bay.

Visible, but really unseen, was Magsaysay Drive — Olongapo's main street, and the singular street that mattered — reachable only by crossing a relatively small canal of inhospitable, evil-smelling water called the shit river. For now, it was better that the ladies couldn't see Olongapo in all its bawdy detail. They'd cross that bridge soon enough.

Behind the group of eight, unseen because of the white concrete building at their backs, was a tangled labyrinth of thick jungle, intermingled with lush green hills rising and falling like tropical waves from the nearby South China Sea. Further beyond, hidden under canopies of green less than twenty miles away, was the path known to the world as the Bataan Death March.

It was a sixty-mile long blemish of unspeakable atrocities by the Japanese that began just four months after their unprovoked attack on Pearl Harbor. The repugnant scar was a permanent reminder to the world of a malignant cancer purposely inflicted and spread by evil men against several peace-loving nations. Although it blended invisibly into the jungle, it would never conceal the horror or savagery, woven like coarse thread through the thick foliage, of what once occurred.

That they were a long way from the cosmopolitan aura of Singapore, from which they had departed just hours earlier, was clearly obvious to the women. Adding to it was the manner of how their four paths originally came to merge on this day — two because a typhoon couldn't make up its mind where it wanted to go, one from a chance encounter by Mount Fuji best viewed from a former kamikaze airstrip, and one via a communist concentration camp – which, together, created a moment that was uniquely surreal.

The final piece of the equation — that they were standing together on this particular hillside, halfway around the planet from their homes, because of a collision at sea in shark-infested waters — made the gathering absurdly implausible. It would have been difficult for each of the four couples to reconcile it if the indescribable view in front of them hadn't temporarily silenced all thoughts except what their eyes were absorbing.

"If someone could accurately capture this on canvas, I'd hope your art museum would sell prints," said Lauren to Tosh.

"I'm not sure anyone could ever do it justice," Tosh replied.

"Even the smell — a blend of pungent and sweet smells — helps to frame the view."

"Wait until we get to the Subic side. You're going to smell an aroma called what-in-the-hell-is-this."

"Oh my Lord, we surely don't want to miss out on that." The group laughed in agreement.

"Speaking of the Lord, wait until you see the artist just across the bridge who paints Jesus on large velvet wall hangings. That has to be one of the seven wonders, too."

"Yes and amen. Last visit he had painted a Caucasian Jesus with his arm around a Filipino Jesus with dreadlocks, standing next to a water buffalo. That was kinda weird, but cool."

"You know you're in really deep shit if you arrive in heaven and there are two Jesus's and a water buffalo waiting to talk to you, especially if one has dreadlocks."

"Worse if all three have dreadlocks." The laughter from the group continued unabated; they were on a cathartic roll.

"Do you think that's part of a lost parable that one of the disciples left in a South Pacific jungle one night after too many San Miguels?"

"It'd probably have something to do with the parable of nine dumb ass Eagles streaking the Cubi O'Club's main dining room after a few too many San Miguels, Lunker."

"Hey, that was the skipper's idea. I was just there to make sure his steering was good and he'd stay on course."

"Running by the admiral's table was on course? That was your brilliant navigational plan?"

"I was hoping someone knew how to do the Heimlich thing, 'cause it sounded like his wife was choking on her dinner." The laughter from all eight was the best therapy that pesos could buy.

"That was a helluva rug dance the skipper had to do the next day. Maybe he and the admiral did the twist or the shag or something." The laughter was growing.

"I think the skipper was probably twisting in great discomfort. I can still hear that admiral yelling as we ran by." Lunker's emphatic and perfectly timed input kept everyone laughing as two taxis, each a small white sedan with no markings, arrived in front of them.

Willie, Tosh, Gully, and Sharon took the first taxi; Lunker, Mirela, Doc, and Lauren took the second one. Gully and Lunker, each being the tallest in their group of four, took the front seat. Willie and Doc sat between the two women in the rear seat of their respective taxis.

As the taxis made their way down the long hillside from the Cubi BOQ to the road that wrapped around the tropical horseshoe-shaped bay between the Cubi and Subic sides of the base, there was little talking in either vehicle? There was too much to see and absorb as their eyes scanned near and far and left and right. The men were right; the ten-minute taxi ride was a journey all its own. The drive to the Chuckwagon could be longer, and that'd be just fine.

All four men had seen the views countless times, and yet it still captured their eyes and emotions. On this particular trip, their eyes were drawn to Midway, sitting in her berth across the turquoise bay, surrounded by various boats, while two shore-based cranes were moving aircraft and other objects damaged in the collision off the ship. What the aviators really wanted to know had nothing to do with the material condition of their esteemed carrier — the fate of Midway's captain was their greatest concern. It was probable he had already been fired and that his replacement had been selected from the pool of officers who had previously screened for command of an aircraft carrier. It was also likely that the newly selected commanding officer would be flying west across the Pacific before the end of the day. It would be Midway's loss; her captain was one of the best ever.

As for the women, their eyes focused on the view nearest them and then swept to the vista beyond. Closest to them were the hangars, tarmac, and runway of Naval Air Station Cubi Point, upon which sat twenty-three CAG-Five aircraft, including two Intruders, two Corsairs, a Prowler, and four Phantoms that were being prepared for flight. The pending flight operations weren't lost on any of the women's ears as the high-pitched sound of the one of the jets' engines reached out like a shrill voice.

That this change of location for a scheduled port call was a result of a catastrophic event on a dark night wasn't lost on the women, either. Fortunately, that thought was immediately superseded by the spectacular view across the tops of the hangars and the blue-green waters of Subic Bay toward the sprawling naval base — and the view of Midway amid a number of workboats and barges.

157

For the men and women, but especially the aviators, there was something very special about seeing Midway nestled in her berth at Subic. She was a 40's era carrier with 50's and 60's era aircraft and mostly 70's era aviators.

Her keel was laid in 1943. She was designed and built with a straight deck. From a distance, her profile looked more like a World War Two carrier than a modern carrier, even though she had an angled flight deck that was added in 1955.

Midway was the first aircraft carrier to be named after a World War Two battle. Fittingly, the battle of Midway was a noteworthy engagement between Japanese and American carriers in 1942 that proved, once and for all, the critical role that naval aviation would play in the future. In the 60's, Midway's pilots scored the first two air-to-air MIG kills by American forces in Southeast Asia and, almost eight years later, her air wing bagged the final air-to-air kill of the Vietnam War.

Now, like a cherished old hunting dog, Midway remained reliable even as she aged, generating warm emotions as she floated peacefully in the same warm waters she had first encountered over twenty-six years earlier.

The men were very defensive and protective about their ship as she lay resting. The old dog, though nursing an injury, still had a lot of good hunting left in her.

Although Midway's performance and impact was well known within military circles, the press and the public often ignored her, if they even knew that she was still operational. The New York Times once published an article about the nuclear powered aircraft carriers Nimitz and Eisenhower being deployed in the Indian Ocean during the Iranian Hostage Crisis in 1979 and 1980. It reported on their 100-plus days continuously at sea and the emotional and mental toll it took on the sailors, aviators, and their families.

At the end of the article, almost as a comical afterthought, the Times reported that there was 'another carrier' out there. They were referring to Midway, which, from 1979 through 1981, spent more days deployed in the Indian Ocean than any other aircraft carrier.

In many ways, Midway being ignored was par for the course. Few Americans knew or gave any thought to the ships and their crews that rotated in and out of their American ports to foreign seas and lands. Even fewer knew that Midway didn't return to an American port, but stayed vigilant far from her home of birth, either underway or ready to get underway. Midway, the Navy's oldest and smallest carrier, remained America's most operational carrier, and the one that would likely strike the first blow when bad people did bad things to good people.

She was the Navy's foreign legion. Few Americans were aware of her, but America's enemies knew all too well who she was.

The four couples in two taxis remained mesmerized by the views as their journey around the bay continued. Their eyes made a transition from Midway to the legendary city named Olongapo, a crowded collection of one, two, and three story buildings that looked benign from a distance, although that opinion would change with their first footsteps on the equally legendary shit river bridge.

Five minutes later, the group arrived at their destination. Naval aviators were naturally competitive in most areas of their lives, so even now, the men in each vehicle used 'rock, paper, scissors' to determine who would pay the taxi's fare and tip. As they departed the vehicles, the appetizing smell of grilled steaks temporarily supplanted the anticipated smell of the nearby drainage canal.

The Chuckwagon was a perfect metaphor for the allure and magic that made Subic Bay and Olongapo a sailor's most desired port of call. It was simple and nothing fancy, just a melting pot of liberty port essentials available and thriving in paradise.

"So this is the world famous Chuckwagon? Two Quonset huts side by side? That's it?"

"But they're connected by a space packed with slot machines." Doc's voice was emphatic. "And they have good food, good music, and the coldest beer in WestPac."

"Yes, I can read the sign, and the aroma is certainly appealing, but there's more to a world famous place than good food and cold beer and slot machines."

"I'm with you, although I can't say I've seen a place like it anywhere in southern California, coldest beer or not, so maybe that's what makes it world famous." Tosh paused. "Or maybe it's simply because it's in Subic."

Willie smiled at her observation. "Good point, my dear, and before the night is over, you'll see many things that you'll never see in southern California or Japan or Singapore or anywhere else."

"You mean like two Jesus's and a water buffalo painted on velvet?" They all laughed. Not to be forgotten among the required pilgrimage sights was the shit river, but they still wouldn't cross that bridge until they came to it.

Four couples held hands as they entered the world famous establishment's dining side. Inside was an orderly array of picnic tables of different sizes, including some that would easily fit the four couples.

"What's on the other side?"

"Lots of alcohol.

"I don't get it."

"This side is the dining room and the other side is the drinking room. It's a good alternative for sailors who don't need Magsaysay Drive to have a good time."

"Ah, so that's where you find the smart sailors, huh?" They laughed. The women fit right in; it was going to be a very good day.

Over lunch, Sharon, who majored in Asian history at Trinity College in Connecticut, intrigued the group as she connected where they sat to American history. "We're enjoying grilled fish sandwiches and San Miguels looking over the same waters where the Spanish Empire ended and the American Empire began."

"Seriously?" asked Gully. "Really?" He smiled as he stared at his date.

"Yes, indeed."

"Hold on a minute, one of the famous sayings we had to memorize during plebe summer at the academy was Commodore Dewey's famous command, 'You may fire when ready, Gridley,' and that was in Manila Bay, not Subic Bay," said Doc.

"That's true," said Sharon. "Dewey effectively destroyed the Spanish fleet there in Manila Bay, but a few ships escaped here, to Subic Bay, where a Spanish garrison was located. Dewey brought his ships around the corner from Manila, engaged the ships that fled Manila right here in this bay, and put them all on the bottom. With that, the garrison surrendered, the Spanish Empire ended, and the American Empire began. One, two, three, done."

Lunker couldn't resist. "It's the bottom of the ninth, sports fans, two outs, there's the windup, and it's a five hundred mile per hour fastball. That's strike three! Game's over! The Yanks win control of the seas in a devastating shutout!"

Everyone laughed, and Tosh offered a toast with her San Miguel. "Here's to the Yanks and Subic Bay!"

"And Olongapo and Jesus on velvet!" added Doc. The eight friends tapped their bottles, clinking in stereo.

From the picnic table where they sat, Sharon continued to impress them with other historical tidbits, including their proximity to World War Two's Bataan death march, which passed just miles to the east of Subic Bay. What she kept to herself was that Subic Bay was the last place of peace her only uncle saw. He was a fighter pilot who was shot down and killed over Vietnam in the spring of 1966, less than one month from completing a ten month combat cruise on the aircraft carrier

161

Hancock and returning home. He left behind a three year old son and a daughter barely eighteen months old.

"The Philippines' military has always been one of our closest allies. They were in Korea within three months of that war's beginning, and they supported us in Vietnam." She took a sip of her San Miguel and then continued. "And their bravery in battle has never ever been questioned...Never."

As they were wrapping up a delightfully late lunch, and exchanging a wide range of personal and professional topics, Lunker paid Sharon a genuine compliment. "I meant to tell you earlier, Sharon, that your profs at Trinity College should be mighty proud of you. You obviously paid attention in class."

"Why, thank you, Lunker. I certainly enjoy history, but I have to confess that winters in Connecticut made it easy to stay in and study," Sharon replied truthfully, smiling.

"You know, we have a trinity college in the north Georgia mountains," said Lunker. He sounded serious.

"I didn't know that," Sharon admitted.

"Yep, and that trinity college is all about hunting, fishing, and drinking."

Everyone laughed, and several tapped their bottles and nodded their heads in silent toasts to a vintage Lunker comment.

Surprisingly, Gully jumped into the dialogue. "That reminds me of the naval aviation trinity."

"And what would that be, my dear?" asked Sharon, as surprised as the rest of the group at Gully's unexpected prompt.

Without delay, he answered. "Flying, drinking, and sleeping." As Gully finished, the other three Eagles turned toward him with big smiles and 'high fives' as the four women stared at the youngest of the aviators. The naïve Midwesterner was rapidly growing into a bonafide Eagle.

"Yes and amen, brother Gully, you just nailed it!" exclaimed Doc, proudly beaming at the newest member of Bunkroom Eight.

"Nailed it!" confirmed Willie, also beaming like a proud papa.

Tosh smiled and looked at her date. "Gee, Willie. I'm surprised sex isn't one of the three elements in the trinity of naval aviation."

Before he could respond, Lunker answered for him. "There's no need to articulate it, Tosh. Everyone knows that sex is just a natural byproduct of being a Navy flyboy." The other three aviators smiled broadly as they nodded in agreement.

Mirela's instant retort was perfect. "Well, stud, we'll see how that works out for each of you tonight."

"Yes and amen," Tosh added. The four ladies mimicked the flyboys and high five'd each other.

Everyone laughed as the good friends stood and made their way toward the exit. A smile adorned every face. If the close call with disaster less than twenty-four hours earlier — the same disaster that brought them together in a paradox called paradise — was on anyone's mind, it was hidden somewhere far from where Midway currently rested.

Stepping from the air-conditioned coolness of the Chuckwagon's dining area into the sunlight of a Subic Bay afternoon, they were instantly enveloped by heat and draped by humidity that was made more oppressive by the contrast to the air conditioning they left behind. They would learn that humidity would always win; to fight it was futile.

One "Oh, my Lord" and three "Oh, my God" exclamations were the first words uttered as the four ladies made the transition from the Chuckwagon's grilled beef aroma to the unfiltered stench of the wide drainage canal nearby. The men each laughed; once upon a time, they had been in their shoes.

Just as they began their short stroll toward the entrance to the infamous city of Olongapo, the crackling roar of jet engines from across the bay drew their ears' attention, while the indescribable shit river smell began to penetrate every other sense and sensibility. The men slowed their walk considerably as they watched two Intruders lift off, ten seconds apart, from Cubi Point's westerly runway, and begin an immediate right hand turn to the north. The second jet that lifted off became part of an airborne game of catch-me-if-you-can. Its pilot was flying on the inside of the lead aircraft's turn and rapidly closing the distance between them, as if the second aircraft was being pulled in by a strong wire connected to the lead aircraft's right wing.

The two aircraft successfully rendezvoused before completing one hundred eighty degrees of turn and were now flying toward the north side of the bay, aiming directly for the Chuckwagon. They'd continue flying north at six miles per minute, zigzagging across the jungle landscape and villages at two hundred feet above the ground for over an hour and a half before returning to Cubi.

The two jets roared overhead, flying just feet apart, and barely five hundred feet above where the couples stood. Their low but safe altitude was intentional, as was their route over the Chuckwagon and the sailors and aviators streaming into Olongapo. It was a thunderously loud and impressive display of airmanship — an airborne 'I can name that tune in four notes' statement that upped the ante for any pilot watching from below when it was his turn to fly.

"Looking good for the home team," said Lunker, as he and the other seven stared at the two Intruders passing overhead. The jets were low enough that it was easy for bystanders below to believe that they could feel skin-tingling vibrations reaching down from the crackling sound.

"Don't you guys see enough airplanes?' asked Sharon.

"We watch jets no matter who's flying. It's what our brains naturally do," said Willie, "even mentally critiquing them. Besides, we wish we were up there instead of them."

"But not today," Doc added quickly.

"That's what I meant to say," said Willie, correcting himself as he leaned in and kissed Tosh on the cheek.

The group of eight — four couples holding hands on a humid, sun-drenched afternoon — hadn't ventured much further from the Chuckwagon when a question the men anticipated hearing was asked.

"Is my nose smelling the smell of paradise?" Lauren's face had a slight cringe.

"The one and only indescribable smell of paradise," replied Lunker, laughing.

"I think my eyes are starting to water," said Sharon.

"Oh, my goodness, I think I can taste it," added Tosh.

"You'll get used to it," said Doc. "It an acquired taste."

They all laughed and continued to talk among themselves as they slowly walked the relatively short distance toward the main gate of the naval base. As they did, they observed a steady stream of sailors, mostly young, making their way toward a bridge that spanned two worlds — a bridge that was the ticket required to turn a few hours or a few days into lifelong stories and memories.

Lunker and Mirela were holding hands, walking in front of the other three couples, when they stopped unexpectedly. Lunker turned to his right, back toward the others. "As you look at this migration of men, you are looking at a true cross section of America." The other three couples stopped as he spoke.

He turned back to his left for a moment, sweeping his left hand toward the exodus occurring in front of them. "Men from all fifty states, even Alaska, and our territories — Puerto Rico, Guam, Samoa, and the Virgin Islands — are serving on Midway right now. Midway's command master chief gave me that statistic just before I departed the ship for the foreign affairs conference in Manila."

"You are quite the elder statesman, Lunker," said Doc. "Maybe your call sign should be Ambassador."

"The ambassador of love," offered Willie. "That's our boy."

"The ambassador of love didn't realize that he'd wind up in a real foreign affair himself," interjected Mirela.

Lunker, blushing slightly, laughed along with the others, and then added, "Given that I live in the Midway Oasis with you clowns, I'm more like the ambassador of dumb asses."

"Yes and amen," agreed Tosh.

Lunker laughed, and then continued with his observations. "The master chief also told me that the men on Midway represent every ethnic category recognized by the census bureau, including Native Americans, and that over fifty Midway sailors were born in the Philippines." He paused for a moment; he was searching his memory for a specific piece of information.

"What fascinated me most was when he told me that several of Midway's chief petty officers and two warrant officers served during World War Two. In fact, one of the ship's master chief petty officers was on the aircraft carrier Hornet during the Battle of Midway.

"This is real history," said Sharon. "It's easy to forget that the ones who ultimately fight and die or are injured, and make history in the battles we read about, aren't merely photos in a book, but real people, like these." She looked toward the men walking past them and in front of them; it was a sobering thought that touched her soul as she stared at them.

What wasn't said on this balmy day in Subic Bay was that all those currently serving on Midway were volunteers. Besides having served in World War Two, others had combat service during the Korean and Vietnam wars. Over sixty percent were considered to have Vietnam-era service, including Willie and Doc. Having entered the naval service in July of 1974, the class of 1978 was the Naval Academy's last group of graduates to be officially designated Vietnam-era.

Midway's sailors and officers were born into families of every economic class, from ultra-wealthy to ultra-poor, from living in mansions to being homeless. They came from small farms and large cities, from both coasts and each of the Great Lakes, from the Rockies to the Appalachians, and from the prairies and the plains. Remarkably, many had never seen an ocean's waves until they joined the Navy.

"I love looking at the clothes some of these guys are wearing," said Lauren. "They're walking advertisements for their states' and cities' chambers of commerce." She smiled. "They should get paid for that." Some of the clothes they wore spoke of the places they called home or reflected their many eclectic styles — T-shirts with high school and college names, cowboy boots and hats, Kino sandals and tropical shirts, rebel flag t-shirts, blue jean overalls, short shorts and tank tops, bell bottom pants and disco shirts.

"My guess is they're homesick," offered Doc, "and they'd like to be back home, but just not today."

Lunker agreed and then continued his observations on this, his twelfth trip to the Philippines in the twenty-four months he'd been in the squadron. Eight of the trips had been during Midway's port visits; four were a result of cross-country flights, including the midsummer trip running from a typhoon.

"I remember the night before my first visit here. The skipper and I were the last flight to land, and we were in the wardroom having a late night cheeseburger after our debrief. He said Subic was a port visit whose reputation preceded it. I wasn't sure why he told me, since everyone has heard the stories since flight school."

Lunker paused and looked to his left, toward the main gate, and then back to his friends. "Doc and Willie and Gully already know this to be true. The skipper then told me that visiting Subic was a form of bragging rights; that in the Navy there were those who have been here and those who haven't. He also said Subic is a place you can't really know unless you've already visited it."

"The acquired taste or smell, or whatever it is, proves him totally correct," interjected Tosh, as the others laughed.

"You're right, and that's a great example," agreed Lunker. "And now you won't be able to describe it to your friends in San

Diego any better than we could. They laughed, and then Lunker continued.

"The skipper said that what too many don't think about until after their last visit here is that Subic, including Olongapo, is the Navy's last pilgrimage. He said, as Sharon commented a minute ago, that this is more than a tropical paradise; that this is also a place of history tied to our freedoms. But unlike other ports we visit, he said that once we step onto this land, and especially when we cross the bridge, that we'll never be the same — that a piece of Subic will always remain inside of us, and we can't wipe it out of our memory, even if we want to."

Lunker paused again. "Come to think of it, it's a trinity, a pilgrimage trinity — history, geography, and emotions, and by the time Willie buys our first round of drinks at dinner tonight, you'll agree I'm right." He smiled and patted his friend's shoulder. "Thank you, Willie."

They all laughed. "Yes, thank you in advance, Willie. That's very generous of you," said Lauren.

"Thank you for highlighting my natural generosity like that, Lunker," responded Willie, "and thank you for offering to buy the second and third rounds." He laughed and patted Lunker's shoulder.

"Touché," said Lunker, smiling.

"Looks like we're drinking for free tonight, Lauren," said Doc. "And you and Sharon, too, Gully. God bless America and our two bunkroom buddies."

Gully wasn't quite sure whom or what to believe, but he wasn't going to question it. "Lunker, Willie," Gully paused for a second, "Sharon and I would also like to thank you." He paused again. "And we'd like to thank Doc, too."

"For what?" Doc asked, looking slightly puzzled. "For picking up the fourth round." Gully said matter-of-factly, smiling as he gave Doc a thumbs up.

The three aviators looked at Gully in amazement. He fit in perfectly; he had just earned those four rounds, if they made it that far.

As they continued to walk toward the gate that led to Olongapo, the group had momentary glimpses off to their right, between buildings, of the drainage canal a hundred feet away.

What are those boats for?" Tosh posed the first question.

"You'll see very soon," answered Willie.

A minute later, the four couples made a ninety-degree turn to their right and followed a cavalcade of mostly young men getting closer with every step to crossing the infamous shit river bridge. On a steamy, late afternoon under a watchful Philippine sun, the group noticed that many of the sailors picked up their pace, some much faster than others, as they passed through the naval station's main gate.

Less than seventy feet in front of them was a two-lane bridge. It was about a hundred feet, maybe a hundred fifty feet long, they thought, with a single sidewalk area to their right. What captured their eyes, at least momentarily, was not the bridge, but the various buildings on the other side of the bridge. Most of the two and three story buildings were seemingly sturdy, but quite a few appeared to be ramshackle at best. They were densely packed on either side of Magsaysay Drive, a road packed with colorful Jeepneys. It was obviously the primary artery pumping American dollars into the heart of Olongapo's economy.

All along the legendary street they could clearly see a confluence of Filipino and American cultures jamming its sidewalks. The city's reliance on American sailors and other servicemen to sustain its 'adult Disneyland-based' economy sugarcoated, they would soon learn, the actual despair reaching out from half-paved/half-muddy streets, crowded narrow sidewalks, and buildings along the river that looked as if a strong afternoon breeze would bring them tumbling down.

169

Had they stopped short of the bridge and allowed their eyes to take in all the sights in front of them, they would have noticed, less than a mile in the distance, a lush green hillside rising prominently behind the town. They would have also noticed, just across the bridge and to their left, several velvet wall hangings being displayed, one of which had a Filipino Jesus standing next to two carabaos, the Philippine's domestic water buffalo.

In another place and time, all the visitors could easily be streaming through the main gate of Disneyland, eagerly anticipating the excitement and pleasure just moments away. On this day, however, each was approaching a bridge that was a gateway to a storied place far from California. Like the enchanting park across the Pacific, this was a place also fueled by imagination, and recognized by a single word. Many of the carrier's crew would argue, at least for the duration of Midway's time in port, that this fabled city, Olongapo, was truly the most magical place on Earth.

As the four women took their first couple steps along the bridge's wide sidewalk, they noticed, through the swarm of people walking in front of them, several men slowing down or stopping along the bridge's railing — watching, pointing at, or interacting with something or someone in the water. The rest of the men on the sidewalk continued to follow the focus of their attention, whatever and wherever it was along Magsaysay; their quick pace never slowed down.

Before their eyes could rationalize all that they were beginning to see and their nose could categorize the intense 'acquired taste' stench that stung the nose, a young child's sweet voice pierced the air.

"Throw me pesos, lady?"

As if on cue, the four women stopped and crowded against the bridge's metal tube-type railing to their right. The young, brown-skinned girl, with beautiful black hair reaching the middle of her back, stared up at them through clear, dark brown eyes. She was likely no more than four years old, maybe five; her bare feet were planted in the mud at the edge of the putrid water to her right.

They stared back at the frail young child with a bright smile and eyes that telegraphed hope. A thin layer of garbage surrounded the dirty area where she stood, about eight or nine feet below the bridge. She was wearing no shoes and had no basket with which to catch whatever came her way, although her white dress was clean. What they didn't know was that her mother ensured she was dressed beautifully every morning; she always wore one of her three homemade dresses.

Other young Filipino children stood nearby; among them were shirtless young boys whose shorts were soaked and their hair wet. They were more than willing to wade into the wretched water or dive beneath it for their coins. A few of the other young girls were wearing wet clothes; their deep black hair was also dripping with the sickening foul water.

"Here are some pesos," said Willie, handing each of the ladies two five-peso coins. Added together, it was just over five dollars — three to four day's wages for a low-income Filipino worker. "Before you toss them to her, let me get the others away."

He threw a large handful of one-peso coins onto the muddy shore well beyond the adorable child in front of them; the other children eagerly ran toward the coins he had just thrown. As they did, the ladies each dropped two pesos to the young girl, who quickly grabbed them and put them in a small purse belted around her waist.

She looked at the ladies with grateful eyes and said, "Salamat," with the accent on the middle syllable, and smiled; her abundant trove of coins would help feed her family for days, she knew. The ladies didn't understand 'thank you' in her native language, but they clearly recognized her precious and universal tone of gratitude.

Just like the smile of a young girl sitting on a carabao by a village that Willie and Doc once flew over, this young child's smile and voice permanently etched itself straight onto the hearts of eight Americans. The four women on the bridge nodded and said, "You're welcome." Their eyes were all moist as they smiled and stared at the young girl standing by the disease-spawning water, who continued to stare back at them.

Mirela, in particular, was frozen in place. "I don't know if she is envious, maybe dreaming of being on the bridge one day instead of under it, or if she's just thankful that we stopped to give her anything at all, knowing it'll please her parents," she said softly to Lunker, leaning against him for support. "I know what it's like to live among garbage and somehow still be happy." She looked at the young child and smiled, waving softly to her, and then asked Lunker, "Do you have any pesos?"

Lunker nodded and handed Mirela six five-peso and two one-peso coins, just over four American dollars. He took his remaining one-peso coins, five in all, and also threw them beyond the young child, as had Willie. As he did, Mirela dropped her coins to the small child in the white dress. She quickly tucked the coins into her purse; the pesos from Mirela and the other women totaled well over a week's wages for the average worker. Her eyes returned to the women and gave them an adoring smile.

Later that evening, at her home, she'd tell her mother and father about the kind women on the bridge who smiled at her, and especially the "pretty one with the dark hair and dark brown eyes, like mine," who waved and then gave her more coins. Her father could buy almost twenty pounds of monkey meat with the coins she handed him.

Their lots had all been cast at birth — only God knew why. They were standing less than fifteen feet apart, but it may as well have been fifteen million miles. It would take more than money to ultimately bridge a chasm where pocket change for one was a week's wages for the other.

172

Words among the group of eight on the bridge were scarce – the visual experience and the sobering 'welcome to Olongapo' message resonated and echoed loud and clear. Already lost in a strange world less than a hundred feet from the American naval base, the four couples waved goodbye to the precious young girl and the others and began moving slowly and quietly along the bridge's sidewalk.

Having traveled twenty or thirty feet more, each couple stopped walking without realizing that they had stopped. Seven banca boats, each with a single outrigger to its port side, floated less than fifteen feet from the bridge. The narrow wooden canoe-like boats, eight to ten feet in length, were very stable thanks to the outrigger design. As a result, a boat's occupants could safely stand in calm, slow-flowing water. In five of the seven boats, young children were standing near the bow. Their job was to catch or retrieve coins thrown their way.

Six of the boats were occupied by an older teenage girl and either a young girl or young boy. A few of the boys wore white 'dixie cup' hats associated with American Navy sailors. An older teenage girl occupied a seventh boat by herself. The young boys in each boat all had big smiles as they enthusiastically called out to the men walking by. Five of the teenage girls had silent smiles of resignation tinged with despair, although their eyes still radiated hope. The other two teenage girls actively called out in the same way as the young child first encountered by the four couples. They were, by appearance, the youngest of the seven — they could still dream.

In addition to those on the banca boats, four young boys were in the water. Two of the boys were positioned by the boats, hoping to catch or dive for any pesos not caught by those onboard. The other two boys were treading water, hoping to lure pesos from those sailors who found comedic delight in watching the boys disappear under the water in search of the sinking metal coins.

173

The four women on the bridge were frozen by the inconceivable reality below them. Heart-piercing emotions overwhelmed their capacity to accept what they were seeing. If the children in front of them survived the water, it wouldn't be too many more trips around the sun until they were likely stealing or prostituting themselves, maybe both, they thought. They would do whatever it took to survive and to help support their families. Regardless, their likelihood of being mentally and medically healthy by the end of their second decade on the planet was slim. That thought broke the hearts of four women whose maternal instincts had quickly risen to the surface.

Less than a half-minute had elapsed when the women had their first exposure to the young boys diving for coins. "Go fish," yelled a mean-spirited sailor as he callously threw a large handful of coins, at least a dozen or more, out of reach of any of the boats.

"What coins did he throw?" asked Tosh, watching as four boys, two on a boat and two already in the water, immediately dove out of sight.

"It looked like a few pesos, but mostly ten centavo coins," answered Willie. The centavos were noticeably smaller in size than the pesos. "Probably some nickels and dimes, too."

Although the boys would grab any coin within reach in the feces-filled water, their focus followed the peso coins. Fortunately, the majority of sailors tossed their coins directly toward those in the boats, or at least within reach of their nets and baskets, and also within reach of the boys treading water.

Each peso was worth slightly over twelve cents. A ten-centavo coin was worth slightly over a penny; the coins were essentially valueless, and yet the boys still dove deep into water that would cause them problems all their lives.

"Don't they understand how horrible this water is for their health, especially for...for...what is basically pennies?" Tosh's helpless exasperation poured out like an afternoon thunderstorm.

"Maybe," answered Willie, "but health is in the future. A hungry family is right now."

"How long do you think these boys will stay in the water?"

"I don't know, but probably until they've made enough to buy a day's worth of food for their family."

"They may understand health, but most of all, they understand hunger and hungry families. Willie is correct — hunger is today, tonight, and tomorrow morning."

Two sailors heading toward Olongapo stopped just behind where the four couples were standing on the bridge. They stopped and stared at the activity in the water; it was the first crossing for one of them. After a long delay, the 'first timer' spoke. "Man, is this some shit or what?"

"Actually, it is," said his friend in a slow, serious voice. He'd crossed the bridge over a dozen times during his time on Midway.

"Really?"

"Yep.....really."

"Shit. That's fucked up." It'd likely be the first and last time the sailor took notice; like most, he'd simply ignore it in the future.

Several feet away, Lunker and Mirela stood against the bridge's railing and stared at the extraordinary contrast between indigenous people and the outsiders who stared at them or ignored them.

"My family had food, but we weren't free as people. The Filipinos are free people, but they're slaves to hunger and disease. These kids in the water prove we won't put a limit on what it takes to survive."

"I never thought of it that way, Mirela, but you're right. It's so sad that these children and their families have no good options except to be slaves to choices that are certainly unhealthy and may ultimately kill them." What Lunker didn't tell her was that occasionally one of the children in the water would be caught in a sewage grate under the bridge and drown. He had learned that from Eli.

As he spoke, Mirela's eyes moved between the young girls sitting in their boats. She didn't see despair in their eyes; she saw hope. She knew the look and the feeling. She had been there before, and the memory had faded but never departed. Some eyes were smiling; some were faint and sad; some were envious; but they all had a vestige of hope, no matter how dim the actual reality was. She supposed their lives could be worse. "They could die, but then they'd most certainly go to heaven," she thought.

"My life in Romania was harsh, but nothing like this. We paid a price, but at least we had a way out without selling our dignity." Mirela added, as she unconsciously leaned against Lunker. She thought of her father, who endured excruciating blows to his kidneys instead of going to the ground. "Even in our despair, I only remember my parents smiling, just like these kids. Or Eli."

On the other side of Tosh and Willie, Doc and Lauren stood and stared like the others. Their ears had become numb to the never-ending onslaught of loud requests for money coming from the boats and water in front of them. "If these children stood on this bridge and simply walked up and asked or begged for money, I bet they'd be intentionally ignored," stated Lauren.

She paused to watch two young boys disappear under the water in search of pesos, centavos, and American coins thrown out of their reach. It seemed like a full minute before they resurfaced with their black hair glistening from the water and bright white smiles spread across their faces, each proudly taking a few mixed coins, likely worth less than a nickel, to one of the boats.

"But make them sit in small boats in a polluted river or, worse, tread water while pure shit is rubbing against their little bodies, and then they dive under it, and it suddenly becomes charitable entertainment worth paying for...Bastards...Fucking bastards...I ought to throw one of these assholes and his coins off the bridge and tell him to go fish, and see how he likes it."

Doc was stunned; he had rarely heard her swear, and now she was swearing like a sailor. He turned and stared.

Lauren wasn't finished. She was on a roll. "Yeah, the more repulsive the act, the more giddy some of these guys become, like they're experiencing euphoria at their philanthropic goodness when these young Filipino boys finally come back to the surface with coins worth a few pennies in their hands after a long stay under this nasty water." She paused. "At least it seems like only a few are assholes acting that way. I hope they think about it one day and regret it, and hopefully teach their kids to be the opposite of what they once were along this bridge." She paused. "I swear, Doc, I'd love to take one of these jerks back to Ocala and throw his ass right into the middle of Bear Swamp. Right now. Right now in front of all his buddies and see what he thinks then.

"Are there really bears in Bear Swamp?"

"Yes...Big ones...And alligators big enough to eat the bears...Throw his tough guy ass in there and see how tough he really is...He'd be crying like a baby in two seconds. Bastard."

Doc laughed. "Dang, Lauren. You sound serious."

Lauren turned her head and stared into Doc's eyes. "I am. I'd ask the Lord to give me superhuman strength for just five seconds and off his ass would go into his own shit swamp."

Doc laughed. "I love you, Lauren. Shit swamp and all."

"I love you too, Doc."

On the other side of Doc and Lauren, Gully and Sharon stared like the others. "It's ironic, Gully."

"What's ironic?"

"This bridge. This shit river bridge, and this town," noted Sharon as she glanced toward Olongapo. The history teacher then returned her stare to the faces in the water.

"The parents and grandparents of these kids stood so loyally by our troops during World War Two, no matter how tough or

177

how hard it got. Our two countries were staunch allies. Rock solid. But at the end of the war, we said goodbye and sailed across the Pacific to parades and celebrations and prosperity."

She paused. "But for the Filipinos, they were left with a country and cities and towns destroyed and land mines buried throughout this beautiful land." Sharon continued speaking, this time with more emphasis.

"When the Japanese first arrived in Olongapo, its citizens burned the city to the ground...the entire city...all the way to the ground...so the Japanese couldn't use it. It's been thirty-six years since the war ended, and here we are on a bridge over a river of sewage separating our two countries. Americans are still prospering on their side while these children in the water and their families are paying a horrible price. Plus, even now, Filipinos are still being maimed and killed by those same land mines, and they will for decades more."

She paused. "I don't think God could make this up if he tried. I guess it's why the shit river bridge isn't in any of our history books; no one would ever believe it."

Gully nodded. What was in front of them was so easy to believe and yet so impossible to believe.

Thankfully, the group noticed, the vast majority of sailors tossed their coins toward those sitting or standing in the boats, or at least within reach of their nets and baskets, and also within reach of the boys treading water.

After a few more minutes, the group finished their discussions and continued their short pilgrimage toward the legendary city of Olongapo. As the group stepped off the shit river bridge's concrete sidewalk, Lunker asked a comical question.

"Why did the chicken cross Magsaysay?" He answered his own question immediately. "Because it wanted to see a Filipino Jesus with dreadlocks on velvet."

They all laughed and began easing to their left across a busy Magsaysay Drive, safely dodging a convergence of colorful

178

Jeepneys that were picking up or dropping off sailors by the bridge. For now, thoughts of the children in the water were conveniently tucked away, although, as the men had said earlier, the memories would never disappear.

The thin, black haired Filipino man with a ponytail was a talented artist; his paintings on velvet confirmed it. The four men had previously looked at his creations from a polite distance, but had never engaged him in conversation. It was their loss – he was funny, personable, and astutely observing of people.

The velvet artist had glanced to see if there were wedding or engagement rings on any of their hands. Confirming there weren't, he knew this was likely the first trip across the bridge and into Olongapo for the women, and that a part of their emotions was still back on the bridge. They'd be much more relaxed when they walked by on their return to the naval base.

He spoke broken English with a medium Tagalog accent. "Hello, ladies. My name Bienvenido. It is Spanish and Filipino and means 'welcome.' You are welcome here all time, especially today."

He laughed and smiled broadly at each of them. "Boyfriends have good taste in women. You remember visit with group picture on beautiful velvet. For you special deal only right now." Bienvenido was a smooth talker who went straight for the sale. "Your men want to remember visit in Philippines with beautiful women on velvet I paint just for you. Look beautiful on wall in house."

"I don't think we have time to stand here in the sun; we would melt before you even painted one of us." Tosh loved his salesmanship, but wasn't a fan of velvet wall hangings. She was respectfully saying 'no thanks' for the group.

"Beautiful women no melt. I take photo. Use that. Have ready tomorrow." He was a natural marketer. The group looked at his artwork. A few of his velvet paintings were hanging up; the others were flat on the ground.

"You are very talented, Bienvenido." Mirela appreciated people who masterfully channeled their creativity and gifts to get ahead in an unfair world. "Perhaps we will visit you again during our trip." It was her cue for the others to politely say goodbye.

"I think one of us needs to get a Filipino Jesus with dreadlocks before we leave Japan for good," Willie said very quietly to Doc, almost in a whisper. "You know we'll wish we had."

Doc turned toward Willie and responded in an equally low voice. "Maybe on the way back at the end of cruise. We'll flip a coin. Loser gets it." He smiled at his friend.

"So, what's next, my sweet tour guide?" asked Mirela as she took Lunker's hand.

"First, we buy a tote bag or a backpack, and then we stay very close to each other as we cruise Magsaysay." Lunker held her hand a little tighter.

The sidewalks on both sides of the street were crushingly packed like a subway during rush hour. Sailors were enjoying and taking full advantage of the unplanned visit; many of those in a hurry walked along the street's edge. Even still, the street's population of sailors would double or triple, sometimes quadruple, when the sun disappeared and the lustful desires of the night took center stage.

Anything and everything that would occur in the next few days could be easily justified. When the visit was over, these same sailors would see nothing but an endless ocean, day and night, for at least the next sixty days.

The traditional wet season was underway; fortunately, rain had been scarce most of the previous week except for a few scattered afternoon showers. As a result, the dry spell had made crossing the first dirt side street and all those to follow uneventful — mud-free — a genuine blessing as the four couples began their stroll along Magsaysay.

On purpose, none of the men had alerted their dates to what they would see; it would have been a futile effort. Like everyone before them, the women were unprepared for the world in which they entered. In retrospect, a native Filipino painting Jesus with dreadlocks on velvet was the perfect carnival barker to welcome them to a bizarre circus that had been continuously running without interruption for decades.

A trio of options was the foundation of the infamous street: a wide range of bars with endless music and alcohol; open air shops and kiosks selling tee-shirts, Filipino crafts, 'puppy on a spoke' and other local delicacies; and a never-ending supply of women, some in the bars and the rest on the street, all offering a product called "love you long time," although 'long time' was a very relative term.

These three drove the economy, diversions, and the soul of Magsaysay Drive. The alligator in a small pen outside of Pauline's was a bonus for those who found such a novelty an entertaining encore.

At the first shop they passed, numerous versions and colors of tee shirts proclaiming either 'Midway vs. Cactus — Midway won' or 'Midway vs. Cactus — Cactus lost' adorned the framework around the open-air shop.

"This always amazes me," said Lunker. He pointed to one of the shirts that said 'Midway vs. Cactus – Midway won.' It had a depiction of Midway with its airplanes adorning the flight deck, including a few Phantoms that were slightly damaged, and a 'foreign' freighter, also damaged, on the ship's port side.

"We've only been in port for a few hours and the Olongapo grapevine has probably been in high gear since dawn and is as up-to-speed as the Pentagon regarding what occurred. I mean, how would they know it was the Phantoms that were damaged?"

"Someone down at the port or maybe in the communications center must call the mayor and pass the news before they do anything else," added Doc. He had seen it once before — He was on a cross-country to Cubi when two Navy

181

ships arrived unexpectedly in the middle of the afternoon. The town's population of women grew rapidly before the ships were even tied to the pier.

"I'd like to see the place where they create all these shirts so quickly. It must be an impressive operation," said Willie.

"The world's largest and busiest sweat shop, most likely." Gully's comment was accurate. This was his third trip to Olongapo, and yet he was still in disbelief at what he saw.

"I'm going to buy a bag. We'll be right out," said Lunker, as he took Mirela's hand and entered a store to his left.

We'll keep walking slowly," said Doc.

"Okay, see you in a couple."

A few minutes later, Lunker and Mirela rejoined the group with a new canvas-like travel bag and a suggestion. "Hey, let's drop into Old West Number Two and have a San Miguel or two." From a few doors away, they could hear a voice singing *On The Road Again* that sounded very much like Willie Nelson himself.

"Is that a disc jockey spinning records or are these bands really that good?" asked Lauren.

"They're really that good," answered Lunker. "Many of these singers speak very little English, but they nail the songs every time, especially the band in Old West Number Two. How they make their voices sound so realistic is part of what makes Olongapo unique."

"Lunker's right," interjected Doc. "You have to give all the bands credit for their talent, although occasionally they make a mistake with their English that sticks with you. Remember last cruise, the band at the Cubi O'Club singing Dream Weaver? I can't hear that song without singing along and adding weave dreamer instead of dream weaver."

The four couples were laughing as they walked through the door of Old West Number Two, one of the men's favorite clubs in Olongapo. It had great music, tasty food, and cold San Miguel.

The club had an odd smell, one that was noticeable at almost all of the clubs along Magsaysay. It was more than the stale cigarette smoke and alcohol odor prevalent in bars and nightclubs in every city; it was something the women hadn't smelled before — a blend of grilled and fried meat, with lots of spices, strange spices, and something sweet mixed in.

Lunker answered what the ladies were thinking. "What you're smelling is mostly grilled chicken adobo and fried lumpia with meat, everyone's two favorites. They use lots of spices native to the Philippines, but they also use lots of traditional spices and peppers and an Asian oregano that has a mint taste. Lots of coconut-based sauces are used, which are responsible for the sweet smell, most likely."

"How do you know all this?"

"Lots of golf with Eli. He says his wife is a very good cook. When the skipper and I were here this summer, running away from the typhoon, Eli explained the basics of Filipino cooking to us."

The eight friends each had two frosty bottles of San Miguel as they laughed and talked and sang along to country-and-western songs for just under a very entertaining hour. Having decided to shop for a few souvenirs, the group of eight walked out of Old West Number Two and straight into the heated, motionless air that was typical of a late summer afternoon along the streets of Olongapo. It was then when they first heard the news.

"Hey, the old man is staying," said a young man in a loud voice, about six feet in front of them. His comment was directed across Magsaysay to a group of sailors walking back toward the naval base.

"What? Really? You're sure?" The question came from a crusty, older sailor standing nearby who had a very salty air about him. "When did you hear that?"

"I just left the boat. A friend in the ship's admin office told me and then the petty officer of the watch told me as I left the quarterdeck."

"Excuse me. The captain's staying? He's not being relieved?" Willie asked the young man the question they all wanted confirmed.

"Yep. He's staying; not getting fired. It was announced about thirty minutes ago."

"That wonderful!" said Doc to no one in particular. "What great news!"

"You can say that again," responded Gully. "I was sure he'd be fired within the first hour."

"I'm in shock," admitted Lunker. "I'm really happy, but in shock. This will be such a great morale boost to everyone as we start the long line period."

"What happened?" Tosh knew it was positive; she just wasn't sure what had occurred.

"Typically, when there's a collision at sea, the captain of the ship gets fired, no matter who's at fault," answered Doc. "It's pretty much automatic, but Midway's captain didn't, which is just hard for us to believe, although it's the right decision. He's a great skipper; we need him."

Later in the afternoon, Doc would add that Midway magic was also a big winner on this special day; it was a good omen for the upcoming time at sea.

All across Magsaysay, the Subic telegraph was in high gear, spreading the word along both sides of the street and into the bars. The news also reached Moscow within minutes. Soviet agents, disguised as American businessmen or tourists and speaking fluent English, paid local men and women well to keep them informed regarding the movements and plans of the ships and squadrons that sailed and flew in and out of the Navy's deep-water port and airfield. Too often, the agents only had to mingle among the sailors along the street for their ears to hear all the information they were trying to collect.

The couples stepped across a second dirt side street as they continued walking slowly along a crowded Magsaysay sidewalk. Straight ahead, slightly less than three hundred feet away, positioned at the top of the infamous street where it ended in a 'T' intersection, they could see the New Jolo Club with its very prominent sign facing toward them.

In front of them, on both sides of the street, were more shops, cafes, small hotels, and clubs, all packed in as tightly as those in the two large city blocks behind them. The clubs had names like 007, Bali Hai, Wild West, Wigwam, Grand Ole Opry, New Florida, California, Boston, Nashville Room, Tally Ho, Zanzibar, and others that promised an imaginary path back to America, or a make-believe trip forward to an exotic place along one of Magsaysay's three blocks. They all had bands that could pack any bar in America.

"Can we stop here? I want to get a few things to take home," said Lauren. The group was in front of a shop selling traditional Filipino clothes, monkeypod kitchenware, and more t-shirts.

"Me, too," said Sharon.

"You can buy them at the Navy Exchange tomorrow. They carry most of this for about the same price."

"But then we couldn't say that we bought them along Magsaysay. Didn't you say this would give us bragging rights?" Tosh's last comment was argument-proof.

"You have us there, sweetie," Willie answered as he and the other three men smiled. She was right.

After the women each purchased a few monkeypod items, mostly square plates and bowls, as well as a couple oversized VA-115 Eagles tee shirts to wear as nightshirts, they stored them in Lunker's new bag and continued their journey. Every shop, bar, Jeepney, and local citizen passed was a new experience — an authentic, never-ending thieves' market that they wouldn't be able to convey to their friends any better than the men had to them.

"Is that what I think it is?" Tosh was looking across the street at the right side of Pauline's, a three-story club, hotel, and restaurant that sat next to a dirt side street named Gallagher Street.

"Yes, Tosh, it's an alligator." Willie had seen it so many times that he usually forgot that the small chicken wire, wood-framed cage with no top was there.

"Is that sailor feeding it a little chick?" Mirela had seen many bizarre and aberrant sights in Romania, but never anything like this.

"Yeah, but if it isn't hungry, the gator will just ignore it and keep sleeping in the mud." Lunker also rarely paid attention to it any more.

"Oh my Lord," said Tosh. "What else are we going to see here?"

"Depends on the bar and the time of day," responded Doc. "That includes the Cubi O'Club bar, too."

"Amen, brother." Willie high-fived his friend of many years.

"As a teacher, I think I'm going to submit Olongapo to the Webster dictionary as a new definition for indescribable, suggested Sharon as they continued walking.

"I can hear high school students now as they study for a test together. 'How would I know what the hell Olongapo is; it's indescribable.' Yep, that'll make their time in school productive," said Doc.

Gully laughed as he said, "Do you think they'll actually believe such a place exists?"

"Well, for those who actually make it here one day, they'll understand why Olongapo, and not life, is listed as the definition of indescribable. Life would be so much easier to describe." Lauren's comment wasn't flippant; it was right on target.

"Right now, Olongapo is life and the pursuit of living to some of these sailors, apparently." Sharon made her statement just after the group was practically bowled over by three sailors quickly making their way toward the bar at the end of the street.

They watched closely as the men dodged a plethora of packed Jeepneys in the road in order to maintain their semi-straight line toward New Jolo, which was quite possibly Olongapo's most notorious club — an exceptional proclamation considering most of the clubs along the street were notorious in their own way.

"Those three must have mama-sans at New Jolo Club. Hope they have lots of peso-nality," said Lunker, emphasizing the word 'peso.'

"Lots of what? Did you mean personality?" asked Mirela.

"Oh, hell no, we're talking pesos. It's all about the pesos. Pesonality has to be in the dictionary somewhere."

"Probably stuck between Olongapo and goat rope," responded Lauren, laughing out loud. Doc had explained the meaning of 'goat rope' to her during their walk in Misawa on the morning after the typhoon's landfall.

"Maybe that's what you should tell Eli the next time he asks you what's over the horizon," Doc said to Lunker. "Just say goat rope."

"And when I tell him what it means, he may start calling my putting goat rope," answered Eli's favorite golfer.

"What does goat rope mean?" asked Mirela. "I haven't heard that before."

Lunker smiled as he answered his European sweetheart. "Goat rope is a situation that is so fundamentally screwed up that it can't be unscrewed without God's own hands."

"In Romania we call that varza."

"No kidding; varza, huh?" Lunker nodded his head. "That's a good thing to know, Mirela. What would you say in Romania if it's like really screwed up varza?"

"Really screwed up varza." Everyone laughed.

"Mirela one; Lunker zero," announced Doc.

Willie interrupted the discussion about goat ropes and varza. "Hey, let's go in here. This band is the best."

They were in front of a bar named Reggae Island, from which they could hear a band finishing an excellent reggae version of Otis Redding's *Sitting On The Dock Of The Bay*. Along with Old West Number Two, Reggae Island was one of Willie's two favorite clubs. Without delay, the band began playing

Dancing In The Moonlight; their reggae version was all the enticement the couples needed.

The bar was at least three quarters full, with a few sailors and their Filipino dates slow dancing. The four couples glanced around the club and then opted for a large table fifteen feet from the band. After ordering and paying for eight San Miguels, Willie walked the short distance to the stage as the group finished the song. He handed the lead singer a twenty-peso bill and said something into his ear; a big smile and a nod was the response.

Their beer arrived as the band began playing the Four Seasons' hit *Can't Take My Eyes Off You.* The band's exceptional talent was on full display, even considering they used an early form of a karaoke machine as an occasional backup.

"I think your new call sign is going to be king," said Lunker, "as in king of romance."

"He may get lucky tonight after all," responded Tosh, as she kissed her blushing date and draped her arm across his shoulder, singing, smiling, and swaying to the tune along with the others. It was easy for her to forget that she was an entire ocean away from her hometown on the southern California coast; right now, this strange new world was the only place in which she belonged.

As the band finished, Lunker walked to the stage and, like his fellow bunkroom buddy, said something to the lead singer that was also answered with a nod and a smile as he accepted a twenty-peso bill. The band was happy to play any song for the equivalent of three American dollars.

"I think Lunker is hoping for a little dancing between the sheets tonight, Mirela," said Doc, as the band began playing *Love Me Tender,* a ballad for lovers recorded by Elvis Presley the year Doc and Willie were born. A few of the sailors and their dates walked to the small dance floor, and joined the couples already there to take advantage of a song perfectly suited for a well-earned slow dance; others just stood and danced next to where they were sitting.

As the song finished, Doc stood and turned toward his friends. "My turn, gentlemen; let me show you how romance is really created." He never backed down from competition, even if it was only imagined.

The lead singer smiled as he watched Doc walk toward him; he liked this generous group of Americans and their dates, especially when Doc handed him thirty pesos. He hoped the four men and their lovely women would stay a long time.

Doc had just sat down when the band began playing an artistically smooth reggae version of *All I Have To Do Is Dream*, a number one hit by the Everly Brothers in 1958. As the four couples sang along with the song, numerous sailors, sitting with dates at tables or on benches along two of the bar's walls, hoisted their San Miguel toward Doc and nodded.

As if on cue, both the band and Gully's three friends looked at him as the song ended. "I'm still thinking; your choices are tough to beat," he admitted, as he slowly stood up. After a few more undecided seconds, Gully made his decision and walked to where the band's leader was waiting.

As he did, Tosh said what almost every visitor to Olongapo thinks and desires. "I'd like to bring some of these bands back to San Diego. What a hoot it'd be to have them there."

"They'd probably pack a bar every night in southern California," agreed Lauren. "I'd like to bring a couple of the bands to Misawa, but in the winter their lips would freeze and they couldn't sing and they'd probably never come back."

Gully handed the lead singer sixty pesos as the two engaged in a short discussion. The band's bass player was summoned to the meeting and nodded a couple times before he responded, in Tagalog, to the lead singer. Had one been taken, a photo of the three huddled together — Gully, with his short, close-cropped hair and six feet, one inch frame, towering over two five-feet-three inch Filipinos with dreadlocks and guitars — would have been a Bunkroom Eight classic.

Gully walked back to where the others sat and, instead of sitting down, offered his hand to Sharon. "Would you like to dance, my dear?" he asked, as the band began playing a fast reggae version of *Cuando Calienta el Sol*, a popular Spanish love song from the early sixties whose title translates as "When the sun heats up."

"Well my, my. Look at Romeo here," said Lunker, smiling. "Gully's growing up."

"Why don't you follow his lead?" suggested Mirela. "Or should I just dance alone?"

Without hesitation, Lunker, immediately joined by Doc and Willie, stood and escorted Mirela, Lauren and Tosh to the dance floor, less than ten feet away, where Gully and Sharon were already dancing.

After a few minutes, the band expertly transitioned the upbeat song to a slower tempo version of *Love Me With All Your Heart*, a love song using the same tune. Five minutes later, and once again perfectly timed, the band transitioned back to Spanish lyrics and a fast tempo. Altogether, the group rhythmically extended the normally three or four minute song to almost twelve minutes, although it still didn't seem long enough.

Three of the couples began to walk away from the now crowded dance floor as the band finished.

"Hey, who said we were finished dancing?" asked Gully. The band had just begun playing a relatively fast version of *Your Song*, an Elton John hit from 1970, which included one of the band's three guitarists switching to a saxophone. It was a reggae-jazz-love song in Olongapo — an unexpected musical treat that caught everyone by surprise in a town where nothing was a surprise.

The band's version had most of the couples in the bar immediately on their feet dancing, along with plenty of sailors without dates, too. As the tempo was increased a couple notches, even more couples stood and danced. That the four couples were almost seven thousand miles from the London neighborhood where the song was written didn't matter. An Englishman's song had become their song, and it fit in perfectly along Magsaysay Drive. Frosty San Miguel beer and dancing at Reggae Island created one more surreal event to add to a day already filled with many surreal events — It was an appropriate way to wrap up the first day in Olongapo for the four aviators and their dates.

There would be a debate, days later in Bunkroom Eight after the ship was underway again, as to who of the four picked the best song. Not surprisingly, Gully won hands down, and he cheerfully accepted the legitimate vote.

Three hours had elapsed since the four ladies had taken their first steps onto Magsaysay. In retrospect, those steps were naïve, sheltered baby steps. Had they stayed a few hours longer, the streets would have become treacherously bawdy and openly scary. Street crime against intoxicated sailors would rear its ugly head, and purveyors of a wide range of debauchery would become as prevalent as beer in the bars.

The couples retraced their original steps, walking across three dirt streets and passing a sleeping alligator in an open-air, muddy cage by Pauline's along their journey back to the Navy's base at Cubi Point. The sun was patiently retreating behind the lush tropical mountains to the west, casting a golden glow that was slowly fading toward darkness.

Stepping back on a bridge that would forever be so much more than just a bridge, they noticed that the river was devoid of banca boats and small children in the water. A few boys stood on the riverbank nearest to the base's main gate, but only a handful of sailors tossed pesos their way.

It had only been ten hours since the memories of what would become a most unusual day had their beginning — in Singapore for the women, and on an injured ship for the men — but it would be a day none of them would ever forget.

For the women, just like their boyfriends before them, it would be easy to believe that the rock band Eagles composed the song Hotel California just for this moment. So many of its lyrics fit so perfectly with the entirety of their first Subic Bay encounter. One of the song's creators once explained that the song was written to convey and portray a journey from innocence to experience.

As the four couples crossed the shit river bridge and climbed into two taxis for the ride back to the Cubi Point side of the base, a single line from the ballad summed up their visit perfectly: they were checking out......but they could never leave.

CHAPTER NINE

Days And Nights Of Danger
Mid-to-Late Summer, 1980

The naked woman, covered only by a soft cotton sheet below her waist, reached across the sleeping man next to her and pressed the snooze button on the alarm clock. It was pitch black in the room, even though the sun had been steadily rising in the sky outside for almost two hours.

"Good morning," Tosh said softly, resting her hand on Willie's chest as she pressed her warm body tightly against his.

"Mmmmm, you'd better be a gorgeous southern California blond named Natasha or I am in really deep shit."

"Yes, you would be in a really deep shit river, Willie Pete, and I'd be throwing a lot more than pesos at you." She slid her hand lower on his body. "Do you see the time on the clock, mister?"

"Who said my eyes are open?"

"I can feel you waking up."

"It's a very healthy way for pilots to start the day. Part of the morning checklist."

She laughed in the unseen darkness of the room. "I'm sure it is, but you were the one who suggested breakfast at Chuckwagon at eight-thirty."

"Tosh, my dear, eight-thirty really means nine o'clock." Willie rolled to his left and faced Tosh, taking several long seconds to kiss her good morning before rolling on his back again. "Only Gully still believes eight-thirty means eight-thirty."

"Hmmm, I see. And where did you learn that interesting fact about time?"

"Everything I know I learned from three great institutions."

"Really?" She paused. "And those institutions would be?" She could guess two of them.

"Archie, Professor Leydorf, and Pensacola."

Willie couldn't see her smile, but he could hear her soft laugh and feel her hands rubbing his bare chest. He assumed correctly that she was contemplating his comment.

"So," she said slowly, "the key to all knowledge is moonshine, slide rules, and airplanes. Is that right?"

"Yes, and while I didn't do well with academics at Annapolis, I do remember one or two things about physics, and right now I'm feeling a strong gravitational pull toward the horizontal axis."

The touch of their bodies, immersed in the erotic tension filling the unlit room, was slowly turning the conversation into an aphrodisiac. "I see, and which of those is responsible for the time warp where eight-thirty is really nine o'clock."

"The snooze alarm." Willie smiled in the dark and rolled to his left, on top of her, allowing his body to softly rub against hers.

Tosh laughed softly. "Then four taps on the snooze alarm are all you get this morning."

"Silly woman. I only need three to have you meet God and an angelic choir." He slowly eased down her warm body.

"The clock is ticking, flyboy."

194

Five minutes before nine, on a sunny but already humid morning in the south Pacific, Willie and Tosh stepped out of a taxi and straight into the acquired taste of the nearby rancid river. As they strolled into the air-conditioned comfort of the Chuckwagon, they noticed that Doc, Lauren, Lunker, and Mirela were already seated, but Gully and Sharon were nowhere to be seen. Several other tables were occupied, including two by aviators in flight suits who appeared to be finishing their meals.

"Sorry we're a little late. We decided to attend church before we came over." Tosh punched Willie in the arm as he finished speaking.

"Gosh, I didn't realize morning mass was conducted in the BOQ these days," said Doc.

"Hey, where's Gully?" Willie quickly changed the topic of discussion.

"Maybe he and Sharon are standing in line for communion." Lunker's response made them laugh.

Gully and Sharon arrived at the large table ten minutes later. "What a nice big smile, Gully. Were you two at church like Tosh and Willie?" asked Doc, with a wide grin of his own.

"Nope. We assumed no one would actually show up at eight-thirty, so we were just taking our time hanging out in the room." As Gully answered, Tosh elbowed Willie very lightly in the ribs.

Lunker, whose golf clubs were leaning in a corner nearby, gave the group their morning brief. "We have a tee time at ten-fifteen, although the course shouldn't be busy this morning. Everyone on the ship who isn't on duty is probably sleeping in or nursing a hangover." As he finished his sentence, a waiter arrived to take their orders. Breakfast burritos and omelets were the selections of choice, except for Gully; he added a bowl of oatmeal and a side order of hash browns to his overstuffed sausage, red peppers, and cheese omelet.

While the orders were being taken, Gully leaned in toward Willie, sitting to his left, and asked very softly, "You and Tosh went to church this morning?"

Willie smiled. "I'll tell you later," he answered quietly.

"It's only a five minute ride to the course, so we're in no real rush. I left a message earlier for Eli to get his three favorite caddies, but he doesn't know why." Lunker was looking forward to his caddy's reaction at the sight of the ladies.

"He's going to be in heaven when he sees four beautiful women step out of the taxis," Doc interjected.

"It'll be a treat for all of us," said Lunker.

"Speaking of treats, the day before I left Misawa on my way to Singapore, I spoke to my sister on the phone, and she told me her boyfriend popped the big question! Is that cool or what?" Sharon's own excitement was palpable.

"So she's pregnant?" asked Lunker.

"What? Pregnant? How does pregnant fit in here?"

"Well, you know, a woman says she's pregnant and the number one big question is 'Are you shitting me?' That's the number one 'popping-the-big-question' for guys. Surely you know that."

Lunker looked at each of his fellow aviators — all three were laughing and nodding. The women were smiling but seemed puzzled. Without hesitation, Lunker continued.

"The number two popped-big-question for guys is the response to a woman saying 'I'm leaving,' and the guy asks if it's leaving like you're going to the 7-11 to get me some more beer, or leaving because you're saying sayonara, asshole. I'm leaving, leaving." The group laughed as Lunker continued.

"Will you marry me is actually number three of three in the list of the top three popped-big-questions. Every man knows that. It's part of the birds and bees lectures dads have given their sons since Columbus drank Bushwackers on Pensacola Beach."

As Lunker finished his comment, and while the group was laughing, Gully quietly asked Willie, "Is that right? I didn't know that."

Willie grinned as he shook his head. Gully still had some innocence to lose; that was good to hear. It meant his roots were still grounded in the naive soil of the heartland.

"My sweet Lunker, you are so very right. In a woman's world, 'Will you marry me' actually isn't the number one question. We just pretend it is." As did her date previously, Mirela now held the group's attention. "Our number one question is are you going to enjoy sleeping alone tonight? We just don't publicize it." The ladies all laughed and high-fived each other; their dates laughed as well.

As they continued to chat, four aviators in flight suits passed by where the couples were gathered. Lunker, like the others, knew each of the four men from the air wing's Prowler squadron. "You guys are flying in Cope Thunder this morning, right?"

Cope Thunder was a military exercise conducted several times a year in Crow Valley, a massive forty-two mile long area, located twenty-seven miles north of Subic Bay. The complex sat in a jungle valley surrounded by mountains of various heights on both sides, including an inactive volcano virtually hidden by dense foliage, named Mount Pinatubo, just three miles south of the southern end of the range. Little could anyone in the two groups imagine that, just ten years into the future, the volcano would erupt and decimate the magnificent Naval Base Subic Bay, where they currently sat, as well as Naval Air Station Cubi Point, resulting in both of them being officially closed.

The Crow Valley real estate included an air-to-ground target range with advanced electronic warfare capabilities. The complex provided aviators with a very realistic scenario — the dangers in the air and on the ground were real. The jungle was full of wild animals and bad men; it was well known that MOROs were spread throughout the complex. They weren't an official part of the exercise, but they were a very dangerous element if an aviator had to eject from his jet.

197

"Yep, a side benefit of being here instead of Singapore," said Jack Muldoon, a lieutenant commander and one of the EA-6B's three electronic countermeasures officers, all of whom would be involved in providing various forms of electronic jamming and support. "We're strictly flying up and down Crow Valley today. Nothing too hard — an easy, plain vanilla flight supporting the Air Force while we do a little jungle and mountain sightseeing."

Lunker introduced them to Mirela and the other three ladies, and then bid them goodbye and a safe flight as they departed.

"By the way, the four of us will be flying late morning, day after tomorrow." Lunker directed his comment to both the men and women. "Zero-nine-hundred brief; eleven-hundred wheel's up. Back on deck by thirteen-hundred." He looked at Willie. "You and Gully will lead a flight of two; I'll be with Chicklips in the second jet. Doc and Socks will lead the second flight of two."

"What will you be doing?" asked Tosh.

"Heading south a couple hundred miles — cruising the string of Philippine islands, mostly around the big island of Mindoro, but lots of little ones dotted all around the sea," replied Lunker.

"Sounds beautiful," she said. "Can I sit on Willie's lap?"

"I'm okay with that," responded Willie, smiling. "Any bombs?"

"Nope; giving the ordies a break." The 'ordies' were the squadron's ordnance handlers. "I'm betting we'll get a week of bombing at Tabones, Los Frailes, and Scarborough Shoals when we pull out, which will keep them very busy, but tomorrow is just a back-in-the-saddle flight to stay current."

"I think we ought to head south to Simara Island." It was one of Willie's favorites among the over seven thousand islands, of all sizes, shapes, and beauty that comprise the Philippines. It didn't have tall waterfalls like many of the fantasy-like islands, but it was still a masterpiece. He turned toward Gully. "You'll enjoy seeing it. It's about five miles long, about fifty miles or so east of Mindoro." Mindoro was a very large island, approximately a hundred miles south of Olongapo.

"That sounds good to me. Beautiful long, white beaches and lots of lakes, rivers, and lagoons all blended among the palms," offered Lunker. "Plus some cute villages. The skipper and I flew over it a few times last cruise."

"That's the one," agreed Willie, "and there's a very old Spanish fort on a hilltop, too. But, there are lots more islands just as pretty, so we'll just have a mark one, mod zero boondoggle sightseeing tour in the name of official Navy training, sir." They all laughed.

After finishing a delicious and filling breakfast, the eight departed for the golf course, a short five-minute drive away.

Eli was sitting on a faded white wooden bench when the two taxis arrived at the Binictican Golf Course. If he noticed his four dear Navy friends, it wasn't immediately apparent. Eli was focused on the four divinely lovely women walking his way.

"Hello again, Eli." Mirela's words delicately flowed like warm cream as she walked toward Lunker's dear friend and hugged him.

"I brought you Mirela and three new friends, Eli," said Lunker, as he and his caddy shook hands and embraced.

Eli still hadn't spoken. He was numbingly stunned by his good fortune; his smile reflected the joy of the surprise.

"This is Tosh....Sharon....and Lauren." Each of them gave the overwhelmed man a light hug as Lunker introduced them. "I think you know these three knuckleheads with me....Moe, Larry and Curly." Eli laughed as he shook hands with each of his old friends. He had seen episodes of The Three Stooges on a television at the golf course's snack bar.

Behind him, three caddies stared at the group, and especially the women; they couldn't believe their luck. They rarely caddied for any golfers who weren't active duty or retired military men.

Eli introduced them. "Meet best caddies. Lito, Romy, George. Lito my cousin." They greeted each other like old friends with warm smiles and handshakes.

While Doc, Willie, and Gully rented clubs and paid for the round, Lunker stood by his caddy and swept his hand toward the four women. "Eli, now you know what is over the horizon."

Eli made a sign of the cross and smiled as he admired the women next to him. "My wife beautiful. Each of you beautiful. Make Philippines better place being here. This best day of all." His comments and broad white smile melted the women's already emotional hearts.

"Look at Eli," said Willie to Doc and Gully, as they stood together by the pro shop's open-air counter. "He looks like a Filipino host of a beauty pageant standing by the girls. I don't think he's looked at Lunker once in the past two minutes." His friends agreed; Eli was in a heaven of his own.

"I think he's more like Sheik Eli Da-caddy and his forbidden harem of beauties," said Lunker, who overheard them. "We need to get a photo of this." He had a camera. They took a group photo, courtesy of pro shop manager, and then a couple shots of just Eli and the women.

The first hole was a disaster for the men. Lunker, Doc, and Gully each bogeyed the hole; Willie had a double bogey. The four women and all the caddies laughed when Eli suggested the reason.

"Must be looking at pretty women instead of golf ball. No impress girlfriend this way."

"You are a wise man, Eli," stated Mirela, who had moved next to the smiling man. They all laughed; Eli the most.

As they walked to the second hole, Lunker related the story of the skipper and the monkeys from their round of golf during the 'escape the typhoon' boondoggle.

"Do you think we'll see them again, Eli?" Tosh was curious. The monkey exhibits at the Los Angeles Zoo had always been one of her favorites since she was a young girl.

"Same monkeys? Maybe; don't know. Lots monkeys in jungle. Four monkeys right here play golf now." He laughed as he pointed toward Lunker and his fellow Eagles.

As they arrived at the number two tee box, Lauren noticed them first. She pointed toward the tree line to the left of the far side of the green.

"Monkeys come," said Eli. Three large and one very small monkey slowly walked out of the jungle. The small monkey was staying close to the one that was likely its mother. The three adults were the size of very large cats, maybe closer to bobcats, and sinewy — lean and muscular — at least eighteen inches to two feet tall, although the upright way they sat made them look much larger.

"Oh, my goodness!" said Tosh.

"Is that a baby?" Sharon asked.

"Mother, father, baby," responded Eli. "Maybe cousin or best friend," he added, laughing.

The four sat near the left edge on the backside of the green; the mother and baby sat slightly behind and away from the other two. The women were mesmerized at the sight; golf, to no surprise, was suddenly insignificant.

Lunker teed off first, hitting a high arcing shot that landed about twenty-five feet to the right of the hole. As the monkeys watched the ball roll to a stop, they didn't move. They were simply nosy neighbors who happened to live on the same street.

Doc was next; his shot landed short and rolled a few feet to the left of the green. The monkeys watched, but remained motionless, although the baby monkey was constantly climbing on or moving around its mother.

"That easy chip there. Roll down to hole," said Lito, Doc's caddy and Eli's favorite cousin.

Gully hit a low shot with minimal arc that rolled about twenty feet past and to the left of where Doc's ball was resting. "I'll take that," he said, satisfied he could get it cleanly out of the low rough. As he picked up his tee and turned toward the group, he could tell by the reactions of the four women that something was happening behind him.

All eyes watched in silence as papa monkey walked toward Gully's ball. As the monkey reached his destination, there was a gasp and then laughter from everyone, especially the ladies, as a very distant relative picked up the ball, looked at it, and tossed it onto the green, where it rolled to within seven or eight feet of the hole.

"Can you believe it? What a great bounce! I'll take that!" Gully had the entire group, including the four caddies, laughing. No one argued; it was better to have a lucky break than to merely be good.

Papa monkey rejoined his family and watched as Willie hit his shot. The ball was on a direct line to the hole, but, like one of Willie's trends when landing his Intruder on Midway, it had a little too much power at the start and flew over the flagstick and the green like a fast jet, bounced twice, and disappeared into the thick green jungle. He and the others waited several moments to see if a monkey would retrieve the ball and provide him with a lucky bounce. Unfortunately for Willie's ultimate score, the monkeys ignored his wayward shot and simply retreated into the jungle behind them.

Gully birdied the hole; Lunker and Doc made par; and Willie recorded a triple bogey, leaving him five over par after two holes. As they finished, Doc handed his caddy one hundred pesos to buy San Miguels for the foursome and their dates and whatever the caddies desired to drink.

"Take your time, Lito. We'll meet you at the top of the hill."

"I see you there." Lito knew the group would take their time, but he would still hurry. He was enjoying being around his cousin's friends, especially the women.

As the group arrived at the tee box for the third hole, they heard the unmistakable and not unanticipated whine of an approaching aircraft's Pratt and Whitney J-52 engines. It was the engine used by both the Intruder and Prowler.

Cubi Point's single runway, two miles away, was oriented so that an aircraft departing to the east-northeast would fly, on runway heading, directly over the golf course, and then begin a turn, left or right, toward its initial check point or destination.

The Prowler, manned by the four men they had seen earlier at the Chuckwagon, passed almost directly overhead the golfers at an altitude of no more than eight hundred feet above the ground. The late morning's thick blanket of humidity enabled dazzling vapor contrails to peel off the wings as the pilot pulled the aircraft into a tight left hand turn toward the north. It was a fine demonstration of the jet's aerodynamic properties.

As they walked toward the next hole, none of the four gave any warning to their dates regarding how they would reach the tee box.

"Is this cool or what?" added Tosh. "Check this out."

"Are we back in the nineteen forties?" asked Lauren.

The women stared at the packed dirt steps carved out of the steep hill and the seemingly long distance to the top, made more enchanting by the pathway between two walls of thick jungle foliage. Mostly though, they were riveted by the ancient generator and the thick rope they'd hold as they made their way to the top.

Romy pushed a green button, and the ladies watched with rapt interest as the noisy generator slowly propelled the thick, coarse rope in a slow loop between a pulley at the bottom of the hill and a pulley at the top.

"Ladies first," said Lunker.

Mirela, who had made this climbing trip before, paved the way for the women behind her. She never mentioned the view from the top. Her three new friends could experience it, as she had not so long ago, when their unique journey toward the sky was complete. Lauren, Tosh, and Sharon followed her and, upon reaching the top of the steps, were silent for at least a minute as they took in the vista in front of them.

"What do you think?" asked Lunker. "Some view, huh?"

"I can't think," said Sharon. "This is just so stunning." The small part of Luzon Island on which they stood was typical of the breathtaking beauty across the island, the largest and most populous island in the Philippines. It was also the fifteenth largest island in the world.

"This is art," added Tosh. "This is what real art is all about."

"I saw this view just a little over a week ago, and it still feels like the first time," admitted Mirela.

"Okay, no more golf; let's just sit here for a couple hours and enjoy the view." Everyone agreed with Lauren's comment, even the caddies with them.

The Bataan peninsula officially included the Subic Bay Naval Base and Naval Air Station Cubi Point, but not the city of Olongapo. Its history included periods of peace and violence; times of nurturing and times of harm. The peninsula was home to many generations whose way of life and survival rarely changed. The region's original citizens, and those since then, had been witnesses to advances in transportation, electronics, technology, and healthcare; yet, those lifestyle changes were generally relegated to visitors. Most of the local residents' lives remained, in more ways than not, the same as they had been for countless generations.

They stared at an authentic tropical jungle in front of them and positioned two hundred or so feet below them. That land was unchanged for centuries except for a few roads and land cleared while creating the eighteen holes of the course. Their view looked to the east-northeast. Distant dark green mountains with a hint of blue were about forty-five degrees to their left and right; highlighting them was Mount Pinatubo, rising almost five-thousand feet to their left, and another dormant volcano, Mount Natib, forty-one-hundred feet to their right. Between the two, just five miles beyond the visible horizon in front of them, was a sixty-mile long trail of misery that, due to horrific events in the spring of 1942, would be forever known to the world as the Bataan Death March.

A few minutes later, the group heard the pulley moving as Lito arrived with beer for everyone. He was overjoyed when Doc told him to keep the change; it'd feed his family for three or four days. They all took their time and savored the delicious taste of San Miguel beer while discussing many topics.

As the group looked across the now pastoral hills and plains of alluring beauty, Sharon shared more information about this land that had borne the ugliness of war and the brunt of a powerful human force called hatred.

"I apologize in advance for putting on my history teacher hat, but only seventy or eighty miles north of here, in Lingayen Gulf, is where the final drive to Japan began in January of 1945." She paused as each person turned toward her. "My master's thesis was centered on the Battle of Luzon and the drive south from Lingayen Gulf to Manila. It's one of the reasons I requested an assignment to a teaching position in the Pacific. I hoped to see this hallowed ground for myself, and now here I am with each of you." Sharon paused for a few moments, savoring this special moment, and then glanced at Gully as everyone, including the caddies, waited to hear what else she had to share.

"The battle plan was to move south through Luzon, across Bataan and Corregidor and Subic Bay, where we're standing, and then into Manila. My focus, my master's focus, was on the unrecognized human toll of the final Philippine campaign and, in particular, two key areas. One of the two focused on American casualties in Lingayen Gulf, where seventy Allied warships and over one hundred fifty landing craft were amassed to begin the assault. There was an unrelenting barrage of shells bursting over the gulf, trying to shoot down enemy aircraft, and also a massive number of shells aimed toward the ships. Unintentionally, the two created a lethal blanket of shrapnel that rained down on and around the ships and boats and resulted in more American injuries and deaths than from enemy fire actually hitting the vessels or from shooting the men as they came ashore."

"My second area of focus was the high number of Filipino civilian deaths on Luzon during the drive south, about one hundred forty thousand. In comparison, American deaths totaled only ten thousand, and most of those occurred on ships in Lingayen Gulf. For a little perspective, the Filipino civilian deaths alone were just slightly less than the entire population of Miami at that time."

Sharon paused as her mind took her back to interviews with Filipinos who lived through the campaign. It was impossible to forget their vivid recollections and emotions as they spoke, each with sad eyes. "What I learned from eyewitnesses, which shocked me and the professors who reviewed my thesis, was that the overwhelming majority of Filipino casualties weren't soldiers who were fighting the Japanese, but civilians of all ages — almost one hundred thirty thousand noncombatants, from babies to the elderly, slaughtered because of a small piece of fabric."

"In the frenzy of villages and towns being overrun, many citizens had lost, or could not quickly locate, a small cloth tag the Japanese required every Filipino, from the oldest person to the newest baby, to wear prominently at all times on the front upper part of their shirts or dresses. It measured one and a half inches from left to right, and two and a half inches from top to bottom. It was white, with a solid red circle in the center, and had Japanese kanji writing vertically on the left and right sides of the circle, as well as centered vertically below the circle."

"Anyone not displaying the small tag was shot on the spot, regardless of age, including babies and children. The Japanese provided only one tag per citizen, so losing it or not wearing it could easily be a death sentence." As Sharon spoke, the four caddies each looked toward the ground or off into the distance.

After a few quiet moments, Eli spoke first. "Mother say grandmother and aunt shot because no tag. Saw two babies shot." His eyes stared out across the lush land to the north, toward his village, as he continued recalling a moment passed down to him in his teenage years. "Me one year old near end of war. Mother just give me bath outside when soldiers come. No tag on my shirt." He paused to gather his emotions. "Uncle stand nearby and pull me against his chest. Put his tag on me. Give me to mother and then run into jungle. Soldiers chase. Mother say she never forget hear guns shoot. Know he die save me."

Eli was too young to remember it, but the story was firmly entrenched in his soul, and the sacrificial gesture's roots were now planted in all those around him, each of whom was stunned by what they heard. There was silence for ten or fifteen seconds, and then Lito spoke. "My grandfather die battle fighting. Have uncle shot since no tag. Teacher in school tell story about tag. Hard to forget. Crazy. Not right."

"After war end, everybody burn tags. Never want to see them again." Eli's twelve-word commentary spoke tragic volumes for a nation whose loyalty to America never waned, even though such loyalty and friendship came at a mortally high cost.

On a single occasion, many rounds of golf earlier, Eli had shared gripping recollections from the wartime years passed down from family members, but none as shocking as these cold blooded murders. Eli then quickly changed the mood from somber to joy by engaging the group with a lighthearted story.

"Mother tell funny story. Japan soldiers like bananas. Want banana trees planted along every road so can eat banana any time. Don't like walking into jungle. Make kids and adults in villages plant banana tree. Japan soldiers complain trees not give fruit. Make village people plant more, but new ones never give fruit. Japan soldiers don't know two kinds banana trees. Look same. One give fruit. One not. Need both kind side-by-side or no fruit. Village people only plant trees not make fruit. They win. Japan soldiers lose."

The entire group laughed; the caddies loudest of all. "That's a wonderful story, Eli," said Sharon. "I've never heard that. I'll start using that story in my history classes. Philippines one; Japan zero."

The caddies smiled broadly. The same pride that never deserted them in the great war remained intact on this sunny day in paradise.

Tosh changed the subject. "Are your daughters okay, Eli?" Willie had shared, with all the women, that Eli had lost three of his five children, including his only son, before any of them reached the age of seven.

Eli nodded and kept smiling. "Everyone good. Life good. What over horizon?"

Lunker answered. "Oh Eli, there is so much over the horizon, but nothing more beautiful than these four women and your four wives." He knew the other three caddies were married; Eli had told him that earlier. "And no land more beautiful than right here, right now."

"This paradise."

"This is paradise." Lunker smiled. "But my golf game is not paradise today. I need your help, Eli."

Eli laughed. Life was so good, he thought.

"Really Eli, I need your help every round, but after this visit, my next visit here will be my last. You have to teach me all you know before I transfer back to America." Lunker had dreaded breaking the news to his friend and caddy; he'd received his orders to Pensacola the day before the collision.

Eli was quiet for a moment. "How many days this time?"

"Probably three more, and I'll be out here every day with you and Mirela."

"Still need three years. But we try together. Make you better than monkey throwing ball on second hole." Everyone laughed, but none harder than Lunker, as Eli continued with his thoughts. "Goodbye come one day. Not today. Today golf, friends, beautiful women."

"Yes and amen," interjected Doc, "and San Miguel." Everyone smiled and agreed.

Almost an hour later, the group of four golfers, four caddies, and four beautiful women were walking from number six to number seven when they heard the sounds of a helicopter's rotors. Less than a minute later, one of CAG-Five's SH-3 Sea King helicopters passed overhead on a heading of north. Its top speed was 120 miles per hour, and it certainly looked like it was moving that fast or faster.

"Something's up," said Willie.

"Why do you say that?" Lauren asked what the women were all thinking.

"Well, one, they were hauling ass. Two, there were three Marines in combat gear sitting inside with M-16's." The M-16 was a combat rifle.

"What do you think is happening?" asked Tosh.

"I don't know, love, but the only jets heading north today are the Prowlers working with Cope Thunder. Right, Lunker?"

"Yep, you're right. It doesn't mean the two are related, but they could be, or the helos are augmenting the Air Force's security team or supporting troops on the ground. It could be several issues; it's hard to know."

As they continued walking, they heard the sound of another helicopter approaching. It too passed within a half-mile of where they all stood; like the other one, it was on a northerly heading.

"That's one of VC-5's helos," said Doc, "and it looked like there were Marines inside of it, too." Once more, golf was irrelevant for the time being; concern for aviators possibly in trouble took precedent. As the sound dissipated, Lunker added a bit of information.

"We did some Cope Thunder work between my first two cruises. If my memory is correct, the Air Force's combat rescue helos were the primary SAR go-birds, and VC-5 was backup." SAR stood for 'search-and-rescue'.

"I hope the Air Force has lots of Negritos on payroll in Crow Valley," said Willie, "like the Navy has for security around the perimeter fence here."

"Who are the Negritos?" asked Lauren. She had a teacher's natural curiosity for learning.

"Negritos are, well, in simplest terms, Negritos are Filipinos who haven't been domesticated," answered Doc. "It's like comparing a bobcat to a large house cat. The Negritos typically live off the land."

Willie added his input. "The Navy uses Negritos for security around the bases here, and they were also some of our instructors when we went through JEST, the jungle escape and survival training at Subic. If a Negrito told me he could turn palm fronds into a functioning radio, I'd believe him. They know tricks we could never think of."

Eli laughed at Willie's comment, and then turned serious himself. "My village use Negritos catch wild animals for food and protect against MOROs. What they do to MOROs not nice. We hear scream for long time, but teach them stay away from village." His cousin and two friends nodded in agreement.

Lunker added an interesting tidbit. "The Navy pays the Negritos at JEST in cigarettes and condoms, with some pesos on the side. It's what the Negritos ask for." The ladies noticed the four caddies also nodding at his comment.

As the group arrived at the eighth green, about ten minutes after seeing the two helicopters, they heard a jet approaching. Within twenty seconds, a single A-4 Skyhawk raced by, about fifteen hundred feet above the ground, in a hard left hand turn toward the north.

"Man, he's hauling the mail," said Doc.

"Something's up, and now we know it isn't good," added Willie.

"Why do you say that?" asked Mirela.

"Because he's carrying rocket pods under the wings, and that isn't normal."

"During Cope Thunder and other exercises over land, I think VC-5 keeps one of their A-4's armed and ready to go."

"That's correct, and my guess is someone had to jump out of a jet in an area where MOROs are known to hang out."

"I agree. Nothing else makes sense." They heard a second A-4 approaching, and then watched as it raced by on a northerly heading.

"He doesn't have rocket pods, but I'm sure he has a full magazine of twenty millimeter BBs to shoot at any bad guys."

"Yep."

The caddies found it all fascinating, but the women were hypnotized, almost paralyzed, by what was occurring over their heads and, most likely, in a valley less than thirty miles away.

"All right, Gully, you still have the honors. Show us again how it's done." The four aviators had switched, in an instant, from discussing danger and bad guys not too far away to their friendly, but competitive, golf match waiting patiently for them.

Gully impressed everyone with his golf shots, especially Sharon, who looked at him with very loving eyes. He had been on fire the past four holes.

"You know, Gully, not to interrupt your focus, but if you get five pars or better in a row, you owe everyone watching a drink of their choice at dinner. It's a CAG-Five rule," said Doc.

"Really?" Gully backed away from the ball and looked toward his friends.

"That's right, Gully, it's right up there with walking into an O'Club bar with a hat on. I can't speak for the others, but my choice will be the scotch of Frank Sinatra and the scotch general in Kwangju — Chivas Regal...in a tall tumbler." Willie smiled at his friend and B/N standing by the tee.

"I think that will be my choice too," said Doc.

"Mine three," said Lunker, smiling.

The four women and the caddies didn't know if it was an actual rule or not, but it was engaging and entertaining. In retrospect, they'd all learn that it was vintage naval aviation. New tactics or traditions could be hatched on the fly to ensure a positive outcome for any target — It was an accepted necessity in combat and in any friendly competition.

"Good thing my credit card balance is at zero." Gully confidently smiled and then landed his tee shot about fifteen feet from the hole on the short par three.

"I can taste that drink right now, Gully," said Lunker, "unless you can't actually handle the pressure of two putts that I could make blindfolded."

Gully laughed and wore a big grin as he looked at his bunkroom buddy. "You're up, Lunker." After Gully picked up his tee, he added, "An appetizer of lumpia says you can't get inside of my shot."

"Oooh, Sharon, bet you didn't know you were dating a man-tiger," said Doc, smiling and laughing.

"I've known it since the night we met." She was standing by her man, and Gully loved it.

"Okay, fight's on," said Lunker, stepping up to the tee.

"Aren't you going to kiss me first?" Mirela's comment took everyone by surprise. "In Romania, before two warriors fight, they kiss their damsel of choice."

Lunker walked over to where Mirela was standing and gave her a long kiss, which drew laughs and applause from everyone, especially Eli. He and the other three caddies were thoroughly enjoying this day under a warm South China Sea sun.

"Okay, let me show you how it's done." Lunker addressed the ball and then backed away. "Eli, my trusted friend, where should I aim?"

Unadulterated joy beamed from Eli's weathered face at Lunker's request; they were more than a team —on this day, they could surely teach an old dog new math if they wanted to. "Aim five feet inside Gully ball. Wind carry."

"Very well. Here we go."

Lunker was the best golfer of the four, and he proved it by precisely following Eli's advice. As his ball rolled to a stop about three feet from the hole, he took a bow and then gave Eli a hug as big as he had ever given anyone.

Two hours later, a very delightful stroll in one of the world's most beautiful settings was drawing to a close. Twelve once-upon-a-time strangers had turned four hours into an unforgettable day among dear friends. During the walk under a warm tropical sun, Eli shared the story of his daughter Diwata, and how his friends' efforts quite likely saved her life and, possibly as well, that of her older sister. His gratitude was reflected in the hint of moisture evident in his eyes.

Lito, Romy, and George had joined Eli as the men's caddies of choice. They each had families, and Romy and George had also lost a child to a common childhood illness that was rarely, if ever, fatal across the big ocean to the east. The group's laughter was a common language easily understood. Their dreams were the same as mothers and fathers around the globe, and all twelve loved the sweet taste of cold San Miguel as they sat together at side-by-side picnic tables under a rectangular gazebo.

Distance would soon separate them, but only in a geographical sense. These memories and emotions would be etched in the part of their soul that never sleeps.

"When back, Lunker?"

"Probably sometime in early December, Eli, but right after that I'll be transferring to Pensacola to become a pilot." There was sadness among the joy in Lunker's statement. He'd miss his time with Eli, and he'd miss his time in the right seat. It was rewarding to guide a fast jet flying low to the ground, dodging mountains at night and in bad weather, and then placing ordnance on an unseen target at the exact time specified.

"So, be monkey follow banana like Willie." Everyone laughed out loud at Eli's comment, and none louder than Eli himself.

"That's right, Eli, and the Navy doctors will remove half of my brain when I arrive so I can fit in with the other pilots."

"That's how we get our irresistibly charming and childlike personalities, Lunker." Willie smiled at his friend as he finished his comment.

"So when do we get to see your charming side, Willie. I've seen the child." Tosh gave him a kiss and put her arm across his shoulders.

"Tosh smart funny woman, Willie. Maybe train you." Eli couldn't resist. The distance between cultures and countries and friends was negligible as Willie smiled at Eli and gave him a thumbs up.

"If Lunker, Gully, and I can train you, Willie, Tosh can easily train you," added Doc.

"I already have," said Tosh, without hesitation. "Willie, would you stand up for a second, please."

As Willie stood, Tosh finished her sentence. "See?"

Eli and the other three caddies laughed as hard as Willie's friends as the slightly blushing pilot sat back down.

"Thank you for that fourth law of thermodynamics moment, Willie," said Gully. "I guess that's what a gullible pilot does for his B/N, huh?" Naval aviation's fourth law of thermodynamics was a survival guide for aviators: If the heat is on someone else, then it can't be on you.

"I still have a few things to teach my pilot." Tosh kissed his cheek again.

"Can I borrow your owner's manual for pilots, Tosh?" asked Mirela. "It sounds like I'll need all the help I can get."

"Just hold a banana in front of him and lead him wherever you want him to go.

"Need banana tree for Lunker," said Eli, laughing, as he looked at the special woman with the dark hair and eyes, like those of his wife, sitting next to the golfer he'd miss so much.

"Yes and amen."

"See you tomorrow, Lunker?" Eli assumed the answer, but always asked. These were precious moments that he, too, would miss. There had been many 'Lunkers' during the last four years of the Vietnam War, when he was a still a young man. Two didn't return as expected; he never took an aviator's presence for granted again.

"Yes, of course. We'll be here tomorrow." Golf was secondary; walking in paradise with friends was the savory fruit on the vine.

The group agreed to meet for Mongolian barbeque at six-fifteen that evening. It'd be a few minutes after sunset. Doc called the Chuckwagon and made reservations. Until then, they were free to explore paradise in whatever form paradise presented itself.

Willie and Tosh strolled into the downstairs bar at the Cubi Point Officer's Club a little before five-thirty. Before they went to dinner, she wanted to see the hundreds of squadron plaques adorning the walls of the appropriately named Ready Room Bar, a tradition that dated back to the Vietnam War. The area was about half full of men either having an early dinner or enjoying cocktails before going upstairs to the club's more formal dining room. To Tosh, it appeared that there was very little space on the walls not covered by a plaque.

"Two San Miguels, please, Charlie."

"Rather have clean living, Willie?" he asked with a big grin. Charlie, a Filipino with the same polite, good-humored personality of Eli, had been a bartender at the club since anyone could remember. He had difficulty saying the name Glen Livet, so he simply said clean living. His extraordinary photographic memory also endeared him to everyone who had the pleasure of meeting him.

"We'd better start with cold beer. Maybe get to scotch later." Willie smiled. He'd be worried if Charlie didn't offer his own drink of choice. "I'd like you to meet Tosh. She's from southern California."

Charlie was friendly to everyone. "Always nice meet beautiful woman," he said, "Wish could all be California girls."

The three laughed. "Me in Los Angeles two years ago see sister. She live with husband in Point Mugu."

"That's a beautiful place. I live in San Diego now, but was born and raised less than an hour north of Point Mugu. I hope you had a nice time there, Charlie."

"Wonderful time. Here two cold San Miguel. Please enjoy."

"Thank you very much. We will."

Tosh was intrigued by the history the plaques represented, especially the ones that had combat cruise inscribed on them; most of those included an 'In Memory' section that especially captured her focus and emotions. "It would be easy to think of these men that didn't return as just names, Willie, but I imagine most were your age, or just a few years older."

Willie nodded. "I love looking at all the designs and details, and recognizing names of the Navy's senior officers and those of all ranks that I know personally, and thinking of how they were all once young lieutenants."

"All witty and charming, huh?"

"Yes, ma'am, and good looking, too. Don't forget that." They both laughed.

They continued looking at the walls covered with plaques of all sizes and designs, and all of them created by skilled craftsmen in Subic Bay. Along the way, Willie introduced her to at least a dozen of his friends from the air wing's squadrons, including several Eagles. She laughed and politely declined each time one of them humorously offered to take Willie's place so she could date a "real aviator."

Her eyes caught one plaque in particular. The In Memory box had eight names. They were all lieutenant junior grades or lieutenants; young men in the prime of their life.

"You can't replace this with a photograph, Willie. I hope they preserve these plaques forever."

"I agree, Tosh. They're all special." He was staring at a particular plaque from a year earlier.

Tosh watched him as he stared. "Do you know them?"

Willie slowly nodded as he ran his finger along one of the two names in the plaque's 'In Memoriam' box. "I was in this squadron for a month before I went to flight school. Great guys. One had been married for less than two years...hit the back of the ship on a night landing...but...some days you bite the dog...and some days the dog bites you. That's what he used to say." He stared for a few more moments, and then looked at Tosh and smiled. "Ready to take another trip to the Subic side?"

"I was born ready; isn't that what you say?" She smiled and softly kissed his lips. "Can we take our beer?"

"We can do anything in Subic." He returned the smile and the kiss.

After a short taxi ride, they arrived at the Chuckwagon. Doc and Lauren were the first ones there. After a few minutes of small talk, Doc turned toward Tosh. "Have you had Mongolian barbeque before?"

"No," she answered. "I first heard of it when Willie mentioned it."

"You and Lauren are in for a treat. It's like an Asian buffet cooked right before your eyes," he explained. Before he could say anything more, Lunker, Mirela, Gully, and Sharon exited a taxi less than twenty feet away.

"You guys know the rules; last two couples buy." Doc smiled and greeted them with handshakes and hugs.

"Is everything a competition with you little boys?" asked Sharon, smiling.

"Only if we can rig it so we automatically win." Everyone laughed.

"I was giving Lauren and Tosh the Mongolian barbeque primer before we head over to the grill area," said Doc. The buffet was set up outside the Chuckwagon and faced the calm waters of Subic Bay. "It's simple. Pick any combination of meats and vegetables available, and add it to the large bowl you'll pick up at the start of the food line." He paused to take a sip of beer.

"My personal favorite meat combination is chicken, shrimp, pork, and monkey meat. Once you've done that and picked your vegetables, hand it to the chef..."

"Wait, go back. Monkey meat? Are you joking?"

Doc smiled. "Yep, you caught me, I generally don't add pork if I'm having monkey meat."

He laughed and continued. "Yes, I'm only joking. As I was saying before Sharon went into ventricular fibrillation over monkey meat, once you're done selecting meats and vegetables, hand your bowl to your chef, who'll be standing by the large griddle. He'll tell you about the spices and sauces available, and then you pick whatever combination you want."

"If you like, you can stand back and watch him cook it all together, and then he'll put it in a new bowl when it's done. He'll hand it to you and you're ready to enjoy fine Chuckwagon dining." He smiled.

"This looks great," said Tosh. "I wish we had this in San Diego."

"It's only been here for about five years," said Lunker, "and it originated not in Mongolia, but in Taiwan. CAG told me that last cruise."

As they were going through the line, Gully spotted Tonto, who had been part of the great Misawa typhoon boondoggle. "Tonto, come join us!"

"Hey, Tonto, what a nice surprise," said Sharon, who gave him a hug.

"Mind if I break in line here, guys, between a couple beautiful women?" he asked, smiling.

"So good to see you again." Lauren also gave him a warm hug. "You doing okay?"

"Doing very well. Thank you, Lauren," Tonto said, as he shook hands with the guys and then turned toward the other two women. "You must be Tosh and Mirela. It's a pleasure to finally meet you."

They exchanged light hugs, and then the group focused on selecting their dinner ingredients. As they walked slowly through the line, Sharon turned toward Tonto and spoke quietly.

"Jackie misses you. She tells us that at least once a week, Tonto, but then says she can't handle the anxiety and separation. It makes her sad, but it's the reality she lives with." Jackie had broken up with Tonto shortly after he left Misawa to return to Atsugi.

"I know; I miss her, too." He looked down for a couple moments, and then up again. "I guess it takes a special woman to live with it all."

"The crash just an hour after you flew away really spooked her; it's been obvious since then. She had gone back to the hospital and was there when the pilot was brought in."

"It's okay; it is what it is." He took a deep breath and then smiled. "Tonight, we're celebrating good friends, good food, and happy times here in paradise."

The group of nine sat at a large picnic table that could comfortably hold twelve adults. None of the five men had been to Singapore, so the ladies described what they had been able to see during their one day there. As they did, a waiter arrived with nine glasses filled halfway with a white liquid and a couple ice cubes.

"Stingers for my friends," said Lunker. The group stopped eating as the drinks were handed out, and Tosh asked the question all the women were thinking.

"What's in a Stinger?"

Willie answered. "It's white crème de menthe and brandy here on the Subic side, and vodka replaces brandy at the Cubi O'Club, and more than two will put you on a steep path to being as coordinated as a monkey trying to make love to a football." Everyone laughed at his warning.

"Mmmmm. These are very good." Lauren smiled and raised her glass toward Lunker. "Thank you, Lunker."

"These are almost as good as your Bushwackers in Misawa, Lauren, from what I remember," said Gully.

"Yes, they were delicious and potent, too," confirmed Tonto. "I remember them all too well."

As the group continued eating their Mongolian barbeque, Lauren asked about Ie Shima.

A couple weeks earlier, Willie and Doc had been assigned to spend a week on the small island off Okinawa as range control officers. During their stay, they utilized four local Japanese range employees to assist them and to brighten up the range control tower's expansive viewing platform, which overlooked the East China Sea.

Tonto, Gully, and Lunker discussed what they saw from the air over the five days they bombed at the island known by only a few. At the top of their list was their surprise when they flew by for the first time and saw three young Japanese women in graduation gowns and caps on the range control tower, and a Japanese lady off to the side.

Lunker regaled them with the operations officer's response to the first day's theatrics. "Magic Mann was more than furious; I thought his head was going to explode. And then it got even better when CAG walked in the ready room and asked who was responsible, and Magic just slammed Willie and Doc. He looked pretty smug for about two seconds until CAG said he actually wanted to congratulate whoever came up with what he thought was a great idea." He paused as everyone laughed.

Lunker then continued. "And I swear I thought Magic was actually going to detonate right in front of us as he tried to stay calm in front of CAG."

"Lunker's right. All we needed was a countdown, like T-minus 10...9...8..." said Gully. The laughter continued.

Tonto jumped into the discussion. "Later that day, Lunker, whose name will forever be kept secret as the author, wrote the recipe for a new entrée on the ready room chalk board. It said, Wardroom Special Tonight: Magic Mann burrito: eight ounces of jerk chicken and four ounces of asshole." Everyone at the table laughed. "The skipper and XO even laughed at it before Magic erased it."

"Back in Annapolis, Professor Leydorf was probably laughing and didn't know why," added Doc.

"I think we set a new standard for Leydorf-trained men," said Willie, "on the low end." Professor Leydorf was their electrical engineering instructor at the Naval Academy.

"I wish you all could have met Harumi and our three range control officer personal assistants: Miyako, Shiori, and Reika. They were so wonderful and seemed to always be laughing. They would fit right in with us."

"Especially after a Stinger or two," said Willie.

The group continued to share numerous stories from their backgrounds, and Tonto became intrigued by many of Mirela's stories. "Do you have any sisters just like you?"

"I do," she admitted, "and my sister Ramona is more beautiful and funnier than I'll ever be."

"Do you think she would like me?" he asked in a hopeful tone.

"Most likely, but she really loves to laugh. Can you make her laugh?"

Lunker couldn't resist. "Take off your pants, Tonto. That'll make her laugh until she pees herself."

"Thank you, Lunker. Now we know why Mirela is always laughing when she's around you."

"That's not the only reason," said Mirela. "Sometimes he'll tell a funny joke."

The group laughed at Mirela's jab. "And look, how can I not laugh when he makes his face instantly turn red?" She wasn't letting her date off the hook, although her kiss on his cheek and arm draped over his shoulders confirmed where her heart resided.

"Well, now that we've resolved that burning question, what did you all think of Eli?" asked Lunker, smiling. "Is he just the best, or what?"

"Oh my gosh," said Tosh, "I'm a big jazz fan, and all I kept thinking was that Eli has a smile as warm as the great Satchmo, Louis Armstrong. I just wanted to hug him and stare at that smile all day."

"I think he would have been fine with the hug all day part," said Willie.

Just as he finished his statement, a bellowing voice from the past interrupted their discussion. "The last time I saw Willie Pete and Doc, I was saving their sorry asses from an Air Force paper pusher."

Willie stood and shook hands with Captain Jack Pelham. They both had big smiles, as Doc stood from where he sat.

"Hello again, Doc. Good to see you." They also shook hands.

"Hi there, Jack. It's nice to run into a fellow Leydorf-trained man in the South Seas."

"Oh, no. Please don't tell me you and Willie Pete are LTMs."

"How do you think we wound up in trouble and still got the beautiful women?"

"Speaking of which, why don't you introduce me to your friends, or did Professor Leydorf not teach you the refined social skills he taught me?"

"My friends, I'd like to introduce each of you to the Marine Corps' poster child for dumb ass grunts. The one and only Captain Jack Pelham."

As he was introduced to everyone at the table, another round of Stingers appeared. Willie handed his to the Marine next to him and ordered another one for himself.

"As a senior officer, I think this round and every round is on my plebe Willie here. Hope you have a couple paychecks to cash." Pelham smiled and nodded at Willie. Pelham was a senior at the Naval Academy when Willie and Doc were freshmen.

"Hmmm," said Willie, "I wonder if I can do that math in my head, or if I'll need my slide rule to figure out the dollar damages for the meal."

"Slide rule? Who even has a slide rule anymore," questioned Lauren, smiling, but wondering how a slide rule made it into the discussion.

"Leydorf-trained men," answered Doc, with pride in his voice, "who were part of the last Naval Academy class to be issued slide rules, and you're looking at three of the finest examples of LTMs ever produced sitting right in front of you." As he finished his proclamation, he and Willie gave high fives to each other across the table, and then to Jack.

"You guys want to clue us in to this new designation, this LTM thing," asked Tosh, still laughing, "or should we just assume it randomly came in the mail one day."

Doc lowered his voice slightly, both in volume and tone, and spoke reverently, as if he was in church. "Tosh, please, we take being Leydorf-trained men seriously. Only a select group of men can make the claim of being so trained. It's a cherished honor that must be referred to in the most respectful, but hushed, tones. You certainly don't want to embarrass anyone sitting nearby who may have to admit to his friends or a date that he isn't an LTM."

Glenn Leydorf was a grocery store clerk who worked his way through night school at the University of Toledo. During World War Two, as one of the country's early experts in radar systems, he was commissioned an officer in the Navy and, despite requesting a combat assignment numerous times, was handpicked to teach the new art of radar systems at the Massachusetts Institute of Technology for the duration of the war. Professor Leydorf desperately wanted to go overseas so he could have a direct impact on the war effort.

As it turned out, he did. Many historians claim that radar won the war. There was truth to that axiom. During World War Two, battles, and especially dogfights, were overwhelmingly won by the side that was the first to obtain a visual sighting of their foe — enemy airplanes, ships, or submarines. First sightings by Allied forces exponentially increased after the introduction of radar to the battlefield, and especially as it related to the German Luftwaffe. After the end of the war, Professor Leydorf was offered a position as an instructor at the Naval Academy and, ultimately, became chairman of the electrical engineering department.

"Second class year, our junior year, everyone was required to take two semesters of double-E. Even though calculators were allowed, professor Leydorf required all his basic double-E classes to use slide rules instead of calculators. His logic was that we should learn to do math in our heads, as a backup to blindly trusting whatever answer was displayed on a calculator, a gauge, or any other instrument or display." Willie paused, and Doc picked up the conversation.

"He believed it would not only help us in all we did, but that it may save us one day. To his credit, he was right. Professor Leydorf's philosophy has been a life saver on several occasions, especially in the jet," Doc admitted, truthfully. Some of the airborne moments that he was recalling had been with the pilot sitting across from him.

Doc continued. "That was the key to being a Leydorf-trained man. He taught us what was important, what would keep us safe and out of trouble. I really do believe that."

"Yes, he did," agreed Willie, "and we're thankful for his philosophical focus because we didn't know shit about electrical engineering." Everyone laughed as Doc shifted the conversation back to Jack Pelham.

"Were you up in Crow Valley today?"

"Yeah. How'd you know?" Jack was curious. They were trying to keep the episode quiet, especially regarding the role of the base's security team.

"We saw the helicopters and a couple A-4s heading north while we were on the golf course. Kind of hard to miss rocket

224

pods on a jet and armed Marines in a helicopter. What was going on?"

"I thought you would've heard. The Prowler that was on station had a fire, and the four guys had to jump out right in an area where MOROs are suspected to hang out."

"Did they get out okay?" asked Tonto.

"Yep, but one has a busted leg. Otherwise, minimal injuries to the other three."

"Well, at least everyone is back safely." The four women appeared to be frozen as they took it all in.

"We took a small squad and a couple Negritos up there in case they needed us. We stayed airborne the entire time — never had to touch any dirt. I think we'll soon learn that the Negritos working for the range did exactly what they're paid to do and did it very well."

"Do we want to know what they did, assuming they did?"

"They were just keeping the peace." He smiled. "No. You don't want to know. It'd probably give you nightmares."

"Ever think you may need to be institutionalized after this tour, Jack?" asked Willie.

"It'd be nothing new. We were all institutionalized for four years at Annapolis, and that includes you two characters." He laughed along with the entire group. "But hey, I'm meeting a few guys inside. It was nice meeting each of you." He then turned to his former plebes and stared sentimentally at them, proud of their accomplishments. "Glad to know you are both doing well."

He shook Willie and Doc's hands, and then looked at the group. "Can you keep my plebes out of trouble while they're here so I don't have to rescue them, too?"

After Captain Jack Pelham left, Mirela spoke first. "That's crazy."

"It wasn't that long ago that Lunker and CAG almost had to jump out one night," Doc reminded them.

"Yeah, thankfully it worked out okay. I wasn't looking forward to getting my freshly-pressed flight suit wet," Lunker reminded them in a sober tone, and then laughed.

"We didn't want you to get your freshly-pressed flight suit wet, either," said Willie.

"Well, hey. I remember you and Doc having one of those nights during our last at-sea period. The odds were substantial that you were going swimming," Lunker reminded them.

"Doc kept feeding me lots of ripe bananas."

"Yeah, that's right. Had to keep the monkey distracted while the jet was falling apart."

"What happened?" asked Sharon.

Doc spoke first and slowly. "Well, it was a dark and stormy night." Everyone laughed.

Lunker was laughing, too, and his memory accurately supported Doc's comment. "He's half right. It wasn't that stormy, but it was as black as a black horse's ass."

"I think it was darker than that," added Tonto. "I was out there with Pistol, and we both agreed that we needed a new color that was blacker than black." He smiled as everyone continued laughing.

Doc continued. "Most of the pilots were able to get aboard on their first try, but a couple Phantoms and a Corsair were really struggling. The deck was pitching more than usual, and there was a large cloudbank overhead at fifteen hundred feet that covered about three quarters of the sky. The rest of the sky was clear, and there was no moon; it was somewhere on the other side of the world.

Willie picked up the discussion. "The net effect was not only a very black night, but a lot of the pilots had vertigo, which is when a pilot's internal sense of up, down, left, and right doesn't agree with what his airplane is really doing. In this case, the way the sky appeared from the cockpit, a pilot flying toward the ship on the final approach really needed to keep his eyes only on the instruments. If he peeked outside, he could easily believe, by what his eyes were seeing and telling him, that his plane was in a right hand turn and climbing, when he was really straight and level. That is the worst possible combination at the ship at night — having your eyes tell you that you need to turn away from the direction the ship is heading and, worse, push the nose over and descend."

Doc stepped back into the story. "All that Willie described is to say that a few pilots were destined to struggle, and likely struggle, every pass until they could finally get their jet home."

He took a sip of his Stinger and continued. "We call that a night in a barrel, and every pilot will have at least one, usually on some black horse's ass kind of night, but some will have theirs on a perfectly fine night with a bright full moon. You never know when it's going to be your turn." He paused for a second. "I remember Willie's."

Willie nodded at a somber reality known to every Navy pilot. "Doc's correct. I had mine a month before the night we're talking about," he confessed. "I thought Doc was going to shoot me before I could kill us both."

"It looked more like he was having a night in an oak barrel full of whiskey, but unfortunately we only had one pass to land," admitted Doc. "Land on the first try or go swimming."

"I remember it well," said Lunker, smiling as if it were just a game. "We were already drawing straws in the ready room to see who got your Sony Walkman." Willie could feel Tosh stiffen as he said it.

"Thank you for that vote of confidence, Lunker. Maybe I need to ask for an assignment to the training command so I can be one of your flight instructors."

"By the way, Willie," interjected Tonto, "I drew the smallest straw." He smiled at his friend.

"So what happened that night?" asked Tosh, as she held Willie's hand a little tighter.

"We tanked one of the Phantoms and then the Corsair. The Corsair's pilot was able to land on his next pass, but the

Phantom kept going around and around. In the meantime, the other Phantom that was initially struggling had, fortunately, safely landed aboard on his trick-or-treat pass."

"What is a trick-or-treat pass?" Mirela was curious.

"Yeah, I was curious about that, too," added Lauren.

"It's when a pilot either has to land on the carrier or, if he doesn't for any reason, he's required to get fuel from an airborne tanker. On the night we're talking about, we were conducting what is called 'blue water ops', which means we have no land-based airport to send a jet to. The only landing area for a jet when we're blue water is Midway's angled deck. That's it." Lunker didn't need to point out that there actually was one other option, which was to eject from the aircraft and land in the sea.

The women were learning more than they wanted to learn, especially with Midway, docked nearby, undergoing repairs from an accident on a devilish night at sea.

Willie then continued. "On each of the Phantom's attempts to land, we set ourselves so that, if he boltered, meaning he didn't catch one of Midway's three wires, all he had to do as he flew off the angled deck was to look up and to his left, at his ten o'clock position, and we'd be there, twelve hundred feet above the ocean, with our refueling hose extended, waiting for him. Sounds easy enough." Willie laughed. "If it was only that easy on a black night, low to the water."

All the guys laughed as well. The women apparently saw little humor in it; they didn't realize laughing at cheating death was much easier than thinking about the terror of it all. Year after year, a few pilots inadvertently flew into the water on such a rendezvous.

Doc then added a statement that got each of the ladies' attention; Lauren's and Tosh's more than anyone. "The next time the Phantom was at a trick-or-treat fuel state, it boltered, and this is where it became much more our nightmare than his." The table was silent, waiting for Willie or Doc to continue speaking. Even Lunker appeared tense, and he knew how the story ended.

Willie began telling the rest of the story after a sip of his Stinger. "The Phantom's pilot made five or six stabs at our refueling basket, but missed. The wind was steady, so it was just his nerves that were getting the better of him. He was a first cruise pilot, like me, and I'm sure he felt like every set of eyes on the ship was on him."

Willie paused for a moment; he, too, knew the pressure of a night in the barrel. "They probably were, since there are television monitors in every ready room and work space, and everyone on the boat has a stake in what's happening up on the flight deck and in the air."

"We were about two miles behind the boat, flying downwind, heading in the opposite direction of the ship's heading, when he finally engaged our refueling basket, which was a relief to everyone." Willie took another sip of his Stinger as Doc picked up the story again.

"In the meantime, one of our bombers with a refueling pod was redirected to act as a backup tanker, so we had plenty of gas in the air as we were hauling this fighter pilot around in a sky that was like flying in a bowl of black bean soup. We were told to give him thirty-five hundred pounds of gas. As we passed the fuel to him, Willie began a left hand turn back in toward the ship and intercepted the glide slope just inside three miles from landing. We were right where we wanted to be to drop the Phantom off in perfect position to land. We have a counter on our instrument panel so we can see how much fuel he's received from us and, as the gauge hit thirty-three hundred pounds, he unexpectedly popped out of the basket."

"Just as Willie told him on the radio that he was within two hundred pounds of his expected fuel and to continue his approach on his own, we suddenly felt our jet's nose violently lurch upward, as if an invisible hand had grabbed the tail of our jet and viciously pulled it down."

Doc glanced quickly at Willie. Their eyes met in a place that was only known to them, a place in a black sky that had once been their worst nightmare.

"I pushed the stick forward to get the nose back down, and we saw the Phantom directly in front of us, nose high," said Willie. "It looked like he was going straight up. We couldn't have been more than forty or fifty feet from hitting him as we flew directly under him and through his jet wash, which put us in what felt like out-of-controlled flight. I centered the controls and we were stable within a few seconds. That was when it hit us that the asshole had jammed his throttles full forward, reengaged our basket, flew under us and then pulled up right in front of our jet, which is when he ripped the hose right out of our jet."

"Yes and amen," punctuated Doc. "The dickhead was flying away with the same basket stuck on his damn refueling probe that he could barely engage for the previous two minutes."

Willie looked at his friend and cracked a smile before he resumed relaying the drama. "Very astute and colorful observation there, Doc. As I was about to say..." Willie stopped speaking as all the guys laughed; he noticed Tosh, Lauren and Mirela just stared as they absorbed a part of naval aviation that had always applied to someone else. Lunker and CAG's close call, months earlier, suddenly became very real as well.

"As I was about to say," he repeated, "two of our four hydraulic pumps went to zero immediately. Doc hit the emergency shutoff to the refueling system to save our gas, and, at the same time, declared an emergency with the ship and explained our predicament. I lowered our landing gear and flaps and slats right away, since they're all powered by hydraulics, and saw Doc pull the handle to drop our tailhook as I turned downwind to begin maneuvering to intercept the glideslope to landing."

Willie glanced at Doc and then continued. "We were a little under three miles from the ship and on glide slope when Doc reported to the ship that we had lost a third hydraulic pump and were down to only one hydraulic pump, and it was dropping quickly. If all hydraulics were lost, I couldn't realistically turn the jet left or right or make it go up or down in a manner that would allow us to land successfully."

Doc looked back at his friend. "I thought the way I informed the ship of our status was a nice way of telling Willie he needed to do whatever it took to get us on deck on the approach unless, of course, he really had a desire to go swimming or maybe die on a black horse's ass night instead of eating cheeseburgers."

The guys shared another laugh at Doc's comment as each of the women sat in concerned silence. It didn't matter that they knew everything turned out well; they each had various levels of distressed looks on their faces, even Sharon. At the same time, Willie leaned in toward Tosh and quietly said, "Hey, you're squeezing the blood out of my hand." Her pressure eased ever so slightly.

Willie added a couple more comments. "Two miles from the ship, about a minute from landing, Doc reminded me that a Leydorf-trained man shouldn't and couldn't screw up the landing. He said I had to rise above all the external factors and pressure or I'd lose my LTM bragging rights forever."

"Not true," said Doc. "Not true at all. What I said was, you're Leydorf-trained. Don't fuck this up." The group laughed as Doc raised his glass to Willie, who tapped it with his own.

"Needless to say," Willie continued, laughing loudly along with the others, "even though I didn't know up from down, it all turned out fine, and twenty minutes later Doc and I were in the wardroom having the best tasting cheeseburgers and fries we'd ever had." He wore the grin of someone who had successfully cheated death. "That night was just another fine day of Midway magic." Willie drank the remainder of his almost empty Stinger.

A tragedy at sea had brought this group together in a tropical paradise, and now the discussion of another emergency on a dark night was bonding them even closer — everyone involved in operations at sea or in the air has a stake in the outcome, even those not physically there.

"Now," said Lunker, "what neither Willie nor Doc has said is that while we were all sitting together having cheeseburgers in the dirty shirt wardroom, the pilot that ripped off their basket and hose came in and wanted to know who was flying the tanker. When Willie spoke up and said he was the pilot, this idiot jackass told Willie that if he had been smoother flying the tanker, he wouldn't have dropped out of the basket and then almost caused an accident."

Tonto spoke up and articulated each word slowly. "Let's just say that, at that moment, Willie became instantly homicidal." Everyone laughed as he added, "Fortunately for him, Lunker grabbed Willie as he bolted from his chair and held him back."

"Unfortunately for the Marine pilot, it was strike three," added Lunker. "Twice before, his marginal airmanship skills had nearly caused catastrophic accidents. So, as a result, his commanding officer politely asked him to turn in his wings and request an occupational skill not involving flying, which he did."

"What I remember after that night," recalled Doc, "was that we had an impromptu meeting of the Far East Film Society, and Willie became very intimate with mister Jose Cuervo's tequila, the bunkroom buddy hiding in a TV we don't talk about."

"Good memory, Doc," noted Lunker. "We were watching the movie 'The Good, The Bad, And The Ugly' and Willie, with a little help from his friend Jose, went through all three of those in the course of about thirty minutes."

It brought more laughter and a toast from the guys, as if the entire story of a horrifying night was just another comedy worthy of a gathering of the Far East Film Society. The women smiled, but were mostly quiet. A discussion that terrified and unnerved them was remarkably cathartic to the men they loved.

After leaving the Chuckwagon, Tonto took a taxi to the Cubi O'Club, and the four couples walked toward the pier where Midway was tied up. A bright full moon was overshadowed by brighter lights that turned the damaged areas of the ship into daylight. Skilled Filipino workers and numerous technicians from a ship repair facility in California crawled over the carrier, performing their own kind of magic. It was noisy. The legion of sounds — metal being cut or riveted, the pounding of hammers, a multitude of voices shouting directions or acknowledgements, vehicles driving up and down the pier, cranes lifting and lowering supplies, including weapons — impregnated the air as it gave the old carrier a new life.

Amidst the activity, several dozen local vendors were selling t-shirts and other Filipino crafts by the pier's entrance. The most popular shirts remained the ones with 'Midway vs. Cactus; Midway Won' written on them.

Thirty minutes later, the four couples shared two taxis and proceeded back to the Cubi side. The short drive between the Subic side and the Cubi side was now familiar, as was the incessant 'Binictican come in' call from the dispatcher. It had been a busy day for each of the passengers. To the women, in particular, it had been twelve hours that introduced and exposed each of them to the unforgiving elements associated with carrier aviation that were, to their surprise, much more commonplace than they'd ever imagined.

Before they went their separate ways, they agreed to a simple schedule for the next day: meet at the front of the BOQ at nine, and then take taxis to the Chuckwagon for breakfast. Gully asked if it was a real nine o'clock, or a 'nine-thirty' nine o'clock; a real nine o'clock was agreed upon. They would tee off somewhere around ten o'clock for nine holes of golf. Eli would understand the abbreviated round; after golf they planned to spend the rest of the afternoon at Grande Island.

Like a beautiful Greek sea nymph, Grande Island rose from the beautiful blue waters halfway between the entrance to Subic Bay and the half-moon shaped land mass that contained the trifecta of Olongapo, Naval Station Subic Bay, and Naval Air Station Cubi Point, huddled together at the northeast end of the bay's nine-mile long body of water. The island was perfectly located to welcome arriving ships with open arms and, later, bid their departure to the mighty ocean with fair winds and following seas.

The one-hundred acre Navy-operated resort sat like a lone sentry in the middle of Subic Bay, and its pork-chop shape included beautiful white beaches along the northern and eastern shores, perfect for Navy sailors and their families. Along with its tranquil and relaxing beaches, the island's jungle interior included several hiking trails that meandered among long abandoned six-inch cannons and other military fortifications that were strategically placed there in the early 1900's as a first line of defense for Subic Bay.

Grande Island was a sparkling gem in the middle of Subic Bay — a peaceful and restorative setting for families and couples to relax, be spoiled, and, most especially, forget the inherent dangers that were never far away. At least, that was always the expectation.

CHAPTER TEN

It Only Hurts When You're Awake
Mid-to-Late Summer, 1980

Willie looked at the clock as he felt Tosh stirring; it was five-thirty, about twenty minutes before sunrise, and pitch black in their room. He felt her ease herself away from their bed, and then heard her enter the bathroom. It was all he consciously absorbed before slipping back into dreamland.

They had skipped the Cubi O'Club's Ready Room Bar the previous evening, knowing it was a place that habitually turned a well-intentioned 'one drink only' pledge into a disastrously long night. Instead, they cuddled and played and played and cuddled, until Tosh asked again about Willie's dark and frightful night. He soothed her fears; it happened, but it rarely happened, he assured her. It was likely, he had told her truthfully, that it was a once-in-a-career episode. She then settled softly into his arms and fell asleep.

Willie heard a clicking sound, and mentally sensed it was part of a dream, but forced his eyes open anyway. His mind couldn't comprehend what his sleepy eyes were seeing for several long seconds but, once it did, he jolted upright and stood next to the bed, grabbing for his boxer shorts and a shirt.

"What are you doing, Tosh?" he asked as he next put on a pair of jeans. "Where are you going?"

"I have to go home, Willie," she confessed in a sad voice. New tears streaming down her cheeks flowed over the old tracks of tears from barely ten minutes earlier.

Willie was confused. "Is everything okay? Can I help?"

"I can't do this, Willie, this life. I want it so badly, but I can't." Her tears were heartbreaking enough, but the inconsolable tone of her voice roared in its emotions. She walked toward him; they met in the middle of the large room, and she hugged him close.

"Oh my God, Willie, I wanted this so much, you don't know. I thought I could be strong enough, and it all felt so right. I love you, I so love you, and I love the heart of a young boy and all his dreams, but I'd rather remember what it was like to have once loved you than live every day with the fear of becoming your widow." He continued holding her tightly as her tears soaked his right shoulder, and her body was mostly limp, relying on him for support.

"I don't know how you handle the ups and downs, the danger and death, or even this blend of incredible beauty and the miserable poverty right next to each other. You always say the great unknown is still the great unknown, and you say it with such confidence, but to me the great unknown is just too great." Her voice was trembling and her body was releasing small convulsions in a steady stream.

Willie was in shock, and her words tore at his heart, but he responded to this personal crisis the same way he had responded to problems in the air. The priority was to deal first with the items that would cause the greatest harm.

"When bad things happen, we're trained to handle them, Tosh. We're trained to fix the unfixable." He was desperate to reassure her, to plead his case, as they continued to hold each other tightly.

"I know that, Willie, I do, but it doesn't make me feel any better. One day you may not be able to handle it, or someone else may not be able to handle it, and you could get hurt or killed, even if you did everything right, like that night another airplane almost caused you and Doc to crash. On a pitch black night, Willie, over a dark ocean that could be your grave, and you'll be out there again as soon as you leave here."

"Tosh, at Annapolis, and in flight school, our instructors told students who wanted to quit, don't quit today. Quit tomorrow, but not today. I'm asking you to not leave today. Leave tomorrow. I know this has all been overwhelming. I understand that. I understand that what I do is dangerous, but you know what we have is wonderful. I love you, Tosh. Please don't leave today. If you still have to go, leave tomorrow." Willie's pleading eyes were moist. He could instinctively tell she wasn't going to change her mind, and the stabbing pain of the inevitable was pulverizing his heart as he quickly dressed.

"I've already made arrangements, Willie. It's why I got up early. The only way I could be strong is if I did it alone. The Navy is sending one of their cars to take me to Manila, and it should be here in a few minutes." She hugged him and kissed him as if it was the first time, but passion couldn't override her terrified heart.

"I'd like it if you would walk me to the car, but I'll understand if you don't want to."

"Of course I will." Willie heard the sound of his voice as he answered her, but he was still numb, in disbelief, and he wanted so much for it all to be a bad dream. He was dying inside. "Here, give me your bags."

"Thank you, Willie." She smiled through her tears.

They arrived in front of the BOQ where an unmarked blue Navy sedan was waiting. The driver loaded her bags into the trunk.

"Please tell everyone how much I enjoyed meeting them, and how much I will miss them." She hugged him tightly.

Willie nodded. He kept hoping it was just one big early morning illusion, but her touch confirmed that it was real.

"I do love you, flyboy. You will always occupy a very special place in my heart that will be yours and only yours." She kissed him a final time.

She eased into the back seat as Willie held the door, pausing before he closed it. "I'm glad we had the chance to dance, Tosh, even if it was only for a short time." His brain conceded this was goodbye, but his heart still had one more thing to convey. "The feeling of loving you is a feeling I will never forget."

As he closed the door, she could see tears in his eyes through her own tears. They met by the waters of the Pacific on a beautiful sunny morning; they were saying goodbye the same way.

Tosh glanced back a lingering single time as the taxi began moving, and then she was gone.

It wasn't supposed to end this way. Willie stood on the hillside in front of the BOQ and watched as the car made its way down to the bottom by the hangars and the runway. He watched as it traveled around the long half moon shape of the bay to the Subic side, and then followed the sedan as it slowly passed through the base's main gate, crossed the shit river bridge, and disappeared all alone onto Magsaysay Drive.

The warmth of the rising sun, the same sun that was setting over a western horizon to those on the California coast, touched his right cheek as she rode out of sight.

"Should we wait for Willie?" asked Gully. It was five minutes after nine on a typical early fall morning in Subic Bay, except for the lack of rain. The sun was already high in the sky; a warm, humid breeze, peppered with the smell from across the bay, smothered the land. It had been remarkably dry for three days in what was normally one of the three wettest months of the year.

The four couples had agreed to meet in front of the BOQ at nine. It was now eight minutes after nine, and only three couples were present. Two taxis were sitting nearby, patiently waiting to drive them across the bay.

"I'll go to the front desk and call his room," offered Doc.

Doc returned two minutes later, wearing a look somewhere between concern and shock. "The front desk clerk said Willie checked out of his room a little after six this morning."

"Why would he do that?" asked Lunker, barely letting Doc finish his statement.

"He said a Navy driver took Tosh to Manila about ten minutes before he checked out, and that she had been crying."

"What?" asked Lauren. "Maybe there's an emergency back in California with her family."

The group stood in silence for a minute. "That doesn't make sense," said Gully. "If it was her family or a problem at work, Willie would be here right now, telling us about it. Something's not right."

"Gully's right," said Mirela, "or Willie would have traveled with her to Manila; there'd be no reason for him not to."

"Last evening she seemed very tense and anxious during the conversation about the jet that almost caused you to crash, Doc. Maybe that pushed her over the edge," offered Sharon.

Doc responded quickly. "I'll have the taxi drop me off at the ship and see if he's in the bunkroom or the ready room. You can order something for me."

Fifteen minutes later, Doc was quickly walking down the long passageway that led to Bunkroom Eight, crossing through a dozen open hatches before arriving at the Midway Oasis.

Willie was fully clothed, but asleep on his upper bunk, with his bunk curtain closed. "Willie. Wake up," said Doc, as he slid the curtain back and shook his friend. The room was otherwise empty.

He slowly opened his eyes; they were puffy and red. "Hey."

"What's going on?"

Willie took a deep breath. "I think I'm gonna go jump off the shit river bridge." Doc laughed ever so slightly. "It isn't funny, Doc; I'm serious."

"Is everything okay with Tosh? What's wrong?"

"She left."

"I know she left; the front desk clerk told me. Something happen at home?"

"She said she couldn't handle the stress, Doc, the stress of the cruise and the danger and the not knowing, the waiting for the call that may or may not come." His voice was strained. "I couldn't talk her into staying just one more day, just one more day. It was all I asked, but her mind was made up." Willie glanced at his alarm clock. "She's on the airplane now."

Willie closed his eyes again. It hurt to think, or even to be alive. He just wanted to hear her voice, feel her touch and the kiss of her lips; he wanted to smell her delicious scent that filled his heart with beautiful watercolors, and listen to her laugh. He was lost, abandoned. Time was painfully slow; each second without Tosh was ten minutes long. If only he could sleep for a few months, maybe then he would wake up and discover it was just an agonizingly long bad dream.

"What can I do?" asked Doc, his friend for over seven years.

"Go and enjoy your time with Lauren." Willie reached into his pocket. "Here, give this to the caddy I would be using today if I was on the course. He shouldn't have to suffer because of my pain." He handed Doc two twenty peso bills and a ten peso bill. "That'll make him smile."

"Okay. I'll check back before we leave for Grande Island."

"Thanks for coming by, Doc. No need to check on me. I just need to sleep for a couple years." He closed his eyes.

"I understand, Willie. I'll see you in 1982."

"Sounds good. I'll be much better by then." He opened his eyes and offered a partial smile. "Hey, tell Gully I'll be fine. We'll have a good flight tomorrow; I just need to get rid of this terrible monster stomping on my heart."

"Get some rest, Willie. We'll get through this together. I'll see you soon."

"Okay. Have a fun time. I may be up for dinner if you don't mind a third wheel."

"You and Tonto can be a couple — but no holding hands." Doc smiled. "I'll check with you when we get back."

"Hey, Doc?"

"Yeah?"

"Thanks again for checking on me. That's what classmates do."

"Leydorf-trained friends, too."

"LTFs. He'd be proud of you, Doc."

"We cheated death together, Willie. We got through that; you'll get through this. I'm here any time you need me."

"I know that. Thanks." Willie closed his eyes again.

Doc walked the fairly short distance from Midway to the Chuckwagon. A breakfast burrito had just arrived for him. "Hey, Gully, Willie wants you to be a good B/N and throw him off the shit river bridge this afternoon."

"What?!"

"How's he doing?" asked Lunker.

"He'll be okay; he just needs to get through the shock of Tosh leaving. I don't think he saw it coming at all." He paused. "He'll feel better after a quick dip in the river."

Lunker and the ladies laughed; Gully looked serious.

"What caused her to leave, Doc. Did he tell you?" Gully was concerned for his friend and pilot.

"The same thing that kills too many relationships — separations and the angst and fear that go with each one of them, made much worse by the waiting, hoping no one in uniform will ever knock at your door. It's always toughest on the women and the kids at home. Always."

All three women nodded without consciously realizing they were nodding.

"He says he'll be ready to fly tomorrow, though, so not to worry, Gully. He's looking forward to you two having a good flight."

An hour later, Eli was puzzled when his friends arrived at the golf course. "Where Willie and Tosh?" he asked Lunker.

"Tosh left, Eli. She's flying back to California."

"What wrong?"

"Time apart. Time at sea. Fear of an accident and someone dying. A man they love never coming home again. All the above, Eli." He paused briefly. "It's a tough life for a woman."

Eli nodded. "She right. See many divorce men from ship come here play golf. Sad for Willie. I like Tosh, but she worry yesterday helicopters flying. I see it. Worry men get hurt. Maybe die."

Lunker smiled and agreed. "You're a smart man, Eli. It's why you're my number one."

Eli's facial expression spoke several volumes of gratitude. "Always glad see you and help you be better golfer, Lunker. You help me when children sick. I help you if you need. Never want anything happen to you or friends. Or Mirela, Lauren, Sharon." He paused. "Or Tosh, too."

His sentiment wrapped around the group like a warm embrace, and then Eli's tone turned more serious. He stared at the golfer he would miss the most of all those he had known. "Be careful, Lunker. One day soon will be last time together. Don't want it come early before time. Want to say goodbye right way. Tosh worry same."

The entire group soon put danger behind them and made the nine holes enjoyable in a way that spread the fun. The golfers hit the first shot, the caddies hit the second shot, the golfers hit any remaining shots to get the ball to the green, and

242

the ladies did all the putting. They saw no monkeys, but that was fine. They were having as much fun as a greenside gaggle of monkeys would have anyway.

Later, Grande Island was everything they hoped it would be. They enjoyed the long stretches of sandy beaches; they hiked inland jungle trails once patrolled by Japanese soldiers almost forty years before; and they saw artifacts from that ugly war, including large rusted guns and concrete bunkers. They sat under a gazebo and enjoyed cold San Miguel beer and snacks.

Large, dark cumulus clouds looked menacing, but they stayed to the north as the ferry docked back at Subic Bay's pier just after four o'clock. The men wanted to check on Willie while they were nearby, so the couples opted to walk the short distance to where Midway floated at rest. Midway's flight deck and hangar bay were buzzing with activity. The Navy's Pacific Fleet commander had authorized repairs and upgrades to numerous parts of the ship while she was in port, instead of waiting until she docked in Yokosuka again. It was for good reason; the price tag was significantly less in the Philippines than in Japan.

Before they reached the steps leading up to the quarterdeck, they spotted Socks and Chicklips walking toward them. After introducing the women to Chicklips and making small talk with both of them, Doc asked what everyone was most concerned with.

"Have you seen Willie today?"

"Yeah," said Socks, "He rolled through the ready room about forty-five minutes ago; said he was heading into town." He paused. "He told us about Tosh."

"Did he say where he was going?" asked Lunker.

Chicklips shook his head. "No. Said he had an early dinner in the wardroom and just needed to get out, take a walk, and let his head clear." He paused. "Is everything okay?"

"Yeah, we promised him we'd catch up with him. We're running a little late." Lunker told a white lie so as not to alarm anyone. He had an inkling where Willie was headed.

"Great seeing each of you again. Make sure you tell Marti I'm behaving myself." Socks smiled; his last comment was directed to Lauren and Sharon, two of Marti's roommates in Misawa.

"Let's prove it. Let's take a photo," said Lauren. She handed her camera to Doc, who took a photo of Socks with Lauren, Sharon, and Mirela.

"Thanks, Lauren. I guess the next time I see you we'll be in a new year. Doc and I are planning to fly to Misawa at the end of cruise, but you probably already know that."

"I do, and I can't wait, but I'm focused on today and the next few days!"

"Me, too," agreed Doc.

"Catch you later," said Socks, smiling as he waved goodbye.

"It was nice finally meeting you all. Hope you enjoy your time here," added Chicklips, as he and Socks headed for dinner.

As the two men walked away, Lunker looked at the group. "Game plan time. I'm willing to bet Willie's at one of two places we've all been to before."

Gully added critical details. "Sunset is just before six, an hour and forty minutes away, and Magsaysay probably isn't crowded right now, so..."

"We're boys, girls, and Lunker on a mission from God," said Doc, interrupting and bastardizing a line from Blues Brothers, one of the Far East Film Society's most popular movies. "Next stop: Old West Number Two." They all laughed, even in their concern.

To save precious daylight minutes, the three couples jumped into two taxis at the head of a short line of vehicles idling by the end of the pier. The drivers loved making twenty-five pesos for barely three minutes of work.

They walked quickly across the shit river bridge without slowing down; they'd have many more opportunities to enrich the children standing by the water, which they'd gladly do.

Old West Number Two didn't yield Willie, but it did yield a single cold San Miguel for everyone and a surprise. As they stood near the bar's entrance and looked among the crowd for Willie, who wasn't there, they were surprised at whom they did recognize on the club's stage.

Two of Midway's most valued chief petty officers, one a master chief and one a senior chief, both of them incredibly skilled and beloved by everyone, were on stage, standing among the band and singing along. They both worked on the carrier's flight deck and had begun serving on the flight decks of aircraft carriers during World War Two. Together, they had loyally served the nation for over seventy-six years through the great World War, Korea, Vietnam, and many conflicts without names. They were storied legends, like Midway herself — real national treasures who created tens of thousands of brave, dedicated men from inexperienced boys. In fact, they had each been on operational tours of duty for almost eighty percent of their time in the Navy — nearly sixty-one years at sea between them; and still, the oldest of the two was only fifty-seven years old. They had given far more than their fair share. One day into the future, Midway would become a popular museum and continue floating in Pacific waters. These two would simply go home with their memories, a modest pension, and the appreciation of a grateful nation, of whom only a few knew their names.

What made their presence remarkably unique on this day was that they were each wearing nothing but cowboy boots, a cowboy hat, and a smile from ear to ear as they danced to the music. Their value and sacrifices to the nation could forgive their cathartically restorative method of remaining sane. The band seemed oblivious to their presence; they played through it all.

The ladies laughed. "You have to blow off steam somehow," said Sharon, 'and they're not bad dancers, either."

"I agree," said Lunker. "These guys are authentic legends." He quickly summarized their long history of extraordinary service. They all laughed and agreed, even as the dark night sky was still almost an hour away. What they didn't know was that the oldest of the two, a master chief petty officer, was one of the two brave men who dangled over the side of Midway, supported above the ocean only by a fire hose wrapped around him as he sprayed water into the gaping hole made by the impact.

"Only in Olongapo does the unbelievable and absurd make perfect sense," asserted Gully to the ladies. They each agreed without any reservation, and it was only their second day in the legendary town.

"Now we know for sure that we are standing where the latitude of a foreign legion meets the longitude of unbelievable sights," said Doc.

"It's the wild, wild, west," Mirela reminded them, laughing. Very little in the world surprised her anymore, but this did.

"Then that makes Midway the sheriff," said Doc.

"And you should all be famous or in jail," added Lauren, "or both." The laughter from the group signed and sealed the moment.

The group of six stayed for five more minutes to listen to the band's rendition of On The Road Again. The two Midway sailors on stage, joined by three Filipino women, danced and sang, proudly and loudly, replacing on the road again, every time it came up in the song, with "on the boat" again.

As the song ended and the two men on stage returned to their table and dressed themselves, the group departed for Reggae Island, the club at which, they felt certain, would be where they found an obviously distressed Willie.

They were right. After crossing two dirt side streets, they entered the barely half full club and immediately saw Willie sitting on a bench that ran along the left side. He was no more than ten feet from the stage, sitting alone, leaning back, and listening to a reggae band comprised of five Filipino men with dreadlocks; Po City Rastas — that wasn't their name, but it could have been.

He looked relaxed as he sat holding a large pitcher of liquid on his lap, swaying ever so slightly, left and right, to the beat of the music, a rendition of the song Buffalo Soldier that sounded as if Bob Marley himself was on stage. The women assumed Willie's detached posture was a good sign.

Doc stared at his best friend. "Oh my God! I think he's drinking Mojo!" Doc's alarming tone surprised all three ladies.

"Shit!" echoed Lunker. "Oh, shit! This isn't good. Shit!" They walked quickly toward where he sat.

"I think he has a double Mojo, Lunker. That's a large pitcher, and it looks like it's almost half gone," observed Gully as they neared Willie. He'd tried Mojo once, and then only a very small amount. That was enough for him to know that what was in front of his pilot — a mixture consisting of a pint of rum, a pint of cherry brandy, two San Miguels, a couple sodas and some fruit juices — was very bad news.

"Shit," said Lunker, who then repeated it twice more. "We can't let him stand up by himself. He'll find the floor if he does."

The men arrived quickly to where he was sitting and sat down next to him. The ladies followed and sat at a small table that Gully slid tightly against Willie's table.

"Hey...bendeckos!" exclaimed Willie loudly, "My bendecko brothers!"

"Bendeckos?" Mirela asked Lunker; she was curious.

"It's a Far East Film Society thing. I'll tell you later."

Although clearly three sheets to a South Pacific wind, Willie smiled like a Cheshire cat at the sight of his dearest friends.

"Hey, Willie...How're you doing?" asked Doc, speaking slowly.

Willie smiled broadly at the sight of his friends. "Did you know buffaloes could be soldiers, Doc? That's so cool — a buffalo as a Rasta with dreadlocks. I never knew that. Buffalo soldiers. I bet they don't carry guns; they just spread world peace through superior rum and ganja across Rastaland." He continued to rock slowly to the music. Willie looked fine, but his brain resided in a foreign place known only to brave adventurers deep in the throes of Mojo. They needed to get the pitcher out of his hands quickly before any more damage was done.

"Can I have some of your Mojo, Willie?" asked Lunker.

"Sure, Lunker. Share the Mojo. Like a Leydorf-trained man but share-the-Mojo-man." He smiled as Lunker took the large pitcher and placed it on the ladies' table next to where he sat. Almost half of the original amount had vanished. Lunker looked at the ladies with a half-smile and shook his head. It was just another day as part of the Navy's foreign legion — funny and not funny at the same time.

"Come on, Willie. We have reservations at the Chuckwagon, and we don't want to be late," said Doc. They had to be careful. If he stood up on his own, he'd likely kiss the floor just seconds later.

"We have to wait. I paid for a song the band leader said was perfect for me being ditched by a beautiful woman, and he said they're playing it next, but you go ahead and save three or five or maybe two cheeseburgers for me...I'll be fine and I need to finish my Mojo anyway. This is the first Mojo I've ever had, Doc, and let me tell you the gospel truth that this is one kick-ass drink.

"I'm glad you like it, Willie, and we're looking forward to hearing the song, too." Doc wanted to keep him talking so he'd forget they'd taken his drink away.

"We should take some Mojo to Professor Leydorf, Doc...His classes would rock with Mojo...Who needs slide rules when you have Mojo?...Everything's perfect no matter what answer you get."

Willie eyes and ears were prominently focused on the band on the stage; he was waiting to hear the song that was promised. In the meantime, his brain, memory, and voice continued to operate completely independently of each other.

"Maybe give some to Captain Jack, too...He could be the first Leydorf-trained Mojo Marine...Run into some MOROs and they won't know what to say or do but run away...Kick their ass without having to kick a single ass...That's good math I could do with two slide rules in stereo...Bam! Go Navy Beat Army."

The ladies laughed out loud. Willie never noticed. He was traveling through several locations and places and locales at once — the transforming speed of Mojo — and yet part of him consistently remained focused on the band. They were starting to play the song, *I Don't Want To Talk About It*, for which he had paid them a hundred pesos. The band's leader was right about the selection — It was the perfect song for where Willie's heart resided. After hearing the chorus for the first time, Willie sang along each time it came up after that. As the alcoholic influence kicked in even stronger, the Mojo he had been drinking found and engaged a reggae beat somewhere deep within Willie's vocal chords, even as he mixed the words.

"I can't tell my bunkroom buddies, how my heart broke in two." He didn't have tears in his eyes, but he sounded as broken-hearted as a man drinking Mojo could sound, even as he smiled and continued to rhythmically sway back and forth.

The song ended after seven minutes; the band stretched it out from its normal four minutes — a hundred pesos would do that every time. Now, though, it was time to get Willie back to the boat. He and Gully were on the next day's flight schedule with a briefing time of ten o'clock and a takeoff time of noon. Although they were well outside the Navy's twelve-hour 'bottle-to-throttle' rule, Lunker had been in his shoes before. He knew twelve hours of sleep or more was the perfect antidote to the lingering overnight effects of a drink more mysteriously powerful than...everything.

Lunker looked at Doc and Gully and nodded. They both nodded, as did the women, who were watching, and they imperceptibly understood the plan.

"Hey, Willie. I smell a cheeseburger at the Chuckwagon with your name on it," said Mirela. She hoped a woman's voice would motivate him. "Maybe two or three."

"Are there a couple with the scotch general's name on them, too?"

"There sure are, Willie. I can smell all of them," asserted Lauren. "Fries, too."

Willie smiled and tried to rise from his seat as Doc supported him on his left side and Lunker on his right. Gully stood behind him to nudge him forward or catch him if he fell backwards. It was a total team effort, just like getting an Intruder off the front end of the boat and bringing it safely home.

The group kept Willie surrounded on both sides and behind him as they slowly guided him toward the door. Two feet from departing Reggae Island, Doc said, "Right for lineup, Willie." During a carrier landing, from a pilot's perspective, the angled deck is constantly moving from his left to his right. Making small corrections to the right to compensate for the inherent movement is a required part of a successful landing.

With a nudge from Doc on his left, Willie made a very natural 'right for lineup' turn out of the door and onto Magsaysay's sidewalk; they were now heading toward the bridge and the base's main gate. Fortunately, the sun hadn't completely disappeared below the horizon, and there was more than enough light to highlight any obstacles along their path toward Midway. Also, in Willie's favor was that the sidewalks weren't as crowded as on the two previous days. A sailor's money disappeared quickly during the first days in port, especially when an unconfirmed rumor was sweeping the ship that Midway's repairs were ahead of schedule.

Thanks to the 'Midway underway' experience and his supportive friends, Willie quickly found his sea legs; like a good sailor, he made adjustments for a sidewalk that seemed to have a slow roll from side-to side. As a result, he could focus on sharing the visions that a half pitcher of Mojo and the band at Reggae Island had infused into his brain.

"I can see Jesus as a Rasta man with dreadlocks, you know, about as tall as Gully, hanging with the camels in the desert and living in a tent...singing a good Bob Marley song in harmony with the disciples in his squadron on Midway, you know, Peter, Paul and his sweet momma Mary. That'd have to be some hard rocking harmony, and you know they loved having Jesus around, 'cause if anyone could grow top shelf sugar cane in the middle of a desert, snap his fingers and make instant rum, it'd be Jesus at full power on the port catapult..."

Willie's friends caught him as he stumbled slightly; he never noticed. His voice continued to articulate colorful visions and random thoughts that were as entertaining and illogically normal as the two chief petty officers at Old West Number Two.

"I can see the disciples sitting under a tent and saying, 'Hey Jesus mon, you're the best, but my jet has a low fuel light so can you sprout some more sugar cane so we don't have to go to Bunkroom Eight to get some rum that is not there but is really there if you know where to look and can you explain it to us one more time...One night I go to sleep happy after an okay two wire and some vanilla dog with chocolate syrup, and the next morning I wake up in a big sandbox with a bunch of camels and donkeys and three disciples named John, Paul and Jones and, hey, was that band at Reggae Island the best? I love that song..."

Willie never stopped talking, even as he stumbled slightly while navigating the three-inch drop from the sidewalk onto General Vincente Lim Street, the first of three dirt side streets they'd cross on their Reggae Island-to-Midway journey.

"We must have done something really bad for this desert assignment, like maybe eating all the chocolate dog without sharing, or Doc losing that blue Air Force truck in Okinawa, or I bet it was Samson, the big guy, and I'd go to him and say I bet it was you, Big Sam. We told you not to go after the married chick 'cause she doesn't like long hair, but, you know, Sam the man

251

had a thing for her and she finds this knife the size of Lunker's three wood and becomes the first barber in the Bible, like whack, whack and history changes…"

As they approached the other side of the dirt street, Lunker and Doc timed Willie's steps perfectly and eased him up, and then down, to the sidewalk as they continued their journey to the small 'home within a home' known as the Midway Oasis.

"And whoa, Nellie, can I get a thank you Jesus for that burble moment…did I nail that landing or what, Gully? I mean nailed it…that's an okay two wire for sure…" The 'burble' is an anomaly that occurs when landing on an aircraft carrier; the wind hitting the ship's island structure creates a brief downdraft just behind the ship that a pilot has to compensate for less than ten seconds from touchdown.

"Very impressive," underscored Mirela to the three men. "I think you've done this before."

"Oh, maybe once or twice," answered Lunker, laughing as he kept his focus on his friend.

The men eased Willie toward his right to avoid a couple sailors walking swiftly past them; their eyes were intently staring straight ahead toward the end of the street. They were on a one-way mission to trouble — the New Jolo, the club at the end of Magsaysay, was their likely destination. The men didn't even glance at the alligator in a pen to their left, in front of Pauline's. Neither did the three women or anyone else in Willie's entourage; the alligator was just par for the course along Magsaysay.

"Hey, wasn't Bam-Bam the kid in the Flintstones?…little strong on the rum there, long-haired preacher mon. I bet Matthew, Mark, Luke Skywalker, and John Lennon wore tee-shirts with Fred and Wilma and Barney Rubble on the front, and do you think Pebbles and Bam-Bam ever got married?"

"Where did the Flintstones come from," asked Gully, as everyone laughed.

The group had just passed four large stores, each with an open front wall, selling tee-shirts filled with several dozen designs for Midway and its individual squadrons, as well as the myriad 'Midway vs. Cactus' designs.

The only thing Willie hadn't covered so far in his Mojo-influenced sermon was why Jesus didn't simply turn water straight into rum and skip the sugarcane, or why he ultimately chose the fruit of the vine over sugarcane. This journey wasn't about logical outcomes; it was simply about a flight path the directionless mind of a brokenhearted man was trying to navigate.

"His Mojo mind seems to be focused on religion, cartoons, rum, and flying," observed Lauren. "From my limited experience, I'd say he just summed up the essence of you Navy flyboys remarkably well." They all laughed as Willie's three bunkroom buddies kept him solidly on course and on glideslope.

"That's right, Lauren. Flying is a religion, and God has saved my ass more than once," acknowledged Doc.

"What happened to sex in that list? Oh, that's right. Never mind. I remember now; it's a natural by-product," rehashed Mirela, as everyone laughed. "I think I heard a priest mention that in church recently."

"When do you think Willie last went to church?" asked Sharon.

"Define church," answered Lunker quickly, smiling as he continued to steady his friend.

"May I remind you that we are on a mission from God, and right now, we're saving Willie from the devil's own brew." Gully's comment kept them laughing as Willie kept his own vocal chords meandering on a kaleidoscopic course.

"Marley heard our Eagles choir and Dick the Donkey singing together and said, 'Hey, you wanna hear a jamming' reggae song?' and they say 'Yea, mon, like flying down the Nile to Mount Zion,' and then he starts singing Exodus to Moses, who was sitting in the skipper's ready room chair, and he's singing about

253

movement of ja people and ja animals but not ja big ass asp snakes."

Willie slowed his pace for a moment, but his friends nudged him lightly to keep his momentum where it had been. They were approaching the second dirt side street that they'd cross on their path to the shit river bridge. The third, and last, dirt side street was the one by the artist who painted Jesus and carabao and ships and planes on large felt wall hangings. If he was provided photos, he'd paint Marley, Moses, and Willie sitting together on a carabao — The painter had exceptional talent.

"...And I think Jesus probably said to Noah, who was like old as the dirt along the banks of the Nile, but who would be flying Intruders if they had jets back then...you know, flying low and fast over Cairo and freaking out all the dudes building the pyramids, and have you ever thought what's with that giant lion laying in the sand by the pyramids getting a tan?"

A loud noise inside a club to the right caused Willie to look that way for a brief second. "At least his ears work normally," observed Mirela, "even if his brain doesn't." The group laughed as Willie picked up where he left off.

"I could figure out electrical engineering before I could figure out that lion in the sand and why he doesn't just go hang out by the Nile and have some chocolate dog or something, but laying in the sand? I'd call him lazy lion hanging out in the sand and I did that on Pensacola Beach one afternoon but I fell asleep and spilled my Bushwacker and then woke up sunburned and it hurt like a bitch putting my torso harness on to go flying the next day."

"Willie's brain is in ancient Egypt and Pensacola and eating chocolate ice cream and drinking a Bushwacker at the same time. What actually is in Mojo again?" asked Sharon. "It sounds like it could give new life to my boring history lectures." Her comment produced laughs in stereo. They weren't laughing at Willie; they were laughing along with him, even if he wasn't laughing. That was also one of Mojo's hidden side effects.

Unlike his initial crossing at the first dirt side street, where he stumbled, Willie's stride was as smooth as a calm sea as he navigated the three inch drop from the sidewalk onto Gen. Antonio Luna street, the second of two dirt side streets they'd cross on their Reggae Island-to-Midway journey. They were at the halfway point to the taxi stand.

A large group of sailors, also apparently on an urgent mission from God, aggressively moved down the sidewalk in the opposite direction, brushing against the group several times on the crowded narrow sidewalk during their own short, but familiar, journey to a foreign place.

"Hey, Gully, we're catching a little turbulence here; it could make landing a real bitch tonight, so I need you and Matthew, Mark, Luke Skywalker and Johnny Walker Black to keep a good eye on me."

"You're doing just fine, Willie. Keep your scan going." Gully made it sound as if they were side-by-side in the air, service buddies looking out for each other all the way to touchdown.

The group had one more dirt side street to cross on their way to the safety and security of the Midway Oasis. With the ladies leading like a wedge, they parted a large flood of fast walking sailors heading toward them. They, too, most likely, were each on a mission from God.

"Willie's trapped in a world that makes no sense except to him," said Lauren.

"I know the feeling of being trapped in a world that doesn't make sense. It's called life as a Romanian Baptist, but it wasn't as funny. I wish Lunker had flown in and rescued me." Mirela turned around and quickly kissed Lunker, even as the group barely slowed its movement. "I would've sat on your lap, flyboy."

The group kept walking. They were getting closer to the final dirt side street. That was good; Willie's stride was starting to noticeably lag behind his still-racing brain, making their journey with Willie slightly more perilous.

"Hey Doc, my best bendecko buddy forever, how many more days until we arrive in Subic? I could sure use a cold San Miguel and a Cubi Dog..."

"Three more days, Willie. Just three more days."

"That's awesome...I hope Tosh doesn't miss her flight, 'cause I want her to meet my new friends, Matthew, Mark, Little Luke McCoy and John Deere. Can you believe we found the tractor man hanging out in downtown Olongapo?"

Before anyone could respond, Willie continued; his brain had conveniently and quickly moved the memory of Tosh to a hidden place, and wouldn't bring it back again until he again woke up in the trusted confines of Bunkroom Eight.

Willie was rapidly running out of airspeed, but not random and absurdly disconnected thoughts. It was more obvious to his friends with each step — Mojo still had control of his brain, although the drink's horsepower was slowly fading into a western Pacific horizon.

"Hey, that looks like Tonto, my bunkroom buddy, or is that his twin? My eyes can't see that far but he looks like he's just two feet away." Tonto reversed his course and joined his friends.

They arrived at St. Columbian Street, the third and final dirt side street between Reggae Island Club and the shit river bridge.

"Hey, you guys hungry? Man, really, I could eat some puppy on a spoke right now. Hey Gully, you think it's really puppy? Puppy on a spoke makes me think about Lassie and Rin-Tin-Tin, and then I couldn't watch them on TV anymore and say get along little doggies without feeling bad that I ate a couple...I think I need a combat nap...you know, have a siesta fiesta like that carabao we saw laying in the mud."

Willie's mind remained in foreign parts of another world, but the animation in his voice was slowly receding back toward planet Earth, along with the rest of his body, giving way to the reality of a tired heart and soul.

"Remember that, Doc? That sweet little girl waving to us sitting on the big water buffalo? Man, I sure would like to find a place to lay down right now, even in the mud with that carabao, and snuggle up with my Russian friend Natasha Tosh..."

By the time they passed the Filipino man painting Jesus with dreadlocks standing by a carabao on felt, Willie was quiet. The women noticed it first; his eyes were moist.

Mojo couldn't heal a broken heart; it simply took it to a world where life was still fun and there was no pain. Whether Willie was just tired or sadly resigned to his fate at losing Tosh didn't matter...He would shuffle his way across the shit river bridge with the help of his friends, especially Tonto, who did what good shipmates do. He rode with Willie in a taxi for the less than half-mile distance to the ship.

Tonto helped his friend crawl safely onto his top bunk in Bunkroom Eight, the Midway Oasis, whose motto, 'It only hurts when you're awake,' was never more appropriate. Before he fell asleep, Willie's mind returned to the reality of the current moment — a long enough moment for a final comment to his friend and bunkroom buddy. "It was a good ride with Tosh, Tonto. It just ended way too soon."

Willie fell asleep immediately. Tomorrow would arrive with a new dawn; a healed heart would take much longer. Tonto survived losing an Indian maiden named Pocahontas. Willie would survive losing a tall blond southern California girl...but no one would ever win an argument with God about time, tides, weather, or an inability to teach an old dog new math. As with every other time, the gospel of Eli held true.

Yes and amen.

CHAPTER ELEVEN

The Gospel Of Eli...Now And Forever
Mid-to-Late Summer, 1980

"How was Manila, shipmate?" Doc greeted Lunker as he stepped out of a taxi at the Subic Golf Course.

"It was wonderful." After holding the door for Mirela, Lunker turned toward his caddy, smiled, and shook his hand. "But not as wonderful as being here, Eli."

Wearing his trademark smile, Eli retrieved Lunker's clubs from the trunk and hoisted them up onto his bony left shoulder. Even though he knew Midway would be underway in less than twenty-four hours, Lunker's comment froze a smile on his brown weathered face that wouldn't leave for eighteen holes.

"Driving in to the city, there were parts that looked just like Olongapo and Magsaysay, and I was a bit leery. But as soon as the marina district along the waterfront came into sight, it was an entirely different world. Our restaurant looked over the water and the sailboats, and it was like a postcard." Lunker glanced toward Mirela and smiled. "Beautiful like my Romanian date."

The previous evening, he had accompanied Mirela to a late-notice dinner in the Philippines' capital city, hosted by Mirela's Hong Kong-based employer. "Before dinner, we walked up to an observatory in the hotel where our restaurant was located to watch the sun set. On the horizon, just to the left of the sun, we could see the island of Corregidor, rising from the sea like a WestPac Rock of Gibraltar." He didn't have to elaborate; the irony of that island's history next to an idyllic view was obvious.

"My two closest friends fell in love with Lunker and asked if he had any single friends he could bring next time." Mirela made eye contact with Willie, who was standing next to Doc and Lauren, and smiled. "They're smart and beautiful. Interested?"

"I'm married to the Navy, remember?" He smiled at her. "But thanks for thinking of me."

"How you marry Navy, Willie?" Eli was confused, along with Lito and Romy. They would be the caddies for the threesome this morning, the last round of the inport period.

"Just a figure of speech, Eli. It means the Navy controls everything I say, do, and think."

Eli laughed along with the other two caddies. "Same with marry wife."

"Excellent observation, Eli. I agree," echoed Lunker, nodding. He laughed as Mirela poked a finger into his left shoulder. "Where's Gully? I thought he and Sharon were joining us?"

"They decided to spend their last day at Grande Island," said Lauren.

"Good for them. You guys ready?" queried Lunker.

"We were born ready," said Willie. "Let's tee it up."

Midway would be returning to sea the next morning, one day ahead of schedule. She would pass Hoover Mountain by eight thirty, saying goodbye to Subic Bay as she greeted the warm waters of the South China Sea, a transition the carrier had made countless times before. None of the sailors and officers on board the great ship would touch land or hear the voice of their loved ones for at least seventy days—likely more. On a few occasions, the aviators would fly over islands and coastal areas, but none would feel the firmness of their soil. It would be the longest uninterrupted time at sea during the one hundred fifty-five days that would be remembered as Midway's 'Fall of '80' cruise.

As the threesome approached the tee for the fifth hole, a flight of two Intruders raced across the sky in front of them — two aircraft moving as one, close enough for a human to jump from one wing to another, at over three hundred forty miles per hour and barely two hundred fifty feet above the ground. The heads of the golfers, caddies, and guests moved as one, from right to left, as they followed the side-by-side sources of ear-shattering noise.

"Speed is life; flying fast and low is living," noted Lunker, as the two Eagles' jets roared toward the low mountains along Luzon's western coast. Doc and Willie nodded at his observation.

"Saw you fly yesterday. You in first two go fly by. In back plane, right Lunker?"

"That's right, Eli," answered Lunker. "I'm glad you saw us."

"I smile see you fly. Going fast. Watch go out of sight. You told me you be in first two. Willie and Gully in front plane. You in other one."

"That was us," acknowledged Willie, always humbled at his good fortune to do what so many would love to do. "Doc was in the second group of two that flew yesterday morning."

Eli smiled. "What over horizon?" If he could never leave the touch of planet Earth, at least his friends did, and he would live vicariously and imaginatively through them.

"We saw a school of small whales as we crossed the southern coast of Luzon, Eli. We were about three hundred feet above the water and could see them as clearly as you can see the flag on the green." Eli looked that way as Lunker spoke. "I thought about you and wished you could have been with us."

"Me, too. Would like see whales swim in group." Lito and Romy agreed with Eli; all three were nodding at the thought of a dream mutually longed for.

A few hours later, the group approached the tee box for number eighteen; Lunker was quieter than usual as he looked out toward the fairway and all that was around him. His demeanor had been unusually subdued the last couple holes, and now he moved close to his caddy.

The two dear friends, from opposite sides of the planet, stood side-by-side as they had since their first round together, a short twenty-five months earlier. Uncharacteristically, the tall aviator bit his lower lip and then put his arm across Eli's shoulders. "Did I hit the jackpot or what?"

Lunker looked at the assembled group, none of whom immediately grasped the timing or focus of his comment, although Doc and Willie silently guessed that it likely had to do with the extraordinary man standing next to their fellow Bunkroom Eight resident.

"What jackpot mean?" asked Eli.

"You," answered Lunker, his eyes staring at his caddy. Eli's brown eyes stared back. "You. Jackpot means the best prize of all; a larger than large prize, a treasure better than anything else...and that's you, Eli."

The group stood in silence at this special and endearing moment under a foreign sun. The sad reality was that this could indeed be the last time Eli and his favorite golfer would ever share the same patch of earth. Lunker was taking no chances — Midway's long-range schedule projected a return to the aqua blue waters of Subic Bay in early December, two weeks before Lunker's scheduled transfer, but there were no guarantees.

Willie and Doc had seen the smothering cloak of sadness in Lunker only once before; it was when he returned from taking his wife and daughter to the airport as they bid Japan, and him, sayonara. For weeks afterwards, he performed like the professional he was — in the air and on the ground. In the closely held confines of the bunkroom and ready room, though, his naturally spunky wit was noticeably sedated.

It was Eli, during two rounds of golf, courtesy of a weekend cross-country flight from Atsugi to Cubi Point, who resurrected his friend's spirit. Lunker never revealed what Eli said or did during their time on the course together, but his words and actions were obviously cathartic and healing. Upon his return to Atsugi, the north Georgia man they treasured was himself once again.

Lunker turned so that he was facing the dear man he would never forget. "You are a very dear friend to me, and you have been the finest caddy a golfer could ever have. You know that, and you know how I feel about our friendship and the time we've spent walking this beautiful land." He paused; his voice had a slight tremble to it. "We're supposed to be back here in a few months, and we probably will be...but if we don't..."

His voice stopped again, this time for several seconds — Lunker was clearly emotional — he'd always known this day would come, and yet he was still unprepared. He made no effort to wipe the tears forming in his eyes.

"...But if we don't, I want my friends to know how I feel about you." Lunker took a deep breath. "But more important than that, Eli, I want you to know how I feel about our time together, and our friendship" — the words on his tongue fought fiercely and desperately against verbalizing a nightmarish thought — "in case today, right now, this is the last piece of earth that you and I will ever have the pleasure of sharing."

Lunker was silent as he focused on the green grass under him, searching his brain for the thoughts and emotions that would convey the message he wanted Eli to hear. His breathing had deepened as his voice reached out with boundless respect and pierced the heavyhearted air.

"Seeing your smile always made me smile, and you were so comforting to me when my wife and daughter left. I will never forget your words to me during our first round after they returned home. You restored my spirit and what you said will always stay with me." Lunker stared at his dear friend and spoke as slowly and affectionately as he could. "I always knew I could trust your advice on the golf course, Eli, but it was knowing I could trust you as a friend and that you would never compromise your honesty or our friendship that meant the most to me." Lunker took a deep breath.

"I will be old and gray one day, Eli, and my mind may not work as well as it does today, but I do know this." He took another noticeably deep breath. "Any time my thoughts and memories take me back to happy times and places, no matter how old I am, you will be there." Lunker had exhausted the last of his emotional energy; a deep breath and a single tear on his cheek silently confirmed it.

Eli was quiet for several long seconds as he looked into his friend's moist eyes, and then he turned and pulled a golf club from the bag. He handed the three-iron to the tall American next to him. The weathered, brown-skinned man was wracked with emotions as well, although he was able to keep them hidden. That he was emotionally stronger than Lunker was no surprise. Having said too many final goodbyes of his own to golfers and, most poignantly, to three of his young children had taught him how to manage his personal reservoir of sentiments a long time ago.

"Time hit ball, Lunker. See you next visit. Say goodbye then."

Lunker looked at his trusted friend, smiled, and slowly teed his ball. He then smashed a monster drive that sliced over the palm trees and foliage to their right and, most likely, landed on the far side of the fairway for the first hole.

Eli turned and stared at the tall golfer next to him. "Good start for next round, Lunker, but have to finish number eighteen before play again." Eli's comment generated a cathartic laugh from the other caddies, golfers, and observers. The target of his comment grinned broadly as well.

"Please, Lunker, I know you don't want to say goodbye, but I don't think my feet can take eighteen more holes." Mirela couldn't resist; her comment was followed by more laughter and verbal jabs from all those watching.

Ten minutes later, the group walked off the eighteenth green as one. Willie and Doc each shot par on the final hole; Lunker carded a double bogey.

"Can't finish with double bogey. Have to come back again," noted Eli. His smile sent a heartfelt message, spanning the continents that would one day soon separate them.

"Would you believe that was part of my plan?"

Eli laughed harder. "Maybe believe after two three San Miguel."

After two rounds of drinks, it was time to say goodbye. Although Lauren and Sharon would likely have many opportunities to visit Subic Bay in the future, this was ostensibly Mirela's last visit to the lush tropical paradise, at least for the next several years. "I may not see you again either, Eli, but I won't ever forget you." She gave him a tender hug.

"Lunker lucky man. I tell him after meet you first time."

"Thank you, but I think we are the lucky ones." She hugged him again as tears formed in her eyes. "I hope I can meet your wife and children one day."

Eli smiled and nodded. "Like that. Will like you. Be good time. Always friend over horizon."

Ten minutes later, Doc, Lauren, Lunker, and Mirela took a taxi to the Cubi BOQ; Willie took a taxi to Midway. Before they departed, each of the men had given their caddies large tips, enough to feed their families for a few weeks. They also gave Eli a similar amount of money for George, who would have been Gully's caddy had he joined them. Gully had thoughtfully given them the amount before he and Sharon left for Grande Island.

Thirty minutes later, Eli rode in a red, orange, and blue Jeepney to a rutted, uneven dirt road, almost eleven miles north of Olongapo, and then walked slightly over two miles to his village. His wife was cooking rice over an open fire when he arrived; unseen under the hot coals was fish wrapped in banana leaves. Eli told her to close her eyes and, when she did, he placed a delicate, medium length coral necklace around her neck.

He spoke in Tagalog, the beautiful language of the Philippines.

"From Lunker. I tell him how beautiful you are. He say this necklace perfect for beautiful woman. His girlfriend pick out in Manila when they have dinner there."

Violetta, his wife, was speechless. She adored Eli and loved his many compliments, and she knew he treated the golfers for whom he caddied with great respect. That the golfer he spoke of often, and who had already supported their children so unselfishly when they were sick, would think of her this way was overwhelming. She ran the coral strand through her hands and fingers over and over as Eli stared. The luscious orange beads were dazzling against her copper brown skin; in all her years, she had never seen nor worn anything so alluring or fashionable — tears spoke for her gratitude at Lunker's gift.

"When Lunker visit next, invite village. His friends too. We celebrate together. Cook fish pig."

Eli smiled and nodded in agreement. "Be great feast with great friends."

Morning arrived too early for everyone assigned to Midway. All personnel, except those flying aircraft from the Cubi Point runway to the carrier's flight deck, were required to be aboard by six a.m. Commander Singer, the Eagles' skipper, would lead a flight of four to the ship with an arrival time overhead the ship of ten o'clock. Lunker, Doc, Socks, and Gully would be part of the four crews flying aboard instead of walking aboard. They would have a few extra hours to say goodbye to the ones they loved.

As the morning dawned, Olongapo and Magsaysay Drive would be significantly less crowded, as would the shit river bridge and the golf course. The impact on the economy was significant when Midway was in port; five thousand men in search of anything not painted gray, smelling like jet fuel, or rolling from side-to-side would be responsible for that. The impact was felt just as significantly when five thousand men sailed away.

The men on Midway would miss the extraordinary people and the beautiful land that made the Philippine Islands — the 'P.I.' — the memorable place it was, but it was clearly time for the men on Midway to depart. Many were out of peso-nality, and others were starting to answer to 'Hey, Joe' when that wasn't their name, but all of them were ready and eager to get back to doing what they were paid to do — steadfastly sail across foreign waters toward another distant horizon.

At 8:15 a.m., slightly over two hours after the sun peeked above the horizon, the pilots and B/N's who would fly the four Intruders to Midway's flight deck walked out of the Chuckwagon, accompanied by four of the five women who had met the ship days earlier. From where they stood, waiting for taxis to take them to the Cubi side of the base, they could see Midway, with a deck full of aircraft, steaming through aqua blue waters on a southwesterly course. She was approaching the slightly less than two-mile wide passage between Grande Island and lush green land to the west. Three miles later, the ageless carrier would pass Hoover Mountain on her starboard side as she eased into the warm waters of the South China Sea, a sea in which she had first sailed twenty-three years earlier.

At 8:30 a.m., as their loved ones donned their flight gear in preparation for their journey from Cubi Point to a ship at sea, the 'women of Midway' watched as a Navy C-9 passenger jet made its final approach to the naval air station's nine-thousand foot long runway. Two hours later, with Lauren and Sharon, among others, sitting comfortably in the back, the airplane would depart from the Philippines enroute to Okinawa. After a short delay, it would continue on to Atsugi and then proceed to Misawa in northern Japan.

On Midway, activity throughout the ship was well underway; the carrier was once again a true floating city. She would be abuzz with activity around the clock until her next port visit, wherever that might be. Olongapo was recent history; spending the next seventy-six days at sea was the present and the future.

Back on the Cubi Point Naval Air Station's tarmac, the air was humid and sticky and the aura surreal, as a group of four women and four men, standing by the four Intruders ready for flight, said goodbye.

"Two and a half months is nothing. It'll pass quickly."

"I'll try not to worry, but you know I will. Please be careful."

"Our time together is worth any wait. I wouldn't change a thing."

"I love you so much. Believe me when I say that meeting you was the best thing that's ever happened to me."

"Your smile will be with me every day, and I hope you will feel mine."

From the open-air gazebo near the first tee, Eli stood and watched the large gray aircraft carrier steam across Subic Bay toward the South China Sea. Her wake lingered behind, cutting a telltale trail through the water like a long goodbye; it would soon fade away, unlike the memories recently made. He continued to watch as Midway quickly covered the ten miles between her dock and the open sea, and then made a slight port turn, disappearing to his left.

Less than forty-five minutes later, the roar of jet engines drew his eyes to the runway across the bay. Eli watched as four Intruders lifted off to the west, about ten seconds apart. The first aircraft slowly began a turn to its right, and the other three quickly joined in formation. He smiled as they rolled out after just over ninety degrees of turn and, seemingly flying just feet apart, took aim for the land on which they had played golf just a day earlier. They roared overhead, in a starboard turn, just a few hundred feet above where Eli stood smiling. In the right seat of the jet in front, leading the other three, he could easily see an aviator waving. Eli waved back; Lunker had made good on a promise. Within two minutes, they were out of sight, and he could no longer hear them. He knew where they were going, and he would keep them in his daily prayers.

Eli would forever long to see over the horizon; what was there would continue to elude him, but he was certain of this — he would always have dear friends over the distant line where the water met the sky...So addeth to the Gospel of Eli, yes and Amen.

CHAPTER TWELVE

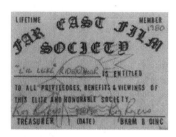

Education At Sea
Early Fall, 1980

After fifty-two uninterrupted days at sea, the long night of the collision and the short Subic inport period were well behind Midway's crew. Events and emotions from the two events weren't forgotten; for now, though, they were securely compartmentalized in a safe place among the crew's memories.

Midway's current home was in the heart of the South China Sea. In exactly three weeks, the carrier would arrive in Hong Kong. As the first launch cycle of the morning was completed, a C-2 Greyhound lined up behind the carrier and touched down on Midway's flight deck. The aircraft had launched two hours earlier from Naval Air Station Cubi Point; among its passengers were four American journalists from San Diego — two men and two women; all four in their thirties.

Throughout their short two-day stay, the journalists' cameras and questions were predominantly focused on the activity on the flight deck, and for good reason. The four had seen movies and photographs of flight operations at sea, but they had never experienced anything as breathtakingly daunting as the professionally orchestrated chaos actually unfolding in front of and all around them.

Actually, breathtaking was an understatement. The flight deck was saturated with scorching exhaust fumes so dense that the journalists could literally taste the pungent air. Like the smell of the shit river in Olongapo, the acrid taste from the jets quickly became an acquired sensation.

The activity had all the elements required to capture the new visitors' every sense and emotion. Against a backdrop of water, water, everywhere — three hundred sixty degrees of endless horizon — they watched fast jets being launched by the world's largest slingshot, and then jets trapped by one of three wires, a slingshot in reverse. They observed the constant danger faced by seemingly fearless men wearing green, yellow, red, blue, white, brown, or purple jerseys that represented their specific duties on the flight deck. All these men were battling skin-melting heat and leaning into gale force winds from the jets' exhaust that could easily blow an inattentive spectator down the flight deck and off the fantail in one long and final scream.

It was why an experienced petty officer was assigned as a chaperone and guardian angel to each of the four newest visitors.

As their eyes watered and stung and their ears ached from an assault of blistering wind, noise, fumes, and heat, the journalists — seasoned, world traveling professionals who believed they had seen it all — were paralyzed and overwhelmed as they took their first steps on Midway's flight deck. Far from home and the eyes of their country, the men on the flight deck made it all look as artistically routine as an afternoon matinee at the ballet, although they constantly fought, day and night, elements that the journalists only had to endure for a short twenty minute period.

Forgotten against the choreographed dance with danger was recognition by the newest visitors that, in the two seconds it had taken a steel cable to bring their flight to the ship from just over one hundred miles per hour to a complete stop, they were now part of a unique and prized fraternity — the small group of human beings who could stake a claim to a seat within the fraternity of tailhookers.

No one could ever take the entirety of the Midway-at-sea experience away from them. It was all theirs. Equally important, it was a privilege they would have in common forever with each sailor and aviator that ever called Midway home.

They would get a printed Midway Tailhooker certificate for their 'I love me wall' that confirmed their arrival. There was no certificate for the catapult launch that would accelerate them from zero to one hundred thirty miles per hour in less than three seconds the following afternoon. Arriving alive on Cubi Point's runway was the prize for that ride.

During their stay, the story the journalists discovered and ultimately reported was predominantly that of the brave young men who, for hours at a time, worked so perilously amidst the many dangers of the flight deck — a four-acre piece of steel moving through the ocean at over twenty-five miles per hour with no place to run from, and crowded with lethal jets taking flight in the name of peace. From midmorning until well into a dark and frightful night, these men, the majority of whom were under twenty-three years old, conquered the seemingly chaotic activity on the flight deck and made it appear easy. It was a remarkable dance performed to perfection every day.

The stories they discovered onboard the legendary carrier were part comedy club and part intriguing tales from the far side of the globe. These stories, found in the many levels of work and living spaces on and below the flight deck, were tales that would entertain, impact, and stay with them forever.

As a long day turned into a very dark South Pacific night, the journalists didn't want to sleep. There was so much to take in, and their once-in-a-lifetime experience would be over much too quickly. They could sleep when they're dead; that's what the Eagles' skipper would have told them.

Forty-five minutes after the very last aircraft, an A-6 tanker, had landed, the four journalists entered the officers 'dirty shirt' wardroom for a midnight snack. Eight bells had just sounded over Midway's public address system, indicating the clock had struck midnight.

As the four walked toward the serving line, they noticed the wardroom was empty except for eight men, all of whom, they assumed from their sweaty flight suits and discussions, had been flying in jets that were part of the night's final recovery. The aviators were seated at a long table in two groups, about twelve feet apart.

One of the groups was comprised of two pilots assigned to one of Midway's two A-7 Corsair squadrons; the other six aviators were the Eagles' pilots and B/Ns who, like their two comrades nearby, had once again safely mastered the art of drinking from the cauldron of the night's treacherous darkness.

Within both groups, the majority had chosen burgers, French fries and soft drinks. Gully, sitting next to Willie's right side, had added a made-to-order cheese omelet to two burgers; he skipped the fries. A few of the aviators had already graduated to dessert, which was, in all cases, either a soft vanilla or chocolate ice cream cone from the auto-dog machine, or a bowl of soft ice cream with chocolate syrup, even though chocolate cake and two types of pies were available to them. As they ate, the two groups of aviators paid little attention to the four Midway visitors who were selecting their desserts of choice along with cups of coffee.

Landing on a dark and moonless night had been exacerbated by low clouds lurking less than a mile away on the starboard side of the carrier. With those clouds to the right and pure darkness to the left, a pilot's eyes could easily convince the brain that his aircraft was in an acute angle of bank to the right, while the instrument panel was indicating to the brain that the aircraft was actually straight and level. The net effect of the disconnect between the two created a scenario ripe for a potentially disastrous case of vertigo, which made landing more difficult than usual on a night as black as a black horse's ass, as Lunker would later say.

"So, Willie, did you bolter because you wanted to pad your logbook with a little more flight time, or did you really just want to delay me from rendezvousing with my dutifully earned cheeseburger?" The question came from one of the two Corsair pilots who had been a landing signal officer on the night's final event. All eight aviators, including Willie, laughed as he finished his remark.

"Flight time is flight time, Chunks, and my extra trip in the landing pattern gave Gully a little more time to admire the beauty of all those stars that were out on this lovely south Pacific night."

"Way to try and use the fourth law of thermo, Willie, but I think Gully would rather have gotten to his cheeseburgers and eggs than sitting through an astronomy lesson."

"Didn't you learn during plebe summer at Annapolis that time and tides wait for no man?"

"Yeah, sure, but I don't recall anything about time and LSOs having to wait for the Intruder pilot who was afraid of landing." They all laughed and continued eating.

The four journalists, like the aviators, chose burgers and fries. They stood at the end of the serving line and looked around the wardroom, possibly deciding where to sit among the several dozen empty seats, or wondering if they could join the aviators already there.

"The four best seats in the wardroom are right here," said Lunker, smiling at the group and extending his hand toward four empty seats next to where the Eagles were sitting. "We've been saving them for you."

"I think this whole ambassador bullshit thing has gone to Lunker's head," said Chicklips, as the journalists smiled and took the seats.

After introductions between the two groups were complete, a brief description of the Intruder and its mission was provided in response to a question from one of the journalists. Another journalist then asked a follow-up question all four were curiously thinking. "Why did you pick that jet?"

Lunker answered quickly. "Well, it goes back to flight school. A common question we were asked was do we want to be responsible adult aviators or would we like to fly the Intruder." The journalists laughed.

They would soon discover the question appropriately fit these men. "Were you flying out there tonight, just now?"

"We were," said Lunker, nodding. "By design, we land last. Where were you watching from?"

"We watched the launch from up on the bridge, by the captain, and then we were taken down to the flight deck, right by the island, to watch the landings." The answer came from one of the two women.

"Even with the stars, it seemed pitch black without the moon," added the other woman.

"Black as a black horse's ass," added Lunker proudly, as the journalists laughed.

"I think your ambassador skills still need a little work, Lunker," suggested Doc, smiling, as the visitors laughed.

"Do you get scared at night?"

"Well, the pucker factor goes up when the sun goes down, and even more so when there's no moon."

"Pucker factor? I think I get what that means, but maybe not."

Willie took the question and answered slowly. "It's a very personal measure of the stress level of a situation, anatomically defined by the sphincter tension in the deepest part of one's..."

He paused, trying to find a word that would be respectful of their guests.

"Ass?" suggested one of the journalists.

"Bingo." The entire group laughed.

"But, this is what we do to earn a couple greasy sliders and some chocolate dog."

"Chocolate dog?"

"Did you ever have a dog? Watch him do his business in the yard?" Lunker held up his ice cream cone for several illustrative seconds so the four visitors could make the implied connection with the soft brown swirl. "Chocolate dog. In a cone."

The four journalists laughed hard at the new term they had just learned. This group of aviators surprised them. The men had just landed at night — a pitch black, no moon, high pucker factor kind of villainous night — and yet, the four visitors thought, they humorously conversed with the easy tranquility of a group of friends having a glass of chardonnay at a sidewalk café. A Bushwacker at the Sandshaker Lounge would have been a better analogy, but it was unlikely that the journalists had been to Pensacola Beach, so the reference would have been as foreign to them as chocolate dog was until a few seconds earlier.

The atmosphere amazed each of them — stunned them, actually. On the enlisted mess decks, where they had dinner, they found the same attitude of relaxed professionalism among the men who had been slaving so strenuously among the frenzy of the flight deck and throughout the bowels of Midway all day and into the additional danger of the night. The thought silenced them as they absorbed that fact — so far from home, performing dangerous work day and night in anonymity, and yet were unflinchingly professional on a ship that relatively few people actually knew existed.

"Where did you fly in from?"

"Subic Bay."

"Good to know there's still something besides water over the horizon. We haven't seen land in almost two months." Gully's comment startled the new guests. They hadn't given it much thought before then.

"Even better to know Subic Bay is still there." Lunker's comment made them smile.

"Did you cross the shit river bridge?" asked Willie.

"What's that?"

"A unique place you can cross when you return, assuming you're returning to Subic."

"How do we get there?"

"Ask anyone you see. They'll point you toward it if your nose doesn't do it first."

"Sounds interesting." The journalists looked at the aviators; the sentimental expressions on their faces silently confirmed that the bridge was now high on their 'must see' list.

One of the journalists, Tom Reeder, a man likely in his early thirties and the youngest of the group, asked a question each of the four visitors had been pondering after spending a day and evening on the ship and, especially, on the flight deck. "Do you ever worry about being hurt...or dying?"

Silence hovered over the table for several protracted seconds. In the past twelve months, thirty-two Navy jets had crashed. Some involved student pilots, but most involved tactical aircraft doing what tactical aircraft are designed to do. Among the Intruders that crashed, half involved fatalities.

"Nope, not really; although we'd all rather die than look bad." The journalists weren't sure if Socks' answer was real or make believe, and none of them asked for clarification.

"We say that as a reminder not to screw up in the first place." He smiled as he responded to their perplexed looks and answered their unasked question.

Willie added a thought. "You may not have enough time at sea with us to pick up on this, but time isn't real out here. Like now. It's after midnight, but the time of day is irrelevant. Time is for people somewhere else. At sea, time only matters if you're late — late to the brief, late to standing watch, late back to the

276

ship for landing, late to get a critical message sent — Early is overrated; being late is death."

"You must learn a great deal out here. Sailing the seas and oceans, seeing what are strange lands to most Americans, meeting people from foreign shores." The well-articulated comment came from Alexandra Burgos, called Alex, a beautiful, raven-haired journalist born in Cuba and a very astute observer of people. "What are some of the things you've learned during your time on Midway that would fascinate four laymen from southern California?"

After a long thoughtful pause, Doc responded. "We learned a new application of the Southeast Asia domino theory. If you can take over a country in thirty minutes, the pizza's free." Everyone laughed as Doc continued. "And being around Lunker here, we have learned and confirmed that, if you try and polish a turd, you just get a bigger mess."

The group continued laughing as Sock's offered additional commentary. "And that we're part of ten thousand years of war and terror and crazy men. Do you think we look like crazy men?"

"Yes, indeed," interjected one of the A-7 pilots. "That is, in fact, a true statement if you're talking about these chuckleheads." He and the other Corsair pilot stood and bid the Eagles and the journalists goodbye.

Moliver jumped into the fray. "We have also confirmed, hypothetically of course, that a five passenger rental car is not only the fastest accelerating, hardest braking, most durable off-road sedan in the world, but can accommodate seven aviators, four cases of beer, two female hitchhikers, and three large pizzas without using the trunk." Everyone laughed; the visitors the most.

"I'll bring the beer and pizza if I can sit on your lap in your jet. I'd like to see what landing on this ship looks like from your point of view." The proposal came from Patti Elias, a shapely brunette with dazzling brown eyes and a sultry voice as smooth as fine wine. Her suggestion and her sparkling smile had all the aviators volunteering loudly and immediately. What they didn't know, but would soon learn, was that this natural beauty had earned a doctorate in chemistry and possessed a remarkably quick wit.

"I think you probably just created the Navy's recruiting commercial for the next fifty years," interjected Willie.

"I'm the selection chairman, and I select myself," announced Chicklips. "Welcome aboard, Patti. I'll find a 'size beautiful' flight suit for you."

"It's official. Chicklips' new call sign is Romeo," said Lunker.

"As long as his call sign isn't crash, I'm ready to go," said Patti. "What time do we launch?"

The group was laughing when Doc added another fascinating and true story, although it was embellished for effect.

"Midway made a port visit in Kenya a year ago, in Mombasa," he told them, "and we had a chance to play golf at the Royal Nail Golf Club, the oldest course in Kenya. If you've never played on a parched golf course in Africa at the end of the dry season, just before the monsoon season, you need to add it to your to-do list. It's a unique kind of beautiful setting, and quite interesting to play."

"We stepped up to the first tee; I think it was about a three hundred fifty yard par four, and our skipper pulled out a five iron. We all looked at each other, thinking he must fancy himself as superhuman now that he's our boss, and watched him tee off. The ball flew out about a hundred twenty or thirty yards and hit the center of the fairway, and then it bounced high up in the air and continued bouncing before it rolled to a stop about twenty yards short of the green, or the short brownish patch of dirt that was called the green."

Doc continued. "The skipper looked at us and reminded us that the course had been baking under an African sun without rain all summer. He then added a comment about playing golf on a concrete road as a helpful hint on how to approach our round."

"When it was his turn to hit, Lunker being Lunker, well, he pulls out a driver and just smashes the ball. Smashes it." He looked at Lunker as he said it and gave him a thumbs up. Lunker sported a grin like a Cheshire cat. "His ball sailed over the green on the second bounce and kept bouncing until it was far out of sight. We all agreed that ball probably bounced and rolled across southern Africa for at least three days."

Doc paused as the group laughed loudly. "Hard to imagine how many local villagers from Kenya down to South Africa saw Lunker's ball bounce through their town before its chamber of commerce tour rolled into Cape Town."

"Eli loves that story," added Willie.

"Eli," said Lunker in a melancholy tone, 'He's my guy."

"Who is Eli?"

The aviators all looked at Lunker, who gave the group of journalists a brief introduction to Eli. The four visitors were especially touched when Lunker mentioned Eli losing three young children to diseases that Americans cure with a trip to a pharmacy, and also his lifelong dream of peeking over the horizon. They laughed when Lunker relayed his story of a lucky bounce while playing a recent round at the Binictican golf course.

"So I hit a nasty slice that is surely destined to go deep into the jungle. Tarzan deep. Eli is already reaching for another ball when we hear a sharp knock and my ball kind of stumbles out of the jungle and rolls onto the edge of the fairway. I look at Eli, who's laughing, and ask him how to say lucky bounce in Tagalog, the language of the Philippines. Eli makes a sign of the cross and looks at me." Lunker paused to take a sip of water.

"So I ask him, again, how to say lucky bounce and he makes another sign of the cross. Finally, he says to me that only God could have thrown my shot out of the jungle. After that, every time I have a lucky bounce, we both make signs of the cross." Lunker then added a few more thoughts regarding his dear friend in Subic Bay.

The four visitors, each of whom had traveled extensively, were moved by Eli's lifelong dream of seeing over the horizon. Their fondness for a man they would never meet was further cemented when Lunker mentioned Eli's admonition not to debate God over issues of time, typhoons, and trying to make a monkey meow.

The journalists felt at ease with the aviators. Like them, they were professionals simply pursuing perfection in their chosen field. Unlike them, they weren't likely to die if they made a mistake. They were eager to hear what the aviators had to say — what they pondered and what made them tick.

Socks stepped in and added his thoughts and inputs. "We debate questions as we ponder life, you know, because we're always trying to learn something new, especially things that don't make sense to us."

"Like what?"

Doc answered first. "Here's something we can't get our arms around. Our enemies are intelligent people doing terrible things, really horrible things, and yet the leadership in Washington acts like our enemies are reasonable people. Seven of our presidents, seven of them, had a covenant, a promise, with South Vietnam, and then we turned our back on them, and so many of their citizens were killed and we did nothing to stop it. More recently, we trained Iranian flight students in Pensacola and Texas, up until a couple years ago. We were there; we knew them and they became our friends. We had lunch and dinner with them and made trips to the beach together and there were many wonderful conversations between men who had the same desire for peace, to be good fathers, good pilots, and to make the world a better place."

"When the Shah was overthrown, they all asked for asylum. All of them. They knew they'd be viewed as loyal to the Shah and would most certainly be killed if they returned home. They knew it and we knew it, and what did we do?" He paused. "Nothing. Not a damn thing. Our country turned its back on them and sent all of them home. These were good men, really good men — solid aviators — and they were our friends. Several had wives and children, and now they're all dead. Good men and their families. Gone. Wiped from the face of the Earth like crumbs off a table." There was silence for ten or fifteen seconds.

"Doc's right; we screwed those guys," said Lunker. "They never had a chance once their ride back home cleared our airspace. None of them deserved dying when keeping them in the states probably wouldn't have changed anything." He paused briefly. "But on a lighter note, here's a question that recently came up in the ready room. In our squadron, we have a pilot named McDonald, call sign Burger, and one named McAfee, who happens to have a sister. If a McDonald marries a McAfee, do they give birth to a double scotch?

The drastic shifts in the conversations shocked the journalists. This group of aviators appeared able to go from funny to serious to funny with the ease of crossing an empty street. What they didn't yet know, but would discover as they spent more time with the officers and enlisted men on the ship, was that all the men on Midway were simply human beings doing what they had to do to adapt to friendly, foreign, and hostile environments, all at the same time.

As the discussions — funny to serious to funny — continued, the four journalists observed that the collective topics were cathartic to those who lived in a world few would ever know. Like the professional terror of night carrier landings, it only made sense to those who had experienced it.

By its very nature, a Navy ship at sea was an unnatural environment that would drive sailors and aviators insane if they couldn't occasionally act half-crazy. After just two days at sea, the four journalists would understand that sentiment well, especially the one who, as a young child, had spent time adrift in a boat at sea.

Gully posed the next question. "Lunker's last name is Fishman, and we also have a pilot with the last name of Trout. If a Fishman marries a Trout, what does that produce?"

"A dumbass," answered Socks, quickly. Everyone laughed.

"Please excuse my friend here with the brains of a Mattel toy," said Lunker, pointing across the table at his bunkroom buddy. "If you want my two cents worth on aviators, I think there should be a requirement that all aviators, and probably doctors, too, must have been divorced so they understand perfectly why you need to have a plan 'B' during a critical operation."

The group continued to laugh as Willie spoke up. "Take Lunker's bit of wisdom with a grain of salt. It's coming from the lead singer in the divorced men's choir."

"Aren't you glad you asked us about the fascinating things we learn floating around at sea on a ship older than all of us?" asked Chicklips.

"I'm glad I did," answered Patti, smiling. So far, she had been the most inquisitive of all four journalists. "I didn't expect this...this lightheartedness and then deep thoughts, and questions that bounce back and forth. I guess I was expecting everything to be serious and all about your flying and missions."

"We are on a mission...a mission from God."

"I've seen that movie many times," said Darrel Kerr, referring to the movie *The Blues Brothers*. Kerr was the son of a career Air Force officer and the oldest of the group of four journalists.

"My parents and I were once on a mission in a rickety boat running away from Castro; a ninety-three mile, one-way trip at sea," offered Alex. When she was five years old, her family had escaped in a barely seaworthy boat across the Florida Straits to America.

"That's incredible," said Lunker. "I guess your boat didn't have chocolate dog, huh?"

282

Alex laughed. "No, but I remember having ice cream soon after we landed in Key West. They may have refused us entry if we said we wanted some chocolate dog when we stepped ashore." Everyone laughed, and then, over the next five or six minutes, she added several of the harrowing details that had been permanently lodged in her memory since she was a child on the high seas herself.

Lunker smiled. Alex's story of escape reminded him of Mirela, and it made him miss her. "All right, who has another good story to share?"

"Not a story, but a thought," answered Willie. "I think Jimmy Buffett must have been on a Navy cruise in another life."

"Why is that?" asked Patti.

"Well, he wrote *Changes in Latitudes, Changes in Attitudes* and *Margaritaville* at about the same time. I'm thinking he must have been inspired by a few crazy nights in WestPac."

They all laughed.

"How about Doug Hegdahl's story. Remember him from SERE school?" offered Socks.

"I saw him last November. He spoke at a Veteran's Day event I attended," offered Tom Reeder, who had served eight years as a Navy Reserve intelligence officer after college.

"Remarkable, huh?"

"That's an understatement. I've witnessed countless speeches, but none held my attention like his."

"Who is he?" asked Patti, "and what is SERE school?"

"SERE school is the Navy's week-long survival and POW camp experience for aviators and aircrewmen," said Willie.

"Sounds like a summer camp except for the POW part," said Alex. It intrigued her and piqued her curiosity.

"And being waterboarded," added Lunker.

"Amen to that," said Gully. Being waterboarded in the mock prison camp was a very personal memory they had no desire to discuss. Some were waterboarded more than once.

"Back to Doug Hegdahl. He was a young enlisted man..." began Socks.

"An incredibly bright young enlisted man, probably a genius," interrupted Doc.

"As I was saying," continued Socks, smiling at Doc, "Doug Hegdahl was an incredibly bright young enlisted man, probably a genius, who fell overboard from a Navy ship a few miles off the coast of Vietnam. He was ultimately captured by the North Vietnamese, and was taken to the infamous Hanoi Hilton prison camp. Within a week, he was able to convince his guards that he was just a young country bumpkin sailor who could barely read or write."

"He was so intelligent that, when an interrogator asked him what he'd like more than anything in the world, he said a pillow. Since he didn't say he wanted to go home, the guards started calling him the "incredibly stupid one," and essentially gave him the run of the prison camp. Ultimately, he memorized not just the names of 256 prisoners in the camp, but their capture dates, how they were captured, and other personal information, and could recite it all by singing it to the tune of *Old McDonald Had A Farm.*"

"Fortuitously, the prison officials deemed him so useless in terms of military value that he was released early. Once he was released, our government officials took him to the Paris Peace Talks in 1970, where he confirmed the mistreatment of prisoners. He also provided the names of many men being held who the North Vietnamese had claimed weren't in their camps. When he finished his speech to us at the end of SERE, he spent a minute singing and reciting names."

"That's an incredible story," agreed Darrel. "I'd never heard that before." The four journalists asked questions about the SERE school experience for several minutes, before the discussion became light-hearted again.

Doc encouraged his best friend to share a funny story. "Tell them about the Bond girl in Pensacola, Willie."

"This should be interesting," suggested Patti. "A Bond girl, huh?"

"It was a blind date," began Willie. "A fellow student pilot promised me I'd be pleased with his girlfriend's friend. The two were visiting him in Pensacola in late March to escape the cold in northern Minnesota, so I agreed."

"Anyway, she was everything he promised. Very attractive, smart, funny, current on world and national events. It was a really nice evening until, out of the blue, she tells me that she firmly believes she was a Bond girl in a previous life." Everyone laughed as he finished his sentence. "At first I thought she was joking, but then she became annoyed because I was laughing." He paused briefly to take a sip of water. 'Seriously, I can't make this up."

"Willie's right," interjected Lunker. "He really isn't smart enough to make anything up."

"Thank you, Lunker. For five minutes, maybe ten, she tells me all the reasons why she believes she was a Bond girl in a previous life. My first clue as to where this was leading was how she was dressed, more business-like, sorry, Bond-like, than first date casual. While she's doing that, I'm trying to remember when the first Bond girl actually appeared. So, when I mention to her that the first Bond girl hit the big screen in 1962, five years after she was born, it was like a 5-4-3-2-1 countdown and she blasts off into near Earth orbit." The group laughed loudly.

"I swear it was worthy of a NASA astronaut lapel pin or something. all that was missing was smoke and flames and a hole in the roof of the restaurant."

Patti, laughing with the rest, asked what everyone was thinking. "So how long did the date continue after that?"

"Oh, about twenty seconds to the restaurant's door and a very quick two mile drive to my friend's apartment."

"Willie mentioning near Earth orbit reminds me of waiting to land tonight," said Lunker. "We were orbiting high over the ocean, waiting for the exact time we were assigned to commence our approach. While circling overhead, we turned our instrument lights down as low as we could. On a crystal clear, moonless night like tonight, black as that big black horse's ass, Midway is just one small dot of light on a big dark ocean." He paused for a second before continuing.

"And above us, the Milky Way honestly looked like a cloud, a dense white cloud with bright twinkling lights, from horizon to horizon. It's a spectacular sight, hard to accurately describe, all those billions of stars clustered like that. I guess it's one of the positive aspects of being out here."

The journalists tried to picture such a sight, and Patti asked a question worthy of a gathering of naval aviators. "Was that dense cloud as white as a white horse's ass?" Everyone laughed at her question.

Lunker made her an offer. "Stay with us, Patti. Please. Each of you. You'll fit right in."

"Yeah, stick around," said Willie. "Lunker may even play his banjo for you." He could also play the guitar, but preferred the former, which he kept in Bunkroom Eight.

"I think I speak for all of us and say we wish we could." Patti's sentimental statement was accurate. The journalists, well, they felt at home; they were among friends. Staying a little longer would be just fine.

The four were glad they had stopped by the officers' dirty shirt wardroom for a late night snack and beverage. Nothing about their experiences on Midway, day and night, had disappointed them. The American ship on which they resided was, for all practical purposes, a foreign land in foreign waters; that was the best way they could describe it. Fortunately, what was so much easier to describe was that it was filled with America's best — young patriots they'd remember for a long time.

Tom then changed the subject to something near and dear to each of the aviators. "We really enjoyed our time meeting with the sailors in various parts of the ship. They had lots of stories, too, mostly tricks they played on each other," she said.

Darrel provided some recently learned insight into the discussion. "They told us how they'll send the new guys on the ship, the ones right out of boot camp, to find impossible items, like a radar contact, or some glide slope, or a vapor lock." His comments brought with them a new round of laughter. "They told us they send them for fallopian tubes, and some of the work spaces have created their own to give them."

"It's true. Our squadron's engine shop has a box of them," said Willie, smiling. "The guys that work for me once sent a guy to get flight line, and this young kid came back with fuel hose some shop had given him that must've weighed fifty pounds. He was so proud of being successful in his hour-long search, my guys sent him to get some more, and didn't let him in on the joke for two days." The group laughed loudly. "They're professionals at that. They even catch us on some of their pranks at times," admitted Gully, "and I think I was their favorite target." As the group laughed, Gully, who was caught by them more than everyone at the table combined, confessed his innocence. "In my first month in the squadron, I went looking for chem-light batteries, fallopian tubes, exhaust sample kits, buckets of jet wash, and, yep, some vapor locks." The group seemingly laughed heartily for minutes

The Eagles at the table asked the journalists to share stories from their professional world, and they did so for over forty-five minutes.

As the late night grew longer, they migrated to a more serious tone.

"In a few days, we'll be back in San Diego with our families and friends and all the creature comforts of home, and you will still be out here, serving so far from home," admitted Patti, whose beauty was easily matched by her tender heart. After a short pause, she exposed a personal sentiment. "That makes me sad in a way, but I know we're all glad we had the opportunity to connect the faces of real humans, brave Americans, to a hard but dedicated way of life we knew very little about."

"This is my fourth back-to-back cruise," responded Lunker. "No one promised it'd be easy, but what I've learned is that shared misery or pain is not only okay, but it can, in fact, be turned into something good. Look at the great sports teams. They are built around a core philosophy of team, purpose, mission, or goal, or some combination, but never self, even when the rigors of their training surpass human capabilities. When a group of people becomes centered on self, then the first areas to be focused on, especially when misery or poor performance creeps into a team, are race, lineage, geography, personal traits — you know, items that can't be changed. As our skipper preaches to us, as long as we ensure our men have clean bathrooms, clean living spaces, good food, and a sailor gets his own laundry back and it's clean, then we'll have no morale problems as long as we keep our focus on team and mission. He's right. Quality of life, a team mentality, shared purpose, and a successful mission go hand in hand."

Socks added his thoughts as the four journalists leaned in, riveted by what was being said. "Sure. It sucks at times out here. We miss a lot of events that matter. Last cruise, Willie's mom died, and Lunker got a divorce by mail. Doc's sister was fighting cancer, our maintenance officer's son hit a game-winning home run in his conference championship game, and our admin officer's daughter took her first steps, and that's with just a few of the aviators in our squadron."

"Our enlisted men had the same issues last cruise, and similar things have already occurred during this cruise. Collectively, these things that we're not home for are the biggest prices we pay out here. But, to Lunker's point, the team and the mission is more important than the price we pay, and it's something we take pride in, even with the sacrifices."

"When I have a chance to see him, my grandfather always reminds me of something he told me when I was young," said

Willie. "He says we're doing what everyone wants done, but no one wants to do themselves. That may apply to you. In fact, I'm sure it probably does in ways we don't know, like it does with firemen and policemen and others like them." He paused briefly to take a sip of water. "It reinforces the difference between life and living, something you can only understand if you have personally experienced it." All four journalists nodded.

Lunker stepped back in. "We know you had a chance to spend some time with the enlisted men earlier, and you'll likely spend more time with them after you wake up later this morning. Those guys are the real heroes, the unsung heroes. We can't bring the jet back better than it was when we launched. It's the same, or something's broken that they'll have to fix so we can go flying again." He paused, clearly trying to articulate a thought.

"We reap the prize on their backs, and it's very humbling. If they didn't do their job, then this ship, our airplanes, and all of us, well, we couldn't defend our country at sea or in the air. All we'd be is a floating museum in a harbor somewhere. I don't know what you will write about regarding this experience, but I hope you will let your readers know that the men who will never have a chance to launch off this great ship and soar through the skies are our heroes, and they should be their heroes, too."

"I've only been in the squadron for less than a year, but what I have learned is that the nature of our business is all about hello's and goodbyes. Just like with you now; this may be our first and our last meeting." Gully's comments were straight from his roots in America's heartland.

"We've said hello to you and, too soon, we'll say goodbye. It's what we do, and it's tough. You all know that. And in our business, and in your business, the hellos and the goodbyes never stop. We enjoy the highs of the first meeting and lament the sadness of the last farewell, whether it's people or places or experiences, like this early morning on Midway." He paused briefly. The others could tell Gully had something to add; the emotions on his face gave it away. "Most likely we won't ever see any of you again," he said in a melancholy way, "and there is something very sad about that." He hesitated as he searched for the right words. "But would you trade this time tonight for us not meeting at all?" He looked at each of them. "I know I wouldn't."

The following afternoon, the four journalists, waiting to board the aircraft that would soon catapult them from Midway's flight deck, were overwhelmed as they said goodbye to the ship and the men, and most especially when Willie and Gully, walking in full flight gear toward their jet, smiled and waved as they passed by their new friends. They remembered Gully's words as they waved back.

In a few days, the four of them would be back in the comfortable surroundings of America, far from the men of the Navy's foreign legion who, they all now knew, would still be on patrol, loyally doing their duty somewhere over the horizon.

A week later, back on dry land in sunny southern California, each of the four penned their thoughts for the readers of their publications. They wrote eloquently about the many different facets of life on Midway. Among their articles, the common thread was that the men with whom they had associated so far from their homeland — the sailors and aviators and other members of the crew — were part of the nation's best and brightest and bravest and funniest citizens...and, without a doubt, the most endearing. In keeping with their promise to Lunker, they each articulated, artfully in their own way, the warm affection felt by those who flew toward those who kept them in the air.

Most poignantly, the four journalists had experienced two very special emotions known all too well to Midway's sailors and aviators. After landing back in Subic Bay, but before they left for California, they crossed the shit river bridge. Only once...across and back. That was enough.

And, equally impassioned, although they had said goodbye to Midway, they knew that their experience on the remarkable carrier would remain with them forever.

CHAPTER THIRTEEN

Elixir For The Soul
Fall 1980

On a balmy mid-afternoon, Willie and Doc launched from Midway, nestled off the northeast coast of Malaysia, and headed north-northeast as they climbed to an altitude of flight level 280, or twenty-eight thousand feet. Their final destination was Naval Air Station Cubi Point in the Philippines, fourteen hundred miles from their starting point on Midway. They were the CAG-Five's representatives to a pre-exercise conference regarding an upcoming airwing 'surprise strike' against the aircraft carrier Coral Sea, currently seventy miles northwest of Cubi Point.

Doc checked the readout on his navigation display. "...on deck with a cold San Miguel by the Cubi O'Club pool in one hour and thirty-six minutes, assuming we can be in the bar twenty minutes after landing." He was optimistic; thirty-five minutes was the normal time to put the Intruder to bed, check in with air ops, get a taxi to the Cubi Bachelor Officers Quarters and be on the receiving end of a cold San Miguel beer by the pool.

Predictable afternoon storms over the southern Philippines required them to play 'dodge clouds' as they began a descent toward their tropical home for the evening. Both had flown this path several times previously, and the sights along the way never failed to astonish, impact, and humble them. As they had on previous visits, they canceled their instrument clearance and flew the final two hundred miles south to the Subic Bay area under visual flight rules.

Green rolling hills, filled with lush tropical trees and dense jungle foliage, provided the perfect backdrop for unparalleled tactical navigational training at just two hundred feet above the ground and covering each statute mile in seven seconds. To say that tactical navigational training was all it was, though, would be to describe a fast walk along the floor of the Grand Canyon as nothing but decent aerobic exercise. The Philippines were a lot of things, but a boring place for flying wasn't one of them. Time was frozen in a large percentage of this small part of the world; it was both mind numbing and heart wrenching for those blessed to fly low and fast over such a beautiful country.

As they passed less than a couple hundred feet over beaches, rivers, and streams, quite often occupied by small wooden boats or individuals fishing, the two men were incontestably reminded that, as the world's second largest archipelago, the Philippines is the home to sons and daughters of the sea, people whose lives were, like those of the sailors and aviators on Midway, inextricably linked to the water.

Weather required them to circle in from almost thirty miles north of Naval Air Station Cubi Point. Fifteen miles east-northeast of their ultimate destination, flying just two hundred feet above the ground, they saw a small village, about three miles in front of them, less than thirty seconds away. It was a carbon copy of so many villages they had seen along their route while flying north across Luzon, the largest island in the Philippines, during the past thirty-five minutes. Like the others, this village was nestled next to a small rice paddy at the edge of a forest of palm trees. The only paved road they saw was two miles or so west of the village, a road that made a sharp turn to the north. Nearby was a small flowing river and two agricultural fields, side by side, separated by two parallel rows of palm trees and small rolling hills located on the north and east sides of the village.

A snapshot of the village itself revealed two thick clumps of tall palms, arranged by nature in two arcs facing each other, surrounding ageless small, fragile-looking homes, open communal fires, and several carabaos — big docile water buffalos, resting in wet, muddy areas scattered in and around the village. Like a boat is to a fisherman in undeveloped parts of the planet, carabaos are a beast of burden to the Filipino people. They represent a source of income and a ride home to those who toil daily in the fields.

The large, domesticated draught animals were disciplined, strong, and loyally supportive to the hard working Filipino villagers and farmers who couldn't afford machinery or modern equipment. The carabao was so revered, in fact, that it was the national animal of the Philippines.

Nearby, a small river, or perhaps a large stream, was flowing toward the sea a little faster than normal, a result of almost constant rain the previous two days. Although the village was only four or five miles from a small town of probably a thousand people, there was no sign of electricity or any other modern creature comfort that indicated the year was 1980, except for the aircraft racing toward the timeless settlement at three-hundred sixty knots, over four-hundred miles per hour.

At the edge of the village, the fliers saw a group of young children, most of them barely clothed, whose brown skin blended in with a game they were playing in a large open dirt field by a rice paddy. The game could be best described as soccer, although the ball they were kicking didn't appear to be a traditional kind. Willie adjusted the Intruder's course and altitude so they'd pass about fifty feet away and one hundred fifty feet above their heads. As they did, the children all looked up at the loud interruption flying low over them, excitedly jumping and waving as Willie rolled the Intruder slightly to the right so Doc could wave back, keeping a little back pressure on the control stick to keep them from descending toward the trees.

Even there, on the edge of their makeshift field of sports, two carabaos rested in mud, cooling themselves like spectators. It was strikingly surreal to see a place on the planet where time stood still. Likewise, the distinction between beast of war and beasts of burden could not be more apparent, and yet both were doing exactly what was required for them to be ready to perform their duties when called upon.

"Did you see that little girl sitting on that water buffalo, by herself, waving at us?" Doc continued to look out the right side as Willie kept his eyes scanning forward, left and right.

"I sure did. Was that a genuinely sweet smile or what?" A quick glance was all Willie safely had, but it was more than enough to be emotionally captivated by a precious young girl, with long black hair, who had her left hand against a large but gentle carabao with wrap-around horns, and her right hand waving excitedly to them.

"Yeah, sweet, sweet smile is right, and waving as hard as she could." Doc paused, staring at the country racing past them. "I'd love to go down there and tell her she made my day."

Just as he finished his statement, Doc felt the Intruder roll into a hard left turn. "Let's go back and tell her the only way we can," replied Willie, as he maneuvered the jet to fly by the village a second time. As they approached the village, Willie slowed the jet to two hundred forty knots, just under two hundred eighty miles per hour, and descended to barely a hundred feet above the treetops. As they passed the children and the young girl sitting on the carabao, Willie slowly rocked the Intruder's wings as Doc waved at them. The young girl, probably five or six and still sitting all by herself on the carabao, slid off the animal and waved at them with both hands while jumping up and down.

The Intruder, back on course to Cubi Point and accelerating, covered several miles over lush ground as its two aviators sat in silence, trying to digest the heart-tugging emotions of twice seeing the small Filipino girl, an innocent child whose smile transcended distance and cultures and hugged them right where they sat. Their minds still longed to see her and her smile once more, even as their hearts silently ached with the knowledge that it was impossible. What a shame. There was so much they could probably learn from her.

The last village, which they named 'smiling girl village,' was the final one of at least a dozen such villages they had passed enroute to their destination. Each injected a full dose of humbling reality into the Americans. In particular, the young children's bright smiles and joyful greetings, all along their path, were emotionally infectious to the two men, separated from them by more than just a fast jet.

"We'll miss this, Willie, one day when we've been ushered out to pasture like that big ol' water buffalo lying by the rice paddy," observed Doc. Consciously or unconsciously, Willie, Doc and the CAG-Five aviators who flew low over this special land left a small piece of themselves behind each time they bid it goodbye, just as they did each time they bid farewell to Midway. It was one of the foreign legion's blessings and one of its curses.

CHAPTER FOURTEEN

One Final Round
Early Winter, 1980

Lunker was asleep in Bunkroom Eight when the telephone rang. He could reach it from his bunk.

"Lieutenant Fishman." He glanced at his watch. 0601. One minute after six. His alarm was set for seven.

"Good morning, sir. Petty Officer Winslow here. I have a message you need to see right away."

"I'll be right down." As the squadron's flight schedules officer, Lunker often received calls from the Eagles' administrative office in the early hours of the morning. Generally, they involved an urgent Navy message regarding changes to target times or other operational issues that impacted the day's flight schedule or missions. He quickly dressed: gray cotton work out shorts, a Bunkroom Eight t-shirt, green flight suit, white athletic socks, and black flight boots — Naval Aviation's version of business casual attire. Two minutes later, he departed the Midway Oasis.

Although the ship was relatively quiet inside, excepting the constant low hum of a massive ship underway, Lunker could hear voices, the dragging of chains, and the sound of airplanes being towed just feet above him on the flight deck. In slightly less than three hours, the airplanes assigned to the day's first launch would be manned and their engines turning; in four hours, they would all be airborne.

The ship's rolling motion was minimal, making for a smooth walk and, most importantly, a safe 'step-over' through the endless steel hatches — kneeknockers — along the way. The seas must be relatively calm, he thought, just as the weather-guessers predicted. That was good.

Five minutes after receiving the call, Lunker strolled into the Eagles' admin office and was greeted by a smiling face.

Petty Officer Winslow handed Lunker a single piece of paper. As anticipated, it was a Navy message, but it wasn't urgent or related to the flight schedule. "Congratulations, sir. We'll miss you."

UNCLASSIFIED
R 082154ZDEC80
FM BUPERS WASHINGTON DC
TO FISHMAN, CARL E/LT/1320
INFO CO ATKRON ONE ONE FIVE
CARRIER AIR WING FIVE
BT
UNCLAS

SUBJ/PCS ORDERS ICO FISHMAN, CARL E/LT/1320//
UPON RECEIPT OR NLT 21DEC1980, DETACH FROM
ATKRON ONE ONE FIVE AND PROCEED TO NAVAL
AVIATION SCHOOLS COMMAND, NAS PENSACOLA,
FLORIDA FOR DUTY IN A FLYING STATUS INVOLVING
OPERATIONAL OR TRAINING FLIGHTS AS A STUDENT

NAVAL AVIATOR. DESIGNATOR CHANGE FROM 1320 TO
1390 UPON DETACHMENT APPROVED.
REPORT NASP BLDG 633 NLT 0800 30DEC1980.
BT

It was official. Lunker was leaving the Eagles, Midway, and Eli to begin a journey culminating, he hoped, with the gold wings of a Navy pilot. A one-page document was the key to taming the great spaces in the sky, and he would soon be doing the driving. Lunker could still barely believe it, and he made a mental note to again thank CAG for his input to the Pentagon. He had anticipated receiving the orders for the past couple weeks, and yet their arrival, nine days into December 1980, still felt like an early Christmas present.

"Thank you, Petty Officer, Winslow. I'll miss you and all the guys. All of this." He looked around the office. He'd truly miss the interaction with all the fine men and the jets and every other part of Midway, but he was suddenly eager to begin the next chapter in his Navy adventure.

Lunker extended his hand to the senior enlisted man in front of him. "Thank you for the best wake-up call I could ever receive."

"Last time in the P.I. coming up, sir. Pensacola is a great place, but it ain't Subic."

Lunker nodded slowly as he smiled. "Yep. No place but Subic is Subic." He always knew there would be a last visit to the place everyone casually called the P.I. — Republic of the Philippine Islands was far too formal for places as marvelously simple as Subic and Cubi and the Binictican Golf Course.

He glanced at the message again; it was bittersweet. One part of him was happy and the other part was sad. He was ecstatic at actually having his official orders in his hands, but Pensacola was a long way from his dear friend and caddy and all the wonderful men on Midway, especially the brotherhood of the Eagles and Bunkroom Eight.

"It's hard for everyone to leave. It's why I volunteered for a second tour on Midway after my last duty station back in the states." Petty Officer 'Arizona' Winslow smiled.

"I can understand that. Maybe you can get orders to Subic or Cubi when you roll out of here. That's only, what, seven months away?"

"Yes, sir. That's a blink of an eye in this man's Navy, and I'm already talking to my detailer about it."

"I hope he comes through for you."

"Thank you, sir. You need to work out an actual departure date with the skipper, and then we'll get the orders drafted."

"Thanks again, Petty Officer Winslow. You're one of the guys I'm really going to miss."

"If you get back to WestPac, sir, you'll know where to find me."

"Yes, I do. Old West Number Two." The two men smiled and shook hands.

Lunker returned to Bunkroom Eight. As he entered, everyone was still sleeping except for Willie and Gully. They were flying the tanker on the first event of the day.

"Everything okay?" asked Gully. He glanced at the paper in Lunker's hand. It was easy to see that it was a standard Navy message.

"My orders to Pensacola. I'm a short timer."

"Congratulations," said Willie, his smile beaming at his friend's news. He and Gully shook Lunker's hand.

"Thanks. I'm not sure it's sunk in yet."

"I'm not sure Eli is ready to hear the news."

"Well, I'll just have to hit a couple holes-in-one to make him smile and forget I'm leaving." They all laughed.

"You'll need help from some friendly greenside monkeys to pull that off."

"I think they've helped him all along. We just didn't see them."

"You guys are jealous because I'll be having a Bushwacker on the beach while you're having shit on a shingle with a bunch of smelly guys on an old gray ship."

They all looked at each other, smiling in silence for a moment. "It's gonna be a helluva farewell party in Cubi."

"Yes and amen," added Doc, who had heard the discussion and stood up next to his bunk in order to shake his hand. "Congratulations, Lunker, but it doesn't mean I'll ever voluntarily fly in your right seat."

Lunker smiled. "You may be part of a long list." They all laughed.

The second week of December flew by quickly. Midway was less than twelve hours from arriving in Subic Bay for a six day visit. The last jet to land before the inport period began had snagged a two wire at exactly twenty fifteen hours; eight fifteen p.m. to most of the world. It was an Intruder with Willie flying and Lunker sitting to his right.

There was a large sheet cake waiting for Lunker in the ready room. He received an Eagles' plaque with a gold metal tag that had his name, call sign, and arrival and departure dates.

LT Carl 'Lunker' Fishman
22 Jan 1979 - 13 December 1980

Four hours later, it was deathly dark on Midway's quiet flight deck. Although a quarter moon was peeking very slightly above the horizon, it was positioned behind the ship. The two men had been strolling the deck, chatting, and reminiscing for almost thirty minutes; it was well after midnight, but the time didn't matter.

"I have to ask you something, Lunker. Do you have a death wish? You're the schedules officer and you scheduled your last flight in the squadron as a last event tanker on a night when there's no moon."

"Willie," he spoke slowly, "I wanted a final reminder that if you could do this pilot shit, then even I could do this pilot shit."

They both laughed. "I should have intentionally boltered a few times, maybe gotten really low and been waved off. That would have messed with your brain just a little bit. But being a good bunkroom buddy, I sent you off with an okay pass and a fresh dose of confidence."

Lunker laughed. "I'm glad you landed on the first pass. I was really eager to cut into that standard Navy-issue cake and drink whatever that nasty punch was."

As they laughed and continued a slow walk past the island toward the bow, their discussion shifted to a sad reality that had been part of both their journeys on Midway. They each had lost a woman they loved to the stress of naval aviation.

"It's true," said Willie. He glanced to his right at the man next to him. It was difficult to make out specific features in the darkness that enveloped them both.

"What's true?" asked Lunker.

"The Bunkroom Eight motto. It only hurts when you're awake."

"I remember that feeling all too well, Willie. It plants itself deep into places you never knew you had, places that never seem to sleep, or don't allow you to sleep." Lunker paused for several steps, as they were walking slowly toward Midway's bow, packed with jets at rest. "Sometimes, when I think of my daughter being so far away, I wish I could cry, but I haven't cried in a long time."

"I understand, Lunker. I'm not even sure I remember how to cry." They walked in silence for about thirty seconds and then stopped next to the Intruder they had flown just hours earlier. The jet was parked with its nose pointed toward the ship's two o'clock position.

Midway's bow was less than seven feet away as they leaned against its port wing. From where they stood, no one could see them. Only a blanket of stars and God knew they were there.

The two men stood in silence, listening to the sounds of the South China Sea as its warm, eighty-degree waters met

Midway's bow. It was a rhythmic, soothing sound, despite its imbedded power — cathartic and appropriate for their discussion.

"It's like Moses," said Lunker.

"What's like Moses?" asked Willie.

"Midway's bow is parting the waters."

There was silence as Willie absorbed his thought. "Maybe that should be your new call sign in Pensacola."

They were quiet, and a sense of peace surrounded them. There was no hurry or urgency to their conversation. After a minute, Willie continued. "How do you say Moses in north Georgia?"

Midway's bow was steady and firm as she continued to slice through the dark ocean. Time was irrelevant as a stiff warm breeze refreshed their faces.

"Moses."

"Well, at least something makes sense up in those hills." Willie smiled in the darkness. "Do you miss the mountains, Lunker?"

"Many times," he admitted. "Sometimes all the time."

"I feel what you're saying." Willie paused for a few seconds. "I worry that I've already had my last walk in the mountains with Archie, my grandfather. He's eighty, you know, and it makes me sad to think we may never share that land together again."

They were quiet for a minute or two, listening to the sound of dark water being split and choosing sides as it flowed down the port and starboard sides of Midway, only to rejoin behind the ship when the short journey apart was over.

"I do believe that the drinking lamp is lit, Willie." The tall man spoke slowly.

"You have something up your sleeve?"

"Nope. In a pocket in my flight suit." He slowly pulled two vodka miniatures from a small zippered compartment on the inside left arm of his flight suit, in the bicep area.

"Thank you, my dear bunkroom buddy," Willie said gratefully as he accepted the gift. "It won't be the same when you leave and head back to P-Cola, so let's drink to remembering these days."

"Deal," agreed Lunker. "We likely won't pass this way again, so here's to us, mi amigo, and Eli and all the others."

Willie nodded. "Yes and amen, my friend. Yes and amen." They tapped their bottles in the near darkness, drank the smooth burning liquid in a matter of seconds, and tossed the empty miniatures into the warm, vast sea.

Eight hours later, Midway approached the Hoover Mountain passage, the entrance to Subic Bay. The morning was so clear that it would be easy to believe that Eli could climb to the top of a tall hill and see all the way to California — if it weren't for that well-placed barricade to a dream called the horizon.

The Binitican Golf Course was active with golfers taking advantage of the Philippines' winter weather. It was seventy-seven degrees with a light breeze. The high temperature was forecast to be eighty-three, with a slight chance of a late afternoon shower. The previous afternoon, via whatever official or unofficial sources they had access to, numerous Subic Bay residents had confirmed that Midway would be arriving at just after nine o'clock in the morning.

Eli was waiting patiently at the course when it opened, and was immediately selected to carry the bag for a member of the first group to hit the course. His hope was that if Lunker was still on Midway he would see his dear friend in the early afternoon. It was important enough to him that, forty-five minutes earlier than he would normally leave his home, he walked the two miles from his village to the road where he would board a Jeepney for the thirteen-mile ride to Olongapo.

"Five iron, please." The older golfer, a military retiree, held out his hand, but Eli's thoughts and eyes were temporarily focused on Hoover Mountain and the watery passage that Midway would pass through sometime soon. "Eli, can I have my five iron?" His voice was louder and his tone was one of irritation.

"Sorry, sir. Right away." He pulled the club from the bag and handed it to the golfer.

"You seem distracted this morning. That's not like you. What's going on?"

Eli was a professional, and he was instantly angry with himself for allowing his focus to drift somewhere it didn't need to be. "Will be okay, Nelson. Time play golf. Help get lower score than last time."

Thirty-five minutes later, Eli was walking between holes when his eyes saw Midway through a group of palm trees nestled just beyond the next hole. She had cleared the Hoover mountain passage and was, from his perspective, passing the right side of Grande Island. Every time Midway came into sight after that, Eli stared, hoping his friend was on the big gray ship. He would be devastated if their last visit three months ago was actually their last time together.

Two holes later, Eli could tell that if Midway wasn't already tied to the pier on the Subic side of the base, she was just minutes away from being officially inport. He tried to hide his elation, but he failed as he said a silent prayer that Lunker was onboard.

"Driver, Eli. I think I'll see if I can get in position for a birdie." Eli didn't immediately respond, which wasn't like him at all, thought the man for whom he was caddying.

"Eli. Driver. Please." He was more emphatic and slightly annoyed.

"Yes sir. Sorry, sir."

"What's going on, Eli?

Eli took a deep breath. Absolute honesty was the only path he ever traveled. "Have friend on Midway. Flyer." His eyes glanced westward across the lush green Binictican course and blue waters of Subic Bay toward the pier where Midway rested.

Eli looked back toward Nelson Cryor. "Caddy for him over two year. Last trip before leave America. Hope he on ship and not gone. Will know this afternoon."

Nelson understood the toll the Navy took not only on the families, but also on friends, found and nurtured in America and around the world, who were temporary by the very nature of Navy life. He also knew of Eli's desire to see over the horizon. Like Lunker and others, he shared with Eli many stories from and descriptions of the places he had visited.

"Eli," Nelson said in a soft, fatherly tone, "We only get one lifetime. If we don't pursue our dreams in that lifetime, there is no second chance. We don't get a second chance on dear friends, either." He paused. "You look at that ship all you want. I understand. I hope he's on there, as eager to see you as you are to see him. If he feels the way I feel about you, I'm sure he's chomping at the bit to get up here and play a round of golf with you."

Eli's eyes were beginning to imperceptibly moisten as Nelson spoke. The God who held three of his children in His hands had blessed him with good friends on this beautiful land. "Okay. Thank you." He paused. "Thank you."

Four hours later, to both their delight, Lunker and Eli were reunited with big smiles.

"Glad you back. Not leave go home."

"I'm still having a little trouble with my short game, Eli. I thought maybe you could help me fix it if I came back here one more time."

Eli laughed loudly. "Still need three year, maybe four."

"It is so good to see you, my dearest friend of all." Lunker put his arm across Eli's shoulders. "There was no way I was going to leave and not see you again, even if I had to jump off the ship and swim to Subic."

"Thought you bad swimmer."

"I am a bad swimmer, Eli. I practically drown every time I take the Navy's swim test, but I'd try and swim here to play one more round with you."

"Glad you here. Time play golf. Have fun."

"And cold San Miguel and hot dogs," added Lunker.

A dozen carabao couldn't pull Eli's grin off his brown, weathered face. "What Doc say? Yes and amen?"

"Yes and amen." The tall aviator laughed. His smile was seemingly permanent as well; he was right where he wanted to be.

The two friends laughed and talked like two young boys through the first two holes, discussing flying and that which Lunker had recently seen over the horizon, which was mostly water. Like young lads, they decided to climb the steps up to the third hole without assistance from the generator-driven, rope pulley system.

At the top, the two friends sat on a wooden bench that had recently been added and looked across the lush tropical land. The scene was as familiar and comforting as a well-worn, soft cotton shirt. Small rolling hills, dotted sparingly across the landscape a half-mile or so away, and taller mountains, green with a slight blue hue at their ten o'clock and two o'clock positions in the distance, had never lost their Eden-like allure. They were old friends, too — always there, patiently waiting for the next visit.

"How Mirela?"

Lunker smiled. "She will be pleased that you asked about her, Eli. She's fine, and we had a nice time in Hong Kong, but we left one day earlier than planned."

"Why leave early?"

"The aircraft carrier Coral Sea, old like Midway, had a problem and couldn't launch its airplanes. We left early to take its place."

"Coral Sea here four five week ago for six day. What problem?"

"Oh, it had a broke-dick air conditioning system and some other problems."

The weathered caddy looked at Lunker and smiled. "Didn't know aircraft carrier have dick." Eli was laughing hard as he finished his comment.

Lunker's laughter echoed that of his caddy. "Well, apparently the Coral Sea does. Fortunately, an A-6 B/N who had previously been an enlisted man threw on some coveralls and had it fixed in about thirty hours. Unfortunately, by then we had already departed Hong Kong."

He looked into the brown eyes of the rarest kind of a man — a man who still managed to embrace and smile at the life he was given despite all the unimaginable heartache he had known. "I miss you already, Eli. No one makes me laugh like you do." He paused, looking out across a land he would sorely miss. "Seriously. I can't remember a single time being around you when I wasn't laughing or smiling."

"Except hit ball in jungle and can't find. Lose stroke."

"Okay, but c'mon, that was only one time, I think."

Eli laughed hard again. "Five time. Remember better than you. But will forget. Pretend no time hit ball there."

"Thank you, Eli." Lunker was laughing as well. "How's Violetta?"

Eli smiled broadly. Only Lunker had ever asked about his family and his wife. "She good. Me no good without Violetta. Keep me on toes you say."

Lunker laughed. "Yes, indeed, my friend. We men would be so boring and incomplete without women."

Eli quickly responded. "What Doc say?"

"Yes and amen," the two friends answered together in stereo, laughing as they did.

Eli was soon quiet, leaning forward on the bench. Time was irrelevant. There were no golfers behind them at the moment. He seemed apprehensive. "When leaving?"

Lunker took a slow, deep breath. "Four days."

308

"Play golf tomorrow?"

"Tomorrow and the next two days. I leave the morning after. I'll fly one of our jets to Japan, then fly on a commercial airliner back to America. Mirela is going to meet me there."

Eli was quiet. The entirety of their friendship had been born and nurtured on a small patch of ground, a geographic miniscule of a dot. There had been other naval aviators he remembered fondly, but only a couple had ever returned. Even then, it was never like the first time. None had been like Lunker. He couldn't find the words to say why, but he knew why. Maybe they really were brothers.

"Time go fast. Remember first time met. You birdie first hole."

"You have a remarkable memory, Eli." Lunker looked to his left. Eli hadn't changed in the almost two and a half years they had known each other, he thought. He remembered the first time they met, but he didn't remember the birdie.

"Always remember friends." Eli paused and took a deep breath. "You special friend, Lunker."

Lunker was quiet, but nodded. There was unspeakable beauty in the land where they sat, and there was unspeakable beauty in their friendship. Any attempt to define it with human words would be woefully inadequate. They would carry the emotions forever; that was all that mattered. No words were necessary; the voices of their hearts spoke for them.

The two friends continued to look across the landscape, savoring the moment for a couple more minutes, and then they stood up. Both were smiling.

"Hit three iron. Best club you hit." Eli reached into the bag.

Lunker took the club and walked toward the tee box, where he bent over and teed his ball. He stood upright and slowly looked back toward his friend. "Seriously, Eli? You think the three iron is my best club?"

Eli nodded. His face wore a half smile, but his heart was serious. "Know you better than you Lunker. You good golfer.

Very good man. Always try be better. Listen to someone teach; not get mad. Hope you listen when learn be pilot. Make you safe. Not crash."

Eli's observation and sentimental concern for his safety hit Lunker's heart the way Lunker hit a three iron. Hard and straight.

The ageless caddy was acutely aware of the ever-present dangers attached to those who flew the Navy's fast jets. He knew that, too soon, he'd again be thinking about his friend, somewhere over the place where the water and sky bonded, and hoping he was safe. The great unknown would be painful at times, he knew, but arguing with God for an answer as to Lunker's fate would be fruitless. He had been blessed with a gem of a friend, and their cherished memories would make him smile until he left this paradise for a better one.

Eli continued. "Be safe for me you. Be safe for daughter. Be safe Mirela too."

Lunker could barely speak as his friend's concern landed upon his ears. He always knew their last visit would be emotionally difficult, but he didn't expect this. "I promise, Eli." He nodded. "I promise."

As the round continued, a symbolic countdown timer, connected to their time together, was ticking faster than either of them would like. The round was over too soon, but they were smiling. Lunker finished the final hole, a par four, with a birdie, due in large part to his listening to Eli's advice instead of his own intuition. He was sure a three wood was the right club, but deferred to Eli's insistence and used his three iron instead. As they walked off the green toward the open-air snack shop, their bright smiles could have illuminated a dozen dark rooms.

Sitting on a wooden bench among a small grove of palm trees, the two men enjoyed hot dogs, cold San Niguel beer, and each other's company for almost an hour. Most recently, Eli had been regaling him with stories of his two daughters, Macaalay and Diwata, now eight and six. They loved to play soccer, although they had to use a makeshift ball made from tightly intertwined palm fronds.

Eli became quiet for a minute and then spoke. "Not play last day here." Eli's words surprised Lunker. He had hoped to play every day he was in Subic Bay.

"Is something wrong? Is it your family, Eli? I'd like the two of us to play every day I have here."

"Wife invite you friends come our village. Doc. Willie. Gully. Other friends live with on ship. Have feast. Cook pig fish. Meet family friends. Best way say goodbye you, Lunker. Better than golf."

Lunker was speechless. He never expected this. His hometown in north Georgia was a long way from the Philippines, but not really. Family and friends meant everything in that part of the world. It was the same in this South Pacific paradise, too. He wasn't surprised that Eli felt like his brother.

Lunker spoke slowly. "I'd like that, Eli, and I'm sure my friends will as well. Is there anything we can bring?"

"No. Just you. We fix everything. See village. Play with children. Best way say goodbye."

Lunker nodded. "I can't wait, Eli, and I am very honored you would think of me and my friends that way." He paused. "But you will now have to work extra hard the next two rounds to make me a better golfer." He laughed as he finished, as did Eli.

"Still need two three year."

The second day of golf began late. As they had said goodbye at the end of the first day, Lunker had told Eli that he'd be at the course just after lunch, probably around one or one-thirty, and explained why. His going away party was going to be a long raucous night at the Cubi Officer's Club. Now, under a bright south Pacific sun, he and three of his bunkroom buddies were living proof that beer on whiskey is mighty risky and, further, why a morning tee time would have been foolish.

"Okay, Lunker? Look tired."

"I was at death's door most of the morning, Eli. I'm a little better now. But no beer today. Just water or soda."

Eli laughed. "Long night at go away party? Too many San Miguel?"

"And other assorted drinks, too. Too many toasts. One would have been enough." Lunker paused; his bloodshot eyes confirmed the fun of the long evening at the Cubi Officer's Club, and the misery of the late morning wake-up call."

"Lunker's right," agreed Doc. "We were knocking on death's door with him, Eli, and it was a long way from paradise."

Eli laughed harder. "Order coke and hot dog. Will feel better once start walking paradise."

Gully and Fish were quiet. They, like the other two Eagles, had struggled waking up, but a promise was a promise. Playing golf and drinking beer had sounded like such a wonderful idea just after midnight. Only Willie exhibited good judgment; he didn't pretend he could be productive on the golf course. He was still asleep when the four departed Bunkroom Eight.

Over a lunch of oatmeal and wheat toast at the Chuckwagon, the four friends all swore, as they had done on previous occasions, that the previous evening was the last time they'd make the mistake of randomly drinking San Miguel, stingers, and tequila shooters.

The group of four was joined by the same three caddies used during the previous inport period: Lito, Romy, and George. They were glad to be reacquainted, and looked forward to a walk with old friends in a place that seemed like home to all eight. First, though, they all enjoyed a lunch consisting of two hot dogs and a soda.

Added to their late breakfast, the second wave of food injected a healthy dose of rehabilitative power to the four aviators. In fact, it was restorative enough that, when Eli asked about the previous evening's events, they regaled the four caddies with the Eagles' fight song, a song they had sung loudly and proudly at least a dozen times during the long night of youthful festivities at the Cubi O'Club.

You mention attack,
We're the best in WestPac.
We will fight night or day,
We will fight anywhere you say,
And don't forget we're Eagles,
We're Eagles, we are the best.

Eli laughed and asked them to sing it again, which they did. The Eagles were feeling better by the minute.

"Thank you, Lunker. Like song. Now time play golf." Eli's declaration was perfectly timed and well received.

Fortunately, large, puffy south Pacific clouds hid the sun for much of the eighteen holes, and the round went by quickly. On four separate occasions, one of the caddies was sent for sodas — no beer. All four aviators were sweating much more than usual and needed plenty of fluids. The four caddies laughed each time the request was made, and all four shared in the generous tips. At several points along the heavenly course, they paused for photos. If Lunker and Eli had their impending final round on their minds, it didn't show. They looked like two best friends simply glad to be spending the afternoon together.

As the round was completed, Lunker and Eli agreed to meet at twelve-thirty the next day. They'd have lunch together and then play eighteen holes — just the two of them — for the very last time.

The next morning, the eight residents of Bunkroom Eight, the Midway Oasis, met for breakfast at the Chuckwagon at nine. They each wanted to shop for Christmas gifts for their friends and families before Magsaysay Street became congested with sailors later in the day. With the exception of their upcoming visit to Eli's village, this would, most likely, be the last time the eight men would be together as a group. No one had to articulate it; the significance of the morning gathering hung over the group like the early morning clouds overhead.

Unless someone dicked the donkey in a very bad way, no one, not the enlisted men nor the officers, could escape his turn saying a final goodbye with the friends he had made on Midway.

This was Lunker's turn; his goodbye would be in Tagalog — Paalam, pronounced pah-ahl-lam, with the accent on the middle syllable. Appropriately, it'd be in a simple building with lots of charm and a row of slot machines between the two attached Quonset huts. The Chuckwagon was vintage Subic; he wouldn't want to say goodbye on any other land but this illustrious soil.

Lunker arrived at the Binictican Golf Course five minutes early. As Lunker paid the taxi driver, Eli retrieved Lunker's clubs from the white sedan's trunk. The two men smiled and shook hands as they had countless times before.

"What that bag for?" Eli motioned toward a small backpack-like bag Lunker was holding.

"Cold beer." Eli laughed. "It's called a soft cooler," said Lunker. "It's lined with a material that is supposed to keep ice from melting for three hours. I thought we'd see if it actually works."

Eli laughed harder. "Why wait last round golf bring? Should have every round full with beer."

"It's new, and the Navy Exchange just got them in." The Navy Exchange was the Navy's version of a large, tax-free department store. Lunker had already put ice and four cold San Miguels inside the bag. "I also have another treat for us."

"What that?"

"You'll see in a minute."

Eli hoisted Lunker's bag onto his shoulder, and the two men walked to the first tee box. The nearest golfers were three holes ahead of them, and there were no other golfers waiting. The noon sun, almost directly overhead, would likely keep other golfers away for at least another hour.

Eli looked inside the bag's compartment that held golf balls and made a funny face as he pulled one out. "Why you have different color balls, Lunker?" Red, green, yellow, blue, purple, and orange balls were numerous.

"I thought you'd enjoy them on our last round instead of the boring white ones."

Eli laughed. Rounds of golf were always enjoyable and amusing, and he was emotionally impacted at the thought Lunker had put into their last round together. "Like them. Where you get color balls?"

"You can get anything you want in Olongapo."

Eli laughed and nodded. "Yes. Some good, some bad."

Lunker smiled. "Some fun, and some scary." They both looked at each other and smiled.

"Some cold. Some hot."

"Some tasty. Some not so tasty."

Eli's heart was already aching at the thought of no longer having the company of the dear friend who always made him smile and laugh. "Some tall. Some short."

Lunker laughed. "Some skinny." Lunker spread his arms wide. "Some not skinny."

Eli laughed harder. "Some..." He used both his hands to depict large breasts and then small breasts.

"And then your wife cuts your balls off with a sharp knife, my friend."

Eli smiled. "No. Use dull knife. Take longer. Hurt more."

Lunker laughed as he nodded, and then put his left hand on Eli's right shoulder. "We are just alike, Eli. We are brothers from different mothers."

"But same father." Eli made a sign of the cross; Lunker did the same.

"Yes and amen, and now it's time for us to play a round of golf."

"Make best round ever."

"Oh Eli, every round with you has been the best ever."

Eli was silent for a few moments as he contained his emotions. "Will miss time on course, Lunker. Won't be same."

Lunker stared at Eli as his dear friend handed him his club. Eli wasn't known as a great man, but he was a great man. He stared for a moment more. Where had all the rounds and all their time together gone? For so long, there was always a tomorrow in front of them. There was always a next visit just over a distant horizon after a short or long separation, and then more rounds of golf. Each disappearing minute of this final round was palpable, and Lunker hadn't yet teed off.

The first two holes were played the way they'd played them every time before. Discussions were predominantly centered on what both had been doing since they last saw each other and how their families were doing — Eli's family in Subic Bay and Lunker's family onboard Midway. Lunker had two pars, although a great recommendation by Eli regarding where to aim saved Lunker from bogeying number two. They rewarded each other by opening two beers from Lunker's new backpack cooler.

"I remember the first time we came to this hole," said Lunker, as the two arrived at the rope climb to the number three tee box. "You turned the old generator on and I thought time had turned back forty years."

"Wish could turn back time." The two men looked at each other and smiled.

"Me, too," said Lunker in a melancholy voice. "It's been a wonderful ride, Eli."

The two men turned the first sixteen holes into a nostalgic walk of the most joyous kind, especially with cold San Miguel along for the journey. On two separate occasions, monkeys sat by a green and looked at the men. "Maybe we should let them hit and we'll stand by the green and watch," said Lunker.

Eli laughed. "Think monkeys come say goodbye, Lunker. Miss you too."

"That's a nice thought, Eli. Let's give them a treat." On both occasions, although the monkeys didn't touch the ball Lunker hit, the two men each selected several colored golf balls and threw them toward the spectators as they walked closer to the green. The monkeys seemed pleased and carried their gifts into the jungle.

Between holes nine and ten, they stopped to have a hot dog and a soda. As they stood together at number ten's tee box, Lunker made a confession to his friend. "Do you remember the time when we tried to play a hole blindfolded?"

Eli stopped walking and smiled. "I go first. Hit two of three balls. Miss third." He laughed.

Lunker nodded. "I have to tell you something, Eli. You hit those first two pretty good for being blindfolded, and I wasn't sure I would even hit one, much less two, when it was my turn." He paused. "So, after you lined up to hit the third shot, and I tied the blindfold on you, I went quickly and moved the ball and tee about two inches further out."

Eli laughed hard. "That funny. Glad you tell truth. Now I tell truth." He paused and looked into Lunker's eyes. He'd miss these moments with a man he'd never forget. "Remember you swing two time at first ball and not hit. I took ball off tee put back on after you swing each time."

"You little shit, Eli. We are brothers. Sneaky little shit brothers." They both laughed. "I think it's time for another beer."

"Fine with me. I buy."

"Nope. I'll buy. I'm the visitor here. You live here. Visitor buys."

"No. You backward. You always buy. Caddy buy last round golf. New rule." Eli reached into Lunker's backpack and retrieved two beers as they both laughed.

"Okay, Eli. Thank you."

Later, as they walked off number sixteen's green, Lunker stopped and looked all around the course — a soothing blanket of emotions and experiences lingered like the sweat on his brow — three hundred sixty degrees of memories he wanted to sear into his brain. He would miss the unique and flavorful smells, the sounds of the indigenous animals and birds, the taste of San Miguel, and the beauty of a land half a planet away from his home. He'd even miss the heavy sweat that soaked his clothes for most of the daytime hours and the mosquito bites when he forgot to use repellent in the early evening. It was a five-senses experience like no other; Eli's sixth sense in suggesting club and shot placement was icing on the cake.

He looked at Eli standing a few feet away, a man diminutive in physical stature, but a giant as a human being and a friend. "From the day I first arrived onboard Midway and joined my squadron, the Eagles, I knew one day I'd leave, and I instinctively knew on that last day that I would miss it all — the carrier, the squadron and the flying, and the men who fixed our jets and those who flew them. I knew I'd miss Bunkroom Eight and my friends who lived there with me." He paused and moved a little closer to Eli, close enough so he could put his hand on the shoulder of the only caddy he ever used.

"What I never anticipated, Eli, was that I would miss a Filipino caddy the most. But it's true...I will miss you and our time together more than anyone or anything. I love the airplane, the Intruder, but it will never love me back. You were there for me during my toughest time, when my wife and daughter left, and times when I was unsure of myself, of what I wanted to do in life, and your words always kept me going, kept me pushing forward. You kept a smile on my face when I didn't have the energy for one." Lunker had tears as he stared into Eli's eyes.

"I will never forget you. Never."

"You help me, Lunker. You save Diwata life get medicine. You only golfer ask about children wife every time. Treat me like best friend. We best friend. Even far away. Now have two holes to play. Be best holes. Then good time tomorrow my village." Eli was also wracked with emotions, but he had conditioned himself to keep them in control.

Sooner than they would like, the two friends stepped off the number seventeen green. Lunker had, twice, questioned Eli's recommendation for the aim point on a long putt, but his dear friend was insistent. Thanks to Eli's guidance and keen ability to read the break of the green, Lunker birdied the hole with a putt from eighteen feet away.

As they arrived at the tee box for the final hole, Eli reached into the bag. "No club," said Lunker softly.

"Why no club?" Eli looked at his friend from far across the horizon. He was puzzled; he had always hoped Lunker would birdie the final hole with a long putt for which he had suggested the proper aim point. Just as he had done on seventeen, Eli was looking forward to doing it again, one final time, on number eighteen.

"If I play this hole, then we have no more holes to play together." Lunker paused and looked toward the green and the pin flag waving in the warm breeze. He had thought about this moment for a long time. He looked left and right, and then stared at the dear man next to him. "This way, you and I will always have one more hole to play, no matter where we are in this world."

He spoke slowly as he looked at the treasure of a man in front of him. "You will probably always need three years to make me a better golfer, and I know you would never stop trying, but it's okay." Lunker paused to compose himself and to wipe away several tears. His voice was slightly shaking. "What is important, Eli, is that you made me a better man by simply being the man I should hope to be, and that will stay with me forever. Golf or no more golf."

Eli was overwhelmed as the two men, both with tears in their eyes, stared at each other. He looked at Lunker, struggling to find the right words. "You gift from God, Lunker. Never forget time here. Will remember always special." It was all he could think to say.

"I told you this before, Eli, but I want to tell you again because I know it's true." Lunker spoke slowly as he looked at his friend. "One day I will be old and gray, and my mind may not work well." He paused and took a deep breath, and then another. It was difficult to form the words he had to say. "But when my memories take me back to my favorite times and places, I know I will find you there."

Two men from different sides of the globe walked slowly down number eighteen's fairway and then bypassed the green on the left side. They walked in silence, listening to nature's cacophony of sounds emanating from the jungle so near. When they arrived at the pro shop, Lunker retrieved his camera from his golf bag and asked a waiting golfer to take several photos of the two of them. The scenic beauty of the course to their rear was a perfect backdrop.

Fifteen minutes later, after a final beer, the two men stood together watching the arrival of the taxi that would take Lunker back to Midway. "What you do tonight?" asked Eli.

"I'm going to be very low key tonight, Eli, and go to bed early. Get a good night's sleep." He paused. "I heard there's a very special party being held tomorrow, and I want to be well rested."

Eli smiled and nodded. He was full of emotions, but out of words as they shook hands.

CHAPTER FIFTEEN

Return To Paradise
Early Winter, 1980

The next morning, a brightly colored Jeepney crossed the shit river bridge and stopped at the entrance to Naval Station Subic Bay. After being cleared for access, the driver continued to the pier by which Midway was resting. Waiting for the Jeepney were the eight residents of Bunkroom Eight, the Midway Oasis. Next to them was an assortment of shopping bags and cloth laundry bags, plus several boxes and three canvas seabags, all filled to capacity; Lunker carried both a banjo and a guitar.

"Nice meet you. I am Doneng, Eli's cousin. Call me Don. Live in Floridablanca, in Pampanga province. Five miles north Eli. Let me help you." They all shook hands and then loaded a few of their large bags onto the area between the two bench seats that ran fore-and-aft in his Jeepney. The remaining bags and boxes were secured on the large luggage rack on top of Don's vehicle.

"Banjo? Play banjo?" Don asked.

Lunker nodded. "I do. I began playing when I was a young boy."

"Have friend in Angeles City play banjo. Air Force man. Like banjo. I drive Jeepney for Clark people." Clark Air Force Base was twenty-seven miles northeast of Olongapo. Eli's village was halfway between the two.

Don's Jeepney was a smorgasbord of bright colors; an elongated, open air Jeep with a long bench seat positioned lengthwise on both sides and no glass in the windows. Above each bench was a long silver rod for passengers to hang on to.

"We love your Jeepney. A Filipino fiesta on four wheels," proclaimed Lunker.

"Salamat. Thank you." Don was proud of his Jeepney; he had painted it himself. "Began with American Jeep and add Japanese engine, but built with Filipino hands." Eli's cousin beamed.

Don and Lunker sat in the front; the remaining seven Eagles sat on the benches in the back.

"Four plastic horse statues, huh?" Lunker smiled and pointed toward the front of the Jeepney.

Don nodded broadly at his question. "Yes. All beautiful." Plastic horse statues as hood ornaments represented the number of girlfriends the driver was dating at the time.

The sun was already high in the sky as the Jeepney traveled east on a two-lane highway, variously bounded on both sides by views of rice paddies, flat fields of green, small rolling hills, and roadside kiosks selling an assortment of food and household items. Each of the eight aviators had flown over this particular road as they were inbound to Cubi Point's runway, but were generally preoccupied with navigating their Intruder toward the arrival checkpoint and watching for other air traffic. Unlike then, their eyes were now riveted outside at the passing landscape and sights. A couple miles outbound from Subic Bay, Mount Santa Rita dominated the view to their right as they traveled on a northeasterly heading. The small mountain, painted in a lush dark green color by the morning sun, reached almost sixteen hundred feet in the sky above the flat fields surrounding its base. Sitting prominently on its peak was a building with numerous antennas on its roof.

"Building on top for Navy radios. Use with ships and bases in Philippines. Lots of monkeys there. Sometime race Jeepneys up to top then down." Don laughed at the fun he and the other drivers had on the mountain.

After fifteen minutes of passing a mixture of flat agricultural fields in various shades of green and brown, and rice paddies on both sides of the road, they approached Dinalupihan, a city of over eighty thousand people, and skirted to its southeastern side. The men looked north across the city, prominently dotted with a large number of Spanish-style churches, toward Mount Pinatubo, a dormant volcano resting peacefully twenty miles to the north, rising almost six thousand feet toward the heavens.

As they passed the city, Don left the main highway and turned right toward the southeast, driving slowly for almost a mile on a small paved road that turned ever so slowly to the south. Flat fields, dotted with small hills of palms and other indigenous trees, and small rivers and streams were scattered across the landscape.

Agricultural fields and rice paddies seemed to be in equal numbers as they slowed to enter a narrow dirt road to their left. "Hope road dry. Get stuck if too muddy. Two mile to village." As Don communicated the distance to their destination, all eight aviators narrowed their focus to the front of the Jeepney. Their hours in the air above the Earth's lands and waters were filled with new places and dazzling sights, but none carried the electrified sense of anticipation at seeing Eli, Violetta, their children and relatives, and the place they called home.

Although the road was very rutted, Don determined he could drive the two miles to Eli's village. Along the way, they passed through two very large clusters of palm trees, where the trees bent over the road like welcoming tunnels. Both times, the sounds of the jungle surrounded the Jeepney, and the temperature noticeably cooled several degrees as they drove slowly through nature's arches. The land of the second cluster rose gently, probably twenty or thirty feet, before easing back down to where they could see a stream paralleling the road. The men were silent; their eyes were wide, and a fragrant smell enveloped the Jeepney as it had in the first cluster of trees.

"Sampaguita," said Don, pointing out the white flowers blooming on both sides of the road. "Philippine national flower. You call jasmine." The men nodded as they stared at the lush land all around them.

"Smell sweet. Good give girlfriend as surprise.

"Is that all four girlfriends," asked Lunker, "or just the most special one?"

Don laughed. "All four special." The eight men smiled and laughed with him.

The Jeepney cleared the second group of trees and entered an area blending low tropical foliage and small open fields. As it did, Don honked his horn, which bellowed a very loud trio of musical notes. Soon, a third cluster of tall palms, rooted in two prominent arc-like patterns facing each other, came into sight less than a half mile away, and Don honked his horn again. At the same time, the men could see a few one-story homes nestled close to the tree lines.

"Willie. Look." Doc, sitting next to Willie at the front of one of the bench seats, pointed at the two sets of trees ahead and slightly to their right. "Recognize that?" He paused. "I think this is smiling girl village."

"You think so?" Willie leaned forward and stared. "Seriously? You think so?"

"Look at the trees," implored Doc. "They're big arcs, like quarter moons facing each other, and the houses set close to the trees...and the opening leading to the field on the right...That's where we saw the young girl on the water buffalo...by that creek. It's gotta be, Willie...I'm sure...and Don said we're about twelve or thirteen miles northeast of Subic."

The two friends looked at each other, not wanting to get their hopes up only to be disappointed. "Frankly, I was trying to keep the jet out of the trees, Doc. We were kind of low."

"I remember that well, but I swear I think this is it. We didn't see any other village with trees arranged like that." A tingle swept both their bodies. Even from ground level, the view generated a definite déjà vu moment. Imperceptibly, their breathing deepened ever so slightly and their eyes became more focused as the possibility took hold that they could actually meet the young girl who had waved so energetically at them.

Soon though, another sight superseded everything else within the range of their curious eyes. From a couple hundred feet away, Eli's bright smile was a welcoming beacon like no other, made all the more electrifying by the beautiful Filipino woman standing next to him, a coral necklace draped softly around her neck. Each of the men in the Jeepney instinctively smiled back.

For Lunker, the moment was emotionally overwhelming. He was a long way from the north Georgia mountains, but not really. Friends, family, and reverence were entrenched in this divine piece of earth, just as they were in the hills of his birth.

Like his Bunkroom Eight friend in the front seat, Gully, too, was overwhelmed. He was far from his home in Iowa, but he felt the same warmth he felt in America's heartland as his eyes stared at the couple standing together in front of him, the small homes behind them, and the children playing in the distance. He was solidly in the heart of the Philippines, a place where families were still the roots that kept the soil in place.

Ahead of them, numerous adults were slowly walking from the village toward where the Jeepney would park. Precious children, all barefoot, could be seen running excitedly toward the gathering crowd. Some had been playing in the open areas between the homes, but most were running from the flat fields beyond the village.

Soon the colorful Jeepney rolled to a stop, and the eight aviators began exiting the vehicle. Their many bags of gifts remained on board for the moment. Eli's smile was electric as he shook hands with them, one at a time, and then introduced them to Violetta.

"This Lunker."

Eli only needed two words to convey the bottomless depth of their friendship and its impact on his family.

Violetta's dark eyes stared at the man who had so blessed her husband and their family. As their eyes met, so did their hearts. She knew her husband's friend had likely saved the life of Diwata, their baby girl, just months earlier. Similarly, Lunker would never forget that Eli had rescued his soul at its lowest point, barely a year earlier, when his wife and daughter returned to the north Georgia mountains.

"It's nice to finally meet you, Violetta. I've been looking forward to this since the day Eli invited us." Lunker stared back at the woman whose light brown skin was as smooth as warm caramel. Her long silky-black hair flowed to just above the small of her back, and her beauty was as natural as the land on which they stood.

"Thank you, Lunker. Happy meet you. Your friends. Have good time. Good food. Thank you all do help children." Her soft smile conveyed a sentiment of gratitude known only to mothers. She paused and then continued. "Thank Mirela necklace. Most beautiful ever saw." In person, its orange beads were more dazzling against her skin than Mirela or he could have imagined.

"It is perfect on you. A beautiful necklace for a beautiful woman. Mirela will be happy to know she made the right choice."

Violetta nodded and continued to stare at Lunker. There was no way to place a value on a child's life. Neither was there a way to place a value on her gratitude. Uncharacteristically, she moved close and hugged the tall man from across the ocean. As she released the embrace, her eyes glistened with tears.

"This Willie." Eli continued introducing the remaining members of Bunkroom Eight to his wife before introducing the aviators to his adult family members and friends congregated around them.

Like most villages, this one was anchored predominantly by family members and extended family members — brothers, sisters, children, and cousins. Eli was the village elder at the ripe old age of thirty-six. His next birthday was seven weeks away.

As Eli began introducing the children to the aviators, two young girls moved close to Eli, one on each side, and leaned against him. Willie and Doc's eyes were riveted on the smaller of the two. She wore brown homemade shorts and a light yellow cotton tank top. Her hair was blacker than the night and cut short, barely reaching the bottom of her neck. It complimented her dark eyes, which were filled with curiosity as she stared at the men her dad called friends.

"This Macaalay," said Eli to the men, motioning to the young child against his left side. She smiled as he said her name. "And this is Diwata." The smaller child to his right looked shyly at the men in front of her. In Philippine mythology, Diwata was the guardian spirit of nature.

Each of the aviators, in turn, smiled and gave his name.

"Eli, would you ask your daughters and the other young girls here if any of them remember a jet flying by the village really low about five or six months ago, right over where she was sitting on a water buffalo, waving at us?" Doc asked as he was introduced to the two young girls.

Eli asked the question in his native Tagalog and looked at the young girls in the group. One of the older girls answered quickly, followed by a couple boys.

"Remember jet fly low. Very loud when play ball in field." Eli pointed toward the field closest to the village.

As he finished, Diwata, still tucked in tightly against Eli's right leg, spoke in Tagalog and held up two fingers. As she did, Willie and Doc leaned ever so slightly forward in unison.

327

"Diwata say jet fly over two time. She stand wave."

"Was she sitting on a water buffalo?"

Eli asked his daughter the question and she nodded. As she did, Willie and Doc looked at each other, their eyes frozen in stunned disbelief. They were at smiling girl village, and Eli's daughter, Diwata, was the smiling girl.

"Willie and I were flying that jet," said Doc. We saw them all playing ball in the field and decided to fly by one more time. We flew right by where Diwata was sitting so I could wave at her."

The children responded immediately with excitement, Diwata particularly. The small child, Eli's baby, was no longer shy as she left her father's side and walked next to where Willie and Doc stood.

"Want go fly." Her voice was serious.

The entire group laughed. Diwata's comment was the icing on a great start to a great day.

Six months earlier, Willie and Doc had longed to see her smile just one more time. That wish had just been granted. The two friends had also believed there was so much they could learn if their feet were ever planted on this soil. That wish would be answered soon enough.

Lunker spoke next. "We have some things for the children." He and his fellow Eagles unloaded the bags from Don's Jeepney that contained their gifts. As they did, all the children gathered around with curious eyes and large smiles, talking excitedly among themselves in Tagalog, wondering what they would soon see. Their reaction when the first large duffel bag was placed on the ground was more rewarding than a hundred Christmas mornings.

Three soccer balls and two rubber kickballs tumbled out quickly, only to be immediately engulfed by the sounds of the younger children's glee. As Socks videotaped the activity with a recently purchased Sony Betamax video camera, Lunker emptied the first bag by dumping out an additional soccer ball and two more kickballs.

As he did, 'Molly' Hatcher and 'Fish' Trout emptied duffel bags containing plastic bats and balls; fishing rods, lines, hooks and nets; crayons and coloring books; picture books and other assorted books, pencils, and paper; kites and string; more soccer balls and kickballs, and much more. There were three bags with an assortment of shirts, shorts, and pants for the children, which they set aside for the parents to select from. For now, they left the bags that specifically contained items for Eli onboard the Jeepney. Don had agreed to move them discreetly into Eli's home when no one was nearby.

Two young boys grabbed fishing nets and quickly ran toward a nearby stream, while the remaining older children swarmed the plethora of gifts scattered at the edge of the village. They were clearly overwhelmed by the unexpected generosity, but soon each had found the perfect item for the current moment.

"Want show you village." With the happy sounds of the children now scattered around the village and fields, Eli was eager to give the eight men a tour of the village of his birth. His stride was slow but strong, and he walked erect, hiding any damage caused by nineteen years of carrying heavy golf bags.

Eli was filled with ancestral pride. He had held his family and their dwellings together through nature's storms and the wrath of disease. This was God's land, but God had granted it to Eli, and he would care for it as if it were heaven. Eli's pride in his village was obvious, and it hit Lunker particularly hard. As they drew nearer to the homes in the village, with Eli leading the way, a cavalcade of thoughts and emotions raced through Lunker's heart in the blink of an eye.

"Look at him...smiling...beaming...so proud of his meager piece of the earth...a place so inconsequential to the world, but all the world to him...why didn't I ever look at him and realize he was so resolute and steadfast, like an anchor, an anchor keeping his village and his family in place, through good days and bad days, through nature's wrath and fury out of his control. He's

such a dear friend; he works so hard; and he's always smiling. In his life there must have been so many days and weeks, maybe months, of turmoil and heartache and grief, immeasurable despair, so many more than the short period when Diwata was so sick. How does he still wake up and smile alongside golfers who will never know or care about his lot in life — so many rounds of golf when I didn't ask the questions that matter. Oh my God, I feel horrible, and I can't go back and make up all those days. How much did I miss where I could have helped? How did he keep smiling through those moments and days and weeks? I wonder if he thought I didn't care, or that he'd be a burden to me if he spoke of the demons of death and illness and despair that haunt every village like his...He ain't heavy, he's my brother...He showed us the krait that killed his daughter — how many more krait-like moments has he endured when death was closer than life? The actual heartache he's endured must be so much more than I've ever considered...and his family's safety, his village's safety, is just one bad storm away. How does he live with that burden when he sees the dark clouds on the horizon...and look at him now...smiling, laughing, and focused on our happiness. I know he accepts that you can't argue with God about wind, rain, storms, or why you can't teach a monkey to meow, but how my precious friend keeps that smile on his face is a miracle in itself..."

The eight men had big smiles and wide eyes as they followed Violetta and the ageless caddy into the heart of their small village. Two thick groves of palm trees, curved and facing each other like mother nature's own parentheses, one-hundred-fifty feet apart, served as storm protection and as the city limits for the seven small homes positioned along the edge of the trees — three on one side, four on the other. Each was blended into the grove like children trying not to be seen in a game of hide-and-seek.

Each home had the appearance of two modular rooms loosely joined together. Each was conspicuously constructed with a combination of vertical and horizontal bamboo stalks, one-to-three inches in diameter, and both rooms had a thatched roof piled almost a foot high. Several of the walls included a random few panels made of thin aluminum, most likely salvaged from the remnants of earlier typhoons in the nearby city. Each home rested on large bamboo supports that elevated each room about two feet above the village's hard dirt, in respectful deference to the devastating impact even a small flood would have. Neither room was sealed from the elements like the homes in which the aviators lived — they each wondered how the families survived the rainy season, from June to November, but didn't ask.

Straight ahead was an old hand-cranked water pump, upright and erect. Fifteen feet beyond it was an open fire, tended by a young woman. She was probably in her mid-20's, and her sweet smile, a seemingly genetic trait of the Filipino people, extended a warm welcome to the eight Americans.

"Mmmmm. I smell paradise."

Violetta smiled at Lunker's comment as the others nodded in agreement. "Salamat. This Tala." Violetta gestured toward the woman. "She cook pig. Fish in ground. Under fire. Best way cook."

"Older brother daughter. Tala name mean bright star," Eli added proudly. He stared lovingly at the petite young woman. What Eli didn't say was that she was only eleven when her father, Eli's brother, had died, and he had raised her as his own. She was now married to Rodrigo, whom they had already met. Their two young children were playing in a nearby field with the first real soccer ball they had ever seen.

"Nice meet you. Glad here with us. Food ready one two hour." Her clean, innocent smile and honest eyes bridged any divide between people from different countries and cultures.

Each of the aviators continued to behold the simple but perfect practicality of the village; there was no wasted space. On countless flights, they had all glimpsed and stared at dozens and

331

dozens of native villages such as this, most of them similarly surrounded by tall palms and thick, lush foliage, as they flew the Intruder low across the landscape of Luzon and dozens of other islands of the Philippines. Each village obviously had its own nuances, but they all tended to look the same at six, seven, and eight miles a minute. "Speed is life," they each thought, "but how much more we could have learned by slowing down for a few moments."

Right now, though, the eight men were immersed in an evolving surreal moment. There was certainly a world beyond where the aviators' feet were firmly planted, but it was irrelevant. As Eli took them on a slow tour of the seven homes, and then to a small field where the smiling children from the village were playing, each aviator knew that he was standing in a place on the planet that would forever rest in a special place in his heart.

Within minutes, as two carabao rested lazily in mud nearby, all eight guests, along with Eli and a few of the adults, were playing soccer with the children on a parched dirt field next to a rice paddy. If there really was a paradise somewhere over the rainbow, the heartwarming sound of happy voices from children and adults kicking a ball in a large field was proof of its existence.

"Hope fly airplane better than play ball." Doc was picking himself off the ground for the second time in a few minutes, and Rodrigo's comment brought a smile to his face.

The children seemed to flow over the bumps and dips and furrows of the field with ease; the Eagles' aviators were less nimble, earning a bellyful of laughter from the children each time they took a spill. Fortunately, the dirt was closer to firm mud than skin-scraping gravel. After at least an hour, perhaps two — time was irrelevant — Violetta called to the group. The feast was ready.

Served on brown hardwood plates made from a nearby monkeypod tree, the feast featured a veritable Filipino surf and turf. The pork was tender and sizable, and servings suitable for two were served to each individual aviator, along with a large filet of fish. Slices of mango, the national fruit of the Philippines, were served over the fish, and slices of a yellowish fruit, which smelled like a blend of pineapple and bananas, were served over white rice.

Not unexpected, Eli sat between Violetta, to his left, and Lunker to his right. They sat on rudimentary wooden benches built by the hands of the men in the village. On a nearby bench, Diwata sat between Doc and Willie, while Macaalay sat between Socks and Gully. Some of the remaining children sat by their parents. A few sat on the ground near the aviators from across the big ocean as they all energetically savored and devoured the food placed in front of them.

"This is incredible," said Lunker, looking at Tala. "Everything. So tender and delicious. So many flavors."

On a nearby bench, with a bright sun peeking between cumulus clouds, Tala smiled. "Salamat," she said, as Rodrigo put his arm around her.

"Tala good food every day. Make me fat. Have work hard stay shape." He laughed; he was lean and he carried a sinewy muscular body built from tending their fields and homes. Like Eli's, the smile and eyes on his weathered face reflected a primitive pride in what he created from the earth.

"What is this?" asked Gully, as he pointed to the yellowish fruit on the rice. "It's so good, very sweet." He thought it tasted like a cross between a mango and a peach, and it could have easily been their dessert. On their plates, Diwata and Macaalay had eaten the savory fruit first and then received seconds.

"That langka. Pick from tree. Grow all year. Langka very big. Heavy." Eli extended his hands three feet apart and then pointed to a tree about seventy feet away. "Weigh fifty, sixty pound. Give energy." All the aviators looked at the tall tree. The langka resembled two or three overgrown, yellowish-green cantaloupes connected to each other in a squiggly line.

What Eli didn't know was that langka, called jackfruit in America and much of Europe, was the largest tree-borne fruit in the world, easy to cultivate, and often called a miracle fruit because of its many nutrients.

"Langka over horizon?" Eli laughed at his own question.

Lunker put his arm over his friend's shoulders and spoke slowly. "Eli, there is probably langka somewhere over the horizon, but it will never ever taste better than right here...right now." Everyone smiled and nodded at Lunker's response. Life was good halfway around the world from his village in the mountains of north Georgia. They shared the same sun and moon and stars and, on this day, a taste of heaven on earth.

As the group finished their meals, interspersed with constant laughter from the sharing of humorous stories that took place in two countries, on the sea, and in the sky, Lunker turned to his left and looked straight into Violetta's dark eyes. He spoke slowly as he gathered his thoughts. "Your husband has been the best friend I could have ever asked for. He is a blessing to me. And now you..." He glanced at everyone sitting together, including the children, and then his eyes returned to Violetta.

"Each one of you has blessed my friends and me by opening up your village and your home to us. Today is a day we will never forget. Today our home is right here, and we wouldn't want to be anywhere else." Lunker took a deep breath as he tried to find words to convey feelings as deep as the ocean itself. "Tomorrow I have to say goodbye to the Philippines, but I can never say paalam, because a part of me will always be here...and with each of you." Lunker paused again as he turned to the most precious man he would likely ever know. "And you, Eli, my dear friend, especially you."

Eli stared back at Lunker. "Salamat. You always friend. Now take friends for walk." As he finished his short statement and stood up, tears bred from deep-rooted heartache began to fill Violetta's eyes. She knew where they were going.

Eli stood, and immediately eight aviators, each from a place a world away, stood along with him. No words were spoken as Eli began walking out of the village, passing through an opening in the grove of trees and onto a flat field. Instinctively, as if guided by a mystical influence, the men walked behind him, mostly in single file. Lunker walked behind Eli, followed by Doc, Willie, Gully, Socks, Rooster, Fish, and Jackal.

Eli's path was steadfast and true. His every step was as measured as the notes in a symphony, a tragic melody replayed at moments he couldn't always predict. He needed no guide; he made this trip often, but usually alone. It was his burden, as was being responsible for the village and its residents. Occasionally, he would be accompanied by Violetta or family members, but never outsiders...until today.

None of the men spoke. As naval officers, they were trained to lead and to follow and to respect their role based on the mission at hand. Eli was leading; they dutifully followed.

There was no turning back as the group took dead aim at a very large and thick grove of trees, approximately a half mile away. It was significantly more expansive, hilly, and densely packed than the grove in which Eli's village resided. To its right, near the base of the tall hill, flowed a large stream that exited the grove near its base and made a sharp turn to the east, toward a set of rice paddies.

The only sounds penetrating the humid air around them came from indigenous animals and birds — predators, prey, spectators — each of which contributed to the unfolding crescendo of foreign sounds as the men drew closer to their destination.

Approaching the tall palms trees that framed the grove, Eli's pace didn't falter. He alone was the guardian, custodian, and curator of this sacred piece of God's creation. A few minutes later, as if entering a forbidden room, Eli eased his body between two trees, barely eighteen inches apart. They were situated among a group of densely packed trees that formed a

335

thick natural barrier across the grove for at least a hundred feet or more in each direction. As each man followed the path blazed by Eli and passed through the narrow opening, he found his feet planted on dirt worn of heartache and indescribable anguish, the threshold of a small but defined path to an unknown destination.

Inside the grove, the temperature cooled, the presence of moisture increased, and the sky disappeared, replaced by a canopy of swaddling green shade. They were surrounded, captured in a way, by a secret place where the hardships of a Filipino child's real life could be suspended and replaced by nature's utopian playhouse. All around were birds and animals they could hear, but not see, invisible playmates surrounding and protecting them like jealous guardians of this consecrated land.

As each foot touched the ground, the elevation rise was evident, yet randomly unpredictable. The flowing sounds of a stream echoed all around them, very much alive but invisibly cloaked, adding its respectful salute to those whose mortal souls were being strained and tested with each step.

Eli stopped walking for a moment. He turned to his left and looked at each of the eight men behind him. No one had spoken since they departed his village. The strain evident on Eli's face told them that they had reached the point where there was no turning back.

No one moved or flinched or made a sound, although their breathing was slightly labored, and the beating of their hearts was palpable. The men stood in a place that made the rest of the human world nonexistent; this was a place where the only language that made sense had no words. Their only comparable frame of reference for such a great unknown was their first night landing on an aircraft carrier; nothing could adequately prepare them, and only at the end of the journey could they appreciate and reconcile the ride.

Eli looked directly at each of the eight men, one by one. Their trust was unmistakable and admirable, especially given that they were blind to their ultimate destination and the impact it would deposit on their hearts. They suspected, he was sure, but only he knew what actually awaited them.

Each of the men stared back at the weathered face of Eli; the foes and hurdles he had faced didn't exist in their world. Neither did the lush tropical backdrop in which they stood, an enchanting place whose dark side took sweet children home far too soon. If grace was amazing, it needed to be extra amazing in this place that outsiders called paradise.

The aviators following Eli were trained to control their emotions during the execution of a mission, but this was different. This journey would forever be memorialized as a date with mortality, a life-changing moment after which they could never be who they were before. They were confidant, and they were ready.

Eight sets of eyes from a land far away stared at the man leading their journey. They each trusted Eli's personal compass and obediently followed his steps. If he were to ask them to pull their boats up on a foreign beach and burn them, they would. Like their ageless carrier Midway, he would find a way to return them safely home; of that they were sure.

Eli began walking again, slightly slower than before as the path in the dense jungle steepened in its angle of climb for thirty or forty feet before turning downhill for double the distance. As they neared the bottom, the sound of flowing water could be heard again. It was nearby, but the density of the jungle acted as a closed curtain, hiding the earthbound misery of a tragic day. Lunker intuitively knew what it was. Twice he had heard the full story. Twice he listened as Eli had exposed his heart as only one father could to another. Twice he wanted to cry a tidal wave of tears.

The group stopped by an idyllic stream, a virtual Eden unspoiled by a material world. The water was clear and unobstructed, and its movement yielded serenading rhythms that could easily lull a visitor into a deep sleep. Eli took two steps to move closer to the flowing water.

"My idea picnic here. Celebrate Ligaya four year birthday by water." He looked down at the earth of his ancestors. He was quiet for almost a minute, tacitly returning to that day. Time had healed many wounds, but not this one. "This where Ligaya stand when krait bite. Die before sun go down." Eli looked to the ground and closed his eyes for at least thirty seconds, reliving a father's worst nightmare. It was a burden he would always carry. His best intentions had turned into his daughter's last day. He made a sign of the cross with his right hand, took a deep breath, and stared at the group. His moist eyes then touched each man, one by one. "My idea," he admitted again after a deep breath, and then turned to continue the journey. His personal guilt was imbedded in each heavy step.

None of the men spoke as their path through the lush land returned to an uphill climb. After five or six minutes, the terrain began to level off, and the men could see a small clearing thirty or forty feet in front of them — a crude man-made area, about eight feet by twelve feet. Their eyes fixated on that which was within its borders — three slightly elevated mounds, nestled together and serenely placed among the untamed disarray of the nearby jungle. The sweet smell of paradise stepped aside as sadness abruptly inserted itself into the peace of this unearthly place, a relative speck on the face of the earth. Each man could feel the heavy burden of anguish as they arrived at the terminus of a father's final journey with his child, a tearful walk they each knew he made three heartbreaking times.

There were no markings on any of the three mounds. Eli slowed the pace and stopped next to the first one. The eight men moved in closely together. A shared purpose already bonded them; it became infinitely strengthened in this place of mortal misery and eternal peace. Their hearts pounded and ached as Eli slowly knelt down on one knee by the grave next to him. As his friends respected the moment by remaining quiet, their silent emotions of distress roared thunderously across a wild jungle landscape so timelessly unfair to the young and innocent.

"No name on grave. I know children. Violetta know children. God know children. Miss every day."

Eli rubbed the mound next to him, and removed several small sticks lying on top. He spoke slowly as new tears appeared on his brown cheeks; each short phrase carried a father's love and his burden of grief.

"My children. Still part my family, even with God." He paused for a moment. "This Dalisay. First child. My first love. Die ear problem three week after six year old. No money medicine." He had made peace with his God, but it hadn't been easy. "I build burial box. Dig grave." He paused for another moment. "Wrap Dalisay soft cloth. Kiss goodbye. Carry here myself. Hard to put dirt on grave first time." Eli remained by her grave for at least a minute, his eyes staring, as if they could penetrate the soil and he could see her once again, maybe revive her, or at least comfort her.

He slowly stood and moved a few feet to the second mound. Behind him, a few sounds of unnatural breathing could be heard. Eight bold aviators struggled to contain the distressing sorrow of their hearts; two were unsuccessful as tears flowed freely, and their muted sounds of grief hung in the air like early morning dew.

"This Nimuel. Only son. Teach be good catch fish. Die trouble breathe. Five year old." Eli knelt down, his knees settling gently to the ground. He put both his hands on Nimuel's mound and smoothed the dirt before leaning over and placing the left side of his weathered face on his only son's final resting place. He was to one day fill his father's shoes and carry the family into the future. That had long been Eli's dream, but the dream and the passing of the family name to a new generation ended before it barely began.

He spoke softly in his native Tagalog, his voice strained in its affection, and then stood and moved slowly to the third mound.

He looked to his left. His eight friends stood shoulder to shoulder, tightly bound by sorrow and support. Their eyes, red and moist, and several more now with visible tears, remained focused on his three children.

"This Ligaya." The story of Ligaya and the krait was fresh on the hearts of all the men as Eli knelt down to tenderly caress the dirt on her grave and speak to her in a silent voice for at least a minute. After kissing her grave, he stood very slowly, his eyes never leaving her until he was upright. He turned and stared at Lunker, a father himself, and nodded slowly.

Lunker took a couple steps and knelt down by Dalisay's grave. By the time he arrived at Ligaya's resting place, the tall man from the north Georgia mountains was overcome by compassion for his friend and his family. His fatherly hands visibly shook as he touched the soft dirt, and the warm tears that flowed down his cheeks didn't embarrass him. He was sad for Eli and Violetta, and for all the other families living in this paradise on earth where children died too young and far too easily.

Time was irrelevant as eight men individually paid their respects to three sweet children they would never have the pleasure of knowing in the human world. Sorrow was painted on the faces of each aviator as he tried to reconcile his place on the planet with all the unique and remarkable sights he had seen from the air. If unique sights and sounds and places had a rating scale, none would surpass where they now stood.

Eli spoke once again. "Visit every week. Talk to them. Tell stories about sisters. Diwata. Macaalay. Growing up. Talk about Violetta." Eli looked up at the eight men from Bunkroom Eight, the Midway Oasis, and especially Lunker and Willie. "Tell how you help Diwata sick, fever. Get medicine. Save life." He paused briefly to control his own emotions. "Tell children miss them. Will see in heaven one day. All be together. Happy. One family."

Eli began retracing his steps back to the village, and the men loyally followed. After a slow walk in which they honored the children's resting places with their silence, they exited the grove

340

of trees through the same eighteen-inch gap and stepped back into reality. From their jets, the aviators had, countless times, seen sights few humans would ever see. Yet, none could be compared to or were as poignant as the sight of three graves, three young children sleeping peacefully in a wild jungle tinged with the sweet smell of jasmine; three graves, maintained and watched over by a loving and protective father who was unable to save them.

Eli turned and looked at his friends. Three precious children born into an unfair world bonded the nine men. Their life's lesson was to continue living for those still alive. His voice was solemn, yet upbeat at the same time. "Time be happy. Special day. Family, friends. Each you." Like Eli, all eight aviators had experience making a quick transition to living life again after saying a final goodbye. They would do it here as well.

Fifteen minutes later, back in the village, Lunker spoke with a smile on his face.

"I think it's time for a little music." The group of nine men were resettled among friends and family back in the village; eight were forever changed. Lunker's proclamation was the perfect antidote to the somber feeling sweeping Eli, Violetta, their relatives and guests.

"Play banjo first," requested Don, smiling. He had a cassette tape of banjo music he played often in his Jeepney.

The group of friends, united across a wide blue ocean, gathered around the same benches where they had earlier dined on savory Filipino food. Now they would feast on the sounds of American music.

"Okay, Eli, you and my Bunkroom Eight buddies have to set the example and get everyone dancing," said Lunker as he began to play the first strains of the Beatles hit *I Saw Her Standing There* on his banjo. He played it with an upbeat tempo perfect for dancing, and made modifications to the lyrics, to include Violetta's name, as he sang a song that put a bigger-than-normal smile on everyone's face, especially that of his caddy.

Before too long, Eli was dancing with his wife, as was Rodrigo with Tala, and soon all the remaining family, friends, and children, the child-like aviators included, were all dancing under a warm December sun in paradise.

Lunker played fast songs and slower songs on the guitar and banjo, including two popular Filipino songs he had learned. When the sun was within an hour of setting, he pulled pieces of paper from his pocket and handed them to several of his fellow aviators and new friends. After doing so, he looked at Eli, sitting between Violetta and Tala, and then spoke to the group.

"I asked Eli whether he had a favorite Christmas song, and he told me Silent Night. He said it's a favorite throughout the Philippines, so I have the words in English and Tagalog. We'll sing the English version first."

On a warm, mid-December early evening, Lunker began strumming his guitar, and voices from two sides of the globe slowly sang as one. As the group transitioned to the Tagalog version, Lunker was overcome with emotions and, as his tears flowed freely, strumming his guitar was all he could do. When the final chords were played, the group stood and began saying goodbye, spreading peace and joy among new friends. Too soon for any of them, the eight Americans slowly began to make their way toward Don's Jeepney.

As the group was leaving, Willie stooped to say goodbye to Macaalay. As he did, Diwata climbed on his shoulders. Willie stood and looked left and right and behind him. "Hey, I want to say goodbye to Diwata. Has anyone seen her?"

She began laughing from her perch on his shoulders. "Go with Willie."

One by one, the eight men slowly began boarding the Jeepney for the return to Subic Bay. As Doc and Willie said a final goodbye to Diwata, their thoughts returned to the day they named her the smiling girl. Little could they have known how special she would turn out to be, and how much they would actually learn from spending time with her and her family.

Lunker's goodbyes were last among the men. He slowly turned to face Eli and Violetta, his body consumed with anguish at the thought of possibly never seeing Eli again. He simply wasn't ready for the reality of the moment.

In his life, there had been many ups and downs, highs and lows, many which had occurred on this land, and Eli had been there for him. This was both a celebration of a friendship forged in mutual good times and tough times, and the sadness of a goodbye, with the great unknown in front of them being...unknown.

"Will I ever see his bright smiling face again? I knew this day would be tough but, oh my God, this is so hard...I want to cry a swollen stream of tears, but even that wouldn't be enough...Will I ever see him again? Will his family still be as intact in the years to come as it is today?...What about his precious daughters? Have I done enough to ensure they will always be healthy? Eli would love to just cross one horizon, just one...that'd be enough to satisfy his lifelong dream, yet it took me half of planet Earth's horizons to find and understand the core tenets of love and life...I wish I could turn back time...just one more day...one more, Lord, one more will be enough..."

"You still leave tomorrow?" asked Eli. Lunker nodded slowly; he'd cry if he tried to answer. "Ten o'clock?" Lunker nodded again. "Work hard. Be good pilot. Your dream." Lunker smiled as Eli looked into his eyes. "Fly safe Lunker. Want see you again one day."

The two men hugged. "I'll always remember you, Eli," Lunker said quietly, a single salty tear began a slow journey down his left cheek, "and think of you and your special family every day." He took a deep breath. "Of all my memories in this part of the world, the ones of us together will always be my favorites."

Eli, who had tears as well, nodded as he looked into Lunker's eyes. "Friend always." Lunker nodded.

The men were quiet as they took seats in Don's Jeepney; Lunker sat in the very back. As the colorful vehicle drove slowly down the rutted dirt road, his moist eyes never left his dear friend until a sharp turn into a grove of palm trees became the final goodbye for both of them.

An hour later, Eli and Violetta opened the two very large boxes and one seabag that the aviators left in their home. One of the packages said 'Open last.' Another said 'Open next to last.' As the couple began sorting through the items, most contained in boxes within the larger boxes, they were quickly overwhelmed. There were two radios and six packages of twelve batteries each; clothes and gifts for their daughters; twenty-four yards of cloth; an adult Bible, a child's picture Bible and a beautiful handmade cross; two Polaroid Instamatic cameras and four dozen rolls of film. There were a dozen bottles each of multipurpose vitamins, Vitamin A supplement, and antibiotics, as well as antidotes for snakebites, and two large boxes of bandages and first aid cream. Two Eagles' shirts and an embroidered nametag Lunker had worn on his flight suit brought a smile to Eli's face. From the seabag, Eli pulled out Lunker's putter. A note attached to it said, *It's no good without you helping me.* Eli stared at the putter and note for at least a minute.

Soon, Violetta and Eli were down to just two remaining packages. They opened the one that said, 'Open next to last.' As they did, Violetta let out an audible gasp. Inside were several stacks of peso bills wrapped in plastic. Attached to the plastic was a note.

I recently received money from a relative. She asked me to use it wisely. I can't think of a better use than to bless your family and ensure you will always be okay. Your friend, Lunker.

The amount was equal to eight thousand American dollars, or what it would take Eli almost seven years to earn. Eli and Violetta hugged each other tightly; Violetta then spoke as tears flowed down her cheeks. "All this. Must share. Not right not share with family friends." Eli nodded in agreement.

Eli then opened the package that said 'Open Last.' It was a color photo of Lunker and Eli, the photo taken by the eighteenth hole the day prior. Lunker held his putter in his left hand; his right arm was across Eli's shoulders. It was signed 'Friends always, Lunker.' A short note was attached to the frame.

Eli and Violetta, I can't bring back your three precious children, but I can do my part to try and keep Diwata, Macaalay, and the two of you healthy and strong. Through all my remaining years, I will never forget you. Eli, I will feel your smile every day, because you will always have a place right next to my heart. May God bless you and keep you, and may He make His face shine upon you and your family for all your days. May you all be forever young. Your friend for life, Lunker

The next morning came early. At eight-thirty, with a Philippine sun rising quickly into the sky, Lunker strolled into Ready Room Five, the Eagles' ready room on Midway and, twenty-eight months after arriving, officially checked out of Attack Squadron One Hundred Fifteen. Ten minutes earlier, six of his seven companions in Bunkroom Eight had awoken to say goodbye and good luck. Some of their paths would cross again in the future, and some wouldn't, but they'd always be friends. Socks had already departed the ship for the air operations office. He'd be flying Lunker north to Atsugi, via Okinawa, and was filing the required flight plan for their trip.

As Lunker reached Midway's quarterdeck, he recognized the officer of the day, a lieutenant and Corsair pilot who was one of the ship's catapult officers.

"Pensacola bound, huh?"

"Yep, can you believe it?"

"You earned it, Lunker. Good luck back there. Fly safe."

"Thank you. Request permission to leave the ship, sir."

"Permission granted." With that, Lunker permanently closed a chapter in his life. As he did, the sound of four bells loudly penetrated a clear Subic Bay morning.

'Ding ding, ding ding.' "Lieutenant Fishman, departing." The announcement was carried throughout Midway's corridors and spaces. Bunkroom Eight's residents slept through it. Life on the ship and in the squadron wasn't dependent on a single person. They had all arrived, and one day they'd all leave. Only the magic of the ship would permanently remain.

Lunker rode a taxi for the short trip from Midway to the transient line hangar at the naval air station across the bay. His eyes tried valiantly to absorb every final view of this precious land. One half mile into the trip, a now quiet Binictican golf course came into view to his left. His friend Eli was likely standing at the pro shop, hopeful at carrying the bag of one of CAG-Five's aviators, he thought. He missed him already.

Seventy-eight minutes after Lunker departed Midway, with the aviators strapped into a fully fueled Intruder and all prelaunch checks complete, Socks signaled the plane captain to pull the chocks holding the jet's two main landing gear tires in place. Quickly thereafter, the plane captain began signaling the jet to begin moving forward.

Lunker was off to pursue a lifelong dream. The countdown timer for his time with Midway, the Eagles, and Eli was officially at zero; it was a bittersweet final tick of the clock.

"Steering is direct to Kadena," reported Lunker. "North-northeast for seven hundred ninety-nine nautical miles."

Socks smiled. "Now that you're going to be a pilot, Lunker, eight hundred miles will do just fine."

Lunker laughed. "Roger that."

Reaching the taxiway that would carry them to the end of the easterly runway, Lunker and Socks quickly completed the takeoff checklist. A minute later, all that remained between them and being airborne was two hundred feet of concrete taxiway and takeoff clearance from the tower. Lunker was focused on entering two final waypoints into the navigation computer when Socks' voice broke the silence.

"I think there's someone who wants to say goodbye."

Lunker looked up from his system's keyboard and scanned left and right. "Straight ahead," said Socks, "against the fence."

Then Lunker saw him.

Eli.

He was holding a handmade sign in front of his chest with two unmistakable words in large black letters. *Friend Always.* Lunker was speechless.

"Tower, Eagle Five-Zero-Three." Socks had a plan that required the tower's approval.

"Go ahead, Five-Zero-Three."

"Roger, I'd like to taxi to the edge of the hold short by the fence line and stop there facing south for a couple minutes."

There was a slight delay and then a different voice came through the Intruder's radio.

"Five-Zero-Three, tower supervisor."

"Tower, Five-Zero-Three, go ahead," replied Lunker.

"Is that Eli?"

Lunker smiled as he placed his oxygen mask against his face and responded. "Yes sir. You know him?"

"He's the only caddy I use."

"Roger that. Me, too. The best caddy on the course. I had my final round with him a couple days ago." Lunker's voice had a slight tinge of sadness attached to it.

"You're cleared to stop and park wherever you need."

"Five-Zero-Three. Thank you."

Socks positioned the Intruder at the edge of the concrete tarmac so that only seventy feet of clear air and a chain link fence separated Lunker and a dear man he'd never forget. Eli watched as the Intruder's canopy began to slide back approximately two or three feet.

The friends stared at each other through the noise of the jet's two engines, deafening even at idle. Lunker pointed toward the sign and gave Eli a thumbs up. Eli's bright smile and head nod returned the gesture.

The two men continued to stare at each other for a few more moments, not wanting to succumb to the inevitable, and then Lunker lifted his right hand in a salute.

Eli was unsure of why his friend was saluting him, and then, after several long seconds, he remembered what Lunker had once told him regarding the protocol of a military salute. It was a sign of respect for one's rank, always initiated by the lower ranking person. It was the only way Lunker could tell him that, while they were equals as humans on the planet, he viewed Eli as more than equal as a man.

Eli slowly lifted his right hand in the first salute he had ever attempted. It seemed strange, holding it in place, but he acknowledged and returned the message Lunker wanted to convey. The aviator's salute remained fixed until Eli dropped his salute, at which time Lunker dropped his.

Just moments later, Eli watched as the Intruder's canopy began closing again and the jet began to move toward the end of the runway. Intruder Five-Zero-Three was cleared for takeoff.

"Tower, Five-Zero-Three."

"Go ahead, Five-Zero-Three."

"After takeoff, we'd like to remain in the pattern for a low approach before we depart for Kadena."

The tower supervisor responded. "Five-Zero-Three, your goodbye pass is approved. Give him your best."

"Five-Zero-Three, roger that."

Eli watched as the noisy jet accelerated down the easterly runway. He saw the nose lift up and the Intruder break free of the earth. Instead of flying straight ahead, like two earlier airplanes that morning had done, he observed the jet begin a left hand turn, flying over the golf course and then Olongapo. It flew westerly, toward the opening where Subic Bay met the Pacific Ocean, and then began another left hand turn. Eli watched the jet as it passed over Grande Island, and then took aim for where he stood. Only then did it dawn on him what was occurring.

The Intruder was no more than four or five hundred feet above the water as it flew through the extended centerline of the runway, from Eli's right to his left. The jet descended slightly lower and leveled out as it pointed back toward the runway, and then began a shallow right turn to pass just in front of and over where Eli stood. Socks was expertly flying the jet at a speed fast enough to be safe and stable and yet slow enough to give two friends a few extended moments to share a final goodbye.

A half-mile away from where Eli stood, Socks had the Intruder perfectly positioned. He had descended to one hundred fifty feet above mother earth in a thirty-five degree angle of bank to the right. Eli was draped in noise and emotions as he waved vigorously at his friend so close, but so far away. Lunker had his oxygen mask off and his dark visor up; Eli could clearly see his eyes and his smile and his right hand waving back, as the two men savored their last moments occupying the same spot on the planet.

Lunker looked at the smile on the face of the most precious man he had ever known. It was as bright as the sun that warmed the sparkling blue bay. Eli was one of a kind — one for a lifetime. Lunker always knew their time would end; fortunately, the past twenty-four hours had been the perfect goodbye. Still, it ended too soon, and suddenly his dear friend was disappearing behind him at over six miles every minute.

"Tower, Five-Zero-Three. Thanks for the gesture. We'll pick up our IFR clearance to Kadena now."

"Roger, Five-Zero-Three. Contact departure on two-ninety-four point six. Have a safe trip."

Eli wouldn't argue with God about wind, weather, making monkeys meow, or wondering if he'd ever see his aviator friend from the north Georgia mountains again. Like the short time with three of his children, he'd live with the memories of Lunker and hold them close. Their abbreviated time together was better than never at all.

Still standing at the end of the runway, Eli's sharp eyes kept sight of Lunker's jet until it became a black dot disappearing over a horizon formed of lush mountains. He then returned to his village — smiling girl village — the most special place on the planet, his friends had said. He'd surprise his family with an early return. That's what Lunker would hope he would do, he guessed, on their last day together.

To no surprise, just like reading the greens for his friend, Eli was right on target.

CHAPTER SIXTEEN

Midway Magic
Christmas, 1980

Lunker's absence in Ready Room Five and Bunkroom Eight was felt immediately. His respectfully irreverent observations regarding the Navy were always welcome. Such observations kept the officers and sailors sane in an environment that would drive humans to drink heavily in foreign ports. However, no Navy unit rotated around one person. Although Lunker and his sense of humor would be sorely missed, the squadron would not miss a beat. Sooner or later, everyone who arrived would leave.

Midway's 'Fall of 1980' cruise was nearing its end. Christmas was eight days away. A new year was fifteen days away. If the schedule held as planned, a return to Japan was thirty-two days away. Midway would conduct flight operations for thirty of the thirty-two days remaining. Idle sailors and aviators were dangerous sailors and aviators; the key to keeping them alive was to focus them on dynamic tasks that could kill them.

Three days before Christmas, 'Magic' Mann stood up from his front row seat in Ready Room Five and strolled to the podium. It was 0900, nine o'clock in the morning, and a meeting of the Eagles' aviators had just begun. The primary purpose was to brief the aircrews on an upcoming seven-day exercise with the Air Force.

"First, an update to our operating schedule. Today through Christmas Eve we'll be flying seven cycles per day — four day and three night. Christmas day will be five cycles, beginning with the first launch at 0730. Last plane on deck will be approximately 1830, about forty minutes after sunset. There will be an hour-long Christmas celebration on the hangar bay at 2000."

"Over the next five days, you will notice the ship slowly moving its operating area north, and our primary divert airfield will switch from Cubi to Kadena. The water is going to get colder, and the sun will be setting just after 1700, so plan accordingly."

As the time to a Christmas day at sea drew closer, and Midway plowed her way north, the wind across the flight deck and the air circulating through the hangar bay grew chillier by the day. A noticeable increase in the pitching and rolling of the carrier was apparent to everyone throughout the ship, whether they were walking, standing, or trying to sleep. It was especially frightening to those working on the icy slick flight deck, where walking and working in such conditions froze exposed skin and kept the specter of injury or death just one careless moment away.

Walking below decks became a balancing act in three dimensions; each step was carefully measured throughout the ship. Sailors either quickly rediscovered their trusty sea legs once again or invited bruises as they stumbled against steel

352

bulkheads and other immovable obstacles along Midway's passageways.

Midway's pilots weren't immune or exempt from the perils of winter flying at sea. They taxied their jets on a flight deck that, too often, had the frictional qualities of a freshly swept Central Park ice skating rink. On the catapult prior to launch, they watched, as straight ahead, just a couple hundred feet away, Midway's bow rose smartly above the horizon and then fell well below the horizon, straight into an angry, roiling sea.

Their heart rates elevated rapidly during the times when they saw the catapult officer touch the deck with his hand and raise it, the signal to launch, even as the bow was too often still pointed straight into the sea. Three or four seconds later, as they felt the unmistakable jolt and immediate bodily pressure from the catapult firing, only the carrier's bow rising from King Neptune's watery domain would ease their angst.

Once safely airborne, thoughts of a pitching deck didn't disappear. Lodged in the back of an aviator's brain was the recognition that in two hours, as they returned to land on the only runway available to them, a slick, pitching deck would greet them with the agitated ire of an ornery next-door neighbor.

The three days remaining before Christmas passed quickly, and soon it was Friday morning. Fourteen hundred miles to the north-northeast of Midway's position, American families in Japan had a head start celebrating in their homes the same way that families in America would do half a day later. A few chose to delay the opening of gifts until their loved ones returned from sea, but the overwhelming majority kept life as normal as possible.

On the ageless carrier, Christmas day was simply another day of flight operations at sea, except that one of the catapult officers was wearing a red Santa suit. At 1825, 6:25 pm, five minutes ahead of schedule, the last aircraft on the last event of the day landed on Midway's angled deck. On this blessed day, as almost always, it was an A-6 tanker.

Dinner in the officers' wardroom and on the crew's mess decks included the same delicacies and desserts as Christmas dinner tables across all fifty states. There was turkey and gravy, beef roasts, cornbread stuffing, mashed and sweet potatoes, and much more, including pies, cakes, and vanilla and chocolate dog. The setting was the same as would be found in homes across America, except that those dining on Midway were wearing flight suits, flight deck jerseys, engineering coveralls, or other standard Navy uniforms, and their dining room tables were slowly rocking from side-to-side and moving through the water at just over fifteen miles per hour.

At 2000, eight pm, with a blanket of stars keeping watch over the ship like shepherds in the night, the majority of the crew was sitting or standing in Midway's cavernous hangar bay. Joining them were a few of the flying machines that made the ship a lethal killing machine, even as the birthday of the 'Prince of Peace' was celebrated.

The last time the carrier's crew was gathered as a collective group in this place was on a foreboding night with low hovering clouds, the night of the collision, as a disaster of Biblical proportions slowly unveiled itself. On that night, the answer to the question of whether the ship and crew would see another sunrise was known only to the father of the one whose birth they now celebrated.

Midway's captain presided over the evening's short holiday program. He began by acknowledging and thanking the crew for their service, so far from home, during a time set aside for family gatherings.

"Good evening, Midway, and a very Merry Christmas to each of you. Tonight, as you do every night, you dutifully serve far from our home shores, far from those you love. You labor and sacrifice on a daily basis without fanfare, serving a nation and world who will never know your name, never see the price you willingly pay, or feel the loneliness that slips into your mind like an unwelcome neighbor."

"On behalf of every American citizen, I want to acknowledge and thank each of you for your commitment to the critical missions that have been assigned to us. On a personal level, I want to extend my heartfelt gratitude and appreciation to each and every one of you for your loyalty to this ship, her mission, and to your fellow sailors, airmen, and Marines on this Christmas Day."

"In our homeland across the Pacific, our citizens, neighbors, friends, and families are waking up with freedoms that you guarantee through your service at sea."

"The last time you were all here in the hangar bay together, you gathered as one on a dark night. Looking at the gravity of the damage to our ship, conventional wisdom held that we were doomed, that Midway Magic had fallen victim to events beyond its control. However, you prevailed, and you continue to prove to the world that our mission is a not only a worthy one, but a burden we shall willingly bear and in which we shall not fail."

"On this night, I would like to put our place in perspective by recalling words from the Bible: For a child will be born to us, a son will be given to us; and the government will rest on His shoulders; and His name will be called Wonderful Counselor, Mighty God, Eternal Father, Prince of Peace. Suddenly there appeared with the angel a multitude of the heavenly host praising God and saying, Glory to God in the highest, and on earth peace, good will toward men."

"Jesus was one man sent to bear all our burdens. On this night, all of us are far from our homes, willingly bearing the burden of preserving peace, of protecting the freedoms of our countrymen, and serving to liberate people across the world for whom freedom is only a dream — so that all of Earth's citizens may celebrate their Prince of Peace...in peace."

The carrier's captain paused and looked across the men sitting in front of him. "You are Midway, and you make the magic. I believe in Midway magic, and more than anything, on this sacred and silent night, I believe in you."

They ended the evening with a single song. The men sang *Silent Night* as one voice. There were few dry eyes as the words reverberated off the hangar bay's steel walls, filling the enclosure with a solemn reminder that preserving peace and freedom isn't free or easy. This night, like so many others, would link those serving on the flagship of the Navy's foreign legion together across the ages.

CHAPTER SEVENTEEN

Heroes and Villains
Early February, 1981

The end of a cruise, already a month longer than originally scheduled, was four days away, but this was the Navy's foreign legion, so an unexpected surprise Thursday evening wasn't a surprise at all.

An eighteen plane 'CAG-Five Photo Flight' was added to Friday's air plan, which had been published just thirty minutes earlier and was already disseminated to the squadrons. Unusual was that dissemination of the added event was limited to squadron commanding officers, who were given instructions on what they could and couldn't tell their maintenance and operations officers regarding preparations.

Equally perplexing was that no squadron commanding officer or executive officer was allowed to fly in the exercise. In fact, the preference was that junior officers be used to the maximum extent possible. Normally, commanding officers would lead their squadron's participation.

The flight included four A-7 Corsairs as the lead diamond, with CAG Evans in the lead jet. The other three diamonds included six A-6 Intruders, two EA-6B Prowler electronic jamming aircraft, and four F-4 Phantoms. Two Marine photo reconnaissance Phantoms would fly outside the flight of sixteen aircraft to take photos.

No weapons would be carried; however, the six A-6 Intruders would carry a highly unusual external load of five drop tanks.

The 'photo op' was scheduled to launch at 0630 Friday, the first event of the day, with CAG Evans flying an A-7 Corsair as the strike leader for the large event. A brief for all participants was scheduled at 0430.

At 0400 Friday morning, Rooster, Preacher, Willie, and Gully, all scheduled on the first event launch, were enjoying breakfast together in Midway's wardroom. At 0415, they departed and made their way to Midway's intelligence spaces, where the presence of two armed Marine sentries guarding the door surprised them. After their identities were confirmed, they entered the space and went to the large briefing area, where they joined eight other Eagles, all of whom knew that the level of security meant they were there to fly something that was clearly more than a public relations photo flight.

At 0430 sharp, "Attention on deck" was called, as CAG Evans, wearing his flight suit, entered the briefing area, followed by Rear Admiral John McElroy, the admiral in charge of Midway's battle group. Rear Admiral McElroy was wearing his summer khaki uniform with the gold wings of a Navy pilot.

"Seats, please," announced CAG Evans, as he walked to the podium. "I suppose you're wondering why the Marines were out front and the admiral is joining us at the brief for a public relations photo. He paused and looked around at his aviators, a slightly mischievous smile on his face that signaled something unusual was going to follow. "Who better to tell you than Admiral McElroy himself." He nodded in the admiral's direction.

Rear Admiral McElroy stood and walked to the podium. "Good morning," he said, and continued without delay. "A couple years ago, the Soviet Union sent troops into Afghanistan in 1979, and our country's response was to boycott the summer Olympics and institute a grain embargo." He paused, letting those facts register with the crowd.

"We have a new president who believes those actions hurt our athletes and farmers a lot more then we hurt the Soviets. More importantly, those actions did nothing but send a signal that if you throw sand on us, we'll just move to another sandbox." He paused for several long seconds, as the aviators wondered where this geopolitical statement was leading and what it meant to them and their public relations photo.

"The president wants to send a signal that a new sheriff is in town, and a good spanking has absolutely nothing to do with games or wheat. The message being delivered to the Soviets by each of you sitting here is that Olympics and grain embargos don't sway bad men. Peace through superior firepower is what bad men understand, and right now a gaggle of eighteen white hat-wearing messengers are announcing that our new President is leveling the sand in the only sandbox that matters."

"The Soviet aircraft carrier Minsk departed her homeport of Vladivostok approximately twelve hours ago, heading south to the North Korean port of Wonsan. How we know it and why she's going there isn't important to our mission today. Our mission is to take a photo of sixteen Carrier Air Wing Five aircraft up close and personal, right alongside Minsk in her cozy corner of the sandbox." The silence in the briefing room was deafening. That would be one hell of a photo op. One hell of a 'who blinks first' photo op.

"CAG will give you specific details of the formation, since he'll be leading the flight, but we'll have two Marine RF-4 Phantoms flying above the big diamond taking photos. Each B/N and RIO will have a camera that will be handed out at the end of the brief. CAG has the ultimate decision on how many passes you make by the Minsk, but our plan right now is to make three passes, all of them under three thousand feet, and the final pass at two thousand feet." Rear Admiral McElroy took a sip of water and continued.

"You'll be intercepting her, if she's where we believe she will be, just outside North Korea's territorial limit of twelve miles. Our intelligence convinces me that we'll catch her completely by surprise. It'll be quite the wake-up call for them to see CAG-Five's airplanes appearing out of a rising sun. We'll have two E-2 Hawkeyes airborne to give you any updates, and I'm hoping the A-6's will be able to pick her up on their radars and get a confirmation with their forward-looking infrared system that she isn't launching aircraft. She ought to have a big radar signature and be easy to see on this nice day. If she wants to reverse course and run home or steam inside North Korea's territorial waters, we'll have photos of that, too, but we believe she will stay her course toward Wonsan." Rear Admiral McElroy paused to let it sink in. As he did, he slid a panel on the wall behind him to his left, revealing a large map of the Sea of Japan, displaying the two Koreas.

"You may have sensed that the ship was steaming pretty hard late last night and into this morning. Right now we are about one hundred miles east-southeast of Wonsan," he said, pointing to a large black dot on the map in North Korea, "and here is our launch point." The launch point was seventy miles southeast of Wonsan. "After launch, you will proceed on an initial heading that will put you just south of the border between the two Koreas. If anyone is tracking you, it won't look a lot different from the two twelve-plane flights that went to Nightmare Range the past two days. As you approach the coast, about twenty miles away, you'll turn northwest toward Wonsan and parallel the coast, staying just outside North Korea's territorial waters, until you make contact. If lady luck is on our side, Minsk will be ten to twelve minutes away when you make the turn north, and she'll be refueling aircraft in preparation for her first morning launch. If our intel is good and that's the case, she won't have the time or available aircraft to send up your way before you're headed back home."

He paused, knowing the question each of the young aviators wanted answered.

'If the Soviets decide to take offensive actions against aircraft abiding within internationally recognized and approved boundaries and guidelines," the admiral paused, looking around at the men with a personal interest in his answer, "well, they'll have to decide if they want to take the risk of having to launch planes from underwater in the future." This was 'Liar's Dice' on the high seas, and they were sitting at the table. That was all they needed to know.

"Do I think they will have every tracking and guidance radar painting you?" He looked around the room again. "Hell, yeah. I think your radar homing and warning gear will be singing and flashing like songbirds, but it doesn't mean they'll launch. Just ignore it and treat it as a teachable moment. How many opportunities will you have in your life to tell your kids and grandkids that you were lit up and actively tracked by a Soviet aircraft carrier?" He smiled and sat down.

As planned, every aviator on the launch was strapped in and ready as the electrical and air start units were methodically connected to the air wing's aircraft at 0530 sharp. The Eagles' crews in the division of four Intruders were Rock and Jackal in the lead, Rooster and Preacher in dash-two, Willie and Gully in dash-three, and Socks and Doc flying the slot position as dash-four. The Eagles in the division that was comprised of two Intruders and two Prowlers were Angus and in the lead, and Pistol and Barkus in the slot as dash four.

Willie and Gully sat with their helmets on, dark visors down, and oxygen masks dangling in front of their faces, attached only to their helmet on the left side. Their canopy was open, allowing them to enjoy the warm Pacific breeze sweeping Midway's flight deck as they waited their turn to start their engines.

"That's odd," said Willie, as they sat relaxed in their jet.

"What's odd, Willie?" asked Gully, as he noticed Willie pointing toward the E-2 Hawkeye sitting across the flight deck from them.

"That tall guy with the beard standing by the E-2. See him?"

"Yep," answered Gully.

"He's a civilian based in Misawa with some spook unit there. I attended an intelligence brief where he spoke right before the last cruise. He's brilliant and conversationally fluent in several dialects of Russian and Asian languages. Must have a fifty pound brain."

"Wow."

"That's what I said, and I guess the admiral is planning to put it to good use today."

"Interesting," said Gully. "I guess he'll be listening for any intel about their intent."

"Yep, but what's more interesting is that he and I have something in common." Willie sounded quite serious.

Gully looked to his left. "Really? Seriously?" He paused. "What's that?"

Each time he spoke, Willie put his oxygen mask against his face so he could respond. "He has a fifty pound brain." He paused for a few seconds. "I have a fifty pound dick."

They both laughed as Willie turned toward his B/N. "You know I'm just joking, Gully. That isn't true."

"I know it isn't true, Willie," said Gully, still chuckling.

Willie glanced toward his B/N and smiled. Putting his mask against his face again, he completed his confession. "His brain only weighs forty-three pounds." The two of them looked at each other, not needing the Intruder's internal communication system to hear each other's laughter.

What wasn't a lie was that they each found it hard to believe they were sitting in a flying slice of metal on a big chunk of steel floating in a foreign sea — one of thirty-four Americans who would deliver a personal message from their president that a new sheriff was in town.

High above the carrier's flight deck, the ship's captain left the bridge and stood alone on a catwalk, surveying the planes parked below him that would soon be on their way toward hostile lands. He looked into each cockpit, wishing he could see the faces covered by dark visors and oxygen masks. It reminded him of the days when he, too, flew off Midway as the skipper of the Eagles, operating off the coast of Vietnam during the 1972 offensive.

After a silent prayer for their safety, the captain reentered Midway's bridge area as the first aircraft began moving toward the ship's two bow catapults. He wondered what his counterpart on Minsk would think when he saw the jets approaching, what decision process he would use, how he would react. He also knew it was probable that Minsk would launch a flight toward Midway as a show of retaliatory strength. Only time would tell, but he was ready, and the ship would be ready.

In the White House, the President, Vice President, Secretary of Defense, Secretary of State, Director of the Central Intelligence Agency, Chairman of the Joint Chiefs, and the National Security Advisor discussed the pros and cons of the mission one final time. The clock was ticking, and the window of opportunity would only be open for a short period.

"We will have several layers and methods of irrefutable confirmation that our aircraft were always over international waters, conforming to long established International Civil Aviation Organization rules agreed to and accepted by both the Soviets and North Koreans," stated the Secretary of Defense, emphatically, one more time.

"Our subs are in place?" asked the President.

"Yes, sir."

"They can put the Minsk on the bottom?"

"Quite quickly, sir. They have both had valid target solutions since she exited her port."

"Are we sure there are no Soviet, Chinese, or North Korean subs of either kind in the area?" The President was referring to diesel and nuclear submarines.

"Yes, sir. We're confident that our decoy plan pulled them all to the north."

"Is there an AGI in the area?" asked the President. An AGI was a generally decrepit, barely seaworthy looking fishing ship operated by the Soviet Union. Although the Soviets referred to them as trawlers, the United States and its allies referred to them as AGIs, for Auxiliary General Intelligence, because they were packed with surveillance electronics.

"Not as of six p.m. local time there yesterday, Mister President," responded the Chairman of the Joint Chiefs. "That's the only wild card." Little did he know that an AGI had unexpectedly departed Wonsan, Korea late Thursday to sit off the South Korean coast in order to observe the American jets that would likely be flying into Nightmare Range.

"Very well. Send the signal. God be with those aviators. It'll be a turkey shoot if the Soviets panic." The President looked around. "And the cold war will suddenly become very hot." With that, the President departed for the Kennedy Center to host England's ambassador to the United States at a previously scheduled performance of selected music from Giacomo Puccini's opera Turandot. The chairman of the Joint Chiefs of Staff would join him, as scheduled, in order to not give any astute reporters an opportunity to wonder why one, or both of them, would be absent from the scheduled event.

The rendezvous at three thousand feet was expeditious and safe. A single, seemingly innocuous, statement from Midway confirmed the mission's authority to proceed, and that the target was where they thought she'd be.

"Badman, Ops."

"Go ahead Ops."

"Nightmare is open, the range is clear, weather reported clear through early afternoon." It was the same message delivered to jets flying to Nightmare Range the two previous days.

"Badman, copy." CAG was smiling under his oxygen mask. Life was good.

The flight of eighteen had been orbiting in a port turn for almost fifteen minutes when the 'go ahead' was received. Badman's Corsair rolled out on a southwesterly heading, as had been done on the previous two mornings by CAG-Five aircraft. Twenty-two miles northeast of the point where the current flight path would intersect the South Korean coastline if they continued straight ahead, the eighteen aircraft began a slow turn to the northwest. They were twelve minutes from their target.

Using high-powered binoculars, the AGI's captain and political officer were monitoring the progress of the airplanes from Midway flying toward the coast when they visually observed the turn of the aircraft to the north. Although they were seven or eight miles away, and looking into a bright sun, they could still reasonably determine the type and number of aircraft, although they confused the two Prowlers for Intruders and the two Marine photo reconnaissance Phantoms for Navy Phantoms.

More critically, in the excitement of what they were seeing, and in the glare of the early morning sun, they confused the drop tanks hanging below the Intruders and two of the six Corsairs as high-explosive bombs. The AGI's political officer activated a radio channel he had never used, one that connected him directly to Moscow. He reported what he and the AGI's captain had observed, including their observation that significant ordnance was being carried, and the information was relayed to the Minsk, which had observed the American aircraft making the turn northwest on the Soviet carrier's multiple radars.

In Moscow, the General Secretary of the Communist Party, the acknowledged leader of the Soviet Union, was briefed on the events occurring, and immediately gathered his key political and military leaders. Time was critical. The American jets were approximately twelve minutes from the Minsk. It was a bluff or it was for real. There was no other rationale for aircraft with ordnance to make the turn northward toward their aircraft carrier.

On the Minsk, the ship's captain sounded the general-quarters alarm, and ordered all available weapons trained on the incoming aircraft. The captain, unlike the ship's political officer, was very well liked and respected by his crew and aviators.

Within one minute of the CAG-Five formation turning toward the north, each of the airplanes began receiving aural and visual warnings that an unfriendly opponent was scanning their aircraft. As briefed, the formation maintained radio silence.

Jamming radars was considered a provocation of war. The two EA-6B Prowlers in the flight, although capable of effectively jamming the Soviet's radars, maintained electronic silence.

One of the two E-2 Hawkeyes that launched from Midway served as the primary communications link between the White House, USS Midway, and Badman One. The strange man with the beard onboard one of them was listening to conversations between men speaking in a foreign language.

Under the water, two submarines sat in undetected silence, themselves detecting a Soviet submarine approximately twelve miles away. It became their second target.

The eighteen aircraft were fifty-two miles from the Minsk; eight minutes and forty seconds of flight time. Admiral McElroy's description was accurate; neon songbirds were having a field day in the jets' cockpits as the Minsk's radars pounded all of them like insane artists throwing paint on a canvas. Intruder B/N's could see the bright return of the Minsk on their radars. On their forward-looking infrared system's display, each B/N could vaguely see the rotors of helicopters turning, although none had launched.

In Moscow, arguments were being made to justifiably oppose what many saw as an act of provocation or, some even argued, war. The Soviets had four aircraft carriers, but two of them could carry only a small number of helicopters. If the Minsk was lost, it would leave the Soviets with only one aircraft carrier that could carry fighter and attack aircraft.

The counter-argument was that the American jets, although they were apparently carrying ordnance, were in international airspace and taunting them, and that to launch missiles or anti-aircraft fire against the aircraft would justify a debilitating retaliatory strike against their homeland and naval assets, including one from a submarine, although none had been detected in the area.

As Badman descended his flight from three thousand feet to twenty-five hundred feet, a move immediately noticed onboard the Minsk, deliberations took on a new urgency in the Soviet capital as the clock continued to tick. On the Minsk, the ship's captain was in several heated discussions. He was angry that his jets weren't being refueled faster, one of his gun systems had malfunctioned, and the Minsk's political officer wanted him to launch the helicopters as a show of response, although it'd be a pitiful response against the American jets and would delay getting his jets ready. The captain, pushing Moscow for an answer that wasn't seemingly forthcoming, knew he'd be banished to salt mines or be executed if he made the wrong decision. His wife and children would possibly be punished with him.

At the Kennedy Center, the President was calm as the clock continued to tick.

Badman's heartbeat was remarkably calm. His flight of eighteen aircraft was ten miles from the Minsk, one minute and forty seconds away, and flying straight at her. If the Soviets fired, his would likely be the first aircraft hit. He, too, understood the concept of keeping the peace through superior strength and firepower.

However, his 'Midwestern roots' translation to his friends at home would be to say that if you squeeze a man's balls hard enough, he'd find a way to sing Ave Maria in three languages at the same time.

In the six A-6E Intruder aircraft, navigation and radar systems were being closely monitored to ensure that the air wing didn't stray inside twelve miles of the coastline, especially if the Minsk tried to ease inside the territorial limit and drag the jets with her.

In Moscow, heated debate continued. Some thought the new American president was deliberately trying to humiliate their country and its leaders, and to push the Soviets into firing. Others believed the cowboy occupying 1600 Pennsylvania Avenue would preemptively attack the Minsk, daring their country to launch a war over the sinking of a mediocre and ineffective ship. Only a small minority believed it was a harmless flight being legally conducted in international waters.

On the Minsk, the captain was almost hysterical. Through his binoculars, he could see what appeared to be bombs, or some type of ordnance, hanging below the wings of all the aircraft, now nine miles away and flying directly at his ship, confirming the AGI's observation. Whatever type of ordnance it was, it appeared large enough to do lethal damage to his carrier, and he relayed that message to Moscow. The Minsk's captain knew the time to effectively respond was short, and he screamed at the political officer, "Those idiots in Moscow are going to get us sunk, kill us all."

He had waited impotently and impatiently as long as he could, until he knew it was decision time. He was paid to protect his ship and the men who served on her, not to stand by and watch it be destroyed by the Americans. The political officer, already disliked immensely by the officers and crew, responded by telling the captain that Moscow knew what was best for his ship and to "Be silent."

Six miles from the Minsk, the American pilots and flight officers were close enough to see that, unlike Midway, the Minsk's landing and takeoff area was predominantly dark green, not gray. It was a bit of trivia they'd share in an hour if they weren't shot out of the sky in the next thirty seconds. Each aircraft's radar warning gear was indicating that terminal tracking radars were illuminating them.

In Washington, the Kennedy Center audience was appropriately enjoying the defining moment of the classic aria *Nessun Dorma*, not knowing the irony of its timing as it related to an event half a world away.

In Moscow, the moment to make a decision was upon them; they were down to seconds, even as arguments for and against a military response continued to be angrily debated in the room. The General Secretary calmly stood up, shook his head, and softly said, "Nyet."

The stand-down signal was immediately transmitted to the Minsk and received on the bridge of the carrier, just mere seconds after Minsk's captain had turned to the political officer and said, "I'm going to defend my ship! You can rot in the flames of hell, you bastard," and then turned to his fire control officer. "Stand by to fire on my command."

At the very moment that the message from Moscow was received on the bridge, as he was preparing to fire on the American aggressors, the Minsk's captain noticed the American formation starting a slight right turn, one that would parallel his course, albeit in the opposite direction, and would keep the American aircraft just over a half mile from his ship. The captain immediately directed the missile and gun teams to turn off all radars, as the political officer stood in a corner and glared at him. The inflammatory words of the captain were seared into his brain. The captain and his family would pay a heavy price, he promised himself.

As the formation passed the port side of his ship, the Minsk's captain clearly noted that the American jets were carrying no bombs, just drop tanks for fuel, information he passed back to Moscow immediately, hoping his career would survive the political officer's wrath and revenge.

Inside every CAG-Five aircraft, the radar warning lights and sounds ceased. Every aviator breathed a big sigh of relief. Leaders in Great Britain and other countries friendly to America were informed of what had just occurred on the high seas. At the Kennedy Center, having received the information, America's number one cowboy merely smiled and nodded as he gave the Joint Chiefs chairman a thumbs up, and took a sip of red wine that had never tasted better.

In the skies over the Soviet carrier Minsk, the eighteen jets made a total of four passes. After the first pass, each subsequent pass was flown on the same course as the Minsk, roughly a quarter-mile to its port side, creating many wonderful photo opportunities.

For their fourth and final pass, the flight rolled out downwind, setting up so that they were six miles abeam the Minsk, which was heading in the opposite direction off their port wing. They descended slowly to fifteen hundred feet above the ocean. Three miles downwind of the carrier, CAG began a shallow turn to port for a final pass by the Soviet carrier.

CAG Rick 'Badman' Evans wanted to ensure the officers and sailors onboard Minsk had a chance to get numerous close-up photos of Carrier Air Wing Five's aircraft. He also knew this final pass would be memorable to, and its message clearly understood by, the Russian carrier's commanding officer and political officer, and to the AGI they had sighted as they turned north on their initial inbound leg toward the Minsk.

As the flight approached a point where they had ninety degrees of turn to go for their final pass, three 'mike clicks' were heard on all the American jets' radios. Approximately five seconds later, the unmistakable sound of the O'Jay's song *Love Train* was clearly heard over those same radios.

370

As they learned later, it was being played over the U.S. military's UHF emergency frequency, called 'guard.' Every American jet, ship, airport, and air traffic control facility, and most foreign airports and air traffic control facilities, monitored it constantly. So did the Soviet aircraft carrier Minsk and the AGI.

The CAG-Five flight was less than ten seconds from passing Minsk for the final time when it became obvious why the song was started when it was. Playing was the stanza that urged China and Russia to get on board the love train and to keep riding it. It was a not-so-sublime message, delivered as only a Hollywood cowboy in the White House could have orchestrated it, as the eighteen jets flew by the Soviet carrier for the final time.

On the port side of the Minsk's bridge, the Russian carrier's captain cracked a smile as he watched and listened to the music, mixed with the crackling, ear-shattering roar as the impressive jets flew by. He understood enough of the English language to hear its message loud and clear. I just hope our political leaders have ears that hear and understand, he thought.

It was a cathartic moment as he realized that he and the aviator leading the American flight had much more in common than both being Navy flyboys, albeit opposing navies. They would both laugh at the irony of going from near-Armageddon to rock and roll music in just a fifteen or twenty minute span, he thought. The Minsk's captain also hoped that his three sons, ages twelve, fifteen and eighteen, each hoping to be an aviator in the Soviet Navy in the future, would have the same mental toughness as the aviator at the front of the American flight.

On the other side of the Minsk's bridge, the political officer became even more enraged when he saw the captain smile. In the Ukraine, the home of the political officer and also Leonid Brezhnev, the general secretary of the communist party, smiling and laughing was a sign that a citizen was either anti-communist, or had ill-gotten wealth that they were likely hiding from the government. The captain's smile confirmed to the political officer what he had recently begun to believe about him; the captain was an aviator and sailor first, and not a party loyalist. This final straw, he recommitted to himself, ensured the captain wouldn't be laughing when they returned to Moscow. It'd be hard for the captain to smile or sing when he and his family were sitting and starving in a brutal prison.

Deep under the Sea of Japan, two submarines silently left an area they were never in and glided into their Connecticut homeport a day early, right into the arms of many happy loved ones.

As soon as his jets were ready, the captain of the Minsk launched two fighter aircraft to overfly the American carrier, against the advice of his political officer who, in front of several senior members of the ship's crew, informed him that he would recommend the captain be immediately relieved and severely punished when the ship returned to Vladivostok.

On Midway, the fun and excitement and games weren't over. Anticipating that the Minsk would launch a few jets to fly over the American carrier in retaliation, Admiral McElroy cancelled the launch that was scheduled to bomb at the Koon-ni target range. Instead, he urged as many sailors, airmen, and officers, as could do so, to come up to the flight deck and share brotherly love if, as he anticipated, Soviet aircraft flew a retaliatory show of second-rate airpower.

Forty-five minutes later, two Soviet Yak-38 Forger aircraft from the Minsk proved the admiral right, as they made three low passes by Midway, and an estimated fifteen hundred men packed the flight deck to show their appreciation for the Soviet's impromptu air show, including many who used a single middle finger to wave at them.

The sandbox was, once again, an equal opportunity place in which to play.

On the Minsk, in spite of the flyover by Midway's aircraft, morale was similarly buoyed when the Soviet carrier's unpopular political officer unfortunately lost his balance while walking on one of Minsk's weather decks on a dark night. In front of several credible witnesses whose stories matched, he disappeared over the side of the ship. Morale was elevated even further when the popular Minsk captain, who made a personal vow to one day shake the hand of the American pilot leading that flight, was promoted, six months later, to rear admiral.

During the remainder of the night and into early Wednesday morning, as the Far East Film Society's audience finally surrendered to the need for sleep, Midway made the turn around the southern tip of Japan. After a brief transit across the East China Sea, she turned north into the Sea of Japan.

To the two attack submarines invisibly flying very loose 'underwater formation' with Midway, there was no night or day. In fact, their mission was so classified that they weren't there at all. To all but a small handful of people alive, the two boats were conducting seven weeks of well-publicized training operations off the coast of Connecticut, the inherent safety of which allowed the family members of the submarines' crews to sleep very well at night, not knowing their loved ones were actually halfway around the world, sitting at an international poker table with questionable players.

The primary reason for the short at-sea period was accomplished. The flagship of the Navy's foreign legion steamed south, then east, and finally north into the Pacific waters she called home. To the delight of families eager to see their loved ones after the long separation, the ship and her aircraft returned to their highly anticipated homecoming in Japan a day earlier than scheduled.

Midway Magic was alive and doing very well.

CHAPTER EIGHTEEN

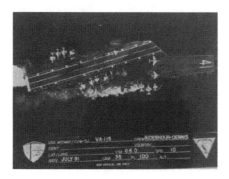

Shipmates
Early February, 1981

The jet that would carry Willie and Gully to Atsugi was parked near Midway's fantail. Sixty-three jets were ready for launch. In less than forty minutes, they would be catapulted from the flight deck for the final time on the 'Summer of '80' cruise. Even though they were over five weeks into a new year, it was the name by which they'd always recall the past six months and a couple weeks together.

The Intruders would be the last to launch, and their departure would effectively close one more chapter in Midway's history. Although one pilot, three enlisted men, and four aircraft would not be coming home, the cruise was deemed a success. Acceptable losses for such an at-sea period were defined as five aircraft lost or significantly damaged, three fatalities involving aviators, and three fatalities involving non-aviators. The men understood the risks and accepted them as part of the profession. Families always struggled with death being an acceptable loss.

The two aviators, both wearing their helmets for hearing protection, stood side-by-side at the front of the jet as noise saturated the air around them. They looked behind them, across Midway's fantail, to an endless ocean. In the carrier's wake was a trail of tears, fears, joy, death, new experiences, new places, sights never to be seen again, and a collision at sea on a dark night. They had been deployed from their home base in Japan for a few days over five months. When exercises and operations away from Atsugi were included, many in the air wing had been deployed from their home for sixteen of the past nineteen months.

"It's time to go home," said Willie.

"Let's go. I'm ready." Gully smiled.

"I bet you are."

Thirty minutes later, with the exception of the helicopters assigned, the Eagles' Intruders were the last aircraft remaining on Midway. All the men on the flight deck were eager to see them disappear; their departure represented the end of another cruise. It would also enable them to escape an outside air temperature of thirty-seven degrees and a twenty-six knot wind down the flight deck that had turned the air's fine mist into millions of frozen, microscopic-sized daggers. To a man, the jets couldn't launch soon enough; getting them off the deck was their ticket to relaxing and preparing for a homecoming in Yokosuka in less than four hours.

Five of the Intruders, with destinations other than Atsugi, would launch first. Socks and Doc sat in a jet with Naval Air Facility Misawa's latitude and longitude logged into their navigation computer, although their personal destinations were the arms of two women who were waiting anxiously for them in sub-freezing temperatures. Marti, from Austin, Texas, and Lauren, from Manitou Springs, Colorado, had both slept fitfully, hoping the men's journey from sea to land would proceed as planned and that they'd soon be warmly reunited with two flyboys on the frozen soil where they first met. The other four jets were flying south like real birds in the winter; their destination was the tropical climate of Subic Bay, Republic of the Philippines.

For several aviators awaiting launch, including Gully, this had been their very first cruise. They, like countless enlisted men, walked into the squadron and on board Midway as inexperienced neophytes. Now, they were leaving as seasoned aviators and sailors, dues paying members of a unique fraternity begun just over two hundred years ago by John Paul Jones, the father of the United States Navy. No matter what they did with the rest of their lives, no one could ever take that away from them.

Gully's juvenile anticipation at reuniting with Sharon was contagious. Willie had accepted that his relationship with Tosh was nothing more than a fond memory, but he was sincerely thrilled for his B/N. Gully had worked hard at becoming an asset in the right seat, and it reflected in their performance as a crew, giving earned justification for the salty swagger Gully had added to his stride and personality.

From their position on the ship's aft port side, Willie and Gully patiently waited and watched six Intruders and their crews accelerate down one of the two catapults for the final time on the cruise. Gully had a good alignment on the jet's inertial navigation system, although they wouldn't need it. They'd merely be tagging along with ten other jets, as Skipper Curry and his B/N led the flight of twelve jets home like baby chickens. Such was the reason that, upon checking in with Atsugi approach control shortly after launch, the controller would ask, "How many chicks in your flight today?"

As the seventh Intruder was preparing to launch, a flight deck crewman, standing in front of Willie's jet, used hand signals to ask if he was ready for the chocks under their jet to be removed.

"You ready to go?" Willie asked Gully.

"Yep. Good on this side," he said immediately, and then watched as Willie quickly gave the yellow shirt a nod and a thumbs up. It was a surreal moment for Gully. There were moments during the cruise when it seemed as if time was crawling at a snail's pace, and even now it seemed that the trip to the catapult for their final launch was painfully slow. Yet, somehow the five months had flown by like a Japanese bullet train.

Seconds later, the yellow shirt signaled for Willie to begin moving forward. He advanced the jet's two throttles and heard the ever-increasing high-pitched sound of the engines as they came to life and began to push the Intruder forward. Without fail, Willie smiled underneath his oxygen mask and a semiconscious thrill resonated throughout his body as man and machine worked in tandem, a reminder that he was still living a dream.

The two friends, their faces hidden by oxygen masks and dark visors, sat in silence as they waited for each of the Intruders ahead of them to launch, at which time they would ease forward about fifty or sixty feet and wait again. All around them, dedicated men were walking or standing with their bodies leaning into an icy wind, doing their jobs as professionally as any human alive, but being paid a fraction of what they could earn in the outside world.

Like all the men in the squadron and on Midway, whether the experiences were good or bad, and the memories fond or sad, a very extraordinary cruise was under their belts, and the two friends had survived. Gully, like all those in the foreign legion, had repaid his debt to the country's forefathers as he voluntarily served on behalf of both the free and the enslaved. It was a source of pride no one could ever take away from him.

Still, as he sat strapped into the aircraft, Gully was humbled by his good fortune and opportunity to experience daily what so many, especially those who toiled on the flight deck around them, longed to do just once; once would be enough.

As they neared the port catapult, with just one jet in front of them to be launched, Willie expressed a heartfelt sentiment. "Doesn't seem right not seeing Buzz up here." Two days earlier, Petty Officer Tessaro was flown to Atsugi to begin the discharge process from the Navy, and also to be the petty officer in charge of the ground crew that would handle the Intruders' arrival at their home base.

"You're right about that, Willie. It was always a warm, fuzzy feeling knowing his eyes were on us."

Two minutes later, with their Intruder having been guided securely onto the catapult shuttle, and as steam rose and blew across their jet's canopy, the yellow shirt signaled for full power.

With the throttles full forward, Willie cycled the flight controls of a jet straining to be unleashed and reported the status to Gully, as he had done countless times during the cruise. "Good engines, good oil, good hydraulics, good throw on the controls. Flaps are set, stab is shifted, no lights." He glanced to his right at his B/N and friend, who, like all the great men who occupied the right seat, made the Intruder the lethal and unique flying machine that it was. "Ready to go?"

"Yep. Let's go."

Willie looked outside, forward and to his right, at the catapult officer on the flight deck and gave him a sharp salute, signaling his and the jet's readiness to get their farewell performance underway. After two seconds of chest pounding acceleration, the next-to-last box in their 'fall of '80' cruise was checked. All that remained was a safe landing in Atsugi.

Mount Fuji, poised dramatically just over a hundred twenty miles away and a beckoning symbol of their adopted country, came into sight on a brilliant sunny morning as the flight passed eight thousand feet on its climb to sixteen thousand feet. Barely fifteen minutes after the flight of twelve said sayonara to Midway, the air wing's hangars located at Atsugi also came into view, thanks to a very cold and clear day in Japan that allowed for unlimited visibility. No one had to point it out; all eyes had been anticipating the poignant moment since the formation began its climb to altitude.

Also anticipating seeing a Japanese city in the distance were Socks and Doc. They were covering the four hundred eleven nautical miles between their launch point on Midway and Naval Air Facility Misawa, where Marti and Lauren were currently waiting, at a ground speed of over five hundred fifty miles per hour. Eighty miles from Misawa, Doc called the air operations office on their second radio to provide an update to their arrival time.

"Misawa ops, Eagle Five Zero Seven." Doc's voice was professional, but accented with a smile. Try as he might, he was unable to mask his enthusiasm at reuniting with Lauren.

"Eagle Five Zero Seven, Misawa Ops, welcome back."

"Five Zero Seven, thank you sir. Overhead in ten minutes."

The voice that answered next was as shocking as if it had been the voice of God. "Well, I can barely wait, Doc, and neither can Marti." Lauren Adams's voice had both aviators grinning and laughing out loud in the cockpit. It was a genuine touch of class, and a nod to the sacrifices of deployed sailors everywhere, that the air operations duty officer had handed the microphone to one of the ladies, who had arrived almost thirty minutes earlier, to respond.

"We're counting each minute, too." It was all Doc could think to say. To the two aviators, the final few minutes seemed to drag on as long as the previous five months.

The duty officer was enjoying the tangible electricity in the air created by the anticipation of seeing the arriving Intruder come into sight. He had been deployed on seven cruises himself, and decided to add his own heartfelt gesture into the reunion about to occur.

"Five Zero Seven, base ops."

"Go ahead, ops."

"Roger, be advised that it's twenty-two degrees Fahrenheit here. I hope you have a way to keep warm."

Inside the cockpit, Socks and Doc looked at each other and nodded, big smiles unseen under their oxygen masks. "Thanks for the heads up, ops. We have a plan we think will work just fine," replied Doc.

Lauren Adams's voice broke the short period of silence. "We also have many plans we think will work."

"I read you loud and clear," responded Doc, allowing his laughter to be part of the radio chatter. An outsider would likely believe that the attitude and atmosphere inside the Intruder's cockpit was relaxed and casual, but it would be as far from the truth as the jet currently was from the deep, dark, shark-infested waters off the coast of Borneo, the site of the collision with the Panamanian freighter. Every aviator knew that a casual attitude could lead to a casual mistake that caused a not-so-casual accident. The embarrassment of an accident was so much a distinct part of naval aviation's culture that from their earliest days in flight school to their last flight naval aviators informally joked that it'd always be better to die than look bad.

Unlike Atsugi's cold and clear day, Misawa was cold but cloudy. The measured visibility was three miles under a solid deck of clouds at eleven hundred feet above the ground. The two women, standing outside the air operations office, first saw Five Zero Seven appear from the clouds slightly under three miles from where they stood. Its three landing gear were down. After five months away, the Intruder was less than one minute away from again touching Japanese soil.

The controllers in the tower simply smiled as they watched the jet arrive. They knew, all too well, the divine thrill of a long awaited homecoming. To a person, they hoped the men in the Intruder and the two women waiting for them would successfully overcome the many impediments that endangered

Navy relationships. For now, though, they'd do their part in making a dose of magic happen.

As the jet touched down and began its long rollout, Socks kept a laser-like focus on making this final segment safe and error free. Soon, he engaged the Intruder's nosewheel steering and turned right at the end of the runway, beginning the slightly over half mile journey to his next turn, which would be to the left and into the arms of a beautiful woman waiting just for him.

When the jet was two thousand feet away, the men in the cockpit became clearly visible, and the two women waved to their flyboys. Socks responded by flashing the jet's taxi light a few times. After making a left hand turn from the taxiway into the area reserved for transient aircraft, the Misawa ground crew directed the Intruder to the parking spot closest to the air operations building. As the jet slowly approached its assigned spot, Doc opened the canopy and blew a kiss to Lauren, who was standing about fifty feet from where they would finally stop. She was the most beautiful woman he had ever seen, he thought, even wrapped in a lavender down parka and wearing a standard Navy set of noise attenuators that covered both her ears. Defying the bitter cold wind, her irresistible smile beckoned like a sunny tropical beach.

Socks eased the Intruder to a slow stop, and a transient line plane director placed chocks under all three landing gear after checking to ensure the brakes weren't overheated. While that was being done, Socks and Doc unstrapped from their ejection seats and exchanged what would, effectively, be their last cruise-related communications.

"System's secured. I'm ready to shut down," said Doc.

"Roger. Waiting for a thumbs up on the brakes and chocks."

A few moments later, the transient line crewman ran to the pilot's side of the jet and gave Socks a thumbs up and indicated, via a hand signal, that it was safe to shut down the Intruder's two engines.

"Okay, we're shutting down," said Socks, as he secured the two engines and listened to them wind down toward silence. The two aviators looked at each other and, having already removed their oxygen masks, spoke in normal voices now that there was no external jet noise to interrupt them.

"Thanks for keeping me alive during cruise, Doc." Socks extended his hand to the friend who also slept above him in Bunkroom Eight, the Midway Oasis. During the cruise that was now over, the amount of time they spent together would make most married couples envious. For all their eagerness to see their awaiting dates, the two men took a few short moments, as they completed a couple remaining cockpit chores, to exchange the professional courtesies due each other.

Doc smiled. "You're a mighty fine stick, Socks. I'm glad we flew together."

"Thanks," Socks said smiling, "my pleasure as well, and now it's time to go see our beautiful dates." He continued to smile as he patted his friend's left shoulder.

As the two men stepped off their respective boarding ladders and straight into the embraces of the women they loved, their 'fall of 1980' cruise countdown timer officially hit zero.

The two couples smiled and laughed and hugged and kissed and held hands as the aviators walked around the Intruder and performed a quick, but thorough, postflight inspection. As they did, a new countdown clock for Midway's next deployment began ticking down from a starting time of eleven weeks and six days.

Unfortunately, another crisis in the Pacific would interrupt that timer in just thirty-four days, and the Navy's foreign legion would be on the move again. For as long as they were tethered to Midway and CAG-Five, they each knew tomorrow would arrive with events planned or unplanned, which was okay. For today and tonight, though, they had the current moment, and it was perfect.

The flight of twelve Intruders inbound to Atsugi approached their initial entry point, five miles from the approach end of the runway on which they'd land, with all eyes in the air and on the ground watching the distance between the two rapidly closing. Within the formation, each pilot began flying a tighter and more exact formation position as they closed in toward the waiting crowd of excited onlookers. Earlier, while still seven miles away and fifteen hundred feet above the ground, the skipper had slowly eased the flight down to eight hundred feet above the ground, adjusting the linear position of the flight so that the aircraft on the far left wing would be over the top of the runway. With the crowd to the formation's right side, it would not only make the visual approach to landing easier for all the aircraft, but it would also create an unmatched audio-visual effect to announce their return in high-fidelity stereo to the waiting crowd.

Mother Nature joined in the reunion. Her cold stiff breeze enhanced the sound from the twenty-four jet engines pushing the flight of twelve Intruders through the air like a high-speed ballet, seemingly close enough to touch. Their approach had been first announced by a high pitch whine, and was soon followed by an ear-numbing, air crackling roar that literally made the air, ground, and human bodies vibrate with joy as the formation passed by where the aviators' families, called affectionately the Eagles' Nest, stood on the tarmac.

Inside the cockpits and among the families and friends waiting on the ground, time seemed to be moving wretchedly slowly, even as the jets traveled at over three hundred fifty miles per hour. The first jet peeled off for landing just as the formation passed the crowd. One minute and seventeen seconds later, Willie banked sharply to the left, almost six miles from the airfield, as 'tail-end-Charlie' in the line of Intruders in the landing pattern. By the time Willie slowed his jet to the appropriate speed and lowered the landing gear, the first four Intruders had already touched down on the runway.

Nine minutes later, after having been directed to parking by Petty Officer Tessaro, who subsequently placed chocks under all three tires and safety pins in the landing gear and external drop tanks, Willie looked to his right at Gully and, with his right hand, made a slashing motion across his throat.

Gully nodded as he gave Willie a thumbs up. Being a precisely choreographed team, it was fitting that their final communication of the cruise required no spoken words.

Willie secured the Intruder's two engines, and a welcome silence finally settled comfortably over Atsugi like a soft cozy blanket. All the returning Intruders now sat quietly at rest in two rows, facing each other just under a hundred feet apart.

Having earlier pinned their ejection seats, and disconnected their harness and leg restraints from the six points connecting them to their seats, the two looked at each other. Willie knew Gully was eager to see Sharon. Many of the other Eagles were already gathered as a group, shaking hands, and acknowledging jobs well done, and they'd be the last to join.

"Hell of a cruise, Gully. You did good." Willie extended his hand and smiled. "And that's the truth."

Gully shook his hand as a smile spread across his face. "Thanks, Willie. Hard to believe it's really over."

"Yep, it was a cruise to remember. But it's over, and I think there's someone special waiting for you."

"Amen to that," acknowledged Gully, with a big grin cemented on his face.

Both aviators smiled as they stood, and then climbed down their respective boarding ladders.

Willie and Gully shook hands with Petty Officer Tessaro, who was waiting in front of the jet for them. "Good jet?"

"Excellent jet, Buzz," Gully answered. "We missed you on the boat."

"I miss being there, sir." His voice tailed off at the end; he was sincere. In fact, he was so sincere that he knew it would be easy at a moment like this to rescind his decision to leave the Navy.

With their quick postflight completed, Willie put his right hand on Buzz's left shoulder, and said, "Let's go join the group." The three of them walked to where the other Eagles were waiting, and joined in shaking hands all around.

"Listen up, guys." Skipper Curry spoke loudly. "Great cruise, great job flying form for the crowd. You guys are the best. I love you all. Eagles on three. One...Two...Three."

"Eagles," resonated loudly across the frozen tarmac.

The aviators who had loved ones waiting walked at a brisk pace or ran toward the objects of their affection, many of whom were already making their way toward them. Some had children in tow, and all were eager for heartwarming reunions that would be tearfully and joyfully consummated under the watchful eye of a very visible Mount Fuji. As they turned toward the hangar, Willie quickly scanned the women on the tarmac. Although he wasn't surprised, he was still disappointed that he saw no tall blond resembling Tosh Collins.

Fully expecting Gully to run toward where Sharon stood, Willie was surprised as he remained next to him for a few steps, so he stopped and turned to his B/N. "Cruise is over, Gully. You're a loyal friend and a great B/N, and we'll be back up in the air again soon." He extended his hand once more as he looked up at his tall friend, "I look forward to it, but now it's time for you to go see the one you really love."

As Gully shook Willie's hand, Buzz smiled at the exchange of emotions and respect between the two.

Gully still seemed unsure, pensive, as if he were breaking an unwritten rule regarding cockpit loyalty, so Willie made it easy for him. "Here, give me your nav bag and helmet bag. You can run a lot faster without them," he said with a big grin.

Gully smiled and handed Willie the two olive green bags. Without hesitation or any more words he began running as fast as his gangly, flight gear-ladened body would allow. Sharon, who had tears in her eyes, was already walking quickly in his direction.

"Let me have those, sir." Buzz reached over and took Gully's two bags from Willie. "You're a fine pilot, but a lousy pack mule." The two laughed as they began walking toward the warmth of the hangar, about six hundred feet away. Eight rows of parked Intruders, one on either side of them, welcomed them back like formal side boys, saluting with their folded wings as they passed.

Although it was cold and windy, there was no urgency in their stride. On their left side were Fish and Donna Ingalls, both of whom waved at them between hugs and kisses. To their right, "Rock" Pyle was on one knee, hugging his daughter, forever the apple of his eye. Willie and Buzz could see tears on both their faces. She had turned eleven just three weeks earlier, and had also grown two inches taller since her dad departed Atsugi. His daughter was crying the last time Willie had seen her, and she was crying now, although tears of unbridled joy had replaced her tears of despair from five months earlier. Later that day, her family would celebrate her birthday with a party, delayed at her request, so her father could help her blow out the candles.

"You know, Buzz, I dreamed of this day since the morning we flew from here to the ship over six months ago. I had a vision of Tosh waiting for me. We'd be celebrating the end of cruise together, a very special moment that we'd always remember even when we were old and gray." He paused for a moment and looked around. "I have to admit I was hoping, had even convinced myself, that she'd surprise me and be here today, and we'd just pick up where we left off and, one day soon, have burgers and beer together in your stomping grounds."

"I'm sure, sir; it's human nature. I was actually hoping it'd be just like you said, including the burgers in SoCal." They smiled and walked in silence for a few moments, and then Willie continued the conversation.

"It's okay. I knew the risks going into it; it isn't for every woman." He paused, looking left and right. "I don't blame her. We can barely handle it, but let's talk about you. You're irreplaceable, my friend. Every time I saw you up there by the catapult giving us a thumbs up before launch, I always knew my jet was good, and that I'd be back unless I was the one who dicked the donkey."

Buzz laughed as the two of them waved at three reunited families to their left, all seemingly oblivious to the biting wind that was, ever so slightly, increasing in its speed. The men continued their slow pace as they passed two more parked Intruders facing each other. "Well, I'm glad you didn't, lieutenant. You know you'll survive and be just fine without me, but I'm already missing this. As excited as I am to get back to sunny California, it's a lot harder than I thought it'd be to actually say goodbye to the guys, and these jets, to Midway and the foreign legion, and even to Mount Fuji watching over us. I thought it'd be easy to walk away one last time, but it isn't."

Buzz and Willie waved to Sharon and Gully, still smiling and hugging and kissing. If not for Gully's flight gear as a hint to his age, the two could be high school teenagers in love for the very first time.

Buzz then struck a serious tone. "I've been thinking about my time with the Eagles and on Midway, sir." He stopped walking and turned toward Willie, who also stopped. The two looked into each other's eyes, each silently but unquestionably extolling the total faith in and professionalism of the man standing across from him.

"I know I was very lucky," Buzz admitted. "I can't imagine there is a finer squadron or ship I could have been assigned to for the majority of my time in the Navy."

Buzz glanced from side to side at the airplanes, and then at the family reunions taking place and the unattached pilots and B/N's making their way toward the hangar. "I'm a seriously strong believer in Midway magic, you know. I believe it's real, and I believe in the Eagles and the foreign legion, but especially the guys."

His visceral emotions could have easily warmed the frigid air as his voice quivered ever so slightly. "It's hard saying goodbye and knowing that it's over, that I won't be a part of it ever again, that it really is over — that this is it, and that I'll be on my way home before any of these jets are airborne again."

Willie nodded slowly. "I'm sure it's hard saying goodbye, Buzz. I see it in your eyes and I hear it in your voice." He, too, looked around at the reunions still playing out across the tarmac and at the men walking toward the hangar. "You were a big part of something very special."

Willie turned toward Buzz and looked into his eyes again. The air had a new bite to it, but neither of them cared. "We'll all be in your shoes one day, saying goodbye to the Eagles and Midway for a last time, but we'll know we served with the best, and you are at the top of that list. You can walk away knowing you did everything and more that anyone asked or expected while you were an Eagle, and you did it better than anyone else. Don't ever forget it, Buzz."

Willie put his right hand on Buzz's left shoulder and stared straight into his eyes. "We never lost an airplane while you were the final set of eyes on our jets. Never. Not once." Willie couldn't emphasize his declaration any more emphatically. "We launched and then we all came back in one piece. Every time. Every single time. That is a fact you can hang your hat on for the rest of your life, Buzz. We owe you for that, and we always will...for the rest of our lives."

Willie paused for a few seconds. "I owe you more than anyone. Your positive attitude on the flight deck and down in the line shack set the tone for the division every single day. You made my ground job easy, and you made sure my jet would bring me home. There was nothing left for me to ask that you weren't already doing."

388

He smiled and looked at Buzz, a young man who ensured they would all safely fly away and return, although he never had the chance to spend even one minute airborne in a Navy jet himself. "That's way more than enough in my book to say you get an endless free drink chit every time I see you in the future."

Buzz warmly smiled as the two men turned and walked into a shivering wind. "That could get costly, sir, but I'll take you up on it."

"It'll be my honor to pay it." Willie returned the smile. "Who knows, I might throw in a burger or two; maybe even some fries."

The two men, young but so dedicated, laughed as they walked at a slow pace, so many special moments encapsulated in their thoughts before they stopped, having finally reached the hangar door and the entrance to the squadron's maintenance spaces.

They both knew they'd see each other a few more times before Petty Officer Tessaro officially checked out of the squadron and then flew over an eastern horizon to his home in California. They'd likely stay in touch for decades more; that was a given. However, this was, emotionally and professionally, the goodbye that surrendered to a countdown timer representing their time together as Eagles and on Midway. Its final tick had reached zero. Their time together in the Navy's foreign legion was over.

With a broad smile of fond memories etched across his tanned face, Willie reached out with his left hand and opened the metal door so that Buzz could enter the warmth of the Eagles' hangar first. It was a symbolic and heartfelt gesture of deep-rooted respect and genuine adoration for the remarkable man standing next to him.

"After you, shipmate."

Buzz knew the ride of his life was over. It was his choice to leave, but he'd miss this. Nothing could compete with the mutual and deep respect and camaraderie of his fellow shipmates, each of them stitched together by a common thread and a noble cause as they served their nation far from its spacious skies and amber waves of grain. There were good times, bad times, and uniquely special times; times of danger and times of thrills; agreements and disagreements; and often moments when they didn't get along at all.

Still, Buzz thought, all those who served together as Eagles, and everyone who collectively served together on the legendary carrier Midway and as part of the Navy's foreign legion, would always be shipmates. No one could ever take that away from them. Maybe their paths would never cross again, but Willie's final word personified the magic that would link them forever.

Shipmate really was what it was all about.

With a simple head nod of humble gratitude, Buzz walked through the open door. His warm smile added the exclamation point.

EPILOGUE

Cradle of Naval Aviation
Naval Air Station Pensacola, FL
Late Spring, 1984

The Emerald Coast could not have been more appropriately named. From the horizon to horizon, the vivid green gem known as the Gulf of Mexico was snugly placed below rich blue skies and next to sugar-white beaches long identified with Florida's panhandle. Under a late spring sun on an early Thursday afternoon, the oceanfront deck of a Pensacola Beach hotel was the perfect setting to celebrate Lunker earning his wings as a Navy pilot.

Not surprisingly, Lunker and Mirela arrived first. He was a student assigned to a pilot training squadron at the nearby Naval Air Station Pensacola. She had relocated from Hong Kong to an office in New Orleans that allowed her the opportunity to work on behalf of new immigrants to the southeast United States. She worked three days of the week in New Orleans and then two in Florida, and remained in Florida through the weekend. It wasn't perfect, but it had worked for over two years.

Doc and Lauren arrived next. The two had arrived the night before after a long flight from Seattle to Pensacola. Doc was stationed at Naval Air Station Whidbey Island, an hour north of Seattle. He was an instructor in the west coast squadron that trained new pilots and flight officers in the Intruder. It was a prestigious assignment and reflected his work ethic and the reputation he had earned while serving with the Eagles. Lauren, a Colorado native, was thoroughly enjoying the cool springs and summers and the gorgeous mountain hikes associated with the Pacific Northwest.

"Over here, Doc," Lunker called from where he sat. He had selected a large round table under a large awning, mere feet from the white sand, that would easily seat ten people with plenty of room to spare. Lunker was wearing jeans. Doc was wearing shorts, as was Lauren. She was stunning in a white halter-top that was dazzling against her light olive skin and emerald green eyes. The temperature in Pensacola was in the mid-seventies, almost fifteen degrees higher than the forecast high at Whidbey Island.

The two men shook hands and embraced. It had been thirty months since they last saw each other, but it was as if no time had passed. Their grins reflected the joy in the reunion, and then they exchanged hugs with the women.

"You two look great," said Lauren, "and so happy."

"We are," replied Mirela, "in spite of Lunker's ego now being in the stratosphere." Everyone laughed as Lunker signaled the bartender for bushwackers.

"It's always been there. I just hid it 'cause I didn't want to embarrass my fellow Eagles," he replied.

"His ego has always outranked his capabilities," offered Doc. "We all knew that. We just didn't let him know." Warm smiles remained glued on all their faces as a waitress quickly delivered four Bushwackers in hard plastic cups.

"Here's to you, Lunker. Congratulations." The two men tapped their cups.

"Thanks, Doc. I appreciate it." Lunker's voice was unusually humble. Learning to fly a Navy jet, especially landing on an aircraft carrier at sea, had been much tougher than he had naively imagined. "I should have paid a little more attention to what was happening in the left seat." He smiled at the truth of it.

After ten minutes or so of catching up, another familiar voice entered the conversation. "I'm looking for a new naval aviator, but all I see is a miserable golfer next to a beautiful woman." On this day, Lunker was fair game.

Socks and Marti walked toward their friends. The men shook hands and embraced, and then hugged the women. "It is so great to see you both," said Lunker. Happiness was painted all over his face. "Thanks for making the trip here." Each embrace reengaged the memories and friendships created and forged together in foreign lands. Doc and Lauren greeted the newest arrivals similarly.

"We wouldn't miss it for the world, Lunker. I heard that you did well in every phase of training, and I'm not surprised. Congratulations." Socks meant every word.

"Thank you, Socks. Truth is, I barely survived the boat, but fortunately the minimum is still good enough." The two men laughed.

"He was just confessing that to us, Socks," stated Doc.

"Let's change the subject," said Lunker, laughing. "So how's San Antonio?"

"It's great," responded socks. I'm the only pilot in the squadron who has landed on a carrier, so it's a novelty they can't seem to get enough of." He was assigned as an interservice instructor pilot to an Air Force advanced training squadron located northeast of the city.

"Are you flying the T-38?"

"Yep; it's a nice jet. It just took me a while to master Air Force landings though."

"You mean soft landings for weenies?" asked Doc.

Socks laughed. "Yeah, and a lot easier to teach than carrier landings."

"We heard you're getting a masters in Austin," said Mirela. She directed her question to Marti.

"I am," she replied, "and it's like I never left the university." She had earned her undergraduate degree at the University of Texas, and was now pursuing an advanced degree in actuarial mathematics. Two more Bushwackers arrived for the latest arrivals.

"Is it a long commute from where you live to the school?" asked Lauren.

"Not really, just over an hour each way, and I'm only on campus two days a week."

"Hey," Doc exclaimed loudly, as another familiar face strolled toward Sandshaker's outside deck area. "Look who it is. Another B/N who couldn't hack it and is being demoted to being a pilot." The group laughed.

"The Navy has truly hit a new low," added Socks. "I guess the guys in Washington still haven't figured out that you just get a bigger mess when you try and polish a turd."

Gully's smile stretched from ear to ear as he walked toward the table where his friends were standing. He was holding Sharon's hand with his right hand. "Is this a great country or what," he remarked. More hugs and handshakes were shared among the group, and two additional Bushwackers magically appeared.

Four months earlier, Gully had been selected for the Navy's NFO-to-Pilot transition program, the same program as Lunker. He and Sharon had arrived in Pensacola from Japan just five days previously. As part of his relocation, he had three weeks before officially reporting to the Naval Aviation Schools Command at Pensacola to begin pilot training. They had spent their previous days looking for a place in which to live, and were then planning to spend their remaining time between Sharon's hometown of Temple, Texas, and his hometown of Ames, Iowa, before returning to Pensacola.

"You know, Gully, you have to believe everything a B/N tells you. Got it?" Doc smiled as he gave Sharon a hug.

Five minutes later, a recognizable voice enveloped the entire group, thundering across the bar's wooden floor to the deck where they stood.

"Who has my Bushwacker, or do I have to get my own?"

The entire group looked toward the voice as their former skipper, 'Spice' Curry, walked toward them. The bartender had the luscious drink was on its way immediately. There were even more hugs and smiles among the group. They had been apart as a group for well over two years, and yet it seemed that no time had passed.

Spice looked around. "Has anyone heard from Willie? Is he joining us?"

"Yep," answered Lunker. "He called me about an hour ago and said he had an urgent errand to run, and that he'd be a little late."

"Did you and Willie ever fly together?" the former skipper asked Lunker. After leaving the Eagles, Willie was assigned as an A-4 Skyhawk instructor at Training Squadron Four, or VT-4, the intermediate and advanced jet training squadron for pilots in Pensacola, and the squadron at which Lunker had just completed his pilot training.

"Yes sir, a couple weapons hops. He was in my backseat on my very first weps hop, and was the lead aircraft on one of my solo flights. I think he was generous with the grades, but he said he was being fair." Lunker paused. "It was nice having him in the squadron. We commiserated often about our glory days in the foreign legion."

Everyone laughed, and the discussions among shipmates continued for almost ten minutes when a tall blond strolled onto the large deck, followed immediately by Willie. They were holding hands.

"Tosh! Oh my gosh!" exclaimed Sharon, who gave her the first hug.

"This is so great!" Mirela also rushed to embrace her, followed by Lauren.

"You look wonderful, Tosh," added Doc, hugging her. Willie had made him aware of the rekindled relationship a few weeks earlier.

"Are you two...?" asked Spice.

"We're taking it slow and steady," said Willie.

"We're in a good place," offered Tosh. She turned and hugged Gully and Sharon.

Willie smiled at Gully. A rush of fond memories swept over both men as their eyes met; countless hours sitting side-by-side and defying death would do that. "Hello, my friend." They shook hands and hugged. "You'll make a fine pilot, Gully. The Navy got this decision right."

Gully was overwhelmed. His heartland roots were still intact. "Thank you, Willie. I'll work hard," he said in a humble voice. "Maybe we'll get to fly with each other."

"I'll make sure we do. You can count on it."

The group continued its collective journey down memory lane. However, this day was all about Lunker, and his friends soon shifted the focus back to him.

They were proud of him, and thrilled that he had successfully completed the pilot syllabus, which included carrier landings in both the T-2 Buckeye and TA-4J Skyhawk. Both of Lunker's carrier qualification periods were conducted on the USS Lexington. She was an aircraft carrier built in 1943 that launched air strikes against the Yokosuka naval base at the end of World War Two. Pilots like Spice, Willie, Socks, Lunker and, soon, Gully would take pride in telling people that they'd been around naval aviation so long that their first carrier landings were on a wooden deck carrier, which Lexington actually was until she was retired at the end of 1991.

As a round of drinks was being consumed, the aviators began asking questions about Lunker's near-term plans.

"Do you have your orders yet?" asked Gully.

"Only verbals, but heading to Whidbey Island at the end of August for a September class date."

"What will you be doing until then?"

"I'll be flying Naval Academy midshipmen on jet orientation flights for the next twelve weeks. Four flights a day, three days a week. Tuesday through Thursday. We even have our own designated airspace out over the Gulf of Mexico."

"Oh, my Lord," said their former skipper. "Those future officers will be dumb asses, mountain-grown hicks, or bad golfers by the time you're done with them."

"Quite possibly all three," added Doc.

Everyone laughed and began to pile on Lunker as the conversation progressed.

"So you're working only three days a week? And it's all flying? Nothing else?" inquired Gully.

"Yep."

"Must be nice," lamented Socks.

"Yes and amen," admitted Lunker. "I can go spend time in New Orleans with Mirela during my days off."

"Sounds like you should return your paychecks to the Navy," said Willie.

Doc changed the subject without letting Lunker off the hook.

"I did a little research, my friend, and discovered that Perdido Key, where you're living now, means lost key in Spanish. Very fitting for you, Lunker. You were lost as a B/N, and now you need a B/N to keep you from being lost as a pilot." Everyone laughed, Lunker more than anyone.

Willie kept the heat on his friend. "I remember Eli once saying that you'd get lost between holes if he didn't point you to the next one."

Socks immediately jumped into the fray. "Well, I remember during my final round with Eli, him saying Lunker couldn't even find his ball when it rolled into the cup."

"If Lunker was a dog and needed to use the bathroom, he couldn't find a tree if he was in a forest." Spice Curry's thoughts kept the comical barrage alive.

"I recall Lunker getting lost walking on a treadmill," added Tosh.

Surprisingly, even Mirela offered her own observation. "Lunker can't find the bathroom even when he's standing in the shower."

"Ouch," said Lunker, grabbing his heart as he laughed with the others. "That one hurt." Life was so good on this sunny day by the beach. He as where he wanted to be.

As the group continued to reminisce about their days halfway around the planet, Gully leaned toward Sharon. "By chance, did you bring Lunker's gift in with you?" She shook her head.

Overhearing his question, Lunker responded with his usual wit. "Thank you, Santa Claus. You didn't have to get me anything, but make sure you hurry right back with it."

"Okay," he answered. He turned toward Sharon and smiled.

The group was laughing as Gully entered the hotel's lobby, and then they continued catching up on their post-Midway lives for several minutes before the discussion was directed back toward future plans.

"When will you be heading to Whidbey?" Willie's comment was directed toward their former skipper, who was currently assigned to the Pentagon, but had orders to be the commanding officer of the squadron that trained pilots and B/Ns in the Intruder."

"Probably late October," he answered, "just in time for the rainy season to start."

"Don't remind me," said Doc. "Lauren and I have been getting in some serious hikes on the weekends. A couple weeks ago, we drove down to Crater Lake."

"Which trails did you do?"

"We did several, but Garfield Peak was our favorite," admitted Doc. "I don't think either of us were acclimated to the elevation, but we were hackers and survived." The high point of the trail was just over six thousand feet elevation.

"It was unbelievable," said Lauren, "as we drove around the rim, looking at the entire lake inside the crater, and then seeing the Cascade Mountains in the distance. Oh my goodness, and then the hike, I mean, it was simply spectacular." Crater Lake, known for its intense blue color, and fed by snow and rain, is considered by many to be the most pristine body of water on the planet.

"That's always been one of my favorites," said Spice Curry. "It never gets old."

"I think Mirela and I will have to try that," said Lunker, his back toward the ocean. "I haven't done any serious hiking like that before, but I promised Mirela that once we were settled in that we'd...uh, that...Oh my God." His eyes were suddenly focused toward the hotel's lobby. It'd be easy to believe Lunker had just seen a ghost. "Oh, my God."

Without hesitation, he began moving quickly toward the lobby's beachside entrance as the group turned to see the cause of the interruption.

Standing next to Gully at the entrance to the beachfront deck was Eli, not looking a day older than when they had last seen him, and flashing a smile that could brighten a clear, sunny day. Next to him, side-by-side, was Violetta, Macaalay, and Diwata. The two young girls had grown taller, but were easily recognizable, especially Diwata, who had the same infectious smile that was once the genesis of 'smiling girl village'.

Violetta was wearing the coral necklace that Lunker and Mirela had bought for her in Manila, and her dress was made from fabric the men had given her on their first trip to her village. Her left hand rested lovingly on her husband's right shoulder, and her eyes looked at the group in front of her and spoke to a level of gratitude only a mother could express.

Lunker was stunned. By the time he reached the dear man who had traveled halfway around the planet to be a part of his special day, his eyes were visibly filling with tears. Their embrace seemed to last an eternity, and neither man wanted to let go. Both of their faces were covered in the tear-strained emotions of two friends finally reunited.

Just as quickly, the entire group joined in the welcoming party, sharing hugs and smiles and tears as introductions of Violetta and her daughters were made to each of the women. As on their visit to her village, Diwata moved to stand between Doc and Willie, who more than welcomed the intrusion.

After at least ten or fifteen minutes of conversation among the group, and a new round of drinks for everyone, the reality of the moment had finally sunk in. Lunker looked toward Gully, and then back to Eli. "How did you pull this off?" He had never been more surprised in the entirety of his lifetime. "I'm in shock...how did you do this?"

As Eli began to explain the details, a warm breeze enveloped the group like an old friend. "Four, five months ago, ask Gully how we go see you be pilot. I use money you give last visit village. He help get passport, tickets, all things to go. Fly Manila, Hawaii then California. Two more flight get here. Now see you be pilot."

His comment almost brought the tall man from Georgia to his knees. After a few long, emotional moments, Lunker responded. "And here I thought it was because you knew I needed a lot of help with my short irons and putting."

"Still need two three year, but will keep trying."

Lunker couldn't stop smiling; neither could Eli or anyone else in the group.

"It's time for a toast I have always wanted to make." Lunker looked at each of the gathered group, and then his eyes stopped at Eli.

"A toast to Eli, the dearest friend I could ever ask for, and his sweet, sweet family." He spoke slowly as he placed his left hand on Eli's back and raised his drink with his right hand.

"To Eli...At long last...Over the horizon." The friends raised their glasses and spoke as one.

"Over the horizon."

As he lowered his glass, Eli flashed a big smile and spoke from a dream fulfilled.

"Yes and amen."

Made in the USA
San Bernardino, CA
22 December 2018